Also by Zev Chafets:

DOUBLE VISION
HEROES AND HUSTLERS, HARD HATS AND HOLY
  MEN
MEMBERS OF THE TRIBE
DEVIL'S NIGHT: AND OTHER TRUE TALES OF
  DETROIT

INHERIT THE MOB

Zev Chafets

FAWCETT CREST • NEW YORK

A Fawcett Crest Book
Published by Ballantine Books
Copyright © 1991 by Random House, Inc.

All rights reserved under International and Pan-American Copyright Conventions. Published in the United States by Ballantine Books, a division of Random House, Inc., New York, and simultaneously in Canada by Random House of Canada Limited, Toronto.

Library of Congress Catalog Card Number: 90-53470

ISBN 0-449-22166-0

This edition published by arrangement with Random House, Inc.

Manufactured in the United States of America

First Ballantine Books Edition: December 1993

THIS BOOK
IS DEDICATED TO
LEORA NIR,
WITH GRATITUDE

THE PHONE ON THE NIGHTSTAND JOLTED GORDON out of a sad dream, and he awoke, as he always did, with a quick check of his vital signs. Beer hangover (mild), piss hard-on, pulse, cigarette wheeze—all the old reliables. He picked up the receiver on the third ring. It was Flanagan, the deputy city editor.

"Hey, pal, I got news," he said. "Your uncle Max just croaked."

"What time is it?"

"Six-fifteen," said Flanagan. "I'm down at the paper. Want me to read you the obit?"

"I've already seen it," Gordon said. His uncle had been dying slowly for more than six months, and one night at the *Tribune* Gordon had read through the obituary, which was first written in 1929 and updated every few years for the next half-century. "It looked all right to me. What's the headline?"

" 'Max Grossman: The Last Gangster,' what else?" said Flanagan happily. "Max was the real thing, pal. They don't make 'em like that anymore."

"Look, Flanagan, I've got an industrial-strength hang-

over," Gordon said. "Let me sleep another hour or so, and
I'll call you back, OK?"

"Jews aren't supposed to have hangovers, pal. Besides,
you've got a big day. Funeral's at one, and I want you to give
us something. Thousand words of color on the widow, the
old cronies, maybe a little something from the shivah. You
can do it first person if you want, I-was-the-nephew-of-the-
Zeyde—type thing. All right?"

It was a request, not an order; Gordon was two Pulitzers
past taking orders from deputy city editors. But Flanagan
was a friend, and he'd have to go to the funeral anyway.
"What the hell," he said. "But no first-person stuff, just
straight color. And no slug about my being the nephew
either."

"If he was my uncle, I'd want the whole city to know
about it," said Flanagan. "The man was a fucking national
monument, a titan—"

"Why don't you go to the damn funeral if you love him
so much?"

Flanagan laughed. "Are you kidding? I wouldn't miss it
for the world. We're going together, boychik. I'll meet you
at your place at noon."

The phone clicked, and Gordon was alone in bed. Being
alone reminded him of Jupiter Evans. Forty-two years old
and in love with an actress. A lesbian actress. Proof that
experience only makes you dumber, he thought; it's no accident that old age ends in senility.

Gordon wondered what his uncle Max would have thought
of Jupiter. Nothing, probably. The old man had been married
for fifty-one years, and Gordon had never heard any gossip
about him playing around. His aunt Ida was a different story.
He already knew her opinion. "Jupiter? The name sounds
like an automobile," she once told him. "A journalist with
a Nobel Prize ought to be able to find a girl with a little more
class."

Aunt Ida didn't know that Jupiter was gay ("bisexual," he corrected himself automatically), but it wouldn't have shocked her. The wives of old Jewish gangsters were supposed to be simple homemakers, but Ida, well past seventy, was still a chachka who had, she once admitted to Gordon, married Max for thrills. She told him this at his mother's funeral, several years before. When she saw the surprise on his face she winked and said, "Death makes old people feel sexy." Gordon wondered if she would be in a sexy mood today at the funeral.

He climbed out of bed, showered and fixed himself a cup of coffee. The hangover was subsiding, the wheeze was under control and the hard-on was in temporary hibernation. Gordon picked up the phone and called his father.

"Grossman," a gruff voice answered. There was, as usual, an implicit, wadda-ya-wanna-make-of-it in his tone.

"Pop, I just heard about Uncle Max. I'm sorry."

"Me, too, Velvel," he said. "You know what time's the funeral?"

"Yeah, they called from the paper. They want me to write a story about it."

"A funeral's a funeral," said Grossman. "Thirty years ago it would have been a real event. Big bouquets from Chicago, shiny cars, the whole shmeer. Today—another old Jew bites the dust. Don't expect anything special."

Gordon wasn't surprised by his father's matter-of-fact attitude; Albert Grossman was not a sentimental man, as his son had learned through hard experience.

"They're going to run his obituary on the front page," Gordon said. " 'Max Grossman: The Last Gangster.' It mentions you."

"My name's been in the papers before," Grossman said in a dry voice. In the late fifties, after Appalachian, when the McClellan Committee was investigating organized crime, Gordon had often read about his father. He was usually described as Max's partner, or sometimes as his front man. Grossman had neither hidden these articles from his son, nor explained them; and since then, he had alluded to that period only once. It was during the Watergate hearings. Gordon was in the States on home leave and before dinner he and his father were watching the evening news. There was a clip that night of John Dean testifying before the Ervin committee. Grossman had listened angrily to the young lawyer's contrite confession. "There's nothing worse than a goy feeling sorry for himself in public," he had snorted. "These potato-heads ratting out their boss make me sick."

"Not like you, huh?" Gordon said, looking for an opening, but his father didn't go for it. "Do I look like a goy to you, Velvel?" was all he had said.

"Pop, I'm bringing Flanagan to the funeral," Gordon told him now. "You think that'll be all right?"

"The one who looks like an FBI agent? Yeah, sure, the more the merrier. He gonna write a story, too?"

"No, he's just an admirer. He says Uncle Max was a national monument."

Grossman laughed, a solitary bark. "Yeah, Max was a regular Benjamin Francis."

It was one of their few jokes. Once, when Gordon was in junior high school, his father had attended a basketball practice. Gordon remembered him sitting in the empty bleachers, wearing a vicuña topcoat and fedora, chewing a Cuban cigar. Coach Kelly kept giving him nervous glances, as if he suspected that Grossman was there to fix a game.

Afterward, Grossman took the starting team out for hamburgers. During the meal he referred to his son as Velvel, a Yiddish version of William unknown to his teammates. When they laughed at the nickname, the old man, typically, had counterattacked.

"Nothing wrong with Velvel," he told them gruffly. "You

shvartzers are all named after wristwatches and electric trains."

"Hey, Mr. Grossman, my mamma named me after Benjamin Francis," protested one of the players with great dignity. "He the man invented the kite."

"Yeah, I heard of him," said Gordon's father. Thirty years later, it was still one of his favorite lines.

"Listen, Pop," Gordon now said. "I've got to get some things done this morning. I'll meet you at the funeral home. Maybe we can have an early dinner, OK?"

"We can eat at Ida's," he said. "Afterwards, I'll take you to the Knicks game. They're playing the Celtics."

"Well, we'll see. I may be meeting Jupiter tonight."

"The hell with it, then. I'll go with Harry," he said. "I'm not playing second fiddle to a dyke Sara Heartburn." Gordon realized, not for the first time, that telling his father about Jupiter had been a serious mistake. "I'll catch you at one, Velvel. And don't forget to bring a yarmulke. Those loaners at the funeral home can give you ringworm." Without ceremony he hung up.

With the whole morning on his hands, Gordon sat down at his word processor to work up some notes on a recent trip to France. He was just starting to make sense of Mitterrand's economic policy when the phone rang again. This time it was Jupiter.

"Hallo," she said, using their special tone of greeting. "I just heard about your uncle on the radio. How you feeling?"

"As James Brown once said, 'I feel good, da da da da da da da.' If you were here, I'd feel better."

"Well, as the Stones said, you can't always get what you want." He could hear her smile over the phone; Jupiter's voice was so melodic that it turned statements into songs. "Seriously, you need anything?"

"Nothing that about two hundred thousand dollars' worth

of analysis can't get," he said. "Where've you been? I've been calling all week."

"I know," she said. "I'm sorry I didn't get back to you, but I've been busy."

"God I hate you," he said. "You want to have dinner tonight?"

"Sure. I'll come by and we'll go someplace in the neighborhood. OK?"

"I'll see you around nine," said Gordon, feeling at once appeased and foolish. She must love me if she's willing to have dinner with me, right? Jesus.

"Give my love to your family," she said, and hung up. He hit himself on the head with the receiver, one good crack, and went back to his notes on the future of the French franc.

At noon the doorman buzzed, announcing Flanagan. He was dressed in funereal black, and he already wore a dark silk skullcap on his red hair. "I look like a yeshiva bucher, no?" he said happily, turning for Gordon's inspection.

"Just like Elie Wiesel."

Flanagan laughed. He had grown up in Brooklyn, and he had a thing about Jews. He called them SATs, after the college entrance exam. Gordon was still wearing jeans and a T-shirt, and Flanagan looked at his watch with alarm.

"You better get dressed," he said. "We don't want to keep your uncle waiting."

"Pour yourself a drink," Gordon told him. "I'll be about two minutes. By the way, my father says you look like an FBI agent."

"We never drink on the job," said Flanagan, splashing three fingers of Wild Turkey into a tall glass. "You think I really look like a fed?"

"Are you kidding? You're a walking J. Edgar Hoover wet dream," said Gordon. Flanagan was six foot two, with a square jaw, pug nose and clear blue eyes. Clear, at least, until the cocktail hour, which often began at lunchtime. Daytime drinking was something the two journalists had in common.

Gordon went into the bathroom to shower and Flanagan, bourbon in hand, followed. "What else did your father say?" he asked. "Was he broken up?"

"He invited me to a Knicks game," Gordon hollered over the pounding water.

"They're playing Boston," Flanagan said automatically. He was not a sports fan, but he kept up for the sake of barroom conversation. Once, years before, he had whimsically founded an organization called Athletes Anonymous. "Anytime you feel like exercising, you call up another member and he comes over to have a drink with you" was the way he explained it.

"Are you sure he wasn't kidding about the 'b-ball' game?" Flanagan shouted. "I mean, it's his only brother. . . ."

Gordon stepped out of the shower and began toweling himself. "My old man? He doesn't kid. Besides, every minute that Max was alive after 1930 was borrowed time. He figures they both beat the odds by about fifty years."

Flanagan followed him into the bedroom, where Gordon began dressing. "They expecting a big turnout today?" he asked.

"I doubt it," Gordon said. "When you're eighty-five, there aren't many mourners left."

"Ever read about the Nails Morton funeral in Chicago?" Flanagan asked. "Five thousand people, half of them rabbis. Morton was in the Bugs Moran gang, and he got thrown from a horse. They shot the horse."

"Who? The rabbis?"

"No, shmuck, the boys. The rabbis came because Nails was a local hero. He protected them from the Polacks."

"From the Irish, more likely," Gordon said. "Anyway, I don't think that Max was too big on protecting people. I never heard any Robin Hood stories about him."

"You could be wrong about that," said Flanagan. "I see him as a kind of Jewish Godfather. Remember that scene where the undertaker comes to Don Corleone after his daughter is raped? 'Godfather, Godfather, give me justice.' Great scene. I'll bet a few people came to Max for justice over the years."

"Chief, did anybody ever tell you that you're a romantic?"

"Uh-huh," said Flanagan. "And you're not. I'm the one who took a wacko thesbian to Mexico for the weekend, right? I'm the one who believes in true love? All I said is that the old man might have helped some neighborhood people."

"If you're going to use the shit I tell you in arguments, I'm going to stop telling you shit," Gordon said. "Besides, Jupiter is bisexual. She just has trouble getting close to men. That doesn't make her a pervert."

"No," said Flanagan. "It makes *you* a pervert."

They arrived at the Riverside funeral home a few minutes before one. As the cab pulled up alongside the brown stone building, Gordon was surprised to see hundreds of people standing outside. "I told you," said Flanagan delightedly. "A great send-off for a great American."

Gordon and Flanagan edged through the crowd, but they were stopped by the bottleneck at the door. Suddenly Gordon felt a hand on his elbow and turned to see a broad-shouldered old man with a hook nose, piercing brown eyes and a white mustache perched above sweet-tempered lips.

"Hi, Nate," Gordon said. Nate Belzer was one of the few people from his uncle's world whom he actually knew, a regular guest at the Grossmans' Passover seder since Gordon's boyhood. He remembered Belzer chanting the Hebrew prayers in a clear, educated voice, and giving him a silver dollar to buy back the matzoh that he ritually stole every year. He remembered, too, that Belzer used to stand outside when the door was opened for Elijah the prophet. "You never know who's coming in with him," he would whisper.

Gordon looked around the funeral home. "Who are all these people?" he asked.

"Friends of the family, children, grandchildren," Belzer said noncommittally. "Max had a lot of friends."

Gordon felt an arm reach over his shoulder. "Mr. Belzer, I'm John Flanagan. I'm a friend of Velvel's," he said, giving the nickname a slight emphasis that made Gordon wince.

"Nice to meet you," Belzer said neutrally, taking the outstretched hand.

"It's an honor to meet you, sir," said Flanagan. "Knuckles Belzer, right? Out of Brownsville. And the Palm Hotel in Vegas."

Belzer gave Gordon a hard look. "He works with me, Nate," he explained. "At the paper. He's a newspaper man."

"A newspaper man," Belzer said evenly. "Well, a friend of Velvel's is a friend. Velvel, Ida wants to see you." He took Gordon by the elbow and gently pushed him through the crowd.

When they entered the small study off the chapel, Gordon went directly to his aunt, kissed her on the cheek and murmured "I'm sorry, Aunt Ida." He shook hands with his father and the rabbi, a small, mild-looking man dressed in a dandruff-covered black robe.

"My nephew is a Nobel Prize journalist," Ida told the rabbi. "Tell him what you're planning to say, see what he thinks."

"Pulitzer Prize, Aunt Ida," Gordon corrected automatically, but the rabbi was already making little "uh, uh" noises, revving up his topic. "Today I intend to talk about Max Grossman the man," he said. "Max Grossman the husband, Max Grossman the Jew. Max Grossman who gave his charity in private, who never forgot who he was and where he came from . . ."

"Sounds just like him," Gordon said, eliciting a sharp look from his father.

"This is serious, shmendrick," he said. "We got a writer in the family, we want a writer's opinion."

"We thought maybe you'd say a few words," said Ida. She was dressed in black and smoked a Kent 100. "Nothing against the rabbi, but he didn't know Max, and you did. Max always said you were a great talker."

"I pass," said Gordon. "Listen, I wouldn't know what to say. There's a guy I came with, Flanagan, he wants to write a whole book about Uncle Max. You ought to let him give the eulogy."

"No goyim," said the rabbi sternly.

"I don't see why not," Gordon said. "Wasn't Uncle Max in business with Italians? Maybe you should talk about what an ecumenical figure he was."

"That's a good point," said Ida, missing the irony. "Max was always friendly with the lokshen."

There was a knock on the door, and Nathan Belzer stuck his head in. "Ida, the Israeli consul general is here to pay his respects. Do you want to see him now?"

The old lady smiled. "Consul *general*," she said, hitting the second word. "Have him come in."

Belzer opened the door wider, and the diplomat, who had been standing behind him, walked in. A man in his late fifties, he gently shook Ida's hand, intoned a Hebrew phrase and then addressed the room in general. "Max Grossman was a great friend of the state of Israel," he proclaimed. "His loss is a loss to all of us."

This was news to Gordon, who looked at his father quizzically, but the old man's face gave away nothing. "You must be William Gordon," said the diplomat, extending his hand. "I am an admirer of your writing. Your series on the Palestinians was first rate, really excellent. I only wish more of your colleagues were able to bring your perspective to the complicated issues that—''

''I didn't know that Uncle Max had anything to do with Israel,'' said Gordon. ''I didn't even know he had been there.''

''I don't believe that he ever was in Israel,'' said the consul uncomfortably, sensing that he had said too much.

''He had passport problems,'' said Grossman.

''Precisely,'' said the Israeli. ''But he was always there in spirit when he was needed, I assure you. And now, Mrs. Grossman, let me convey, once again, our condolences.'' He shook hands all around and left the room.

''What did Uncle Max do for Israel?'' Gordon asked, his journalistic curiosity aroused.

''Here and there, this and that,'' said Ida.

''Perhaps I should mention it in my talk,'' said the rabbi, but Grossman shook his head. ''No business, just personal stuff,'' he said in a gruff tone. The rabbi nodded so emphatically that dandruff swirled off his shoulders.

From the chapel they could hear the swell of voices. Grossman looked at his watch. ''So, you gonna say something or not, big boy?'' he demanded.

Gordon shook his head. ''I come to bury Caesar, not to praise him. No disrespect intended.''

''Forget it, then,'' said Grossman. ''Rabbi, you do all the talking. And remember, keep it short and sweet. Nothing fancy.''

Gordon helped his aunt to her feet, and she stubbed out her Kent. ''We're having Chinese at the shivah,'' she said. ''How's that for a little class?''

The *Tribune*'s late edition hit the streets during the funeral; on the way from the cemetery Flanagan bought a copy, and read the obit aloud as they headed to Ida's East Side penthouse.

"Max Grossman, reputedly one of America's leading crime lords, died yesterday at Mount Sinai Hospital in New York after a long illness. He was eighty-five years old.

"Grossman was born on the Lower East Side of New York in 1897 to Jewish parents who emigrated to the United States from Russia. After leaving school at the age of fifteen, he formed his own gang, known as the Max and Ax mob, with childhood friend Al 'the Ax' Axelrod, who was shot to death in a gangland slaying in Palm Springs in 1951.

"Grossman and Axelrod worked briefly for crime king Arnold 'the Brain' Rothstein before going into business for themselves. Their activities allegedly included extortion, armed robbery, bootlegging and contract killing.

"In 1929, Grossman reputedly helped found the Syndicate, the national crime commission that ruled the underworld for decades. He was closely aligned with Luigi Spadafore and other reputed Mafia figures. He also had close ties with Louis 'Lepke' Buchhalter of Murder Incorporated, Charles 'King' Solomon of Boston and the Purple Gang of Detroit.

"Known as a diplomat and organizational genius, Grossman helped pioneer gambling in a number of Latin American countries, established close ties with leading Democratic politicians in New York and around the country, and founded a chain of department stores run by his younger brother, Albert.

"Over the years, Grossman was the subject of numerous investigations, but his only criminal conviction was for vagrancy, in 1923. Law enforcement agencies were convinced, however, that he stood at the pinnacle of organized crime for decades. In 1957 he was threatened with contempt of Congress for refusing to divulge information to the McClellan Committee.

"In recent years, Max Grossman lived in quiet retirement in his Upper East Side apartment. He is survived by his wife, Ida, his brother, Albert, and his nephew, William Gordon, who serves as a columnist for this newspaper."

"Thanks for the publicity," Gordon said. "I don't remember seeing my name in there before."

"A last-minute addition, boychik," said Flanagan. "Just giving the story a local angle. By the way, when we get to your aunt's, don't mention who wrote the obit, OK? People are touchy sometimes."

Flanagan had nothing to worry about; none of the mourners at Ida's had read the *Tribune*. They filled her large living room, sipping coffee from painted china cups and Canadian Club from standard barroom highball glasses. Along the sides of the room, elderly Jews sat on sofas and munched dim sum delicacies. The mood of the room struck Gordon as decidedly upbeat.

"Aunt Ida, this is John Flanagan, he works with me at the paper," he said.

"I'm sorry for your trouble, Mrs. Grossman," he said,

and she smiled through a puff of cigarette smoke. "You too, Mr. Grossman," he said to Gordon's father, who grunted.

"You ever been to a shivah before, Mr. Flanagan?" asked Ida. "It's like a wake, only for Jews. We have plenty of liquor," she added knowingly. "Get yourself a drink and feel at home." She drifted off, leaving Flanagan with Gordon and his father.

Flanagan scanned the room with intense curiosity. Suddenly he touched Gordon's arm and gestured toward a tanned, dapper, gray-haired man who was daintily chewing an egg roll. "Isn't that Handsome Harry Millman, Mr. Grossman?" Flanagan asked.

"I don't know any Harry Millman," replied Grossman, but Flanagan didn't even hear him. "Sure, it is," he said. "Somebody pointed him out to me at the Carnegie one time. He's a living legend. I can't believe it."

"Who the hell is Handsome Harry Millman?" Gordon asked.

"Don't you know anything about your own heritage?" said Flanagan. "Handsome Harry Millman was one of the hit men in the Dexter Avenue massacre in Detroit in the thirties. He got life. At his trial, he complained that he was only rated number six on the FBI most wanted list. You never met him?"

"I never heard of him," said Grossman again, and looked hard at his son. Gordon shrugged. "Me, either."

"Jeez, this place is like the hall of fame," said Flanagan. "Who else is here, Mr. Grossman?"

"I'm gonna get some more Chinese, Velvel," he said, ignoring the question. He started to move away, then stopped, seized Flanagan's elbow and squeezed hard. "This is a solemn religious occasion," he said to the Irishman in a hard tone. "You wanna eat, eat. You wanna drink, drink. You wanna sightsee, scram."

"Your old man is the real McCoy," Flanagan said to Gordon. "How did you get to be such a pussy?"

"You wanna ask questions, beat it," Gordon said in a passable imitation of his father's gravelly voice. "I'm Wildman William Gordon, and I bump off Irish pen pushers for the fun of it. Jesus, Flanagan, grow up. These are a bunch of geriatric cases. What the hell are you so excited about?"

"Excited? Listen, when I was a kid, my mother used to tell me, 'Eat your dinner or Max and Ax will get you,' " said Flanagan. "And now, here I am, in Max's apartment. Come on, be a guy, who are some of these people?"

"I don't know most of them myself," Gordon said truthfully. His father and uncle had always been extremely careful not to mix business with family. They had expected him to become a doctor, and hadn't been any too pleased when he chose journalism as a career. To them, newspapers were too close to their world, and they had a poor opinion of reporters, whom they considered professional stool pigeons. Gordon was just about to explain this to Flanagan when a small man with a long scar across his right cheek came up and put a gnarled hand gently on his cheek. "Hello, Velvel," he said. *"Vos macht a yid?"*

"Hello, Uncle Abe," Gordon said. "You look good."

"I feel like an astronaut. Why not? You been here long?"

"Just got here. Uncle Abe, this is John Flanagan, who works with me. Abe Abramson."

"Your mudda done it," Flanagan said with a wide grin. Abramson blinked, stared and then burst into loud laughter. Already a little drunk on the Canadian Club, Flanagan turned to Gordon. "It's 1937, right? And one Abe "Bad Abe" Abramson is shot in a card game on Hester Street. The cops arrive. 'Who done it, Abe?' one of them asks. 'Just tell us who done it.' And Bad Abe looks up at the cop and says, 'Your mudda done it.' Right?"

To Gordon's amazement, Abramson laughed again. "Your

friend here is what, some kind of historian?'' he said. ''How'd
you hear that one?''

''The code of silence,'' said Flanagan, drunker than he
appeared. ''The common bond between your world and
mine. Velvel doesn't understand about that.''

''Where'd you find this guy?'' Abramson asked with mock
anger; it was obvious that he was enjoying the attention.

''Maybe we could get together sometime, talk about the
old days,'' Flanagan suggested.

''Sure, why not, I'm the nostalgic type,'' said Abramson.
''I live in Florida these days, you ever get down there, look
me up.'' The old man punched Gordon on the arm. ''Your
mudda done it,'' he laughed. ''Oh, by the way, Velvel, Nate
Belzer wants to talk to you in your uncle's office. He says
come in when you get a chance.''

''I'll go see what he wants now,'' Gordon said. ''Uncle
Abe, show this Mick around, all right? He wants to be Da-
mon Runyon.''

''A fine type of gentile,'' said Abe. ''I knew him in Miami. . . .''

Belzer was waiting for Gordon in Max Grossman's study. He
sat behind the large old-fashioned desk, idly flipping a pencil
in the air. ''Pull up a chair, Velvel,'' he said. ''I want to talk
to you about your uncle's will.''

A few years earlier, *Fortune* magazine had listed Max
Grossman as one of the five hundred richest men in America.
The old gangster had no children, and since learning of his
death that morning Gordon had been wondering if he might
be in line to inherit some money.

''Velvel, you know what your Uncle Max did for a living?'' he said, coming straight to the point.

''He was a retired businessman who owned a chain of
department stores,'' Gordon said, reciting by rote the answer
he had been given as a teenager on the way to a preppy

boarding school. It was a good answer, one that had served him well through twenty-five years, and he had no desire to hear anything different now.

"Your uncle had various interests," said Belzer. "He owned department stores, that's true. Your father and he had a number of department stores. But there were some other things as well. You know what I'm talking about?"

"Not really."

"Come on, Velvel. You're a big boy now. It's time you knew about the family business."

"Where's my father?" Gordon asked, sounding childish, even to himself. "If we're talking about family business, how come he isn't here?"

"He's not here because he doesn't want to be here," said Belzer. "I want to show you something." He opened a leather briefcase and slid a neatly stapled set of papers across the desk to Gordon. It was covered with numbers. Big numbers, with dollar signs in front of them. "Read," he said. "Then we'll talk."

2

GORDON HAD BEEN READING ALL HIS LIFE. WHEN HE was seven, his mother took him for the first time to the main branch of the public library on Fifth Avenue and Forty-second Street. Thirty-five years later, he still remembered vividly how she had browsed through the card catalog, jotted something on a slip of paper and, within twenty minutes, received two thin volumes of Greek mythology, complete with pictures of gods and snakes, from a hole in the wall. She explained that someone called a librarian had filled the order; as the only child of wealthy, indulgent parents, he had imagined that the librarian had written the books just for him.

Seven-year-old William Gordon became a fanatical reader, a fact he was careful to conceal from his friends. He did not want to be considered a bookworm, and he sometimes intentionally failed to answer questions in school to avoid that reputation.

Then, at the dawn of puberty, Gordon discovered a practical use for literature—it was a means of learning about sex. Just after his Bar Mitzvah he swiped a paperback marital guide from the rack in a drugstore. The book inflamed his imagination and gave him a precocious awareness of girls and the fun he could have with them. That year, at summer camp, he employed his knowledge to bluff his way into the cot of a seventeen-year-old counselor from Westchester who smelled of bubble gum and shampoo.

The following autumn, Gordon was sent, under protest, to Grayling Academy, a prep school in Vermont. There he again found a practical use for his reading habit. Grayling was going through a liberal phase, and the emphasis was on "creative processes" and "independent thinking" rather than on memorization and discipline. Gordon persuaded the headmaster to allow him to substitute "extracurricular reading" for classes, and turned in reports on books he had already read, a system that allowed him enough free time to become a better than competent basketball player and to comb the adjacent villages for willing townie girls.

Gordon's mother, Else, was a pretty, somewhat vague woman whose father, a German Jewish snob, founded the Monarch Department Store chain and then lost it through inattention. He was bought out by Al Grossman, acting for his brother, Max; and Al took the daughter along with the rest of the inventory. Else Grossman wanted her son to attend Princeton and become another F. Scott Fitzgerald. Al, who seldom interfered in the boy's education, hoped he would study medicine at Columbia, but not enough to insist. Gordon, who considered authors sissies, and hated the idea of spending his life with sick people, disappointed them both by going to the University of Wisconsin and majoring in journalism.

After three years in a boys' school, Gordon fell in love with the University of Wisconsin. He was delighted by the accessibility of co-eds, beer and a real library. He racked up an impressive number of conquests among blond small-town English majors looking for an intense Jewish intellectual from the big city; joined ZBT and became a star fraternity jock, although he wasn't quite good enough for varsity sports; and, for the first time, brought his reading out of the closet. He concentrated on history and international politics; even then, he knew he wanted to be a foreign correspondent.

In his senior year, he was appointed editor in chief of the college newspaper. He also changed his name from Grossman to Gordon, because he thought it looked better as a byline. The previous editor had been hired by the *Detroit Free Press* as a city reporter, and Gordon expected to travel the same route—a Middle Western apprenticeship followed by a job with a New York paper, and then on to the Orient Express.

During spring break, Gordon flew back to New York to attend his uncle's annual seder. By this time his parents had already moved to the large red brick house in Scarsdale, but Max and Ida stayed in their East Side duplex, which he had visited twice a year—on Thanksgiving and Passover—for as long as he could remember.

By no means religious, Gordon's family belonged to no synagogue and observed few holidays—Al Grossman went to his office even on Yom Kippur unless there happened to be a World Series game. But Passover was special, a time when the family gathered to recall the humble roots from which their present affluence had sprung. The holiday always made Gordon nostalgic, although he was never certain what he was nostalgic for.

That year the seder began no differently from all other seders. Max Grossman sat at the head of the table, a black silk skullcap on his thick white hair and a noncommittal look on his face, while his friend Nathan Belzer chanted the Hebrew prayers. Gordon was, by that time, well aware that his uncle was a notorious gangster, but he could never relate the movie image of a crime lord to the old Jewish man he had known all his life. Max had a soft voice with just the smallest Yiddish inflection, and, unlike his mercurial brother, he was rarely animated. If Gordon had to choose a single word to describe his uncle, he would have picked "ordinary."

Theirs was a distant relationship. Max and Ida were childless, and the old man didn't relate easily to children. Occasionally, as a small boy, Gordon had tried to charm his uncle with self-consciously precocious comments about the adult world, but Max had refused to be charmed. "Your boy is a good talker, Al," he said once, and Gordon, who knew that his uncle had spent a lifetime keeping his mouth shut, realized that it was not a compliment. Since then, he had been as silent around his uncle as good manners permitted. So, when Belzer completed the seder with "Next year in Jerusalem" and Max leaned over to him and said, "Velvel, I'd like to talk to you alone for a few minutes," Gordon had been astonished.

Max took Gordon into the large study off the living room, closed the door and sat at his desk. His nephew sat across from him in a straight-backed chair, trying to remember if he had ever had a private conversation with the old man. He couldn't recall one.

"You're finishing college this year," Max said.

"That's right, Uncle Max," said Gordon, determined to be taciturn.

"Have you decided yet what you want to do?" he asked. It was, Gordon assumed, a preliminary question; the old man must have known from Gordon's father that he planned to become a journalist.

"I want to be a newspaperman," he said, choosing the word for its practical, hard-bitten sound. "Eventually, I'd like to become a foreign correspondent, but that'll take a few years."

"Have you ever thought of going into the business?" Max asked in a flat voice. "Your father could use you maybe."

"I'm not too interested in department stores, Uncle Max. Besides, I don't think I'd be good at it."

Grossman nodded at the justice of this evaluation. "Probably not," he said. "I hear your name is Gordon now."

Gordon flushed with surprise; he hadn't yet told his parents about the name change. "It's a pen name, Uncle Max," he said. "I didn't have it officially changed or anything. How did you know?"

Grossman ignored the question. He took a sheet of paper from the top drawer of his desk and pushed it across the polished surface toward his nephew. There was a name already written on it; clearly this meeting was not a spontaneous whim. "Tomorrow, go and see this man," Max said. "He's a friend of mine. He'll give you a job as a foreign correspondent."

Cy Malkin, whose name and phone number were written in longhand, was the editor in chief of the *New York Tribune*. He was a legendary figure in American journalism. Gordon was so surprised that he laughed out loud.

"Cy Malkin? Why don't I just go and talk to President Kennedy? Uncle Max, it doesn't work that way. I mean, I appreciate it, but Cy Malkin doesn't meet with journalism students. Besides, it takes years to work your way up to getting a foreign assignment—"

"Who's talking about working your way up?" Max said reasonably. "I want to give you a graduation present, Velvel. Somebody gives you something, take it. You're a good kid."

Gordon was more surprised by the compliment than by his uncle's naïve notion that a casual friendship with an editor could get him a job. "Thank you, Uncle Max," he said. "I'll call Mr. Malkin tomorrow." He doubted that he actually would, but he didn't want to spoil the moment.

"Fine," said the old man, pushing himself up from the desk. "Let's go back and get strudel."

Gordon put Cy Malkin's number in his wallet, and walked around New York with it for three days before getting up the nerve to call. He was pretty sure he wouldn't get past the editor's secretary. Finally, on the morning before he was scheduled to return to Madison, he rang Malkin's office.

"This is William Grossman," he told the secretary, instinctively using his real name. "My uncle, Max Grossman, said to call Mr. Malkin."

"Oh, we've been expecting to hear from you, Mr. Grossman," said the woman. "I'll put you right through." There was a brief pause, and then a man's voice boomed through the receiver.

"Grossman, this is Malkin," he said. "Are you free for lunch?"

"Excuse me, sir," Gordon said, certain that the editor was under the impression that it was his uncle on the line. "This is *William* Grossman, Max's nephew. He told me to call."

"I know who it is," Malkin said in an impatient voice. "You like Italian food?"

"Yes, sir," Gordon said, polite as a West Point cadet.

"Fine. Meet me at Castello della Mar on Seventh and Fifty-first at one, can you do that?"

"Yes, sir," said Gordon. When he hung up the receiver, he realized that his palm was sweating.

Cy Malkin was an imposing man in his mid-sixties with a bald head and a large, tubular nose. During World War II he had been America's most famous battlefield reporter, and was wounded at Normandy. After the war, as a syndicated columnist, and later as editor of the *Tribune*, he was a crusader for liberal causes and an eloquent critic of Senator McCarthy. His articles were studied in journalism schools around the country, and Gordon knew parts of his stirring defense of the First Amendment, delivered before the House Un-American Activities Committee, almost by heart.

Gordon arrived at the restaurant twenty minutes early. When Malkin walked in he was greeted like a visiting head of state, and Gordon was almost too shy to approach the great man. But Malkin made it easy. He spotted Gordon near the bar, waved a long arm and called for him to join him. "You look like a Grossman," he said in his large voice. "You old enough to drink yet?"

"I'll be twenty-one in June," Gordon said. The drinking age in New York was eighteen, and he was visibly offended by the question. Malkin smiled. "Twenty-one, eh? You think you're ready for the big bad world?" He turned to the waiter who was standing at attention. "Bring us two Chivas on the rocks," he commanded.

Lunch with Cy Malkin proved to be a monologue. He ate without seeming to notice, and lectured nonstop about the affairs of three continents. It was stimulating talk, spiced with personal, sometimes scandalous anecdotes about international figures. He talked familiarly about Ike and Winnie, De Gaulle and Khrushchev, Ben-Gurion and Nehru. It didn't sound to Gordon like name-dropping; Malkin discussed world leaders with the bored self-assurance of a man gossiping about members of his club.

Under different circumstances Gordon would have been thrilled to be the audience for such heady talk, but after his reception that morning he had dared to hope that Malkin might indeed offer him a job, perhaps as a city reporter. Now he saw that this was no job interview. The editor hadn't even asked him what he was studying. He was being taken to lunch as a favor to his uncle Max, nothing more.

This realization made Gordon relax. He even began to fantasize about how he would tell the story to his professors in Madison. "Stopped off at the *Trib* when I was home and had lunch with Cy, you know, Cy Malkin. He's an old family friend. . . ." He was imagining the look on Professor Jarrard's face when Malkin touched his arm, and he snapped back to attention.

"—and so, I think that the situation in Southeast Asia is going to get worse," he said. "William, do you know anything about Vietnam?"

It had been so long since Gordon had said anything that

he had to clear his throat. "A little bit," he said. "I'm not an expert."

"Good," said Malkin. "I don't trust experts. A reporter should never become an expert, it makes him stop listening. How would you like to go out there for us?"

"Are you kidding?"

"We just opened up a bureau in Saigon," he said. "The bureau chief is a young fellow named John Flanagan, who's been on the city beat for us. He'll need a number two man. Do you want the job?"

"Why are you offering it to me?" Gordon asked. "You don't know anything about me. What makes you think I even want to be a reporter?"

Malkin smiled and signaled for more wine. "Those are reporter's questions," he said. "Shows you've got good instincts. As it happens, I know a lot about you. Max sent me a copy of your college transcript and the articles you've done for the *Daily Cardinal* and I had our guy in Milwaukee check you out."

Gordon remembered meeting the *Trib*'s Milwaukee correspondent. He had come to Madison to research an article on left-wing movements on campus, and he had interviewed Gordon for several hours. Now he realized that the article had been a subterfuge, and it thrilled him to think that Cy Malkin had gone to such trouble.

"You've got the makings of a very fine reporter, William," Malkin said. "So, that's one thing. And I'll be honest with you—people aren't exactly standing in line to go to Vietnam. It's hot, it's muggy, and right now there isn't much of a story there. It could turn out to be a dead end. But I've got a feeling that something's going on that we don't know about, and I want somebody with strong legs. That's why I'm offering you the job."

"My uncle Max said it was a graduation present," Gordon blurted out. He knew it was a fresh thing to say, but an

instinct told him that he had better get things straight right at
the beginning. The truth was, he didn't completely trust his
uncle.

"I don't give away jobs to the nephews of old friends,"
Malkin said evenly. "I've made you an offer. If you want to
think about it, that's all right. Just let me know within ten
days."

"I can tell you right now," he said. "I'll take it. When
do I start?"

"When do you graduate?" Malkin asked.

"June first."

"Good. Take a month off, have some fun. You can leave
for Saigon on the first of July."

In the summer of 1961 Vietnam was not even a name on the
map for most Americans. The U.S. buildup was just getting
under way, but it was still almost imperceptible, except to
the handful of American reporters stationed there. They were
mostly young, ambitious, tentatively irreverent men trying
to become full-fledged trench coats, which is what John
Flanagan called foreign correspondents. Flanagan had a
nickname for everything and everybody. He called Vietnam
"Chinatown."

Gordon met Flanagan for the first time at the *Tribune* bureau, a cramped suite of rooms in a downtown office building
not far from the American embassy. Flanagan had sent his
Vietnamese driver, whom he referred to as Tonto, out to the
airport to collect Gordon. When he got to the office he found
Flanagan sitting in front of an old Underwood typewriter, a
cigar in his mouth and a glass of whiskey on the table next
to him. When Gordon knocked on the open door, Flanagan
looked up and blew a puff of Havana smoke at him. "Dr.
Grossman, I presume," he said.

"Reporting for duty," he said, relieved to see that Flanagan's grin was friendly and welcoming. "By the way, I'm going to use my professional name. Gordon."

"Gordon Grossman?" he said.

"William Gordon."

"I don't care what you call yourself," he said. "I'm gonna call you kid, and you call me Flanagan. When I started out, they called me kid. It's like basic training. Then, after a while, I'll start to call you Gordon. William sounds like an English butler. You'll really appreciate it when I start to use your name. It'll make you feel like you've arrived, know what I mean?"

As Gordon soon discovered, the appearance of candor was part of Flanagan's style; he made a habit of explaining his plans and motives in a seemingly ingenuous way. After they had become friends, Gordon often heard Flanagan use the technique on women. "I'll pick you up, we'll have a romantic dinner, a little walk through the city, and back to my apartment," he'd tell a prospective date. "Then we'll bullshit each other about the meaning of life for a couple of hours and get loaded, but we'll really be thinking about going to bed. Then I'll make a move, and we can make love. In the morning we'll have a big breakfast and then we can see what comes next. Sound all right?" Not everybody appreciated this direct approach, but a surprisingly large number of women found it funny and refreshing, and it often worked.

"Maybe you want me to call you chief?" Gordon said, and Flanagan squinted, thinking about it. "Sure, kid, call me chief," he said. "It's a good act. The chief and the kid. Not bad at all. How old are you, kid?"

"Twenty-one, chief. How old are you?"

"Great, we're bantering already. I'm twenty-seven," said Flanagan. "You want a drink?"

"No, thanks," Gordon said. "It's a little early for me."

"That's a banker's answer, not a reporter's answer," said Flanagan. "A reporter says, 'Christ, yes' or 'I'm on the wagon.' Either way, you want to let the guy you're with drink. People talk when they drink, and this business is about getting people to talk.''

"If I get drunk, I won't be able to remember what they've said.''

"Right, kid. The idea is not to get drunk. How about a cigar?''

"Sorry, I'm on the wagon.''

Flanagan laughed. "A quick study. OK, lesson number two. Cigars are a tool of the trade. You give them to people you want to cultivate, but you've got to smoke along with them, otherwise it looks like you just had a baby. And they fit the stereotype—reporters are supposed to have a certain image, it makes people think they're in a movie. Then they want to tell you things, just to keep up their part of the script, see what I mean?''

"OK, I'll take a cigar,'' said Gordon.

" 'Gimme a cigar' sounds better,'' said Flanagan, handing one over. "Try not to sound too smart. You're an SAT and there's nothing you can do about that, but you gotta be a little bit of an actor in this job.''

"What's an SAT?'' Gordon asked.

"A member of the Hebrew persuasion,'' said Flanagan. "I hear your uncle is Max Grossman.''

"My uncle has nothing to do with anything,'' Gordon said defensively, but Flanagan just laughed. "That's not what I hear,'' he said. "I hear he's got something to do with everything. I hear he's even got some pull with Big Cy.''

Gordon flushed with anger and embarrassment; he had hoped that Flanagan wouldn't know how he had got his job.

"Look, kid, don't sweat it. My old man's a big wheel in the printers' union, that's how I got here. It's nothing to be ashamed of. Let's go have lunch, and I'll fill you in on the local color.''

In the three years they spent together in Saigon, John Flanagan became William Gordon's big brother. Within a month or so he stopped calling him kid and began using "Gordon," and the young journalist was surprised to discover that it *did* make him feel good, just as Flanagan had predicted. It didn't take Gordon long to realize that although they were only a few years apart in age, Flanagan was in a whole other league when it came to street smarts and professional savvy.

One of his constant themes was the importance of stereotypes. "The reason the fuckers exist is because they're basically true," he told Gordon one day that first summer over dinner in a restaurant near the bureau he called the Poison Chopstick. "Micks *do* drink. SATs *are* smarter than everybody else. Shvartzers can dunk a basketball. Generals are stupid. Chinamen are inscrutable. You ever hear anybody say that Norwegians have natural rhythm, or Mexicans are good at business?"

"Can't say that I have, chief," said Gordon. He had learned to encourage Flanagan when he was on one of his flights of imagination. He was aware that a lot of the Irishman's style was rubbing off on him.

"Now, there's only two things you can do with a stereotype," Flanagan continued. "You can play on it, which makes you a pro, or you can play against it, which makes you an anti. There are some advantages both ways."

"How about just being yourself?" Gordon asked, but Flanagan shook his head.

"No such thing, kid. Most people don't have a self. They have to invent one. And they don't have enough imagination to come up with something original. You figure out which way they're going, with the stereotype or against it, you've got them. Then you know what buttons to push."

"You include yourself in this analysis?" Gordon asked.

"Sure," said Flanagan. "First of all, I'm a hack. That's a profession for Irishmen who are too honest to be cops. I drink, I talk tough, I have a certain sweetness of character under the wise-guy facade, you've noticed that, right? The thing is, I know what I'm doing; most people don't. So, in a way, I'm going against type, because nobody expects a Mick to be devious. It's a kind of variation. Sophisticated.''

Gordon raised his glass in tribute to his friend's subtlety. ''What about me?''

''A born anti,'' he said. ''I saw it the first time I met you. SATs have a special problem, because they're so self-conscious. If I was trying to show you how smart I really am, I'd say introspective. Actually, that's why I did say introspective, although I know you've already figured out that my Jimmy Cagney routine is an act. But, anyway, the point is, you don't want to be a yeshiva bucher, right?''

''Go ahead, it's your soapbox,'' said Gordon.

''See what I mean? You already talk like somebody out of *The Front Page*. It's a good pose if you can pull it off; do it long enough, and it'll become your real personality. It'll make you distinctive. Good for getting girls, too.''

Flanagan was right about one thing; Gordon had no desire to be a sensitive, brooding moralist. In any case, Vietnam in those days was no place for idealism. The covert buildup was already under way, and even a novice like Gordon could tell that the diplomats and CIA officials were lying about what was going on.

One day Flanagan returned from a CIA briefing with sparkling eyes and a light step. ''What the hell are you so happy about?'' Gordon asked.

''Gordon, these mo-humpers are bullshitting us,'' said Flanagan.

''Yeah, what else is new?''

''Well said, kid. Like Humphrey Bogart. But do you know what they're lying about?''

Gordon shrugged. ''Everything, probably.''

''Everything means nothing,'' said Flanagan triumphantly. ''They want to start a war, Gordon, that's what they're planning to do. A full-scale, shoot-'em-up, send-in-the-marines bang-bang right here in Chinatown.''

Gordon hadn't thought about it in exactly that way, but he realized that Flanagan was right. "OK," he said, "but what difference does it make? I mean, you can't prove that's what they're doing, and you don't have a story without proof.''

"Correct. Which means we get proof," said Flanagan. "What we really need is to get close to Henderson." Henderson was a senior CIA operative, the kind of Wasp that Flanagan called "a white guy."

"How do we do that?"

"The quickest way to a man's heart is through his gatkas, kid," said Flanagan. "That means underwear, in case your Yiddish is rusty.''

From then on, Flanagan made Henderson his special project. He gave Gordon most of the daily work—attending embassy briefings, interviewing local politicians and writing long color stories on Vietnamese teenagers who loved Hula-Hoops and Elvis that wound up spiked in New York. In the meantime, Flanagan spent his time cultivating the CIA agent.

Flanagan's technique was simple; he pimped for him. First, he took Henderson out to dinner and filled his Yankee skull with stories about exotic Oriental whorehouses, most of which he invented on the spot. Henderson was married to a relentlessly wholesome girl with thick ankles who spent all her time and energy making their stay in Saigon a replica of life in Ames, Iowa. Flanagan guessed that she wasn't much fun to come home to.

At the end of their first dinner, Flanagan suggested that a working acquaintance with Saigon's nightlife was a necessary weapon in the arsenal of a compleat CIA operative. Henderson agreed, and declared himself ready to sacrifice some of his precious personal time in the name of national security. He wanted to go out on the town that very night, but Flanagan sent him home in his chauffeured government limo and let him stew for three days. Then he called to suggest another dinner.

"I've got him, Gordon," he said, putting down the receiver. "He's hot to trot."

That night, Flanagan showed up at dinner with two hookers he introduced as university students. Henderson, turning up the charm, entertained the women, whose English was rudimentary, with racy stories of his own college-boy exploits at Yale. Flanagan took the party back to his large, empty apartment and left Henderson alone with the hookers. He spent the night on Gordon's couch, his long legs draped over the edge.

The next afternoon, Flanagan called the CIA man. "You decadent bastard, what did you do to those chicks?" he said in a tone of locker-room jocularity. Henderson asked if he was free for dinner again that night.

In three weeks, Paul Arthur Henderson became a prisoner of his own sex drive. Flanagan supplied him with an unending stream of single women, sister combos and even, on one occasion, a trio. The girls were always introduced as showgirls, secretaries or students; Henderson never guessed that they were actually being financed out of the *Trib*'s entertainment budget. He had a key to Flanagan's apartment, and Flanagan took to spending most of his time at Gordon's flat.

"I'll tell you something, kid," he said one afternoon, after Henderson called to smugly announce that he had "just scored again." "If these dip-shits do start a war, we ain't gonna win it. They don't know the difference between kenahbee juice and Kool-Aid. I don't think our intelligence operation is ready to take on the inscrutable East."

"Not to mention the devious Irish," Gordon said.

Flanagan laughed happily. "It won't be long now," he predicted. "Henderson is a little leery of being blackmailed, which is what they teach these dumbbells in the CIA. So I'm gonna throw him a fastball right down the middle. I'm gonna ask him for help, guy to guy. Nothing in writing, you understand, just some guidance, a little professional courtesy. Perspective on the American effort to save democracy in Chinatown. If I get some string, I can unravel the whole thing.''

It sounded to Gordon like a good plan. He was rooting for Flanagan, and took a vicarious interest in the story, but he wasn't truly involved. At twenty-two, he was still thrilled just to be working for the *Tribune*, drinking at the bar of the Hotel Continental with the other hacks, being accepted into the fraternity of foreign correspondents. Although he wouldn't have wanted Flanagan to know it, he didn't honestly care if there was going to be a war or not.

One day, coming out of a briefing by an embassy political officer, a secretary Gordon had occasionally dated caught him by the coat sleeve. Her name was Andi Moore, and she had been in Saigon for less than six months. She and Gordon had slept together a couple of times in a comradely way, but they were far from serious about each other. She was having an affair with a married American colonel stationed at the embassy, and she used Gordon as a stand-in when he couldn't get away from his wife.

''William,'' she said in a soft, serious voice, ''there's someone I want to introduce you to. Can you come to dinner tonight?''

''Sure, Andi, who is it?''

''Top secret,'' she said, and winked.

That night Gordon arrived with a bottle of wine and some flowers. He didn't usually bring Andi gifts, but he was hoping that her surprise guest would turn out to be a good-looking woman, and he wanted to make an impression. He was disappointed to find her alone and the table set for two.

''Last-minute cancellation,'' she said. ''But the person I wanted you to meet left you a present. I think you'll like it.''

She went to a desk drawer, unlocked it, and pulled out a large manila envelope. "This is for you," she said, although there was no name on the package. "But you can have it only on one condition. You've got to promise me that nobody will ever know how you got it."

"Sure," he said.

"No, not 'sure.' Say, 'I swear to God that nobody will ever know how I got this envelope.' "

Wryly, with his hand over his heart, Gordon recited the pledge. "What's in it?" he asked.

"Let's have dinner first," she said. "I made spaghetti with a white sauce. The wine will go great with it. Then you can go home and open your present."

They ate the spaghetti, drank the wine and made love with impersonal passion to the strains of Johnny Mathis. Gordon forgot about the package; during his time in Saigon he had often been given "gifts" of this sort by diplomats; usually they turned out to be thinly disguised publicity efforts. Andi had to remind him to take the envelope with him when he left her place about eleven.

It wasn't until he got home and opened the envelope that Gordon realized that Andi had given him an extraordinary gift—a set of memos and cables to and from Washington, outlining the new administration's plan for a major troop buildup. There was a lot of jargon and cablese, but the meaning was unmistakable—Kennedy intended to turn Vietnam into a battlefield.

He showed the cables to Flanagan the next morning. The bureau chief read through them quickly, and then again, slowly. When he was finished he looked at Gordon narrowly. "Where the fuck did you get ahold of this?" he demanded.

"John, I can't tell you," he said. "I promised. But I'm pretty sure it's real. I got it from an inside source."

"Obviously," he said. "Fucking Henderson."

"Listen, it's your story," Gordon said quickly. "You're the chief. Take this stuff and use it. Be my guest."

Flanagan thought for a long moment; he was tempted. Finally he sighed and shook his head. "Nope," he said. "You got it, it's yours. You may stop a war with this shit. And you're definitely going to get yourself a Pulitzer." He lifted his glass of Jameson's, which was half full at ten in the morning. "Gordon, you're going to be a star," he said.

The cables served as the basis for a five-part series on the American buildup in Vietnam. Flanagan was wrong about stopping the war, but right about the prize. Gordon got the Pulitzer for international reporting, 1962. He was not yet twenty-three years old.

On the day the prize was announced, Gordon's mother called from New York and cried on the phone. His father got on the extension in his den and growled, "Nice going, boychik," which was his version of conferring a knighthood. Cy Malkin sent a long congratulatory cable and invited him to a dinner with the publisher in New York. Gordon heard nothing from his uncle Max.

He went home for the award ceremony, and traveled to Madison, where he was hailed as a conquering hero. He told no one that his scoop had been given to him by a horny embassy secretary. When he said that he had been lucky, people took it for false modesty.

Gordon returned to Vietnam, where he was boycotted by the embassy, which conducted a fruitless investigation into the leak. Andi Moore avoided him. Their only meeting was in the garden of the French ambassador's residence on Bastille Day. They stood together on the veranda, glasses of cool white wine in their hands, and spoke in a conversational tone. "Why did you do it?" he asked. She smiled. "Just for the heck of it," she said.

Early in 1964, Flanagan went back to New York, where he was assigned to cover City Hall, which he considered a promotion. Foreign policy bored him, and he loved crooked politics. Malkin offered Gordon the Saigon bureau, but he turned it down, and went to Moscow instead.

Gordon stayed abroad sixteen more years. After Moscow he went back to Vietnam; there was a new set of officials in Saigon, and they treated him more like a celebrity than a pariah. From there he went to Tel Aviv, the first Jew ever assigned to cover Israel for the *Trib*; to South Africa for two years, and finally to London, where he was stationed until 1980.

In Israel he won his second Pulitzer. During the Yom Kippur War, on the day before the Israeli army launched its counterattack across the Suez Canal, he got a call from a general he had met once or twice but barely knew. The general invited him to his home in Tzahala, a suburb of Tel Aviv. There, over strong coffee and homemade cake, he gave Gordon the operational plans for the next day. "Why me?" Gordon asked, and the general smiled. "Somebody's going to have this," he said, "and it might as well be you. The *Tribune* is an important newspaper." For the next two weeks the general kept Gordon one day ahead of the pack, and in the end he had another Pulitzer.

The second prize made him a superstar. He was in demand as a lecturer, wrote a warmly received book on détente and became a well-known face on television talk shows. Viewers saw a broad-shouldered man with a salt-and-pepper beard, thinning black hair and a prominent nose, broken in a pickup basketball game with a group of marine embassy guards in Tel Aviv. For television appearances, Gordon wore a tie and coat; otherwise, he dressed in jeans and a faded corduroy jacket.

In 1980, Gordon returned to the States for good. Not long after, he was profiled by the *Atlantic Monthly* in an admiring article entitled "William Gordon, Mr. Reporter." The writer, who was not much older than Gordon had been when he first went to Vietnam, described him as a profanely wise, cigar-chomping, hard-drinking cynic with a physical resemblance to Abbie Hoffman. This portrait greatly amused Flanagan.

"I know you're still in there, kid," he said over drinks at Gallagher's. "I know you're still a sensitive SAT at heart." Gordon laughed. It was a relief to him that Flanagan knew his act, like leaving a spare house key with a reliable neighbor.

Aside from Flanagan, only Max seemed to see through Gordon's facade. He had visited the old man occasionally during his home leaves, but their relationship remained cool. Gordon realized that efforts to impress his uncle with macho stories from the world's battlefields had little effect; the old man continued to relate to him as a lightweight, a good talker. Eventually Gordon stopped trying, and confined his chats with his uncle to foreign affairs. Several times the old man had surprised him with his knowledge of Latin American and East Asian politicians. It occurred to Gordon that Max probably had business dealings with some of them, but his reportorial instincts, usually sharp, deserted him when it came to his uncle.

The *Tribune* rewarded Gordon by making him a columnist and roving international correspondent. After the grind of foreign reporting, the task of turning out two columns a week was light work, and it left him plenty of time for other pursuits. Flanagan was now deputy city editor, and the two old friends spent a lot of time drinking in various haunts downtown. Flanagan had been married, briefly and indignantly, and now lived in misogynistic solitude in a small apartment near Gramercy Square. Gordon was still single, and his name occasionally appeared on lists of the city's most eligible bachelors. Unlike Flanagan, he loved women, but he had yet to meet one he was certain was good enough for him.

Flanagan's obsession was New York politics, and he usually contrived to steer their conversations to some municipal scandal or local villain. Venality and corruption fascinated and amused him, and he frequently asked Gordon about his uncle Max. He found it unbelievable that Gordon knew and cared so little about his celebrated uncle. One night at O'Dwyer's, a pub on Twenty-third Street, Flanagan was holding forth on the subterranean connection between union pension funds and a Bronx ward leader when he was interrupted by a commotion at the door.

Gordon turned and saw a slender young woman, surrounded by three men in business suits, walk through the crowded room to a table in the rear. Several people called her name, and one or two even applauded. Dressed in sneakers, jeans and a T-shirt, she carried herself regally, shoulders thrown back and head high, as if she were trying to peer over an obstacle. Her most striking features were shoulder-length black hair that hung down in wild curls and a powerful hawk-like nose. She wasn't at all beautiful—special-looking was the description that came to mind—but she filled the room with her presence.

"That's Jupiter Evans," said Flanagan.

"The actress?"

"How many women you think are named Jupiter Evans? Yeah, the actress. She's supposed to be a dyke."

"Too bad. She's great-looking," Gordon said.

"Wanna meet her?"

"Why, you know her?"

"I've met her a couple of times. She used to go around with Lizzie Taylor. That's how I know she's a les. Come on, I'll introduce you."

Flanagan led the way to the actress's table. "Miss Evans, I'm John Flanagan, deputy editor of the *Tribune*," he said. "I'm a friend of Lizzie's."

She nodded and smiled. When she did, her brown eyes flashed and crinkled around the edges, and Gordon noticed little laugh lines. The smile was a friendly gesture of recognition, nothing more, but it stunned and charmed Gordon completely.

"Jesus, I've never seen anybody smile like that," he said without thinking. She turned her head and looked at him full in the face. He blushed.

"Jupiter, this is my protégé, Velvel Gordon," said Flanagan. "He's been away a long time and he's not used to being around women."

"Have you been in jail, Mr. Gordon?" she asked in an amused voice.

"Jail?" he said.

Flanagan laughed. "Worse, he's a foreign correspondent," he told her.

To Gordon's surprise, she looked at him closely. "Are you William Gordon?"

"That's me," he said. "Velvel is sort of a family nickname. It's Yiddish."

"No kidding," she said, but nicely. "I've been reading you for years. I'm a major fan."

"Most people don't care much about foreign stories," Gordon observed, and was immediately sorry. The implication that Jupiter Evans was like most people wasn't flattering, and she picked it up right away.

"My father taught international relations at Yale," she said, letting him off the hook. "I was raised on it. What's the capital of Senegal?"

"Senegal? It's, ah, Dakar," he said.

"Right. OK, I guess you must be William Gordon," she smiled. "Why don't you join us." Flanagan said no at the same time Gordon said yes, and everybody laughed.

"Come on, Flanagan, I'll buy you a drink," she said, signaling to the waiter. "You too, Velvel."

"You've got to call me William. And I'm buying," Gordon said. He wanted to get high in a hurry; it was the only way he was going to be able to get up the courage to ask her to come home with him.

Three bourbon boilermakers later, Gordon felt a warm self-confidence based, he was sure, not only on the liquor but on Jupiter's encouragement. She was frankly flirting with him, making it plain she found him attractive. Thank God, he thought; Flanagan's gossip was wrong.

"What are you doing after the show?" he asked in what he hoped was a cool, sophisticated tone.

Jupiter laughed and fixed him with a direct, brown-eyed look. "Is that an innocent question?"

"I dunno. Are you an innocent girl?"

"Mr. Gordon," she said, "don't you know I'm supposed to be gay?"

He was startled by her directness. "No, I didn't know that," he stammered. "Are you?"

"That's what it says in the papers," she said. "Do you believe what you read in the papers?"

"I don't even believe what I *write* in the papers," he said. "So, you're not gay?"

"I'm not sure," she said. "Sometimes I am and sometimes I'm not. I'm not tonight."

"Then maybe we ought to take advantage of the timing," Gordon said.

"Maybe we ought to," she agreed. "We've only got an hour to midnight."

That was the first time William Gordon made love with Jupiter Evans. In the next three years they went to bed together eight more times. There were single weeks when they had more fights than that.

The fights were always the same. They started out as calm discussions of what she referred to as her "problem," which, Gordon finally understood after months of pretending, was that she feared and resented men. "I want to love you," she said. "I'm trying. But I can't." Inevitably, Gordon's efforts at being a sensitive, nurturing male degenerated into angry accusations and a vow never to see her again. Unable to control what he recognized as a self-destructive obsession, these resolutions usually lasted about two weeks.

Naturally, Gordon discussed the situation with Flanagan. Just as naturally, he was unsympathetic. Since Saigon, his attitude toward women had undergone a slow, negative shift from utilitarian disdain to open hostility.

"The problem with you is that you're still an SAT at heart," he said. "You like being Jake Barnes, or Lady Brett or whoever. You want to get laid, find a girl that likes guys— there must be a few of them left."

"You sound like my father," Gordon said.

"You told him about this?" asked Flanagan in disbelief.

" 'Fraid so. Christ, that was a mistake. You have the same fucking categorical tone."

"Categorical, am I?" said Flanagan. "Does that mean, like, logical, Professor?"

"It means like asshole, asshole," Gordon said, and changed the topic to the piracy of a group of building contractors who were repairing a municipal bridge with papier-mâché. Jupiter Evans was a problem that even the chief couldn't solve.

3

GORDON PUT DOWN THE FILE AND LOOKED AT BEL-
zer. "Jesus, Nate," he said. "Jesus H. Christ. What are we
talking about? In dollars?"

"Probably between three and five," he said. "It's not exactly the kind of thing you get a Merrill Lynch statement on,
you know?"

"Come on, Nate, there's a hell of a lot more than five
million there. Even I can see that."

Belzer looked amused. "That's five *hundred* million, Velvel," he said. "One half of one billion. You speak Jewish?"

"I can understand a little," he said. He felt as if his lips
were frozen.

"*A sach gelt,*" said Belzer softly. "A lot of money. That's
what your uncle had—a sach gelt."

"Why me, Nate?" Gordon asked. His reporter's training
was taking over, trying to organize the chaos in his brain.

"Who else, Velvel? Who else? Ida's an old woman. Your
father's no spring chicken either. Neither one of them needs
the money, and besides, they couldn't do what's necessary
to get it."

"What do you mean, what's necessary? The money's
mine, according to this."

Belzer sighed, a slow, wheezing sound. It occurred to Gordon that he must be close to eighty. Like his father and Uncle Max, Belzer had lived his life among men with guns, but there was a gentle quality about him, quite different from Max's taciturn coldness or Al Grossman's hard-eyed machismo. He would have made a good lawyer, Gordon thought; the phrase "loyal fiduciary" came to mind.

"It's yours but it's not yours, Velvel," he said. "It's there, but nobody's handing it to you. You can see for yourself that it's not the kind of thing you put through a probate court. Fifteen percent of the action on the Brooklyn docks, a third of the union operation, the Colombian business, the lottery tickets. . . . Even a lot of the legitimate stuff isn't written down anyplace. For example, Max had half the Grace Hotel in Vegas with Luigi Spadafore, OK. But where is Max's name? No place. That's what I mean. It's all there, but it's not there. Max had it because he was Max. The lokshen didn't fool with him because he knew where the bodies were buried. But you're not Max. You want it, you gotta take it.''

Gordon laughed. "Take it? You mean go to the mattresses? Bring in the hit men? Shoot it out with Luigi Spadafore and the Mafia? Jesus, Nate, you kidding or what? That kind of stuff doesn't happen anymore—this is 1982. I'm a journalist, for Christ's sake. I've got two Pulitzers. I had dinner last week with Arthur Schlesinger.''

Belzer frowned, trying to place the name. "Arthur Schlesinger? I saw him on PBS. Little fellow with a bow tie. Listen, Velvel, you think the lokshen will hand over five hundred million bucks because you've been on *Meet the Press*? I want you to think about this. You don't have to take the money. You make a good living right now, and when your father passes on you'll get a few million. That's plenty. Max knew that. He said to tell you he wouldn't mind if you passed on the whole deal. It's up to you.''

"And what if I pass? What happens to the money then?''

Belzer sighed again, and shrugged eloquently. "If you pass, there is no money," he said. "It goes to Max's partner, Luigi Spadafore. Some goes to the other Families. It goes to anyone willing to do what's necessary to pick it up."

"How about Max's own people?" asked Gordon. "I mean, some of them must be able to take it, or some of it."

Belzer laughed, a hollow sound. "Max's people? You mean the alter kockers out there in the other room? You gotta be kidding. Most of them make pee-pee into bags these days. Half of them are in Florida, drooling over their gin-rummy hands. We got no people left, Velvel. Just Max, your father and me, and some bookkeepers. And a few dozen safety deposit boxes with a lot of insurance-type information."

"And half a billion bucks," Gordon said.

Belzer nodded slowly. "Yeah, and half a billion bucks."

"Listen, Nate, supposing I decide I want the money. What do I have to do? I mean, specifically?"

The old man raised his hands in a palms-up gesture. "If you want me to say specifically, I have a few ideas," he said. "You'd need to meet with Luigi Spadafore, and discuss things, try to come to an agreement. Basically you'd have to convince them that they need you, or that it would be dangerous for them to fight you. Either way, it won't be easy, I promise you that."

For a moment, Gordon tried to imagine himself frightening a group of mafiosi. "I wouldn't know how to begin, even—"

"I know, I know," said Belzer. "Look, Velvel, you remember that *Godfather* movie? First, Don Corleone had his oldest son in the business. Then he gets killed, and they bring in the young one, what's-his-name—"

"Michael," Gordon said automatically.

Suddenly Belzer's voice became a hoarse whisper, an uncanny imitation of Marlon Brando. "Listen, Michael, after I'm gone, one of the captains is going to try to set up a meet.

And that'll be the traitor.'' His voice returned to normal. "You think that's Hollywood, but it's real life. For them it's a family business, the father passes it on to the son. They grow up knowing how to operate. But for us, it was a whole different thing. Our fathers were tailors, pushcart immigrants. Our kids are doctors, lawyers, journalists like you. For us, it was never a way of life, just a way to make a good living, maybe get a few of the finer things. You think Max ever dreamed he'd end up with five hundred million bucks? Who knew? Who prepared?''

"Nate, I'm going to need some time to think about this,'' Gordon said. "Who can I talk to about it?''

"Talk? You can talk to anybody you want. We don't have a code of silence or blood oaths or any of that goyim naches. But remember this—you talk to someone, he's been talked to. He knows. And you can't make him un-know, if you see what I mean. So I'd be careful.''

"I still don't understand why my father isn't here,'' Gordon said. "Doesn't he know about Max's will?''

"He knows,'' said Belzer, "and I gotta tell you, he doesn't approve. He didn't want to be here, I told you that.''

"Why not?'' asked Gordon. It occurred to him that his father might be jealous.

"I can't speak for your father, Velvel. You should talk to him yourself.'' Belzer reached across the desk and gathered up the folder, sliding it into a drawer and locking it in one practiced motion. Clearly the meeting was over.

"Nate, one more question. Supposing I decide to take the money, or some of it. Will you be there to help me? I wouldn't even know how to find Spadafore, or what to say. And I still don't have a real idea of how the money is tied up, or where.''

Belzer put his hands flat on the desk and pushed himself out of the seat with a perceptible effort. Gordon stood too, and noticed that, despite the air conditioning, the seat of his pants was damp. "I'll be around for a while,'' he said, walking around the desk and taking Gordon's elbow. "I'll do what I can. But I'm an old man, Velvel; and this isn't an old man's game."

That night, almost exactly at nine, the buzzer rang and Jimmy, the night doorman, announced that Jupiter was in the lobby. Promptness was one of Jupiter's virtues, formality one of her defenses. Although she had been to Gordon's apartment a hundred times, she always insisted on being announced. It was, he knew, one of the many ways she had of keeping a small, hard distance between them.

"Jupiter Evans?" he said to Jimmy. "Never heard of her."

The doorman laughed, as he always did. Once, after a rare visit from his father, a friend in the next building had told Gordon that he overheard Jimmy bragging to the neighboring doorman that Gordon was a connected guy. Since then, Gordon had made a point of exchanging Cagney-type wisecracks with the doorman.

"She looks all right to me," he said. "Should I send her up, boss?"

Jupiter came in wearing a Yale sweatshirt, a pair of tight faded jeans and red high-top Converse All-Stars. And a thirty-five-thousand-dollar full-length mink. At the door she posed for a brief moment like a fashion model, one hip thrown out and lips puckered. Then, when she saw the hungry look on Gordon's face, she gave him a chaste kiss on the lips, tossed her coat over a chair and plopped down on the couch.

Gordon poured them each a Wild Turkey on the rocks—her first, his third. He had never lost hope, even after so many years, that he would someday say the magic words that would make her stop being what she always would be. The booze gave him a quicksilver optimism and the illusion of eloquence. It also dulled the pain. Sometimes he could get through an entire night pretending to be as detached and cool as she was; but this wasn't going to be one of those times. Tonight he would reach out for her, and she would, with humor and exquisitely calibrated distance, say no. Tonight it would hurt. And so, tonight, he would be drunk.

"I saw you on the news," said Jupiter. "You looked very handsome in that black suit." She let her gaze run over him, now back in jeans and a Wisconsin T-shirt. "I take it you're out of mourning," she added in a droll tone. "Think you're up to a steak and salad at Barney's? My treat."

"I thought we'd order in Chinese. I want to talk to you about something."

A wary, weary look came over Jupiter's face. "What's on your agenda, William?" she asked.

"Nothing special, really," he said. Gordon still hadn't decided whether to tell her about the will. He was tempted; Jupiter was shrewd about money and people, especially him. It made him uncomfortable to admit it, but she knew him better than anyone; she was the only person in the world who had seen him beg. On the other hand, he was afraid that she would find the story ridiculous, and him comical for taking it seriously. He decided not to decide; he would just talk, and see what came out.

"Did Max leave you a lot of money?" she asked, as if she had read his mind. Jupiter could do that. Sometimes they would be drinking together in a bar and she would casually nod toward a woman at a distant table and say, "She's one," meaning a lesbian. Invariably, it was someone Gordon had noticed and wondered about. Before meeting Jupiter he had rarely thought about lesbians; now they seemed to be everywhere.

"Uh, that depends on what you mean by a lot of money," he said. "It's all sort of up in the air right now. But let's say he did leave me a lot. Would that make a difference?"

"To you or to me?" she asked, smiling.

"To you."

"That would depend on how much it was," she said, still smiling, but paying attention, too. "I've always wanted to own a big boat. Could you buy me a big boat?"

"Let's say I bought you a big boat. Would you marry me?"

"We've been through this before," she said. "You forget Mexico already? Marriage isn't the solution to your problem or mine, you know that."

"Kesef yanes akel," Gordon said. "That means 'money solves everything.' My aunt Ida says that."

"Your aunt Ida is an old Jewish lady with emphysema and vulgar jewelry," said Jupiter in a tight, cruel tone. "If you're going to quote from the sages of your people, pick somebody a little more profound."

"OK, as Moses said to Pharaoh, fuck you," Gordon said. He got up to pour himself another drink and came back with the bottle. Jupiter held out her glass for a refill, and then put a placating hand on his arm.

"I'm sorry," she said. "But you know I don't like playing pretend with you. It hurts us both too much."

"Listen," he said, trying to lighten the mood. "You want a big boat or don't you want a big boat?"

"Goddamn it, you know what I want," she said. "I want a baby. I want to be normal. I want to go home and be by myself." Jupiter was on her feet, already pulling on the mink. Gordon grabbed a sleeve and she lost her balance, falling back onto the couch. He leaned over and held her hard by the shoulders. Their faces were close enough for him to see the flecks of yellow in her brown eyes.

"I can give you a baby," he said, hoping that this time, the magic words would come and open the gates. "I can give you a normal life, and a boat, and any goddamn thing you want. I can—"

"You can give me another drink, sugah," she said, affecting a Southern accent. Gordon cursed inwardly; the magic

words weren't about to open anything that night. He kissed
her gently on the cheek, the way he always did after one of
these scenes, like a man smoothing the sheets of a rumpled
bed.

"I like you when you're sweet, Will," she said. "Be sweet
tonight, and let's not drive each other crazy."

"How big a boat?" Jupiter asked, wiping the juice of her
second nineteen-dollar hamburger off her lips.

Barney's was full that night and, as usual, people were
staring at Jupiter Evans. She ignored them, and for most of
the meal she pretty much ignored Gordon as well, devouring
the burgers with a carnivorous concentration that belied her
quiche-and-mineral-water image.

"You eat like a linebacker," Gordon said.

"I eat like a healthy growing girl. How big a boat?"

"Let me ask you a question. How much did you earn last
year?"

She paused, fork in midair, considering. "With the money
for the movie, and counting past royalties for TV stuff and
so on, pretty close to five million dollars," she said. Although she tried to keep her voice level, Gordon detected a
note of pride; there was more than a little carnivore in Jupiter
when it came to money, too.

"Well, let me put it this way," he said. "Potentially, what
my uncle left me, the interest on it alone is about ten times
that."

"What!" she said, loud enough for the people at nearby
tables to turn and look.

"Yeah, you figure it out, you're good with numbers. Four,
five hundred million at, say, eight percent. Most of it tax-
free. I guess it comes to more than fifty million when you
think of it that way."

"This is a joke, right? Your uncle couldn't have been that
rich." Jupiter had stopped eating and her brown eyes shone.

Plainly she was fascinated. Incongruously, Gordon recalled Kissinger's old line about power being an aphrodisiac, and felt a swelling in his crotch. Next time I see Henry I'll tell him I got a hard-on because of him, Gordon thought.

"Rich, richer, richest," he said to Jupiter, feeling optimistic again. "Crime pays, it turns out."

"Five hundred million dollars," she said, turning the phrase slowly on her tongue. "Just thinking about it gives me a chill. You really could give me a big boat, couldn't you?"

"And a baby," he said. For the first time in three years, Gordon felt as if he might have a real chance with Jupiter Evans. He had suddenly discovered the magic words.

He awoke early the next morning, but not early enough to find Jupiter still in his bed. There was only a hastily scrawled note: "Had to go. Early exercise class. You were wonderful last night. Call you later. Love, J."

Gordon had a high-quality Wild Turkey 101 hangover, but the adrenaline in his body was offsetting it nicely. She loves me, he thought. For my money, OK, but what the hell's money for if not to buy happiness? Now all I have to do is find a way to keep the dough from a group of bloodthirsty Sicilian murderers and I'm all set.

At seven-thirty he called his father's number. The old man picked it up on the second ring and barked "Grossman." Gordon pictured him sitting at the breakfast table with a cup of coffee, a toasted bagel with cream cheese and the sports page. "Grossman," he said in reply. "How did the Knicks do?"

"Won by eleven," said the old man happily. "Beat the spread by three, which is how I went. I think I'll use the dough to plant some trees for Max in Israel." He laughed, and Gordon could almost smell the stale cigars and cream cheese on his breath.

"You're getting sentimental in your old age, Pop."

"Nah, Max would have done the same for me," he said. "What's a brother for, after all? Whataya want, Velvel, I'm in the middle of something here."

"You know about Uncle Max's will, Pop?"

"Yeah, I know," he said. Gordon waited for more, but there was only silence.

" 'Yeah, I know'? Your only son inherits half a—"

"Shut up, Velvel!" Grossman exploded. "What the hell's wrong with you, for crying out loud?"

"Pop, what's the matter—"

"The telephone, you shmendrick. You got something to say to me, meet me where we had lunch last time. You remember? Twelve o'clock, sharp. All right?"

The phone rang while Gordon was in the shower. Hoping it was Jupiter, he stumbled out, wrapped in a towel, and caught it on the sixth ring. It was Flanagan.

"Top of the morning to you, boychik," he said in a carefree tone. It was too early for him to sound like that, Gordon thought; he must be just getting home.

"What's on your mind, chief?" he asked.

"Thought we might go over together, later on," Flanagan said.

"Go over together where?" asked Gordon.

"To Ida's. The shivah. It's a weeklong period of mourning in case you didn't know," he said.

"Ida's probably on her way to Vegas."

"Vegas! She wouldn't do that; Max isn't even cold yet," he protested. He seemed genuinely shocked.

"Listen, Flanagan, do you fuck with a rubber?"

"Yeah, when need be. What's that got to do with anything?"

"Catholics aren't supposed to fuck with a rubber. Jews

aren't supposed to go to Vegas after their husband's funeral. But nobody's perfect. It's an irreverent world."

"OK, so Ida's in Vegas. Why don't you come by the paper, we can go around the corner for a drink and talk."

"What do you want to talk about?"

"Are you kidding?" asked Flanagan. "I want to hear what Nathan Belzer told you."

"How do you know what he told me?"

"I don't. But I saw your face when you came out yesterday, boychik. You know what you reminded me of? Of the way you looked in Saigon when you got the cables."

Until that moment Gordon hadn't decided whether or not to tell Flanagan about his uncle's will, but now he realized that he would. He had to tell someone besides Jupiter; it was too good a story to keep. "OK, I'll meet you at three," he said. "How will I recognize you?"

Flanagan laughed at their old gag. "I'll be the Catholic wearing the rubber," he said.

4

GORDON SPOTTED THE TOP OF HIS FATHER'S HEAD as soon as he walked into the Emerald Isle. Grossman was sitting in a rear booth, wearing a gray tweed sport coat over a black turtleneck, bending over the *Sporting News*. The small restaurant was crowded with the usual mix of workmen in flannel shirts and jeans drinking lunch at the bar and junior TV types from nearby ABC kibbitzing in the booths. On the way to the table he heard the name Reggie twice, and Peter three times.

Gordon had never met Reggie Jackson, but he vividly recalled his last encounter with Peter Jennings. They had been having dinner together at the American Colony Hotel in Jerusalem when Jennings was summoned to the phone. It was New York calling to inform him that he had just been voted one of America's ten best-dressed men.

"It's like a Pulitzer for your wardrobe, Peter," Gordon had told him.

Gordon slid into the seat opposite his father, who looked up from his paper and grunted a greeting. At seventy he still had a head of grizzled gray hair and taut, thick-looking skin that made him seem fifteen years younger. "Pistons against the Knicks tonight,'' he said. ''This city is the sports capital of the universe.''

''Nice to see you, too, Pop,'' he said. ''What do you want to eat?''

''Already ordered,'' said Grossman. ''Try the Irish stew. And the fries here are great.''

''Why don't you just get an order of straight cholesterol?''

''I'd just as soon die from good food as anything else,'' growled the old man. ''I see June Allyson, all them old broads on the tube eating prunes and wheat germ, I want to puke. You think I wanna wind up like Art Linkletter? Gimme a break.''

Gordon ordered Irish stew and a draft Guinness, and waited for the food while his father wolfed down his meal. The stew arrived just as Grossman finished, and he belched loudly as his son lowered his tablespoon into the bowl.

''What's on your mind, Velvel?'' he asked, rubbing his hands together impatiently. ''I'm not gonna just sit here and watch you eat.''

''You know what's on my mind, Pop. What Nate talked to me about yesterday, the will. I want to know what you think I ought to do.''

''Do? What's to do? Max was an old man with a sense of humor, that's all.''

''It's a lot of money, Pop,'' he said. ''Nate was talking about, well, it could be five hundred million.''

''Sure, five hundred million. Why not five hundred trillion while you're at it? Listen, Velvel, there's no money there. The legitimate stuff, the department stores and the housing developments, all that went to Ida, who, if she don't blow it on blackjack and pro wrestling, will someday leave it to you. Personally, I'm planning to spend all mine before I kick off, but you'll still probably get something there too. Plus, you got a hell of a job. That's enough for anybody.''

"Pop, what about the business? I mean, the Colombian thing, the docks, the casinos—"

"That's what I'm trying to tell you, Velvel. There is no business. It belonged to Max and the Spadafores and one or two other greaseballs. Now it belongs to them, period. You think they're going to let your accountant sit down and audit the books, maybe elect you to the board of directors? No way, Moshe." He laughed, a short, amused grunt, and waved to the waiter for the bill.

"Hold it a minute, Pop, goddamn it," Gordon said, his voice rising. "Nate said the money belongs to anyone who does what's necessary to get it. It belonged to Uncle Max. He left it to me. So, why shouldn't I try to pick it up, at least some of it?"

"You're serious," Grossman said, a note of incredulity in his raspy voice. "You wanna do what's necessary? OK, here's what's necessary. You gotta go out and buy a gun. Then you gotta kill Luigi Spadafore, his two sons, eleven cousins and thirty-seven nephews. Then you gotta kill everybody who came from his fucking village in Sicily, and all *their* uncles and cousins. Then you get to keep the money. OK? Can I go now, I got a few things to do this afternoon."

"Well, if they're so tough, why didn't they kill Uncle Max? Or you, for that matter? Or Nate Belzer?"

"Nate's a bookkeeper and I've been retired for years," Grossman said, snapping the check between his fingers. "As far as Max was concerned, well, you ain't Max. For one thing, Max and Luigi Spadafore go back to the old neighborhood. Max took care of his kids when he was in the joint, handled his dough, the whole shot. Plus, Max knew where the money was—a lot of these deals were in his head, and they went to heaven along with him. So they respected Max and they needed him. You?" He made a flipping gesture with his hand, like a man tossing a pancake into the air. "You, my dear Velvel, they don't need and, no offense, they don't respect.''

"Wait a minute, though," Gordon said. "They don't know that Max didn't tell me details about the money. Right?''

Grossman nodded, eyes hooded under his thick brows. "So?'' he said.

"So that gives us leverage. It gives us a chance to deal, a part of the money in return for whatever information Belzer has. We might at least come out of this with a big chunk of—''

"Goddammit, who is this we and us?'' Gordon's father exploded. "I'm not a part of this mishegoss. You want to blackmail the Mafia? You got shit for brains or what? These guys are smart, Velvel—maybe not smart enough to give lectures at the Ninety-second Street Y, but smart enough to figure out that if you give them the stuff we got, they don't need you around anymore.''

Suddenly his voice softened and Gordon saw something in his eyes that hadn't been there before—alarm. "Listen, Velvel, this is your old man talking. I'm not gonna say that maybe I haven't been such a good father because we both know I been a great fucking father. I took you to ball games as a kid. I saw to it you went to the best schools. I always had time, you wanted to talk something over. When you went away to college I bought you a sports car, remember? The Vette with the leather interior. Even after you left home, did I stop taking care of you? Hell, no. I got you that prize—''

"What? What prize did you get me?'' For the first time in years, perhaps for the first time in his life, Gordon saw his father blush.

"Ah, skip it,'' he said.

"No, I won't skip it. What prize did you get me?''

"I'm sorry, I thought you figured it out yesterday when you saw Henderson's name in the stuff Nate showed you—''

"Henderson?''

"Yeah, that Yankee yutz, used to be with the CIA over there. You didn't see his name on the shnorrers list?"

Gordon recalled that there had been a list among the papers he had seen the day before—names of politicians, judges, senior government officials. He might have seen a Henderson, but he had been too much in shock for it to register.

"You mean the cables I got—"

"Yeah, from Henderson," Grossman said softly. "Funny thing, too, we wound up making a bundle with that guy. Arms in Latin America. Anyway, the point is, I did all these things for only one reason. Because I love you. You're the only son I got. And I don't want to see you get mixed up in something you can't handle."

Gordon felt nauseated and numb. The two Pulitzers were as much a part of his identity as his nose or his name—more, because he had earned them. They defined his profession and certified his excellence: William Gordon, Pulitzer Prize–winning journalist. "What about the other one?" he asked thickly.

"The other prize? That one was Max's idea. He was tight with the Israelis ever since the war in 1948. Sold them weapons. Sold some to the Arabs, too, but he made sure to send them the wrong-size bullets. Yeah, Max worked it out with some general, Bar Dror, I think was his name. I think Max was jealous after the Vietnam business, wanted to fix the Pulitzer himself. Speaking of which, sometime I'll tell you about the '38 World Series—"

"Goddamn you," Gordon said. To his horror, he felt tears in his eyes and the start of a sob in his throat. "You rotten bastard, you dirty rotten bastard—"

"You think Luigi Spadafore cries when he gets bad news," demanded Grossman harshly. " 'You dirty bastard,' " he imitated in a whiny tone, " 'you dirty rotten bastard.' Why? Because I gave you a hand? I fix a prize for the opposition, then you can get pissed. But don't blame me for doing what any father would do if he got the chance, OK? Look," he said in an appeasing voice, "you're a top kid, Velvel. You think if you weren't a great reporter they wouldn't have found out about it by now? So you got a little help, so what? The next one, you win on your own." He extended his hand. "Deal?"

The speech gave Gordon time to regain his composure. "You can take that hand and shove it up your ass," he said, rising. "You think that you and Luigi Spadafore and all the rest of your crooked buddies are so smart? We'll see, Pop."

"Velvel, don't do this," he said. "I'm warning you, don't do it."

"Kiss my ass, you broken-down old greaser," Gordon said, turning toward the door. "Goddammit, Pop, kiss my fucking ass."

Flanagan sat at his desk peering into the screen of his computer terminal. As he read he moved his lips, and his normally cynical face had an innocent, almost childish look, like an altar boy in silent devotion. Gordon came around in back of him and read over his shoulder; it was a story about a state senator from Queens who had been caught using his office in Albany as the set for porno movies.

"No wonder the Polacks want democracy," said Flanagan happily.

Gordon grunted, and Flanagan swiveled around in his chair. "You look like shit, kid. What's the matter?" he said.

"Remember Arthur Henderson?" he asked.

"Yeah, that perfidious hard-on. Where did you come up with him?"

"I didn't. My father did. He paid Henderson off in Nam to give me the cables. How about that, sports fans?"

"Henderson? Your father and Henderson? I don't get it."

"It's been a day of surprises," Gordon said. "If you're

done getting your rocks off, let's go over to Gallagher's and
I'll tell you a story that won't be in the paper tomorrow.''

Flanagan sat with a gin and tonic in front of him, so absorbed
in Gordon's account of the events of the past twenty-four
hours that he forgot to drink. It was an edited version—Gordon omitted Jupiter's big boat and the magic words and, out
of habit, some of his father's more incriminating admissions.
Even in its censored form, however, the story had a powerful
effect on Flanagan, who looked at Gordon with something
like awe.

"Each man has but one destiny," he intoned when Gordon finished.

"What the hell is that supposed to mean?"

"*The Godfather*," he said. "It's what Don Corleone says
when he finds out that Michael offed the police captain."

"Christ on a crutch, everybody keeps quoting *The Godfather*," Gordon said. "Can't you come up with something
original at least?"

"Look, let's say your uncle murdered your father and married your mother—"

"My mother's dead," he said. "So's my uncle, in case
you've forgotten—"

"Yeah, OK, but let's say that he did. Don't you think
people would quote you *Hamlet*? Mario Puzo wrote the book
on this kind of thing. There's even an Irish consigliere, don't
forget."

For the first time since lunch Gordon laughed. "Who,
you?"

"Da da da da, da da da da, da da da da," Flanagan
hummed the theme from *The Godfather*. "I will serve you,
Don Velvel, as faithfully as if I were your own son." He
reached over and took Gordon's hand, bent his head and
kissed the third finger of his left hand. "First thing we do is
get you a ring," he said.

5

GORDON GOT HOME FROM GALLAGHER'S A LITTLE
after six, feeling spent and out of focus. He poured himself
a bourbon, lit up a Winston and sat on his small terrace,
overlooking the Museum of Natural History, to consider what
to do next. For twenty years he had been making his living
by sorting out reality from illusion and putting chaotic events
into eight-hundred-word capsules. Now he groped to make
sense of his own situation.

First: All day long he had been thinking seriously about
making a grab for the money. What were his real motives?
Lust for Jupiter. Greed. The sheer romance of the thing. OK,
he conceded, and a desire (probably childish) to prove to his
father that he could do it.

Second: What problems were involved? Number one, getting the money would involve a fight with Luigi Spadafore.
And, number two, even supposing he had the balls to do it,
keeping the money would mean becoming a gangster. What
else could he do—hire a management firm to handle his in-
vestments?

The more he thought about it, the more impossible it
seemed, and the more ridiculous. Max had left him a fortune
in Confederate money; there was no other way to look at it.

Maybe, he thought, I could turn this into a short story some-time, "The Secret Life of William Gordon." He wondered how much *The New Yorker* paid for short stories. . . .

The phone rang and he picked it up on the first ring.

"May I please speak to Mr. Gordon?" said a man's voice he didn't recognize.

"Speaking."

"Mr. Gordon, this is Carlo Sesti." The voice was a cul-tivated, quasi-British tenor. For a moment Gordon thought it was Bill Buckley, playing a joke. A few months before, a Harlem congressman had threatened to sue Gordon for def-amation of character after he had reported that the congress-man represented South African firms in arms deals. The threat made the papers, and Buckley had called in a disguised voice, offering to sell Gordon libel insurance. Like a jerk, he had asked about premiums, and the story made the rounds for several days.

"What can I do for you, Mr. Sesti?" Gordon asked, giv-ing the last name a slight ironic emphasis, just in case.

"We don't know one another, but I was a business asso-ciate of your late uncle's," he said. "I'm calling to express my condolences. I was at the funeral, of course, but I didn't want to intrude on your privacy."

"Very thoughtful of you."

"Your uncle was a unique figure, Mr. Gordon, as I'm sure you know better than I. It was an honor to have done business with him."

"I guess that depends on what kind of business you did," Gordon said, keeping his voice neutral.

"That is the other reason for this phone call," said Sesti. "Your uncle left several outstanding matters that need to be discussed. I understand that you are his beneficiary?"

Goddamn that Flanagan and his big Irish mouth, Gordon thought; this must be his idea of a practical joke. "Mr. Sesti," he said, "no offense, but I don't know who you are or what you're talking about. My uncle's beneficiary is his wife.''

''I appreciate that, Mr. Gordon, but there are one or two matters on which he was working with me and my associates that may not come within the competence of his widow.''

''One of those associates wouldn't be Bill Buckley, would it?'' Gordon asked.

''Buckley? Do you mean William Buckley, the commentator? No, indeed.'' Sesti laughed, obviously amused by the notion. ''I represent Luigi Spadafore. I assume you've heard your uncle mention him?''

Gordon felt a small shock. It's starting, he thought. This is the way it starts.

''Ah, Mr. Gordon, I wonder if it would be possible for us to meet in the next few days. At your convenience, of course.''

''Meet where? A pizzeria in the Bronx?''

''The Bronx?'' repeated Sesti in a frosty tone. ''I was thinking more along the lines of lunch at the Harvard Club. Or at my office, if you prefer. I'm at Fifty-seventh between Madison and Fifth. That's not far from you, I believe.''

''How do you know where I live?''

''I don't, actually. I meant not far from the *Tribune* offices.''

''What do you want to talk about, Mr. Sesti? I mean, specifically.''

''I'd rather save that for lunch, if you don't mind. Are you free tomorrow by any chance? Say, one o'clock?''

''All right, one o'clock. But not at the Harvard Club— they make you wear a tie. Let's meet at Clarke's.''

''P. J. Clarke's it is,'' he said.

''Will you be alone, or is Spadafore coming too?''

''Quite alone, Mr. Gordon,'' said Sesti in his snooty British accent. ''Mr. Spadafore rarely comes into Manhattan these days. I'll look for you tomorrow, then?''

"How will we recognize each other?" asked Gordon, re-pressing an urge to ask Sesti if he'd be the Catholic wearing a rubber.

"Oh, I'll recognize you, Mr. Gordon. You're a public figure, you know. In fact, I believe I've seen you on Mr. Buckley's television program."

"Listen, Sesti, I just want you to know in advance, I don't have anything to do with my uncle's business."

"In that case, ours will be a short meeting and, I trust, a pleasant lunch," said Sesti. "Good-bye, Mr. Gordon. I'll see you tomorrow."

Gordon dialed Flanagan's number at the paper.

"John?"

"Yes, Godfather," he said.

"Come on, cut the shit. Who's Carlo Sesti?"

Flanagan gave a low whistle. "You met Sesti already?"

"Tomorrow. He just called. What do you know about him?"

"He's a colleague of mine," said Flanagan. "Consigliere for Spadafore. Lawyer, got his own firm in midtown. Very smooth operator. Not as smooth as me, you understand, but right up there."

"Jesus, will you stop fucking around? Do you know him or what?"

"I've met him a couple of times, just to say hello to. Once, a few years ago, I talked to him about a Teamsters pension fund story, but he didn't give me anything. I doubt he'd remember."

"Where'd he get that Brit accent?"

"Comes by it naturally. His father was Bruno Sesti, big deal in the Spadafore Family, ran their casinos in London for years. Young Carlo was educated at Downside and Cambridge, don't you know."

"And Harvard law," Gordon said. "What else you got?"

"Nothing, really. I could call up his file, but I doubt there's anything in it. He's never been in any trouble, as far as I know. Do you want me to come with you tomorrow?''

"That's all I need," Gordon said. "Listen, get this God-father shit out of your head, John. It was good for a grunt, but it's not real, all right? I'm telling Sesti that I'm not playing and that will be that."

Gordon spent the next morning working on his column, a piece about NATO and Reagan's Falkland diplomacy. "The President, who made a career of portraying bashful heroes, seems at a loss to cope with the imperious Mrs. Thatcher," he wrote. "President Reagan can no more contend with the British prime minister than actor Reagan could have handled Bette Davis—which is not at all. What she needs are not soft words about the Atlantic alliance but a grapefruit in the face, à la Bogart." Gordon chuckled; he would be hearing from the White House in the morning.

He turned off his electric typewriter, put a tan sweater over his blue button-down shirt, and caught a cab. He was a few minutes early, but he wanted to get to Clarke's first, to size Sesti up as he came in. Apparently the consigliere had the same thought; when Gordon arrived, he was already at the bar, with a glass of Perrier.

"Mr. Gordon," he said, making it a statement. He had a firm, dry grip. Sesti was about his age, an inch or two taller and maybe twenty pounds slimmer. His dark hair was cut short and parted neatly on the left, his dark blue suit under-stated and elegant. Sesti's even features and pale complexion made him appear more New England Yankee than Sicilian.

"Mr. Sesti," Gordon said. "Sorry I kept you waiting."

"I was early," he said with a pleasant smile. "And please, call me Carlo."

"OK, Carlo, let's get a table and eat." On the way down in the cab Gordon had imagined a confrontation with a slick Ricardo Montalban–type hood. But Sesti seemed so ordinary that the tension of the morning evaporated, and Gordon was suddenly hungry. "I can't stay too long," he said. "I've got to get back and finish a piece."

"It must be very exciting, writing on foreign affairs," said Sesti. "I read diplomacy at Cambridge. At one time I even considered a career in the State Department."

"What happened?"

"I failed French," said Sesti, dropping a bit of the British accent. When he laughed he showed white, even teeth, and he seemed surprisingly likable. Gordon realized that he was being disarmed, and cautioned himself to stay alert.

"I would have thought knowing Italian, French would be a snap," he said.

"I'm sure you're right, but, regrettably, I don't know Italian," Sesti lied. "I can understand a bit, but my parents used the language primarily to keep secrets from me."

"Mine did the same thing with Yiddish," said Gordon. "Not that there's much use for Yiddish these days."

"You didn't speak Yiddish with Max?"

"Max and I never talked much," Gordon said truthfully. "I think you may be overestimating our relationship. I really didn't know him very well. Most of the last twenty years I've been overseas."

"Yes, I know," said Sesti. "Vietnam, Israel, the Soviet Union, London. The great and the famous. I envy you that, Mr. Gordon."

"If I'm going to call you Carlo, you'd better call me William."

"Not Bill?"

"William."

"Well, shall we order?" he said, signaling for the waiter. "Since you don't have much time . . ."

They ordered rare steaks and a bottle of Cabernet Sauvignon. "I seldom have wine with lunch, but this is a bit of an occasion," said Sesti, lapsing back into his British accent.

"Is it?"

"I think so. Let me be candid, William, it will save us both time. Mr. Spadafore knows about the will that your uncle left. He intends to honor the spirit of that document in principle."

Gordon had been prepared for almost anything, but not this. A day before, he had listened to his father warn him about being assassinated; now, the killers were offering him a fortune.

"You mean, as a matter of principle, you're turning over five hundred million dollars' worth of business to me? Very generous, Mr. Sesti."

The lawyer gave him a wintry smile. "I'm afraid you misunderstand me, Mr. Gordon. I said 'in principle.' In other words, we accept the fact that you are, in fact, your uncle's heir. But unfortunately there are no five hundred million dollars to be turned over. As things stand at the moment, the businesses your uncle owned in partnership with Mr. Spadafore now belong solely to Mr. Spadafore."

"What you're really saying is that I'm out," said Gordon. "Goddamn it, Sesti, you could have saved us both time by telling me that over the phone. I told you yesterday that I'm not interested in the business." He stood up, relieved and angry at the same time. "You can eat my steak, too, while you're at it. And tell Mr. Spadafore that I hope they put him in jail."

"William, please sit down," said Sesti in a level tone. "I haven't finished. Believe me, you misunderstand what I'm trying to say."

Gordon lowered himself back into his seat. Round One, he thought, and I'm still in the ring. "OK, I'm listening."

"Good. First, please realize that, whatever you may imagine, we are basically businessmen." Gordon smirked, but Sesti held up a hand. "Granted, it's an unorthodox business, which is precisely why a document like your uncle's is not binding. We intend, however, to treat it as a statement of intent, and to try to honor its spirit.''

''You're talking in circles,'' said Gordon. ''Let's get down to the proposition, if there is one.''

''All right. Clearly, Mr. Spadafore, having spent his entire life creating his conglomerate, is not going to simply turn over a portion of it to an inexperienced, if gifted, outsider. It would be unreasonable to expect that. All other considerations aside, our business is, not to put too fine a point on it, confidential. To bring a stranger, especially one with such illustrious credentials as yours, into the inner circle of our affairs would be exceptionally reckless. And Mr. Spadafore is not a reckless man, not by any means.''

Despite himself, Gordon nodded. The reporter's side of his brain told him that Sesti was making sense.

''It would also be presumptuous of us to imagine that an internationally renowned journalist such as yourself would want to enter our world,'' Sesti continued. ''With that in mind, Mr. Spadafore has authorized me to offer you one of two propositions. The first is straightforward. We are prepared to make a cash settlement of one million dollars, deposited anywhere in the world, in return for all of your uncle's documents and papers, and your promise to forget this conversation and anything you may have already learned about our affairs.''

''I'm not putting anything in writing,'' Gordon said.

Sesti winced at this crassness. ''Mr. Gordon, William, I assure you that your word is more than sufficient.''

''What if I took the money and held back some of the papers? Have you thought of that?''

''Naturally,'' said Sesti. ''But were you to do that we would, of course, have you killed.'' He said it in such a neutral tone that it took a moment for it to register.

''How do you know I'm not recording this conversation, Sesti?'' Gordon asked.

Sesti pointed to his briefcase. "I have a device that makes it quite impossible for you to do that. Please don't misunderstand me. This is not a threat. You merely asked a hypothetical question, to which you received a hypothetical answer. You don't imagine that a man like Mr. Spadafore would allow himself to be taken advantage of without retaliation. But, I assure you, if you honor your part of the bargain, we will honor ours."

"Would you be willing to deposit the money before you get the papers?"

"Simultaneously, I believe," he said, "although we could work out the practicalities later."

"You said that there were two propositions. What's the other one?"

The waiter arrived with their food but Sesti ignored him, continuing to talk as if they were discussing stock prices. "Several months ago I had the occasion to look through a collection of your articles," he said. "Over the past few years you've interviewed a great many heads of state."

"Have I?"

"Thirty-seven, to be exact. Of course, several of them are now out of office. But there must be very few people alive who know as many world leaders as you do. Not to mention senior officials and military figures."

"And . . . ?"

The waiter was gone, and Sesti cut a small piece of meat, chewing it thoroughly as he let the question hang in the air. Finally he swallowed, took a dainty sip of wine and traced a small circle on the tablecloth with his finger.

"You may recall that a moment ago I alluded to our world—the world of your late uncle and my employer. It is, of course, smaller than your world. Occasionally the two met—in Cuba, for example, under Batista. But, for the most part, we have confined ourselves to our own circumscribed little planet."

"Judging from what I've seen, it doesn't seem so little or so circumscribed," said Gordon.

"I'm speaking relatively, of course. Our business is highly lucrative, but limited. Our foreign connections are largely with, for want of a better term, members of the underworld. But, of course, the real money, the enormous money, and the freedom to earn it, is controlled by governments. Wouldn't you agree?"

"I suppose so."

"We've made considerable progress since the days of prohibition," said Sesti, "thanks to pioneers like your uncle, Mr. Spadafore, Meyer Lansky and a few others who saw that we required national cooperation to prosper. But this is a new era, William, an international era. To take advantage of its potential requires sophistication, access, expertise. Once—and I'm being blunt now—we needed Jews to handle our money and our legal work. Today, as you see, we have produced our own lawyers and business managers. But we have yet to produce a generation of international diplomats."

"Too bad you failed French," Gordon said. The lawyer acknowledged the joke with a small smile, but his eyes remained serious.

"I'm very good at what I do, William, but I don't imagine that I could duplicate your exceptional experience. As I say, very few men of our generation are as well known and respected internationally. Normally, it would be unthinkable for us to come into contact with a man such as yourself, but you are your uncle's nephew and, by the force of that coincidence, here you are." He opened his hands and smiled, and for the first time he seemed very Sicilian.

"So, you want me to bribe Maggie Thatcher, or Brezhnev maybe? Come on, Carlo, you're smarter than that. At least you seem smarter."

"No, nothing as grandiose as that, William. But we both know that there are a number of places—say, in Latin America, the Far East, Africa perhaps—where there are people in high positions who are, or could be made to become, let us say, amenable to various sorts of business opportunities. They may control small countries, but even the smallest, poorest country is vastly richer than the Brooklyn docks or the Truckers Union. Handled properly, an operation of the kind I envision could be profitable beyond the wildest dreams of even your uncle or Mr. Spadafore.''

''And you want me to handle it, is that it?''

''Handle it, no. With all due respect, you have no training for that side of the business. What I'm proposing is that you take on the role of foreign minister. Locate areas of opportunity. Sound out potential associates. Ensure entrée. And, just as important, keep us from making awkward mistakes.''

''Out of curiosity, what would my share of this international operation be?''

''Twenty-five percent. One quarter of perhaps three billion dollars a year, perhaps many times that. It would make you one of the richest men on the planet. And as a warrant of our good faith, we would be prepared to give you a lump sum of, say, three million dollars.''

''And what if I took the three million and didn't deliver?''

Sesti shook his head, and for the first time in the conversation he seemed a bit exasperated. ''William, I've already answered that. Please don't make me say it again.''

''What about my uncle's papers?''

''No, those we must have in any case. That is not negotiable.''

Gordon was struck with a sudden thought. ''Tell me something, Carlo, was this my uncle's idea?'' he asked. ''Is that why he left me his share of the business?''

A shadow of caution came over Sesti's eyes, like a window shade dropping. ''I never discussed this with your uncle,'' he said. ''Nor, to my knowledge, did Mr. Spadafore. In fact, I must tell you that Mr. Spadafore is skeptical about this proposal. He is, for all his vision, an old-fashioned man in many ways. Distrustful of outsiders. Your uncle was an exception, of course; they were boys together. My first proposal is unconditional, but the second is contingent upon Mr. Spadafore's approval. He'll have to be convinced that you are wholeheartedly and irrevocably committed to our world, as it were."

" 'Make my bones' is the phrase, isn't it?"

"A vulgar expression," said Sesti. He took another bite of steak and fastidiously wiped his thin lips with his napkin; watching him, Gordon realized that he had barely touched his own meal. "I can assure you that you won't be required to do anything violent, now or ever. That isn't your nature; we understand that."

"I have a couple of practical questions," said Gordon. "First, would you want me to leave the paper?"

"Yes. You'd need more independence than it allows. A senior fellowship at a foreign policy research institute would be more suitable. We can, of course, arrange that, although I assume you could do so just as easily."

"Another thing. If I were interested—and I'm saying if— I'd want to bring someone with me, another reporter who was with me in Vietnam."

"Yes, John Flanagan. Well, you would be free to run your side of the operation as you see fit. But you must understand that you will be absolutely accountable for the discretion of whomever you choose. Absolutely accountable."

"Last question. Supposing, again, that I'm interested. What next?"

"I'll arrange a meeting with Mr. Spadafore. But, William, bear in mind that no such meeting can take place unless you've decided affirmatively. I promise that there will not be any additional conditions or obligations. My proposal is solid. But he can, of course, say no. If that happens, we will revert to proposal number one."

"I'll think about it and let you know, Carlo," said Gordon. He raised his hand for the waiter, who moved toward the table with alacrity. "Please, William, this is my lunch," said Carlo Sesti.

"Wrap this steak for me, will you?" Gordon said to the waiter. "And give my friend the check."

WHEN GORDON WALKED INTO HIS APARTMENT, THE phone was ringing. He let it go six more times before picking it up.

"Hello, John," he said.

"Don Velvel," he said. "How did you know it was me?"

"Just a wild guess," Gordon said. "And I told you, cut out this Don Velvel stuff. This whole situation is getting less and less funny."

"Rough meeting with Sesti?" asked Flanagan, all the frivolity leaving his voice. He may have been playing make-believe gangster, Gordon thought, but when it came to getting information, he was an old pro.

"I'll tell you about it tomorrow. I've got to finish this damn article on NATO and the Falklands, and then I've got a talk show to tape at six. Some Middle East discussion. So I'll be tied up."

"What about later on? I could meet you downtown, around eight, get a bite to eat."

"I'd like to, but not tonight. Jupiter."

"Doesn't she have a nickname?" asked Flanagan. "Jody, or Jupy or something?"

"No, she likes Jupiter."

"Yeah, no lie. She likes the hell out of Jupiter. If you'll forgive me for saying so, you'd be better off right now concentrating on business instead of mooning over that muff-diving girlfriend of yours."

"OK."

"OK, what?"

"OK, I forgive you for saying so."

"How about, OK, I'll take your good advice."

"How about, OK, get your ass off the phone so I can do some work? I'll call you tomorrow morning."

It usually took Gordon about three hours to write his column, counting four or five coffee breaks, a telephone call or two and at least one trip to the bathroom. Abroad, Gordon had learned how to write under daily deadline pressure, sometimes in frontline conditions. Sitting in a padded chair, in his own apartment, providing two opinions a week on obscure subjects was, by comparison, a leisurely task.

But today, for some reason, the words wouldn't come. He was suddenly struck by how little he actually knew about the Falkland Islands, NATO, or anything else for that matter. The revelation that he had won Pulitzer prizes because of the intervention of two old Jewish hoods in New York had shaken his normal self-confidence, and now he tried to type it back.

"In the absence of any proof to the contrary, the leadership of NATO must assume that the Soviets may be preparing to support Argentina as it has other Latin American nations hostile to the West. . . ." He looked at the phrase and frowned. How the hell did he know? Really know. Gordon had been around news all his adult life—wars and revolutions, coups and campaigns; had read purloined documents and exchanged information with smooth-faced diplomats in cozy bars—and always he had reported with an authority that approached omniscience. But, he now realized, he hadn't even understood the basic facts of his own life. Maybe Reagan was as complex and deceptively bland as his uncle Max.

Perhaps the British generals were as smoothly lethal as Sesti and his boss. He finished typing the article with leaden fingers, conscious of not only how little he knew but how little it mattered. His father's line about newspapers came back to him; "They wrap fish in them, boychik," the old man once said. That's what his work was, he thought miserably—decorating paper for mackerel.

At five-thirty, Gordon left for the public television studio where he was scheduled to take part in a discussion on the Arab-Israel conflict. The cab was overheated, the driver a young Soviet immigrant who smoked cigarettes with the windows rolled up. Gordon, happy to find a fellow addict, took out a Winston and idly blew a few smoke rings, which wafted through the open bulletproof partition into the front seat.

"Circles," the driver said, noticing. "I too." He blew his own rings and, with his left hand, tried to push them into the backseat for Gordon's inspection. They dissolved into clouds of acrid smoke.

When they stopped at a light the driver turned and said, "I can blow box, too. You believe this?" Gordon shook his head. "Watch," said the cabbie. He inhaled some smoke, puckered his lips and exhaled, moving his head in a rectangular way. "See, the smoke box," he said happily. "You don't know this trick?"

"I know the name of the capital of Albania," said Gordon.

"I know capital of Connecticut. Is Gartford," said the driver. "My brother lives in Gartford. He teach me this trick. For single bars. To get girl's attention."

Gordon looked at the cabbie's license. His name was Jacob Gurashvili, a Georgian Jewish name. "Jacob, when did you leave Tiflis?" he said.

"How you know I from Tiflis?"

"A trick," Gordon said. "Like the squares. You can use it to pick up girls."

"How I know where to say?" the driver asked grinning. He had a gold tooth in front, and his eyes were slightly crossed. He looked, Gordon thought, a little bit like a good-natured pirate. For a second, he was tempted to invite him into the studio and present him to Marty Bronstein as a visiting expert from the Soviet Union. For the first time that day, he smiled.

The meter read $4.50. He handed Gurashvili a twenty. "Keep the change," he said. "And just guess Tiflis. It usually works."

The cabbie regarded the bill with wonder. "Maybe I wait for you," he said hopefully. "Private."

"I'll be about an hour," said Gordon.

"One hour, one more twenty dollars bill," said Gurashvili. "Off clock." He gestured to the ticking meter and flashed Gordon a grin pregnant with complicity.

"What the hell," said Gordon. "Why not?" The paper would pay, after all. Besides, for some reason the thought of this cheerful, gold-toothed pirate waiting for him outside the studio reassured him.

"Drive around, if you want," he said. "Just be back by seven."

"I wait here," said Gurashvili, pulling out a thermos and a well-worn copy of *Penthouse*. "Coffee break, U.S. style."

In the small studio, Gordon was greeted as an old friend by the receptionist. "The others are already here," she said. "You know the way back to Marty's office."

Marty Bronstein was the moderator of *Wide World*, a weekly foreign affairs show. An intense, balding man about Gordon's age, Bronstein taught international relations at Columbia. His specialty was explaining the world in terms of American sports. Urgent international problems were always "fourth and goal," world leaders either all-stars or bush-leaguers, bumbling diplomats "couldn't hit a layup." Recently, Gordon had heard him describe the pope as a "Vince Lombardi–like leader."

Gordon's fellow panelists that evening were Amnon Noy, an Israeli professor on a sabbatical at NYU, and George Haladi, head of the Arab-American Human Rights Commission. Gordon had never met Noy, a slightly built, mild man with thinning sandy hair, but he knew Haladi from past encounters. He was an outgoing type with a loud voice and a mock humility that put Gordon off.

"Well, it is the famous Mr. William Gordon," said Haladi, shaking hands with a strong pumping motion. "Perhaps you can explain to a primitive Arab what it means to say that Yasir Arafat is a lifetime two thirty-five."

"Lifetime two thirty-five *hitter*," corrected Bronstein. "It's a baseball term meaning mediocrity."

"And what is the phrase for an excellent player?" asked Haladi.

"Three hundred hitter," said Gordon.

"Not lifetime?"

"Yeah, a lifetime three hundred hitter," said Bronstein.

"And who would you consider a lifetime three hundred hitter in our region, Professor Bronstein? Mr. Menachem Bee-gin?"

"Naw, he's a midget wrestler," said Bronstein. "The Sky Lo Lo of the Middle East."

Gordon laughed. "Sky Lo Lo? I haven't heard that name in years."

"The difference between your discipline and mine," said Bronstein airily. "For you, only the contemporary matters; but for an academic, context is everything."

"I concur with you on Begin," said Noy, entering the conversation for the first time. "He is, indeed, a small man.

What we need is someone with vision, an Israeli Anwar Sadat." He looked at Haladi for support, but the Arab snorted.

"Sadat? A lifetime three hundred hitter with a very short lifetime," Haladi said, grinning as he used the new expression.

"Another Joe DiMaggio," said Bronstein. "Elegant, stylish, cut down in his prime by injuries."

"What's the topic today?" asked Gordon.

Bronstein flipped some papers onto his desk. "The usual. Peace process. Palestinian self-determination, Israeli security. George and Professor Noy will each present his side, and then you hit cleanup with some sage commentary."

"I could give the Israeli position just as easily," said Haladi with a cynical grin, glancing at Noy. "I know it by heart. Never again!" he intoned dramatically, rolling his *r*. "No Palestinian state, no talks with the PLO, no, no, a thousand times no!"

"Perhaps, then, I shall give the Palestinian position," said Noy. He was a mild man, but clearly he had no intention of appearing to be a pushover. *"B'dam, B'ruh, nev'deh Falestine,"* he chanted. "This means, in Arabic, 'With blood and spirit, we will redeem Palestine.' It is what Mr. Haladi's friends actually want—"

"Never again, never, never, never, a thousand times never—" Haladi repeated loudly, banging his fist into his palm for emphasis.

"B'dam, B'ruh, nev'deh Falestine," chanted Noy, raising his clenched fists like a demonstrator. Both men repeated the phrases again and again, each unwilling to stop before the other.

"On, Wisconsin, on, Wisconsin, run right through that line. . . ." Bronstein began to sing. "Get that ball clear round Chicago, touchdown sure this time. . . ." He turned to Gordon. "Come on, William, where's your school spirit?"

Gordon felt a sudden wave of nausea. Once again he saw

the image of fish wrapped in a newspaper; it seemed to him that he could smell the faint odor of rotting carp.

"You'd better call in a substitute, coach," Gordon said grimly. "I'm out of here." As he started down the hall, both panelists fell silent. Bronstein, face red with anger and surprise, chased after him, catching him by the shoulder.

"What do you mean, 'out of here'?" he screamed. "We've got a show to tape tonight."

"Get Howard Cosell," said Gordon, shrugging off the moderator. "Get Bozo the clown. I'm leaving."

"You can't just walk out on me like this," said Bronstein. "You're supposed to be a professional."

"A professional what?" asked Gordon. "Listen, Marty, wake up. Nobody watches these shows. Nobody gives a good goddamn about foreign affairs, even the foreigners. Hell, especially the foreigners. I'm getting out of the commentator business."

Bronstein's anger was replaced by a look of concern. "William, are you upset about your uncle? Is that it?"

Gordon gave him a sharp glance. "How do you know about my uncle?" he demanded.

"It was in the paper," he said. "Listen, you're upset, that's all. You shouldn't even be here. Damn, I should have been more considerate, but I didn't realize you were that close. I'll try to get Mike Kramer. Tina," he called to the secretary in the next room, "get me Mike Kramer, right away. Try him at home. I'll call you tomorrow, William, maybe we can work something out for next week. It's Ethiopia." He said it in the tone of a man offering an irresistible temptation.

"Ethiopia, Cambodia, what's the difference?" said Gordon, opening the door. "After you hit Turkey, it's all one big Chinatown anyway."

Gordon walked up Sixth Avenue. He felt disoriented, like someone coming out of a darkened movie theater into the sunlight. At the corner of Fifty-seventh he saw Gurashvili sitting in the cab. "You make quickie," the Russian observed nervously. "Is still one more twenty dollars?"

"No problem," said Gordon. "Take me up to Columbus and Seventy-ninth."

Reassured, the cabbie smiled. "A deal is a deal," he pronounced, edging the taxi into the traffic on Broadway.

At the corner of Sixty-fifth Gordon saw a group of black teenagers swagger down the street with ghetto blasters in their hands. Gurashvili saw them too and cursed in Georgian.

"You don't like blacks?" Gordon asked.

"Pushtaks," said Gurashvili. "Hooligans. One hit me on head for money. Next time I shoot. With this." He opened his leather jacket and waved a Smith & Wesson service revolver.

"You'd really shoot somebody?" asked Gordon. Gurashvili nodded emphatically. "I no let nobody take from me my money," he said. "Is the American way, not?"

"Where did you get the gun?" Gordon asked. Gurashvili grinned, his gold tooth flashing under the streetlights. "In New York City, there is everything. Hamburger with works? Hamburger with works. Water mattress? OK, water mattress. Pistol? Pistol. This is all you need." He rubbed his thumb and forefinger together.

"Could you get me one of those?" Gordon asked, surprising himself by the question. He had fired a pistol before, but never owned one. It was a reporter's conceit—the unarmed observer is untouchable. But after today's lunch with Carlo Sesti, he no longer felt certain of his neutral status.

"I give you this if you want," said Gurashvili. "One hundred and seventy-five dollars and no cents. Wholesale price."

What the hell, thought Gordon. "OK. It's a deal," he said.

"Good deal," said Gurashvili. "Business is business."

Gurashvili parked his taxi in front of Gordon's building,

and Jimmy the doorman came out to open the door. "I got a message for you, boss," he said in his Cagney voice. "From a certain dame."

"Jupiter?"

"Yeah, she stopped by in a cab maybe half an hour ago. Said to tell you she couldn't make it tonight. She'll call in the morning."

"Was she alone?" Gordon asked, feeling foolish, but unable to restrain himself.

"Naw, she had another chick with her."

"Thanks," he said. "Keep an eye on this cab for a few minutes, will you?"

"Sure thing, boss," said Jimmy.

When they entered the apartment, Gurashvili gave an admiring whistle. "This real beautiful pad," he said.

"Have a seat," said Gordon, motioning in the direction of the living room. "I'll be right back." He went into his bedroom and opened the small wall safe where he kept papers, his passport and a thousand dollars in cash. He counted out $175 and put the rest back, twirling the combination lock. When he came out of the bedroom he found Gurashvili at the window, looking down at the museum.

"Here," said Gordon, handing Gurashvili the bills. The cabbie looked at them for a moment before placing them carefully in his wallet. Then he removed the pistol and handed it, butt first, to Gordon.

"Is it loaded?" he asked, taking it gingerly.

"Six bullets," said Gurashvili. "If you want more, I can get. Also, automatic pistol. Also, Uzi machine gun."

"What are you, an arms dealer?" asked Gordon. Gurashvili shrugged modestly.

"What about the license for this one?" Gordon asked. "Isn't it registered to you?"

"Is unregistered," said the cabbie. "Is . . ."—he searched for the phrase—"is privately owned and operated."

Gurashvili grinned widely, happy with his command of English.

"Do you have time for a drink?" Gordon asked. Gurashvili looked at his watch, a gold Rolex. "Sure," he said. "Thank you very much."

"Is that thing real?" asked Gordon, pouring two glasses of bourbon. "The watch, is it a real Rolex?"

"Certainly real," said the driver. "You want watch, I get you watch. Six hundred dollars and no cents."

"Not right now," said Gordon. He raised his glass. "L'chaim," he said.

Gurashvili looked surprised. "How you know I am a Jewish?" he asked.

"Another wild guess," said Gordon.

"Ah, you notice this," said Gurashvili, pointing to a gold six-pointed star that hung on his hairy chest from a chain. "Is Mogen David, very good for tips." He leaned toward Gordon, and lowered his voice. "In New York is very many Jewish."

Gordon recognized the confidential tone from a thousand off-the-record briefings with government officials. It was the sound of the obvious repackaged as classified information. How have I stood it all these years? he asked himself. Suddenly the revolver weighed heavily in his hand, and he felt exhausted.

"Thanks for the gun," he said, taking the now empty glass from Gurashvili. "Maybe we'll run into each other again sometime."

The driver reached for his wallet again and took out a small engraved card: *Jacob Gurashvili, import/export/transport*. There was a Brooklyn phone number at the bottom. "You need something, call for quick home delivery," he said. "Like Culligan man on TV."

"Right," said Gordon, moving Gurashvili toward the door. In the hallway the cabbie pointed an index finger at

Gordon. "Tiflis," he said. "Tonight I try. Tiflis." He grinned once more, his dental work flashing. "Hey, honey, you are from Tiflis, I bet. And then . . ." He made a circle with his thumb and forefinger, and ran the index finger of his other hand through it. "America the beautiful," he sighed, and walked down the hall toward the elevator.

7

LUIGI SPADAFORE SAT IN A LARGE EASY CHAIR IN THE
study of his Bensonhurst brownstone, idly spinning a globe
that rested on an ivory end table. It was a custom-made globe,
inlaid with two tiny diamonds—one set on Sicily, the other
on New York—given to him by Carlo Sesti as a sign of respect. Spadafore had deeply appreciated the gesture. Almost
alone among the men of the younger generation, Sesti seemed
to understand and embody the values that Spadafore had
cherished all his life—respect for tradition, elegant manners,
loyalty, ruthless cunning and a finely calibrated sense of
protocol.

Spadafore's own two sons were, by comparison, disap-
pointments. Mario, past forty, was a sour, thick-bodied fellow with bad skin and strawlike hair, which he combed
straight back over his skull like an old man. From boyhood,
he had been exposed to the finest things—opera, theater, the
great books, things that Spadafore himself considered necessary for a truly civilized man. Mario had eaten exquisitely
prepared Italian meals from embossed china, ridden horses
at the family ranch in Arizona, traveled to Europe with tu-
tors. And all of this effort had produced an oaf, a man with
no conversation or culture save the idiotic television pro-

grams he discussed at the dinner table. Mario dressed like
an insurance salesman, drank beer out of cans and wiped his
mouth with the back of his hand, played gin rummy for small
stakes and, Spadafore suspected, cheated. His one virtue was
that he was a hard worker, well acquainted with the family
business. But it pained Spadafore to know that his far-flung
empire, carefully and sometimes brutally acquired over the
course of a lifetime, would go to such a dolt.

Of the second son, Pietro, who called himself Peter, there
was even less to be proud of. The boy had no good qualities,
except for exceptional beauty. He refused to settle down; at
thirty-four he was still "dating," an American custom that
Don Spadafore considered demeaning for teenagers and, for
an adult male, demented. Pietro called the women he squired
around town "foxes," did exercises like an athlete and listened to rock 'n' roll music on a Walkman. On one occasion,
Spadafore had walked in on the boy, stark naked save for the
earphones, dancing alone in front of a full-length mirror in
his bedroom. Pietro had seen his father's reflection, laughed
and said, "Well, you caught me, Pop." Even now, it was a
memory that made the old man wince.

Like Mario, Pietro worked in the family business, but he
had no head for it. He seemed unable to understand the sim-
plest transactions, and, worse, far worse, he couldn't keep
his mouth shut. Don Spadafore knew that he discussed family affairs with his girlfriends. Once he had been forced to
silence a young woman who had learned too much. It had
been an unpleasant experience, made more so by the boy's
seeming indifference to her sudden disappearance. Don Spadafore used violence when necessary—it was a part of his
upbringing—but he tried to contain it within his own world.
Although he had imposed the death sentence, he had done
so with regret; it was far too harsh a penalty for a woman
whose only crime had been listening to the prattle of his
childish son.

No, his true spiritual heir was Carlo Sesti, and for the past several years he had been depressed by the knowledge that Carlo would eventually have to be eliminated. Spadafore intended to pass his business on to his sons. Despite the fact that he despised them, it was tradition, they were his blood; Sesti, for all his fine qualities, was not. Spadafore knew that as long as he remained alive, Sesti would serve him loyally, but once he was gone, the consigliere would swallow Mario and Pietro like sardines. And this he could not allow.

Sesti, the Don knew, was aware of the problem. The two men had discussed the question of succession several times in the past, and always Sesti had pledged to help the boys carry on. But the very fact that he made such a pledge indicated that the consigliere's contempt for Mario and Pietro matched the Don's. Sesti was a sophisticated man, and he understood Spadafore and his traditions. He knew that the Don would protect his sons; and he also knew that they had to be protected, first and foremost, from himself. Spadafore had consoled himself with the certainty that Sesti would understand the deep pain that this would cause the Don, and forgive him.

But Spadafore had underestimated his consigliere. One night, several months before, as Max Grossman lay dying in his hospital bed, Sesti had approached Spadafore with a plan so Machiavellian, so subtle and yet so simple, that the Don had been almost overcome with admiration.

That meeting had taken place in the Don's study. The two men had spoken Italian that night. Spadafore was vain about his eloquence in the language of Dante, and admired Sesti's grasp of it as well. Usually they conversed in English, or in Sicilian dialect; pure Italian they saved for particularly portentous occasions.

"I understand that our friend is seriously ill," said Sesti. It was a title of respect that Spadafore accorded to no outsider other than Grossman. The Don made a sad face and nodded gravely.

"May I ask, Don Spadafore, if you have made any decisions regarding the disposition of our friend's interests?" Sesti inquired.

"They shall be guarded as my own," said Spadafore with an understated smile.

For fifty years Max Grossman had been Luigi Spadafore's partner, his confidant and, most remarkably for a Jew, his friend. Once, when they were young men in the Lower East Side of New York, Grossman had displayed a furious ruthlessness that matched his own; it had been Grossman, along with two of his Jewish cohorts, who had gunned down Marciani and opened the way for Spadafore's control of Brooklyn and, eventually, of much of the Eastern seaboard.

But as the two men grew older, Grossman had drawn inward even as Spadafore expanded. Grossman's Jewish colleagues were either jailed or killed, and he made no effort to rebuild his forces. Instead, he had become Spadafore's partner, relying on the Family for whatever muscle was necessary, and leaving the work of running and administering the organization to the Sicilian. Grossman's own contribution had been largely financial. He taught Spadafore how to hide and protect his money, how to invest it in profitable businesses far from the long arm of the IRS, the police or his rivals. For this, Max Grossman had been fully entitled to his share of the profits; but when he was gone, his interest would naturally revert to Spadafore himself.

"Just so," said Sesti. "But is it not possible, Don Spadafore, that our friend may have other plans? Other, ah, commitments?"

"The wife is well provided for," said Spadafore. "The brother is a wealthy fool. There is no one else."

"There is the nephew," said Sesti. "Gordon, the journalist."

"The nephew is unconnected with his uncle's affairs," said Spadafore. "He is, as you say, a journalist. He is not of our world."

"It has occurred to me, Don Spadafore, that he might be highly useful to us," said Sesti. Speaking smoothly, he outlined his plan. Gordon would be seduced into entering the orbit of the Family, and into using his contacts and expertise to help open doors around the world. Sesti himself would remain in New York as consigliere, "until you no longer require my services"—a delicate euphemism for Spadafore's death. At that time, he would move to London, where he would content himself with running the foreign operation, half of whose profits would go to the Don's heirs, Mario and Pietro.

"You would willingly relinquish your part of the Family enterprises in the United States?" Spadafore asked, and Sesti smiled, tracing a small circle on the arm of his easy chair. "As you know, Don Spadafore, I was raised in London. I find it a congenial, salubrious climate," he said, emphasizing ever so slightly the word "salubrious." The Don had sighed with admiration; no Medici had ever had so diplomatic and subtle a counselor.

"What leads you to believe that Gordon could be enticed to join our enterprises? He is, after all, *legitimate*," he said, using the English word.

A look of cunning came over Sesti's face. The consigliere had anticipated the problem. "I have taken the liberty of gathering some information on our friend's nephew," he said. "William Gordon is a well-known journalist; a man who has lived in the large world. But he is not, I believe, a truly worldly man. In this, he is like many of his American contemporaries." Sesti paused. The Don was aware that this was an allusion to his own younger son, and he appreciated the consigliere's delicacy. "If he were to believe, be made to believe, that he had been made heir to his uncle's fortune, it would, I think, awaken his greed. Of course, we would then make it clear that the fortune itself was not his. A legacy once offered and then withdrawn is a bitter medicine for any man."

"Quite so," said Spadafore.

"Ah, but in that frame of mind, he would then be given the chance to attain an even larger fortune, made an offer he could not refuse." Both men smiled at the phrase. It was common knowledge in their world that the fictional Don Corleone had been based largely on Luigi Spadafore.

"How do you propose to convince Gordon that his uncle has left him a fortune?" Spadafore asked, certain that Sesti had an answer. What a fine fellow, he thought; how unfair that fate had given him Mario and Pietro, instead of this brilliant young Sicilian.

"Nathan Belzer will, I believe, cooperate in this small deception," said Sesti.

"You have spoken to Belzer?"

"I would never do such a thing without your approval, Don Spadafore," said Sesti. "My confidence is based entirely upon my appraisal of his character."

"You may, in that case, approach him," said Spadafore, mollified. "But there are three conditions. First, you must wait until our friend is no longer alive." Sesti nodded; he had expected that. "Second, whatever impression you leave with the nephew, he must in no way receive any true information about the Family business. What you make up is your own affair." Once again Sesti nodded, waiting, but the Don remained silent.

"And the third condition?" Sesti asked, once more tracing a small circle on the upholstered chair.

"The third condition is that you must limit our relationship with Gordon to one year," said Spadafore. "One year will be sufficient time to open whatever doors and gain whatever knowledge he has. It will allow us to begin our overseas operations on, as the Americans say, the right foot. For one year, our friend's nephew can be managed; beyond that, he will acquire too much information. He has not been raised in our traditions, in our world. He cannot be relied upon.''

"One year is a brief time, Don Spadafore," said Sesti.

"Who is to say?" asked the old man, pursing his lips. "Life is precarious, is it not? Who of us is assured of even one more year?" He peered at Sesti through hooded eyes and saw that the message had registered.

That conversation had taken place four months ago, and tonight Don Spadafore recalled it pleasurably. Thus far, things had gone just as Sesti had predicted. Max Grossman had died. Nathan Belzer had been paid handsomely to dangle the bait in front of William Gordon. And Gordon had risen to the hook. Tonight they would cement the relationship with a ceremonial meal at Spadafore's table.

The Don idly spun his diamond-studded globe. Like most of his business, the arrangement with Gordon could have been settled without any particular protocol. Strictly speaking, it was unnecessary; Sesti could just have easily done it with a handshake over lunch. But for Spadafore, the ceremonial aspects of his job were important, almost sacred.

Recently there had been a spate of books about Godfathers and Mafia chieftains, and Spadafore, who liked to read, had been secretly entertained and even delighted by several of them. He especially liked the way that Mario Puzo had captured the dignity and wisdom of the Man of Respect. But Puzo and the others misunderstood the inner motive of men like himself. Don Corleone, for example, had been portrayed as a solemn, somewhat lugubrious fellow entrapped by his old-fashioned nature. Luigi Spadafore, the model for Corleone, knew better.

The most basic truth, he reflected, was that being a don was endlessly entertaining. Like Shakespeare, Spadafore believed the world to be a stage, on which men, even the most successful, are consigned to dreary, tiresome parts. But his was a starring role, one that allowed him to indulge his imagination and his flair for the dramatic. He was no Mustache Pete, enslaved by ancestor worship and the ancient customs of Sicily. He had been born in America and, when the occasion called for it, he could be as contemporary and dry as the chairman of General Motors. But he was charmed by the opportunity to be more than simply a rich man; to become, in fact, royalty, a man whose ring was kissed on bended knee, to whom fealty was sworn in solemn candlelight ceremonies. It pleased him to live in his rarefied world, isolated by obsequious retainers from the humdrum necessities of daily life.

This had been his greatest disagreement with Max Grossman. Grossman had been content to be merely a criminal and a businessman, a man whose personal life was devoid of drama and imagination. The wealthier he got, the more ordinary he became, like one of those contemptibly prosaic Scandinavian kings on a bicycle. When Grossman had, from time to time, witnessed the rituals of the Spadafore Family, he had reacted with a sardonic courtesy, as if humoring an eccentric friend. It gratified Spadafore to know that the shrewd old Jew, who had known him since boyhood, never guessed how detached he actually was from the ceremonial side of his life, or how calculated was the pleasure that he took in it.

Yes, being the Don was a wonderful role, he reflected, but it could only be sustained if it was taken seriously. Not so much by other men—he could bludgeon or frighten them into accepting his authority—but by himself. Spadafore allowed himself no secret deviations or inconsistencies, no private flights from the world he had created. He dressed like a don, in somber, dignified clothing; comported himself with a regal fastidiousness, even when he was alone; spoke like a don, in an old-fashioned, flowery style that had become second nature, the language of his very thoughts. His one hidden pleasure was his own awareness that it was a game; that the distant, self-possessed man on the throne was, in fact, little Luigi Spadafore, a kid from the Lower East Side who had collected baseball cards, worried about adolescent bad skin and cried in his bed the first night at reform school almost seventy years before.

This self-awareness enabled Spadafore to see the world clearly. He knew, for example, that logic dictated that he turn his Family over to Carlo Sesti, and not to his doltish sons. But to do so would be to deny the very basis of his regime, a kind of self-regicide. It would be an admission that he was, in fact, a businessman and not an emperor. He cared little about Mario and Pietro; he had long since stopped believing in eternal life (although he attended mass every Sunday, as a duty of office), and he doubted that he would be forced to look down from heaven on the foolishness of his offspring. What mattered to him now was his place in history.

The Don's speculations were interrupted by a knock on the heavy oak door of his study. It was Pietro's knock. Spadafore spun his globe once more, and straightened his tie.

"It's me, Pa," said Pietro, entering the room with a boyish stride. He was dressed in evening clothes, and his longish hair hung over the collar. "I just wanted to say good night, I'm going out for the evening."

"We have company for dinner tonight, Pietro," said Spadafore evenly. "Have you forgotten?"

"Sorry, Pa, this is something I couldn't get out of," he said. He shifted his weight from one foot to the other, anxious to be done with the confrontation and on his way.

"Pietro, our dinner tonight is a business meeting. I want you there," said Don Spadafore. "Whatever you were supposed to do, cancel it."

"Pa, I'm going out tonight with Julie Morganfield," he said in a proud tone. Spadafore kept his face blank. He knew perfectly well that Julie Morganfield was a blond actress, but it was a part of his old-world pose to pretend ignorance of such things. "She's a movie star, Pa. You should see her."

"It is not her I want to see, Pietro," said Spadafore. "It is you, at my table this evening. There will be other nights for movie stars."

"Come on, Pa, you were young once—"

"Thirty-four is not young, Pietro. When I was your age, I was a married man with children and responsibilities. You have no children but you do have obligations, and tonight is one of them. Cancel your appointment."

"But, Pa. Mario will be here. He can fill me in tomorrow, OK?"

"Cancel your appointment, Pietro," said Spadafore in the same even tone. He was struck by how handsome his younger son was, like a movie actor himself. It gave him an idea. "Remain in your tuxedo, and call Mario and Carlo. Tell them we are dressing for dinner," he said. Normally Spadafore dined in a business suit, but tonight, when Gordon arrived, he would be greeted by four men in evening clothes; his first glimpse of Spadafore's world would be one of memorable elegance. He had already instructed his cook on the menu and the wine, and reminded her to order flowers. The tuxedos would be the finishing touch.

"Pa, seriously, I gotta go tonight," protested his son. "I'll call Mario and Carlo, but I'm going. OK?"

"Pietro," said Spadafore, speaking for the first time in Sicilian dialect. "Do not argue. Do as I say." The young man flushed. "Yes, Father," he said formally in Sicilian, leaving the room.

Sesti and Mario arrived separately but almost simultaneously at seven-fifteen. Both wore black tuxedos—Sesti slim and impeccably tailored, Mario red-faced, looking like a stuffed sausage. They sat in the formal salon, on heavy sofas, and made small talk. Spadafore remained alone in his study, unwilling to engage in idle familiarity, even with his sons and closest adviser.

At precisely seven-thirty, the doorbell chimed, and Sesti, by prearrangement, let Gordon in. The household staff—a butler and two maids, all Sicilians—had been given the night off. Only the cook, a cousin of Spadafore's who had been taken on when the Don's wife died, and a serving girl, another cousin from the old country who spoke no English, were present. The Don's bodyguards were stationed, as usual, around the periphery of the house. They had been instructed to allow Gordon to enter without challenge; no one else was to be admitted that night, no matter how urgent his business.

Spadafore watched Sesti greet Gordon on a closed-circuit television screen. The journalist was dressed in a sport jacket and slacks, and a blue shirt open at the collar, an informality that, to the Don, implied disrespect. In his left hand Gordon held a bottle of wine.

"I wish you had told me you were dressing for dinner," he heard Gordon say to Sesti. "I would have worn a tie."

"Not at all," said Sesti smoothly, taking the bottle and guiding Gordon into the sitting room, where he introduced the journalist to Mario and Pietro. Sesti did not thank Gordon for the wine; as host, that would be Don Spadafore's prerogative.

The Don watched Gordon take a seat and cross his right leg over his left. He seemed to be at ease. Spadafore saw a strong resemblance between the journalist and his father, a vulgar man for whom he had scant regard. Of the uncle he saw nothing.

"Do you get dressed up like this every night?" Gordon asked, genuinely curious. Mario, who had no conversation, grunted. Pietro looked petulant and remained silent. It fell to Sesti to answer. "This is a special occasion for all of us," he said in his British accent. "It isn't often that we are visited by such an illustrious figure as yourself."

Gordon ignored the compliment. "Is it all right if I smoke?" he asked. He already had the Winstons out.

"Of course," said Sesti, producing a gold Dunhill lighter. Spadafore smiled. Sesti did not smoke; he carried the lighter for others. It was the kind of attention to small detail that the Don appreciated and that made the consigliere so valuable.

Spadafore hauled his bulk out of the padded chair, smoothed his hair in the mirror and entered the sitting room. All four men rose. Spadafore opened his arms to Gordon in a gesture of welcome.

"Mr. Spadafore, this is Mr. William Gordon," said Sesti, doing the honors. "Mr. Gordon, Luigi Spadafore."

"You grace my home with your presence," said Spadafore formally, taking the younger man's hand in his. "Please accept my condolences on the death of your uncle."

"Good to meet you, Mr. Spadafore," said Gordon lightly. "I should be offering you my condolences. You were much closer to my uncle than I was."

"Yes, your uncle Max was my brother," said Spadafore.

"In that case, perhaps I should call you Uncle Luigi," said Gordon with a smile. For a moment there was a shocked silence at the lèse-majesté; Mario and Pietro exchanged looks, and even Sesti seemed taken aback. Spadafore regarded the reporter gravely, and then laughed. "Uncle Luigi? Yes, and I will call you Velvel."

Gordon laughed too. "How'd you know about that?" he asked.

"Max spoke of you often," said Spadafore. "And he always referred to you as Velvel."

"A nickname?" asked Sesti brightly, relieved that the tense moment had passed.

"Yiddish," said Gordon.

"A fine Jewish name for a fine Jewish boy," said Spadafore in fluent, Russian-accented Yiddish.

Gordon's eyes widened in surprise. "You speak Yiddish?" he asked.

"Yes," replied Spadafore, still speaking in Yiddish. "Where I grew up, it was a common language. Your uncle and I sometimes spoke it together."

"I'm afraid you lost me," said Gordon in English. "I really don't know very much Yiddish."

"That's a pity," Spadafore said. "Such an expressive language. Mamma-loshen."

Gordon reached for the bottle of Barolo that was sitting on the end table next to the couch. "I hope you like it," he said, handing it to Spadafore. "I brought it back with me from a trip to Sicily."

"You have excellent taste in wine," said Spadafore. "May I ask what you were doing in Sicily?"

"I was there working on a piece about NATO's naval preparedness in the Mediterranean," said Gordon. "It was last year, I think, or the year before. I can't really remember. It didn't turn out to be much of a story."

"Please, tell us about Sicily," said Spadafore, taking Gordon's arm and moving him in the direction of the dining room. "It has been almost ten years since my last visit." The Don seated Gordon to his right, and took his place at the head of the table. Like a headwaiter, Sesti helped the old man into his chair, and then seated himself across from Gordon. The two sons sat at the foot of the table, opposite each other.

The serving girl, Marianna, appeared with an antipasto of smoked beef, artichoke hearts and white beans in olive oil. She handed Sesti a corkscrew, and he effortlessly opened Gordon's bottle, pouring the red liquid into shining crystal goblets.

Spadafore lifted his glass and the others fell silent. "I wish to propose a toast," he said. "To the memory of my friend Max Grossman, who was my brother for fifty years. And to his nephew, William Gordon, who, I hope, will be a part of our Family for the next fifty years to come.'' He sipped the wine and smacked his lips appreciatively.

Gordon held his glass in front of him, untouched. ''That's something we're going to have to talk about,'' he said.

''Yes, but later,'' said Spadafore blandly. ''First, let us eat. And drink.'' His eyes fell on Gordon's glass, still poised in midair. The journalist looked at him steadily for a moment and then sipped the wine.

During dinner Spadafore said little, allowing Sesti to carry the conversation. The consigliere asked Gordon about various foreign trouble spots, expressing extravagant praise for his insights and knowledge and, from time to time, sending significant glances in the direction of the Don, who concentrated on the perfectly prepared scaloppini. To his annoyance, Gordon found himself playing to the old man, trying to capture his attention. Only once did the Don ask a question, inquiring about the stability of the Colombian regime. Colombia was one of the few countries in Latin America that Gordon had never visited, and he confined himself to the kind of general remarks that any reader of *Time* magazine could have made. Spadafore nodded politely, but his expression made it plain that he hadn't learned anything new.

Mario and Pietro ate in silence. Spadafore seemed barely to notice them, and when the meal was finished he dismissed them with a nonchalance that surprised Gordon. ''Pietro has an appointment,'' he said with a slightly sardonic smile. ''And Mario always wants to get home early.'' The younger brother looked relieved, but Mario was clearly disappointed at being excluded. He stood heavily, emitted a small fart, waved his hand in the air, looked at his palm and then extended it to Gordon, who shook it with what he hoped was not evident reluctance.

When the two sons had departed, Spadafore led the way into his study. He seated Gordon in an easy chair next to his own. Sesti gave them DeNobli cigars from a cedar humidor, and lit them with his Dunhill. Then he poured each man some cognac in a large snifter. Spadafore accepted these ministrations in silence. The consigliere's every gesture bespoke a profound respect and a sure grasp of the protocol that sustained his world. The Don stole a glance at Gordon, unable to tell if the journalist was impressed.

Spadafore raised his snifter. "We have business to discuss tonight," he said in a soft voice, "but before we do, I wish to say a few personal words to you about your uncle."

"Go ahead," said Gordon. From the look on Spadafore's face he realized immediately that his permission had been superfluous.

"When I said earlier that your uncle and I were like brothers, you may have taken it as the flowery sentiment of an old man. Perhaps you were even offended, since your father is Max's true brother. But, as much as any two men of different blood can be, Max and I were brothers. We grew up together, prospered together and, yes, we sometimes fought together against those who would take what we had. My enemies were his, his enemies were mine. For fifty years we conducted business together without a written document or a single disagreement about money.

"You know stories about me," he continued. "Some have been written in your newspaper. I will not dishonor you by pretending that I am what is known as a law-abiding citizen. I am not, and Max was not. And yet, I consider your uncle to have been a moral man. Crime is not the same as sin; it is a concept relative to time and place, like beauty. When we were young men we sold liquor and it was illegal; today, you can buy liquor anywhere. The same is true of the numbers. Once it was against the law; now the government runs the lottery. In New Jersey, until only a few years ago, games of chance were forbidden; today, casinos advertise on the television. Even drugs, which are so unpopular, will someday become legal, and people will no longer think of them as immoral. That is the way of the world.''

The Don paused to sip his cognac, sighed deeply, and then continued. ''There are, of course, certain things that are sinful. Murder is one. Murder, I say, which is not to be confused with self-defense. But to take an innocent life is an infamy. So, too, are crimes against the poor, or children, or helpless women. Of these things Max was never guilty, nor was I.'' Spadafore saw with satisfaction that Gordon was nodding in agreement. His message was getting through.

''Earlier you referred to me as Uncle Luigi. I know it was a jest, but I was, I will admit, warmed by the phrase. Although you have never, until now, entered our world, Max spoke of you often. I have followed your career with pleasure and pride. And so, I am taking the liberty tonight to speak to you as an uncle.

''Several days ago, Carlo here came to me with a proposal. You already know its details, there is no reason to mention them now. My first reaction was to say no, not out of disrespect for Carlo, for whom I have great admiration, but out of respect for you and your uncle.''

Spadafore paused and held out his glass. Sesti sprang with an athletic ease from his chair, poured three fingers of the clear liquor for the old man, and refilled Gordon's glass as well. The Don sipped his drink and expelled a huge cloud of DeNobli smoke before continuing.

''Let me explain my reasoning,'' he said. ''First, you are a famous journalist. I thought that you might consider a proposal that you abandon a field in which you have distinguished yourself to be in some sense insulting. Also, I knew from your uncle that you displayed little interest in his affairs. This I took as a sign of disapproval.''

Gordon cleared his throat to protest, but Spadafore held up a thick, powerful hand. ''Please, it is not important if I was correct; I am merely explaining my reasoning. I also feared a disrespect to Max. It was not, I thought, my place to make a proposal to you that your uncle himself had refrained from making during his lifetime.

"Those, as I say, were my thoughts. But I am an old man, and Carlo, who belongs to your generation, thought differently. He pointed out that you are a worldly man, not likely to be shocked by any proposal, or unaware of the relative nature of criminal justice. He also said that, as the nephew of Max Grossman, you could be trusted, whatever your decision, to be discreet. Finally, he pointed out that a great deal of money is involved, and you must, out of respect, be made the offer. You are not, after all, an innocent child; you are a grown man, capable of deciding your own future." Spadafore noted that this last thrust had made Gordon flush with pleasure. Knowing Albert Grossman, it was not difficult to guess the reason for the young man's gratified response.

"Let me say that all of this was persuasive, but I still remained unsure. Carlo," he said, turning to the consigliere, "this is a dangerous conversation. You are learning how easily I am influenced by you." Sesti smiled at the compliment, and bowed his head graciously.

"What finally convinced me that I should allow Carlo to go ahead was a question I put to myself: What would my friend Max want me to do? As I have said, Max was not ashamed of our profession. And I knew of his, ah, legacy to you—"

"I was wondering when you were going to get around to that," said Gordon. "If you really want to know what my uncle wanted, I think his will made it pretty clear." He looked at Spadafore evenly, and the Don averted his eyes. Sesti smiled inwardly; it was an old trick, calculated to make Gordon overestimate the force of his own personality.

"William, let me ask you a question," said the Don. "Suppose the owner of your newspaper died, and left it to his nephew. And, suppose that this nephew had never written for a newspaper, never displayed any interest in newspapers, in fact had never even read a newspaper. Further suppose that a single mistake by this nephew could ruin the entire newspaper, cause thousands of people to become unemployed. Would you consider that a prudent step?''

''No, but it's not exactly—''

''Please, allow me to finish,'' said the Don, once again raising his hand, palm up, toward Gordon. ''You perhaps believe that you understand my world, the world of your uncle Max. That is a common enough illusion these days, shared by the writers of novels, the producers of films and many officers of the law. But you do not. It is more complex, more subtle—and more dangerous—than it is imagined to be. To function in this world, at this level, requires a lifetime of experience. Even the most brilliant novice would flounder; and in our world, floundering would be disastrous, not only for you, but for all of us.''

Gordon looked at the Don, considering the logic of this last statement. Spadafore saw it in his eyes. He is a reasonable man, he thought—a terrible handicap in any negotiation.

The Don leaned toward Gordon and placed an avuncular hand on the younger man's arm. ''For these reasons, I decided to allow Carlo to approach you with his proposal. I insisted only that you be given an alternative—to accept a cash settlement. Our business is no longer as violent as it once was; the day of the gangster is, thank God, gone forever. But there are still risks, particularly with the law. And I do not want you to feel compelled to take such risks if you are not . . .'' The Don let the phrase dangle. He had seen enough of Gordon to be able to guess how he would fill it in. ''—man enough.''

''Exactly how big a risk are we talking about?'' asked Gordon. Spadafore shrugged. ''We would do nothing to intentionally expose you to trouble,'' he said. ''After all, your greatest value lies in your associations, and should you be compromised, they would soon disappear. And of course you would choose your own activities; it would be up to you to decide which countries and which officials can be safely approached. Still, nothing in our world can be guaranteed one hundred percent; in this, we are like the rest of humanity.''

''All right, I'd choose the spots we operate. But I'd have no control over the operation itself, according to Carlo. How do I know that someone else won't foul up and implicate me?'' asked Gordon.

''That is precisely one of the dangers I mentioned before,'' said Spadafore. ''Another would be if we were to withhold from you a fair share of the profits.'' Gordon began to protest, but the old man silenced him with a gesture. ''It is only natural that the question has crossed your mind. I can say only this: You know Nathan Belzer, your uncle's associate. He has been involved with us for fifty years. You have my permission to ask him about our reliability and honesty.''

''I don't need permission to talk to Nate Belzer,'' said Gordon petulantly. Although he had made an effort not to show it, he was uneasy with the way the conversation was going, with the entire evening for that matter. Gordon was not used to being patronized, and he resented Spadafore's Godfather routine—the big musty house full of garlic fumes and outsized furniture, the tuxedos, the sons like rented movie extras, Sesti buzzing around the Don.

It annoyed Gordon that Spadafore would imagine that he could be taken in by such transparent crap. For twenty years he had been interviewing world leaders, people for whom Luigi Spadafore would be less than a peasant, and he had seen the real thing, the imperial style up close. Nikolae Ceausescu, sitting at his desk in a darkened office the size of a basketball court, the brilliant light of three giant chandeliers flashing on at the flick of his finger; Papa Doc Duvalier, the Haitian dictator, who had offered him a cigar from a solid gold humidor and a human skull for an ashtray; Sadat, sitting on the endless lawn of the Abdeen Palace, surrounded by twelve giant Nubian attendants in white *galabias* who stood at rigid attention throughout a three-hour meeting; Golda Meir, making him sit like a schoolboy at the Formica table in her small kitchen while she cooked a nauseating dish of farfel and gizzards and lectured through her nose. He had been up against the greatest stage managers in the world, and he had held his own, asked his questions, got his story, refused to be fooled or intimidated by poses and postures.

Gordon was annoyed at being underestimated; but, he admitted to himself, he was also disconcerted. Secretly he regarded his relations with world leaders as contests; in an image Marty Bronstein would have appreciated, he saw them as professional wrestlers, each dressed up in a costume—the Avenger, the Phantom, the Mad Bomber. For twenty years he had been the clean-cut young athlete, clad in nothing but simple trunks, who grappled with them, tore off their masks and pinned their shoulders to the mat.

But now, after two decades of tossing heavyweights, he somehow felt that he couldn't get his arms around Luigi Spadafore's thick neck. The old man was like a sumo wrestler, fat and slick and elusive. His old-fashioned, flowery speech and avuncular pose made Gordon feel callow and self-conscious, like a teenager unable to keep his voice in the right octave, or his probing fingers off a pimple.

"I believe that you do need my permission," said Spadafore softly. "I assume you understood that this conversation is confidential. I would be very unhappy if you discussed it with anyone outside this room."

"Is that a threat, Mr. Spadafore?" Gordon asked, flushing. "I've already been threatened once this week, by Mr. Sesti, here, and I don't like it. One thing you should know about me is that I don't scare—"

A look of theatrical astonishment came over the old man's face. "Threatened?" he said, turning to Sesti. "Is this true?"

The consigliere seemed suddenly alarmed. "Mr. Gordon asked me a hypothetical question at lunch the other day, and I gave him a hypothetical answer," he said. "In no way did I intend it as a threat."

Spadafore reddened. "Listen to me carefully, consigliere," he said in a harsh tone. "William Gordon is the nephew of my brother. His blood is as sacred to me as that of my own sons." Sesti kept his eyes averted, but his pale face became even paler. "You will apologize to Mr. Gordon," said the old man.

"Yes, of course," Sesti said in a tight voice. "I do apologize, certainly, if my remarks were misconstrued." Gordon noticed that the unflappable Sesti was jiggling his left leg nervously.

Gordon nodded. "That's all right, as long as we understand each other," he said. Out of the corner of his eye he saw the old man's shoulders slump.

"It is not all right," the Don said. "Dishonor is never all right. You have my solemn assurance, my blood oath on the lives of my sons, that neither I nor my associates would ever harm you in any way." The Don's voice was imploring, his eyes watery. Suddenly he seemed deflated, and very, very old.

"Don't worry about it," said Gordon, feeling in control for the first time all night. He had the key now to throwing the old bastard—honor, respect, blood oaths for Christ's sake. He couldn't wait to tell Flanagan. "Listen, Mr. Spadafore, it's getting late, and I think we should talk business. Mr. Sesti has made me an offer; I want you to repeat it, just to make sure we're all talking about the same thing."

The Don nodded. "Carlo," he said. In a clipped monotone Sesti repeated the details of his proposal, including Gordon's conditions.

"I've thought it over," Gordon said when the consigliere had finished, "and I'm inclined to accept. But I want five million dollars deposited immediately, and a third of the operation. I also want it understood that we confine ourselves to legitimate business—government contracts, arms, construction projects, that kind of thing. I'm not getting involved in anything illegal; what you do without me is your own affair, but you can't use my contacts to do it. Agreed?"

"Five million dollars is a great deal of money," said Spadafore, frowning.

"It's a fraction of what my uncle left me," said Gordon. "And a fraction of what you will make."

Spadafore hesitated, and Gordon could see that he had scored a point. Finally the old man nodded. "Agreed," he said. "Carlo, you will see to the money." His voice took on a harsher note. "And you will scrupulously observe Mr. Gordon's wishes. I have given my word."

"Yes, Don Spadafore," Sesti said in a formal tone.

"William, there is one thing that troubles me," said the old man. "That is your desire to interest your friend Flanagan in our affairs. I believe that it is unwise."

Gordon shook his head decisively; he had anticipated this objection, and he wanted to use it to assert his control over the foreign operation. "I've known Flanagan for twenty years, and he's absolutely reliable," he said. "Besides, it would be my business he's involved in, not yours."

The Don sighed heavily. "All right, then," he said. He extended his beefy hand, and Gordon took it, noticing the liver spots and a slight tomato stain on his cuff. "You drive a very hard bargain. Your uncle Max would have been proud of you this night."

"I've learned from masters," said Gordon, and the two men laughed. Sesti managed a smile, but continued to look grim.

"It is late," said Don Spadafore, "and I am tired. Carlo

will work out the details with you, and we will meet again to finalize them. In the meantime, if you will excuse me I will go to bed. Carlo will show you out.'' The Don pronounced the name with such cold distaste that Gordon felt a bit sorry for the consigliere.

All three men stood. Spadafore took Gordon by the shoulders and pulled him near. ''Our association gives me great pleasure,'' he said. Gordon could smell the anchovies and denture paste on his breath. ''My old friend is gone, but the nephew of my old friend has taken his place.'' There was a sob in the Don's voice as he placed his cheek next to Gordon's in a ceremonial kiss. Unsure of what to do, Gordon blew a kiss into the air. Behind him, Carlo Sesti saw the old man stare into space, and then suddenly give him a barely perceptible wink of his watery blue eye.

8

FLANAGAN AND GORDON SAT IN A CORNER BOOTH
in Gallagher's. It was three in the afternoon, but the bar was
crowded with barbered, beefy businessmen and half a dozen
high-priced hookers.

"The auto show's in town," said Gordon. "Jesus, look at
these guys. No wonder the Japs are kicking our ass."

"Japan might be a good place to start," said Flanagan,
stirring his Jameson's with his index finger. "Begin right at
the top."

"Let's not rush it, chief," said Gordon. "First, I want to
get all the details set with Sesti. Then we can start conquering
the world, OK?"

"I've been thinking about Sesti," Flanagan said. "I don't
think it's a good idea for you to meet with him from now on.
I think I should do that."

"Why? Don't give me that Tom Hagan routine, John. Seriously. This isn't a game anymore."

"Look, you said yourself that these people are living in
the Middle Ages. Spadafore's supposed to be the Duke of
Earl and Sesti's his spear carrier. OK, we should establish
some kind of parity. I'll deal with Sesti, you deal with the
Don—otherwise, you lose status in the old bastard's eyes."

"You could be right," Gordon conceded. "I don't think Sesti will be anxious to deal with me after last night. All right, set it up with him. But I want to approve the final details."

"What's the matter, Don Velvel, don't you trust me?" Flanagan grinned, but there was a questioning look in his eyes.

"Listen, John, I think we've got to get something straight," said Gordon. "If I didn't trust you, I wouldn't be bringing you into this. But we're both getting into something that's damn serious. Maybe these guys aren't as dangerous as I thought, but they're not Boy Scouts, either, and it's their ball we're playing with. You and I have to be on the same wavelength and cover each other's ass, especially in the beginning when we don't know the rules of the game." Flanagan nodded and sipped his whiskey, Adam's apple bobbing and blue eyes fastened on Gordon.

"There's something else, too," Gordon continued. "Ever since we've known each other, you've sort of set the tone. Ever since Saigon. I never minded and I still don't. But the thing is, John, this is my deal. Max was my uncle, and Spadafore came to me, not you. If it was the other way around, I'd either be in or out, on your terms. But it's not the other way around, and you're going to have to do this my way if you want to do it at all. And I want to know, going in, if you have a problem with that."

Flanagan looked up from his drink. "Let me ask you a question—what do you want to get out of this?"

"Are you kidding?" said Gordon. "We're talking about millions of dollars, maybe hundreds of millions."

"I don't buy it, kid. You don't give a shit about money, you never have. Are you trying to prove a point for your old man or what?"

"That might have something to do with it, although I hate to admit it," said Gordon. "But I don't think it's the main reason. I'm sick of being a hack, for one thing. I once tried to make a list of the countries I've been in and I got stuck about number fifty-five. It's like trying to count up all the girls you've laid—once you've done it, so what? I know more than any living American about the politics of Kuala Lumpur. I had brunch with Pol Pot. I once saw Maggie Thatcher's underpants—''

"No shit?" said Flanagan. "You never told me that. Where?"

"It was at a state dinner in London. I bent over to pick up my napkin and I got a beaver shot. The point is, so what? I'm ready for a change."

"In other words, you're doing this for the challenge," said Flanagan.

"I wouldn't put it exactly that way, but OK, for the challenge. The thing is, there's not going to be any challenge if we wind up dead."

"Will you relax?" said Flanagan in an exasperated voice. "You think I'm an idiot?"

"No, John. But I know you—everything's a game. I think you don't really understand what kind of trouble we could get into if we're careless."

"And I think you're forgetting something. I may screw around, but I'm forty-seven years old, and nobody's picked my pocket yet. While you were off sniffing Maggie Thatcher's undies I was here in New York, drinking with humps from the Truckers Union who put cherries in their dry martinis and Mafia goombahs whose idea of a free press is stealing newspapers. You think I didn't learn something? I learned what you found out last night at Spadafore's—these guys are retards, dumb fucks—''

"Sesti's no dumb fuck," Gordon said.

"Bullshit. You just got done telling me how he sat there while a hundred-year-old pizza-head who thinks he's Niccolò Machiavelli read him the riot act. What do you call that?''

"What's your point, John?"

"My point is, I don't underestimate these guys. But I don't overestimate them, either. The truth is, both of us are burned out with the newspaper business. It's for young guys with powerful legs who still don't know that puppies shit on yesterday's headlines. But I don't want to leave the paper if we're going to spend the whole time running scared. In that case, find yourself another Irish consigliere."

"Ah, John, come on, you know I wouldn't do this without you. I just want you to calm down a little, that's all."

"Hey, I'm calm, OK? You want me to fix a meeting with Sesti?"

"Yeah, go ahead," said Gordon. "But do me a favor."

"Sure, boychik, whatever you want."

"Be serious for once in your life," Gordon said. "And be careful."

Flanagan left Gallagher's with a nice buzz and walked down Fifth Avenue. The street was filled with yuppie girls in blue business suits and running shoes on their way home from the office. They reminded him of the Chinese women he had seen in Beijing, dressed in drab, clucky gray uniforms. Every revolution, he thought, had its sartorial price.

Flanagan cared little about women, but he had a high regard for proper attire. For years he had been after Gordon about his jeans and corduroy-jacket ensembles. As a boy, he had been subjected to an endless stream of folk wisdom from his mother, a banal woman he had never cared for. The one wise thing she had said, and said repeatedly, was that clothes make the man. Flanagan knew that the first thing that any leader does is to cast about for some accessory that sets him above the crowd—Churchill's bowler, Ike's jacket, De Gaulle's campaign cap, LBJ's Stetson. You dress the part, he thought to himself, you become the part.

Flanagan stopped in front of Morris the Hatter's and looked

in the display window. He saw a gray Borsalino with a black band and tiny red feather. He pictured himself sitting down with Sesti with that lid on, and maybe a pair of shades. It would give him a great pyschological edge—Sesti wouldn't know if he was serious or mocking him. He entered the shop and, although he had half a dozen credit cards in his wallet, bought the hat with cash. "Don't bother wrapping it," he told the salesman, "I'll wear it out." On the street he peered at his reflection in the picture window. "Perfecto, consigliere," he congratulated himself, and started down Fifth Avenue again at a brisk pace.

As he walked, Flanagan considered his next move. He still couldn't believe that Gordon was going along with this. He liked Gordon; he was a willing drinker, a good talker with a sense of humor, and he had a basically lazy, cynical outlook on life—all qualities that Flanagan admired. But there was something soft about him. He remembered Gordon's willingness to hand over his cable scoop. At the time the young reporter had thought he was acting out of loyalty, but Flanagan had recognized it as a reluctance to rock the boat, to get too far ahead of the pack.

It wasn't that Gordon was a coward; if anything, Flanagan considered his battlefield reporting to be foolhardy. But he lacked the fire that comes from real engagement. Like a lot of reporters, Gordon was basically an observer, not a participant. Whereas he, Flanagan, was born to be a player. For Gordon, journalism had been a step down—with a slight push he could have been a U.S. senator. Flanagan, with a small shove, might well have wound up setting type like his old man. For him, the paper had been a way of getting into the big game.

For a while it worked, but recently—not so recently, in fact, but for the past ten years or more—he had been increasingly conscious of the limitations of being a hack. He spent his time around the movers and shakers of the city, and the social convention was that he was their equal, but Flanagan knew better. They made decisions, cut deals, caused things to happen. He wound up in front of his computer writing about them.

Flanagan was perceptive enough to realize that his problems were mostly his own fault. He had no wife, no children, no hobbies and no causes. He belonged to no church, gave to no charities, visited no museums, never traveled outside the city. His life was the paper and the bars. Once, he had found a home in both places, but he sensed that the string was running out.

And then Max Grossman kicked, and he suddenly saw daylight. Finally he was being offered a place at the table and some chips to work with, courtesy of his pal Gordon. He understood Gordon's worries, even sympathized with them, but he didn't share them. Flanagan had no doubt that he was the equal of Spadafore and Sesti and the rest of the greaseballs; but even if it turned out to be a miscalculation, it didn't matter all that fucking much. Everybody dies of something, he thought. At the very bottom of his soul he knew that the only precious treasure he had was his sense of fun—it was the one thing that kept him from standing on the corner with a can of Drano, cursing passing pedestrians. As long as he could indulge himself, he was a man with nothing else to lose.

Flanagan cut across Twenty-third Street to his building, cleaned out the mailbox and opened the door to his apartment. The dingy one-room flat hadn't been cleaned in weeks, and it smelled like dirty feet. He tossed his raincoat on the gray, lumpy couch but left the Borsalino in place, sat down at his cluttered desk and looked for Sesti's number on the Rolodex. One night, high on Irish whiskey and bile, he had written a description alongside each letter—*A* for asshole, *B* for butt-fucker, *C* for cocksucker, *D* for dickhead and so on.

He found the consigliere under *S* for scumbag, sat down and dialed the number.

"Summers, Bravenfield and Sesti," said a woman's voice.

"Carlo Sesti, please," he said.

"May I ask who's calling?"

"Yeah, John Flanagan. He'll know who I am."

"Just a moment, please," said the voice, and a moment later it was replaced by a clipped British accent. "Mr. Flanagan, this is Carlo Sesti," it said.

"Hello, consigliere," said Flanagan. "You and I need to sit down and talk."

9

JUPITER EVANS SAW THE WOMAN AS SOON AS SHE walked out of her apartment house. She was standing across the street, on the southwest corner of Madison and Sixty-fifth. From that distance she looked almost like Jupiter's twin sister: five-six or so, thin, long black curly hair. She even had Evans's posture, a square-shouldered firmness that Jupiter had acquired by dint of her father's daily hectoring.

This was the third day that the woman was out there, but Evans noted her presence without interest or concern. She had been a star long enough to be used to being dogged by fans and to know how to protect herself. Her approach was simply to ignore them. She signed no autographs, refused to pose for pictures and never encouraged strangers in any way. Occasionally someone cursed her for being a stuck-up bitch, but over the years she had acquired a reputation for aloofness that was now a part of her image, and most people seemed to accept it. Sometimes after a show she would emerge from her dressing room and walk past a knot of people who followed her with their eyes but said nothing. Among the fans it was understood that respectful distance was the appropriate response to Jupiter Evans, just as screaming had been the correct reaction to the Beatles. "Jupiter likes her privacy," they would tell one another as if it were an intimate secret entrusted only to them, and by honoring it they awarded themselves an imaginary place in her life.

Jupiter had heard other stars discuss fans. Some swapped "can you top this" horror stories of intrusive admirers that she recognized as bragging. Others wondered aloud what caused the fans to stand for hours waiting for a glimpse of celebrity. But Jupiter didn't brag and she didn't wonder. She cared nothing at all about the lives of her fans and, for that matter, almost nothing about her fellow stars. She lived within herself, thought about herself, and concentrated her energies on taking care of herself.

Often her detachment was mistaken for arrogance, or for humility, but Jupiter knew it was neither. All her life people had misunderstood her. As a girl in New Haven, her demanding, oppressive father had insisted that she become an intellectual, assigning her reading in the classics and the social sciences and then grilling her at the dinner table each night. Professor Arnold Evans had a sharp tongue and he used it to lash her, demanding perfect evening recitations and mocking any girlish lapses. "Come now, Jupiter," he would say if she confused Diogenes with Demosthenes or forgot the year of the Molotov-Ribbentrop Pact. "You'll have to do better. Beautiful girls have the luxury of stupidity but you are not, alas, a beautiful girl." To this day, the memory of those mealtime flagellations nauseated her. When her father died six years ago, she did not attend the funeral.

As a teenager she had presence, even a sort of charisma, which embarrassed her and which she tried unsuccessfully to hide behind a facade of ordinariness, as another girl might try to hide large breasts under a baggy sweater. But despite her best efforts to fit in, she was never accepted by her classmates. Her brown eyes burned too fiercely and saw too clearly for her to be one of the girls. They gossiped about her, invented stories about her sex life and kept their distance. She retaliated by stealing their boyfriends. Jupiter accepted her father's evaluation of herself as an ugly duckling, but she was perceptive enough to know that she was attractive to boys. She never thought much about the fact that they were not especially attractive to her.

Jupiter spent the summer before her senior year in high school as a counselor-in-training at a camp in Maine. She knew no one there, and for the first few days she was even more reserved and aloof than usual. One night after dinner, she went down to the lake to smoke a cigarette. A girl named Claudette Lawton followed her. She walked up to Jupiter, took her by the shoulders, gazed into her eyes and in a gentle voice said, "I know about you. I know who you are. It's all right." The words gave Jupiter a burning feeling in her stomach. Claudette stroked her cheek and walked away.

The next night they met again at the lake. This time Claudette kissed her on the mouth and stroked her body, pulled up her T-shirt and sucked her aroused nipples with a gentle hunger. Jupiter felt overwhelmed by lust and intimacy. She lay on her back and arched herself as Claudette licked and kissed her between the legs until she heard a roaring in her ears and experienced the first orgasm of her life. Then they lay close together in the grass and Claudette kissed her neck. "I know about you," she said. "I love you."

In the morning Jupiter awoke with a start. I'm a lesbian, she thought, and began to cry. She had been sentenced to life imprisonment as a pervert. She would never have a normal life, children, a family of her own. She dreaded what would happen if her father found out; she wouldn't be able to bear the torture of his ridicule. Maybe he already knew. Claudette had seen it, why not others? Perhaps everyone already knew she was sick.

Jupiter climbed out of her bunk in the cabin and put on her bathing suit. It was barely dawn, and the entire camp was still asleep. She walked down to the lake, waded into the water and began to swim. She intended to swim until she drowned.

It took her two hours to cross the lake, and when she crawled out on the other shore, exhausted, she took it as a sign. She had conquered the lake and she would conquer her perversion. Claudette, she decided, was an aberration. She would escape and cleanse herself. That afternoon, while the kids were in an Indian lore workshop, she walked out of camp, hitched a ride to town and caught a Greyhound heading south.

Like thousands of other runaway girls of her generation, Jupiter disembarked at the New York Port Authority terminal. But unlike most of those girls, Jupiter Evans was not out of control. On the lake she had learned that her strongest impulse was self-preservation, and she had no intention of wandering the streets aimlessly, screwing for drugs. She was too strong for that, too proud and too scared.

Instead she borrowed five hundred dollars from her aunt Barbara, her mother's sister, who lived in a large duplex apartment on Third Avenue. She checked into the Taft Hotel, near Times Square, and wrote her father that she was pregnant and had no desire to come back to New Haven. She asked him to send her five thousand dollars for an abortion and to pay her living expenses in New York during her last year in high school. Her father sent the money along with a curt note saying that she was welcome to come home at any time, but that he had no intention of going all the way down to Manhattan to drag her back.

Jupiter rented an apartment on the Upper West Side and charmed her way into the High School for the Performing Arts. There she met girls who openly liked other girls, and discovered that she had a gift for acting. Her drama teacher, an elderly woman with a German accent and an armload of gold-plated bracelets, took her to the Russian Tea Room and introduced her to a feminist playwright named Tamara Rothenberg, who gave her a part in a topical cabaret in the Village. She spent her eighteenth birthday onstage, wearing a bikini made from the flag and telling an appreciative audience that President Nixon was the biggest dick in America. After the show, Tamara gave her a gram of cocaine as a present and took her to bed.

Jupiter Evans's talent was so obvious, and her presence so dominating, that she soon became the envy of her generation of aspiring actresses. She was never forced to work as a waitress in trendy bistros or to make discouraging rounds of casting offices. Producers and directors came to her with offers—leads in small theater productions, supporting roles in serious-minded films, even a part in a socially conscious television soap opera. By the time she was twenty-one, Jupiter Evans was a well-known name.

Two years later, she was offered the starring role in *Sisterhood*, a play about a lesbian love affair. At the time she was in therapy three days a week. Her analyst, Dr. Fried, strongly encouraged her to take the role. "It will help you work through your sexual identity on your own terms," he told her.

Sisterhood ran for twenty-seven months on Broadway, and won Jupiter Evans a Tony Award. She became the symbol of the sexually liberated woman. In a *Time* magazine story about the new sexuality her picture appeared over the caption "Is she or isn't she?" and the article was full of innuendo about her sexual preferences. Her lawyer, a pompous little Wasp named Crispen, deflected her demand for a libel suit by remarking that truth is an absolute defense. "Do you really want to have your sex life examined in a courtroom?" he asked her with a leer.

Two years after the *Time* article appeared, Evans met William Gordon. She found him charming and a bit frightening. She occasionally went to bed with men, sometimes out of curiosity, sometimes to prove to herself that she was not a total lesbian. But she never slept with anyone more than once. She dismissed them by finding fault, picking out annoying flaws and thus giving herself an excuse to despise them.

But Gordon was not easy to dismiss. Not that he was perfect. He snored, for one thing. He talked about himself too much. And he was a little too mannish, too much like the sweaty boys she had necked with in high school. But she liked his humor and his direct manner, enjoyed his sardonic, self-deprecating stories about the life of a foreign correspondent and respected his basic honesty. Most of all, she was drawn to his absolute belief in her as a woman.

Jupiter was cautious with Gordon, but not as cautious as usual. She let him come closer than any other man, allowed him to glimpse her fears and phobias. She let him touch her wounds, expecting him to be repelled; instead, he loved her, wanted her, told her that if she let herself go she would learn to love him. This was something she wanted desperately to believe. The truth was that, no matter how trendy it became, no matter how much she needed the warmth and intimacy that she found from other women, Jupiter Evans never got over the feeling that being gay was a sad abnormality.

Evans walked up Madison Avenue, aware that her look-alike was following her on the other side of the street. For a moment she was tempted to stop and wave, perhaps embarrass the young woman into turning around. But she repressed the urge. Three days was a long time, even for a fan; the world was full of loonies, and some of them were dangerous. She stepped off the curb and raised her arm for a taxi. Inside, she looked out the rear window and saw the girl staring. She gave the driver Gordon's address and sat back gingerly on the cracked leatherette seat.

"I know you," said the cabbie, looking into the rearview mirror. "Jupiter Evans, right?"

"Nope," she said. "I just look like her. A lot of people say that."

"She's some actress," said the cabbie. "You could be her double, you know that?"

"Sometimes I wish I were," she said softly.

10

FLANAGAN ARRIVED AT UMBERTO'S EARLY. A TABLE
in the middle of the room was free, but he asked for one
along the wall. "I like to sit facing the door," he told the
waiter, who shrugged.

"Would you like me to check your hat, sir?"

Flanagan shook his head. "I'll wear it," he said. "Religious reasons."

He was just sitting down when the door opened and Carlo
Sesti walked in. The lawyer was dressed, as usual, in a sober
business suit and carried a briefcase. Flanagan noted with
satisfaction that he was bareheaded.

"Hello, Sesti," Flanagan said, shaking hands.

"Mr. Flanagan, how good to see you again." Sesti gazed
around the spare, simple restaurant. Umberto's had been
Flanagan's choice. "Charming," he said. "I don't believe
I've ever been here before."

"Of course not," said Flanagan with heavy sarcasm. He
had picked Umberto's because it had been the scene of the
gangland slaying of Joey Gallo in the early seventies.

Sesti ignored the remark and took a seat, back to the door,
without evident discomfort.

"How are things with the Teamsters, Carlo?" asked Flanagan amiably.

"You don't mean to say that you've invited me to dinner to talk about that?" he said. "I have nothing whatsoever to do with the Teamsters Union, as you well know. If you're still working on that story, you'll have to find information elsewhere, I'm afraid."

"Naw, I'm not here as a reporter," drawled Flanagan, chewing on an olive. "This is a business meeting. I'm here as William Gordon's consigliere."

A glint of amusement sparkled in Sesti's cold, pale eyes. "I beg your pardon?" he said.

"I beg your pardon?" said Flanagan, mimicking Sesti's British accent. "Who are you supposed to be, Evelyn Waugh?"

"As a matter of fact, I was at school with one of Evelyn Waugh's sons. At Downside," said Sesti.

"Yeah, well, I went to school with Phil Rizzuto's cousin. At St. Benedict's High, old chap."

Sesti picked up his briefcase, which was resting on the chair next to him. "Mr. Flanagan, if you've asked me to dinner to mock me, I assure you that I have no intention of—"

"Sit down, Carlo," said Flanagan, staring hard into his eyes. "I already told you why I wanted to meet with you, to talk about the deal between Big Luigi and my boss. Or don't you know who Luigi Spadafore is?"

"Mr. Spadafore is one of my clients," Sesti said stiffly.

Flanagan snorted. "Yeah, right. Look, Carlo, let's not jerk each other off. Mr. Gordon asked me to sit down with you and work out the details of his arrangement with Spadafore. You don't believe me, drop a dime and ask him. But you do believe me, because otherwise you wouldn't have agreed to meet me in the first place. From now on, you deal with me, consigliere to consigliere. That's the way Mr. Gordon wants it.''

Sesti regarded Flanagan through expressionless eyes. He took in the Borsalino hat, set firmly on the Irishman's head. He saw the tiny red boozer's veins in his nose, his thin lips and the square set of his jaw, the bony fingers resting spread on the table. He sighed inwardly; somehow he would have to get rid of Flanagan. "All right," he said in his clipped accent. "Let's talk, then."

"That's the spirit, Carlo," said Flanagan. He raised his hand for the waiter. "Try the fried clams, you'll love them."

Sesti ignored the advice and asked for a rare steak and a salad. Flanagan, in an extravagant Italian accent, ordered minestrone and an order of clams. "And a bottle of dago red for my friend," he said with a broad wink. "He's a tourist."

When the waiter was gone, Flanagan leaned forward, resting his face on both hands. "Right about now you're thinking, Christ, this guy is a clown. He's fucking around, wasting my time by playing gangster. Well, that's what I want you to think. Then, by telling you that I know what you're thinking, I let you know that I'm not a clown after all. Now you're thinking, this guy's more complex than I thought. Or maybe you're still thinking that I'm a clown, because I'm explaining my strategy as I go along. Either way, I got you puzzled." Flanagan was pleased to note that Sesti did, indeed, look perplexed. "You following me so far, bambino?"

The consigliere nodded, listening.

"I know all about the little play you put on in Brooklyn the other night," said Flanagan. "Tuxedos, candlelight, Christ, I'm surprised you didn't have somebody throw a trout through the window during dinner. 'Lucca Bracci sleeps with the fishes.' We've already seen that movie, Carlo. You think you're dealing with Julius LaRosa? We been to the big city, pal. We're laughing at you. So, point number one, no more bullshit, OK?''

"This is your speech, Mr. Flanagan," said Sesti evenly. "Please go on."

"That's the second thing, I don't like your attitude," said Flanagan. "It's disrespectful. You want to call me something, call me John, or consigliere. You can't help that Brit accent of yours, but don't look at me like I've got shit on my shoes. Don't patronize me. That's not a threat, it's a warning." Flanagan paused, and for a long moment there was silence. Finally he grinned. "Good line, huh? Non sequitur. It's supposed to be 'That's not a threat, it's a promise.' You missed it, didn't you, Carlo? Tell the truth."

Sesti was making an effort to keep his face expressionless, but it wasn't working. Involuntarily, he nodded, and then looked annoyed.

"Fifteen-love to Consigliere Flanagan," intoned Flanagan in an announcer's voice. "Now, Carlo old chap, let's understand one another. What exactly did you have in mind for my boss?"

Speaking with a chill precision, Sesti reiterated his plan, while Flanagan, Borsalino still on his head, noisily ate his soup. It was the same basic idea that Gordon had outlined. When Sesti was finished, Flanagan wiped his mouth with the red-and-white checkered napkin and stifled a belch.

"That sounds good," he said. "Now, maybe you'll quit fucking around and tell me what you really want. It'll save us both a lot of aggravation later on."

Sesti gave an exasperated sigh. "I've just told you what we have in mind. There is nothing more. It's a straightforward business proposition. Surely you see that?"

"Surely you see that?" Flanagan mimicked. "What I see is a fucking goombah with a law degree and a good tailor. What I hear is bullshit in a butler's accent. I expected more from you, Carlo. I really did."

"There is no more, consigliere," said Sesti, allowing

himself to get angry. He rose to leave, and this time Flanagan didn't try to restrain him.

"Here's what I think, Carlo," said Flanagan, looking up into Sesti's face. "I think you're trying to set us up. I think you want my boss, Mr. Gordon, to open some doors for you overseas, and then you plan to dump him. And me. Don't bother to deny it, just listen. I think you and your pal Big Luigi are going to screw us out of our strawberries."

Sesti stood with his briefcase in one hand. With the other, he sketched small circles on the tablecloth. He wondered if Flanagan could have possibly bugged Spadafore's house, and made a mental note to have the place gone over the next day. "I'm not responsible for your fantasies, Mr. Flanagan," he said. "If that's what you believe . . ." He shrugged, a Sicilian gesture that contrasted strangely with his frosty Anglo-Saxon demeanor.

"Put yourself in my place, Carlo," said Flanagan in a tone of utmost geniality. "Imagine you were dealing with a couple of slimebags like Luigi and yourself. Would you trust them? Be reasonable, old chap. You want a deal, OK, we're ready to make a deal. The conditions you outlined with Mr. Gordon are acceptable. I tell you right now that I would have driven a harder bargain, but what's agreed to is agreed to. That's a sacred principle in our Mishpocha. You don't know what that is, ask Luigi. Anyway, the terms are settled. But I want assurances, Carlo, something ironclad that guarantees you won't stiff us. What assurances, you ask? I don't know. You decide, make me a proposal. You're better at this kind of thing than I am, after all; I'm just an Irish hack. But until I hear something that calms my jittery nerves, we won't help you do business. *Capisce?*"

Sesti stood over Flanagan, shifting his weight from one foot to the other. "In that case, Mr. Flanagan, I'm afraid we have no business to conduct. Mr. Spadafore would consider your demand demeaning, and so, frankly, do I. If that's all,

I'll be going. Thank you for dinner.'' He turned and started for the door.

Flanagan let him walk five or six steps before calling out to him. "Yo, Carlo," he said, loudly enough for people at nearby tables to overhear. Sesti turned to Flanagan with a look of anticipation; he had been expecting the Irishman to call him back. For all his tough talk, Flanagan would be a pushover.

"Yes?" he said.

"Carlo," said Flanagan, "I hate to tell you this, but you got a bugger in your nostril."

On the night of Flanagan's dinner with Carlo Sesti, Mario and Pietro Spadafore met in the basement rumpus room of Mario's split-level in Great Neck. The upstairs was decorated in Catholic modern, but downstairs Mario had built himself a fantasy room. There was a white leather wet bar along the wall, a gigantic television screen, a pool table and two pinball machines. There was also a bar bowling game, a refrigerator stocked with beer and soda, a candy machine and about ten thousand dollars' worth of stereo equipment on which he played Rosemary Clooney records. In the basement of his $750,000 suburban home, Mario Spadafore had created a Brooklyn cocktail lounge.

Recently, however, he had almost stopped using the room. He had long since figured out how to cheat the pinball machines, quit drinking the hard stuff on his doctor's advice, and had grown to hate the sound of Rosemary Clooney's voice. There was no one to play pool with, either; Mario had no friends. Occasionally he came downstairs to see a ball game on the giant screen, but there were too many blacks in professional sports these days for him to really enjoy it. When he thought about the rumpus room it was with regret: one more fine dream down the drain. I should be a prince, he said to himself; instead, I'm a fuckin' frog.

Pietro stood over the pool table, a cigarette dangling from his lips, banging balls into the pockets with a crisp, professional stroke. Mario watched his brother with wonder. Everybody else in the family looks like Mussolini, he thought; this guy's built like Travolta. He watched Pietro rise on tiptoe, skinny ass cocked, and blast the seven ball into the side.

"Will you get away from the fuckin' pool table and sit the fuck down?" he said in a thick voice. "This is serious."

"I can shoot and listen at the same time," said Pietro, chopping in the nine ball with a soft stroke.

Mario rose from his seat, grabbed the cue out of his brother's hand and pushed him hard in the chest. Pietro stumbled backward, hit the couch and plopped down. Since they had been kids, this had been their primary mode of communication. "That's better," said Mario. "Stay put."

"You got fifteen minutes, Mario," said Pietro, unperturbed by the shove. "Then I'm gone like a cool breeze."

"I wanna talk about the old man, Pietro," said Mario petulantly. Instinctively he looked around. Even here, in his own dream room, he was afraid that his father might overhear him.

"Yeah, what about him?"

"He's gonna cut us out, Pietro, that's what about him." Mario hoped that his brother would deny it, but he merely looked bored. "Maybe you don't give a shit about being uninherited, but I do."

"Get outa here," said Pietro. "Pa wouldn't do that. We're his blood."

"That's what you think," said Mario. "You see Sesti the other night? Sittin' next to the old man, acting like he owned the place. Fuckin' Sesti—"

"I saw him, so what?" asked Pietro. "Sesti's the consigliere, he's supposed to be there."

"He ain't supposed to sit up at the head of the table, asking all the questions. And how about the old man showing respect for that Jewboy. We're the sons, not them. You see how the old man got rid of us after? I'm tellin' ya, we're gettin' cut out."

"Nah, Pa knew I had a date. That's why he let us go early," said Pietro, looking at his watch.

"Hey, dumbo, wake up. You think the old man gives a fuck about your dates?"

Pietro shrugged. "Maybe he doesn't but I do. And I got one in an hour, a real piece of ass. You ought to get a little more, Mario, you'd be less nervous."

"Are you with me on this here or not?" demanded Mario impatiently. "You gonna let that fuck Sesti steal our birthright?"

"Come on, Mario. Pa's gonna do the right thing, you know that. He goes, you take over. Don't get your balls in an uproar."

"I ought to wack that fuckin' Sesti out," Mario muttered.

"Yeah, right," laughed Pietro. "Wack out the old man's consigliere. Why doncha burn down his house while you're at it? Listen, Mario, do me a favor, you decide to take out Sesti, lemme know so I can arrange to be out of town, huh?"

"Pietro, you ever think about what it's going to be like when the old man croaks? You wanna stay in the business or what?"

"What."

"Whaddya mean, what?"

"I mean what. You said, do you wanna stay in the business or what, and I said what. Meaning I don't wanna stay in the business. It's yours, Mario. I got better things to do with my life."

"What makes you so fuckin' superior?" Mario demanded, grinding a thick finger into his ear.

"Nobody's saying I'm superior. I've just got different values from you, ya know?"

"Yeah? Different values? Like what kind of values?" Mario asked, wiping the earwax on the leg of his trousers.

"Travel," said Pietro. "I like to see new places, learn new things. And girls." Mario waited, but Pietro had finished.

"That's it?" he exploded. "That's your values? Vacations and pussy?"

"Sure, what's wrong with it?" asked Pietro. "You got something better to offer?"

"I ought to wack you out along with Sesti and that fuckin' Gordon," said Mario. He wasn't mad, though; he liked his little brother, and he would have smiled at him if he knew how. Especially now that he was sure that the little dumbfuck wasn't going to be a problem.

Jupiter arrived at Gordon's place just as the sun was going down. She found him on his small terrace with a gin and tonic and a biography of Trotsky spread on the wrought-iron coffee table. The book had been sent to him by its author, a reporter he had worked with and liked in several foreign postings. Normally he would have offered to review it, but right now he could barely get past the first page.

Jupiter's eyes fell on the book. "Trotsky, eh?" she said. "Interesting choice of reading matter for you these days."

"Yeah? Why's that?"

"Jewish intellectual in over his head with a thug he thought he could manipulate. Have you got to the part yet where Stalin had him stabbed to death?"

"Jeez, you're a pain in the ass when you're showing off," Gordon said fondly. It constantly amazed him that Jupiter knew or cared anything about the world of international politics. In his experience, most women were basically uninterested in issues that didn't affect them directly. Those who did care usually struck him as shrill. It was, he knew, a sexist attitude.

As usual, Jupiter read his thoughts. "If Flanagan said that, would you think he was showing off?" she asked.

"No," Gordon admitted. "But John is a hack, not a beautiful actress."

"That's what you think," said Jupiter with a crooked smile. "Your pal Flanagan is the best actor I know."

"John's all right," said Gordon defensively. He hated it when his friends criticized each other, especially Jupiter and Flanagan.

"Well, I didn't come by to talk about John. I came to talk about the other night." Suddenly she looked abashed and vulnerable, like a little girl. Gordon wanted to hug her, but by this time he knew better. Affection frightened Jupiter. Most women wanted to know they were loved, but she was terrified by that kind of responsibility. After each of their few previous sexual encounters she had disappeared, often for a month or more. The thing, he knew, was to keep it light.

"The other night?" he asked. "Let's see, what was the other night . . ."

"Gordon, the other night was a mistake."

"Shit, I knew it," said Gordon. "OK, that's the last time we go to Barney's. Those bastards always overcook the burgers."

"Come on, Will," she said softly. It was a nickname she used when she was being intimate, and the sound of it in her throaty voice thrilled him. "Let's not fool around. All the booze and the talk about money and gangsters, and you looked so damn serious and cute, it just put me in the mood."

"Which you're out of now?" asked Gordon, not wanting to hear the answer.

She looked at him steadily. "Will, you're torturing both of us. You know what I am, what I can and can't be. Leave it alone, and let's be friends. Isn't that enough?"

Suddenly Gordon was furious. "No, it's not enough, goddamn it. Don't insult my intelligence. I don't want to be friends, and I don't think that you do, either. Otherwise you wouldn't be here right now, after all these years. You always leave, Jupiter, but you always come back, too."

"Gordon, I don't find you attractive," she said in a cold, cruel voice. This was part of the routine; when she was cornered, Jupiter lashed out without even thinking about the consequences. "You have a potbelly and a hairy body and you stink of cigarettes and whiskey. You're condescending and insensitive. It was a mistake to come here tonight, and I'm leaving—"

Suddenly, without warning, Gordon unzipped his pants. "What do you want me to do, cut it off?" he demanded. "OK, get a knife from the kitchen, let's cut it off. I'll go to Puerto Rico and get a disbarred surgeon to put in a poo-poo. I'll go on the Scarsdale Diet and start smoking Virginia Slims. Come on, Jupiter, get the knife. . . ."

She started to laugh, a low, melodious sound, and the lines around her eyes crinkled. Gordon breathed a sigh of relief. It would be all right this time.

He fixed her a drink and they sat together on the balcony, watching the lights come on. "Listen, Jupiter, I want to make you a serious proposition," Gordon said. "Are you in a good enough mood for a proposition?"

"Will, please, please don't start—"

"I told Spadafore yes," he said. "I'm going to do it."

"How about the paper?" asked Jupiter.

"I asked them for a two-year leave of absence to write a book. I'll get a gig at Brookings, just for a cover story. Hell, maybe I'll even write a book if I get the time. But the thing is, I'm going for it."

"I hope the other night didn't have anything to do with

your decision," she said. "I don't want to sound egotistical, but if you're doing this because of me, don't. I mean it, Will."

"Everybody talks to me like a teenager these days," he said. "My old man, Spadafore, Flanagan, even you. Whatever happened to William Gordon, two-time Pulitzer winner? Hey, I'm doing this because of me, for my own reasons. But one of those reasons happens to be you."

"Happens to be me," she repeated in a flat voice.

"Happens to be you, yeah," he said. "Listen, the other night when you said that half a billion dollars changes everything, you may have thought you were kidding, but we both know that that much money does change things. At least it can. Will you admit that much?"

"I won't admit anything until I know exactly where you're going with this," she said.

"OK, I want you to marry me," Gordon said, raising a hand to keep her from arguing. "Just wait, let me finish. I want you to marry me, not right this minute, but within a year, providing this thing is working the way it's supposed to. If it does, I'll be so rich that we can have anything we want, including each other, on our own terms. Your terms."

"Are you trying to buy me?" Jupiter asked mildly.

"No, I'm trying to buy a certain kind of life," said Gordon. "A brownstone here in town, a place in London, a house in the islands, a private plane, a yacht and enough money to make things perfect. You could work when you wanted on what you wanted, without having to think about the financial side. You could travel anywhere, anytime. When you wanted to be alone, you could be alone, and when you wanted to be with me, OK, then we'd be together. That's what I want the money to buy, a life together."

"What's the point, Will?" she asked. "I mean, aside from buying a bunch of houses and planes. What would it change?"

"We'd be married," said Gordon. "We'd live in the same world. No matter where you were or what you were doing, I'd be your husband, we'd be connected. And we'd have children." This was a powerful inducement, Gordon knew; Jupiter wanted very much to be a mother. "As many children as you want. Plus, we could have a hell of a wedding—"

"You paint an idyllic picture, you silver-tongued devil," Jupiter laughed. She leaned over and ruffled Gordon's thinning hair. "I don't know what to say."

"Say yes and trust me. I know more about you than any other person in the world. You think your problem is that you like women, but that's not it. The real problem is that you're afraid to make a commitment to anything or anybody. I know that sounds like bullshit, but that's what all the therapy comes down to, isn't it? This is a way for you to make a commitment and still be free, have a family and go on being on your own. If I can accept that, why can't you?"

"I'm not going to turn you down, Will," she said softly. "But I'm not going to say yes, either, at least not now. I want to think about it. You said it's a few months down the road, give me some time, OK?"

"OK, if you promise to say yes."

"No, I promise to think. But I love you very much right now." She leaned over and kissed him softly on the lips.

"God, I love you, too," breathed Gordon, as much to himself as to her. He rose and gently lifted her to her feet. They stood in each other's arms, and Gordon felt tears of joy just behind his eyes.

"Let's go in the other room," he said, stroking her cheek. Suddenly he felt her grow rigid. She pulled back, and he could see clouds of panic in her eyes.

"Not tonight," she said. "I'm sorry, but I've got a date,

I can't stay.'' She stepped away from him, picked up her pocketbook and walked out without another word.

Gordon stood alone on the balcony feeling a sense of total detachment, like people who claim to have died and seen their own bodies on the operating table. He watched himself sit down, light a Winston, pick up the Trotsky book and calmly begin to read. That's odd, he said to himself; I was expecting you to cry.

FLANAGAN WAS NOT SURPRISED WHEN, THREE DAYS after his meeting with Sesti, he got a call from the consigliere. Sesti gave no indication that he was in the least upset or angry about their last meeting; he merely said that he had considered Flanagan's request, and had several suggestions as to how he could accommodate it.

"Thank you, Carlo," Flanagan said with warm sincerity. "I really appreciate it."

That was on a Monday. On Wednesday the two men met for lunch at the Harvard Club. Flanagan wore a dark suit and no hat. He refused a drink, and allowed Sesti to do the talking, listening with a cordial, almost deferential air as the consigliere offered various assurances, bank guarantees and even a five-million-dollar life insurance policy for Gordon and himself. Flanagan had no idea if these constituted adequate protection, and he didn't care. He had wanted to make two points, and they were both made. By crawling back, Sesti had admitted that he needed Gordon more than Gordon needed him. And he had forced the consigliere to deal with him as an equal.

"Carlo, I'm sorry I had to put you to this extra work, but

I'm new at this. I'll learn the ropes as I go along,'' he said modestly.

''John, I probably would have done the same thing in your place,'' said Sesti. ''I respect a man who protects his client's interests.''

They shook hands solemnly. ''Carlo, now that we've ironed out the last details, Mr. Gordon would like to reciprocate your hospitality of the other night by inviting Mr. Spadafore, and you too, of course, to dinner,'' said Flanagan. ''He wondered if Saturday night would be convenient?''

Sesti frowned. ''Mr. Spadafore rarely leaves Brooklyn,'' he said. ''Of course I very much appreciate the invitation, but I'm just not certain that—''

''Please, Carlo, it would mean a great deal to Mr. Gordon. He very much wants to have the opportunity to show his respect to Mr. Spadafore.''

''Well, I'll do my best,'' said the consigliere briskly. ''I'll let you know this afternoon, if I may.'' Two hours later he called to say that Spadafore was honored by the invitation and would be delighted to accept. Dinner was set for seven-thirty.

That night Flanagan dropped by Gordon's. Gordon was aware that Flanagan had met Sesti at Umberto's but knew nothing about the conversation itself, or today's capitulation. No need, Flanagan reflected, to disturb the boss with details.

''We're all set,'' he said. ''We can start at the beginning of the month. Carlo will deposit the money in any bank we say, and the organization pays all expenses. Now all you have to do is figure out which world leader you want to turn into Al Capone.'' Flanagan snapped his fingers. ''Speaking of which, you've got company for dinner on Saturday night.''

''Company? Like who?''

''You're not going to believe this, but Luigi wants to break bread with you.''

Gordon stared at Flanagan. "Luigi? You mean Spadafore? Wants to have dinner here?"

"Sesti dropped the hint. It's customary, especially after he had you to his place. Cement the deal, drink out of the same cup, all that sort of shit. I think you ought to serve Chinese. Those hors d'oeuvres that Ida had at the shivah were delish."

"Goddamn it, Flanagan, are you out of your mind?" Gordon exploded. "I can't have those guys over here. The FBI sticks to Spadafore like white on rice. I got a doorman who already thinks I'm connected and this'll be all over the neighborhood. You gotta get me out of this—"

"Look, they're your friends," said Flanagan. "You're the one who went there for dinner. I can't help it if they're big on protocol. Besides, it's no big deal. We'll get a caterer in, set the place up. The doorman? Fuck the doorman. As far as the feds are concerned, Luigi Spadafore was an old friend of your uncle's and this is a condolence call. What's to worry?"

Gordon looked dubious. Finally he uttered a resigned sigh. "OK, OK. I guess I don't have any choice. What the hell do we serve them? I gotta get some wine, too, and liquor. Goddamn it all to hell, Flanagan, I ought to make you pay for this."

"Relax, we'll take it out of expenses. I'm serious about the Chinese, by the way. Make a nice change of pace for the old boy. I don't imagine he gets much lo mein out in Gnocchi City." Suddenly he clapped his hands together and laughed. "Hey, I got a great idea," he said. Let's load the fortune cookies, put in little messages like, 'Carlo, you're under arrest.' "

Gordon laughed in spite of himself. "Yeah, or 'Luigi, you have just been poisoned. Signed: The boys.' "

"Or how about, 'Mafia girls do it with Ricans.' That ought

to get 'em.'' The two old friends giggled like a couple of schoolboys.

'' 'Go on a diet, Luigi,' '' said Gordon.

'' 'You talk like a sissy, Carlo,' '' laughed Flanagan. "Let's do it, it'll be great for a laugh.''

Suddenly Gordon was sober. "Forget it, chief. No loaded cookies. And no Chinese. Just get some caterer to bring in steaks and potatoes, regular old American food. A tossed salad. And something for dessert, maybe from that place on Mulberry, what's-its-name. Have them serve the food and leave. And a few bottles of liquor—Wild Turkey, Jameson's, Sesti probably drinks Chivas. And some wine. As long as they're paying for it, I might as well stock up.''

"Your wish is my command,'' said Flanagan, looking at his watch. "I got to go home for some z's. I got a late meeting uptown.''

"What's uptown?'' asked Gordon. "You taking night classes at Columbia? Criminology 101, maybe?''

"Naw,'' said Flanagan. "I'm going to see an old friend, guy I went to high school with. You don't know him.''

"OK,'' said Gordon. "I'll talk to you tomorrow. And I'm counting on you to handle dinner.''

"Don't worry about a thing,'' said Flanagan. "Just leave it all to your consigliere.''

At five minutes after two in the morning, feeling rested from a long nap, Flanagan climbed out of a cab on the corner of 125th Street and Amsterdam. The ride cost him twenty dollars.

"I ain't got cancer,'' the elderly driver had said when Flanagan climbed into the cab near his building on Twenty-third and asked for the Harlem address.

"Glad to hear it,'' said Flanagan. "What's that got to do with anything?''

"I figure, someday I find out I got cancer, I drive up to

niggertown at two in the morning, get it over with all at once," said the cabbie. "But this ain't the night."

"I'll give you a twenty and you can turn off the meter," Flanagan said. The driver had shrugged wordlessly and headed north. When they reached his destination, Flanagan was barely out of the backseat before the cabbie skidded into a U-turn and headed back downtown.

Flanagan walked along 125th going west. The block was deserted, but he could hear loud music from several of the apartments. He stopped in front of a darkened barbershop and rang the bell three times. A moment later, he heard the latch unfasten, and he walked in, past the chairs to a door on the side wall. He knocked and a buzzer went off.

Flanagan pushed the door open, and walked into a long, narrow windowless room full of smoke and music and the smell of barbecue. Several dozen middle-aged people sat at card tables playing tonk. A few couples danced between the tables to Gladys Knight and the Pips' "I Heard It Through the Grapevine." Along the side wall, a knot of men shot craps. In the rear, a group was gathered around a small bar, drinking and eating ribs from plastic plates. There was not a single white face in the room.

Flanagan's appearance, in a dark blue raincoat and the Borsalino, had a freeze-frame effect. The crapshooters held their dice, the dancers came to a stop, and the people at the bar suspended their drinks in midair. The only sounds were from the jukebox and from the large fan attached to the corrugated iron ceiling that whirled overhead.

"What's the matter, you never seen a mulatto before?" demanded Flanagan in a loud voice. Nobody laughed.

"Man, what the hell you doin' in here?" said one of the cardplayers. "You don't belong here." An angry murmur arose from the gamblers.

Suddenly there was noise at the end of the room, near the bar. Flanagan saw a medium-sized brown man in a white chef's cap emerge from the kitchen. He squinted through the smoke in the direction of the door. "John Flanagan like to do the Dixie Do, yes he do!" he said with a grin, and waved.

Flanagan felt the tension drain from the room. He walked over to the chef and shook his hand. "Hi, Morgan," he said. "Looks like your white clientele has fallen off."

"Long as it ain't my dick, John Flanagan," he said. "Good to see you, young man, where you been at?"

"Here and there," said Flanagan. "Boatnay around?"

"Be here in a minute," said the chef. He reached for a bottle of Jameson's and poured four fingers without being asked. "How 'bout something to eat?"

"What's on the menu tonight, Morgan?"

"Red beans and rice soufflé, ribs à la Morgan or the special-tay of the house, our famous assortment of pork delicacies," he said grandly.

"Downtown they call those chitlins, I believe," said Flanagan.

"Yaas, indeed," said Morgan. "Well, up here we pride ourselves on speaking the King's English."

"Yeah, B.B. King," said Flanagan. "I'll have some ribs but go easy on the Tabasco. I'm feeling a little queasy."

"Well, you lookin' good, my man. Look like Don Juan, Ali Kahn and Ponce Daily-on."

Flanagan was halfway through the ribs when the door opened and Boatnay Threkeld walked in. As always, Flanagan was struck by the remarkable resemblance between Boatnay and Sonny Liston. There was one difference, though. The ex–heavyweight champ was dead; Boatnay was indestructible.

He took his time walking over to the bar, stopping at the tables to say a word to the cardplayers, winking at the dancing ladies. Finally he slid his bulk gracefully onto the barstool next to Flanagan. "Hey, John, what's happening?" he said in a soft voice.

"Hi, Boatnay. Your old man looks great," Flanagan said, pointing in the direction of the kitchen. "How come colored people never get old?"

"Laughing at white folks keeps you young," he said. "What brings you up to Harlem in the middle of the night?"

"I was looking for you. They told me at the precinct that you were working late, I figured you'd drop by here eventually."

"Yeah, I've gotta be the only po-lice captain in New York City got him an after-hours joint for a hangout."

"Ain't nothin' the matter with an after-hours establishment," said Morgan, overhearing. "It's not but eleven o'clock in California, and this place runs on Hollywood time."

"More like Las Vegas," said Flanagan, gesturing toward the crap game.

"Yaas, this is the Caesar's Palace of Harlem," said Morgan. "I provide drink to the thirsty, nourishment to the hungry and entertainment to the greedy. I don't permit drugs or thugs, coke or smoke, prostitution, retribution or air pollution on my premises."

"You also don't have a license," said Boatnay. "If you weren't my father, I'd bust you."

"If you weren't my son, I could pay you off, 'stead of letting your big rib-eating self come in here and devour up all my profits. Be a hell of a lot cheaper," said Morgan. He moved off to talk to some people at the other end of the bar, leaving Flanagan and Threkeld alone.

Flanagan's parents were both dead, and his only sister lived in Denver. Morgan and Boatnay Threkeld were the closest thing he had to a real family in New York. Flanagan had known them for more than thirty-five years, ever since Boatnay transferred to St. Benedict High School in Brooklyn.

They met on the first day of school. Even at fourteen,

Boatnay was massive and scary-looking, and word of him spread within an hour throughout St. Benedict. "You gotta see this new jungle bunny," Artie Cassidy told Flanagan. "He looks like he just walked out of a King Kong movie."

Flanagan had never met a black kid before, and he was curious. At lunch he sat down next to Boatnay Threkeld, who was eating his sandwiches in splendid isolation. "My name's John Flanagan," he said, introducing himself.

"That a fact?" said Boatnay, and continued eating.

"You a Catholic?"

"Chippewa Indian."

"You got an attitude for a new kid," Flanagan said.

"I'm not new, I'm almost fifteen," Boatnay said, draining a cardboard container of chocolate milk in a gulp. He opened another one and took a swallow. By this time, both boys were aware that they were the center of attention in the crowded lunchroom. Boatnay picked up the milk container and handed it to Flanagan. "Have some," he said.

Flanagan took the cardboard holder and considered. "This is a test, right?" he said. "See if I mind drinking out of the same spout." Boatnay looked at him through dark brown eyes and said nothing. Flanagan handed him back the container. "I don't drink people's spit," he said. "I don't give a shit who they are." Boatnay shrugged.

"That what they do where you come from, drink each other's spit?" asked Flanagan.

"I live over on Flatbush Avenue," said Boatnay.

"Didn't know they had an Indian reservation in Brooklyn," Flanagan said. He saw the black boy's mouth twitch, but he couldn't tell if it was with anger or amusement.

"Lot of things you don't know," said Boatnay.

"You mean like, the mysterious mysteries of the ghetto?" said Flanagan. "You're a real asshole, you know? I come over here to welcome you to St. Ben's and you act like a jerk."

Threkeld looked at him steadily for a moment. "You're not afraid of me, are you?" he finally said.

"Why should I be?" asked Flanagan. "What are you gonna do, untie my shoes?"

Boatnay Threkeld laughed, a loud bark that resounded through the quiet lunchroom. "My name's Bernard Threkeld," he said, smiling for the first time. "My friends call me Boatnay."

A week or so later, Boatnay Threkeld took Flanagan to meet his father, who owned a small bar called the Shrimp Hut in Bedford-Stuyvesant. "Daddy, this is John Flanagan, the kid I was telling you about," he said.

Morgan looked at him with warm, laughing eyes. "Nice to meet you, John Flanagan," he said. "Did you ever eat a rabbit stew?"

"Not on purpose, no sir," said Flanagan.

"Well, I was fixin' to feed my boy some stew, and with your kind permission, I'll make you a plate, too." There was a musical quality to his voice that reminded Flanagan of the evenings when his father and uncles sat in the parlor, drinking and telling stories about the old days in Hell's Kitchen.

Morgan Threkeld set two bowls of steaming stew in front of the boys, and then walked around the bar and put a quarter in the jukebox. The song was Muddy Waters's "Mannish Boy" and Morgan sang along, snapping his fingers and shaking his shoulders and hollering *whews* of approval. He didn't look like any father Flanagan had ever seen before. His own dad would have played Bing Crosby and banged his hand on the tabletop.

"You like your studies, John Flanagan?" Morgan asked. Flanagan nodded. Despite himself, he loved school. "That's fine," said Threkeld. "I'm a strong believer that the younger generation will someday rule this nation, as long as you don't lose your, er ah, refrigeration. In other words, be cool, stay in school and use your education as your most important tool.''

Afterward, Boatnay walked Flanagan part of the way home.

''Your old man's a really cool guy,'' Flanagan said. Threkeld gave him a serious look. Suddenly he seemed a lot older than fourteen. ''My dad is a man,'' he said. ''Around here, that's a lot harder than being cool.''

Throughout high school, John Flanagan and Boatnay Threkeld were best friends. The balance of power between them was almost even. Flanagan was a brilliant student, who effortlessly got straight A's and edited the school paper, but Threkeld was an A student, too, mostly through diligence. Flanagan was also a good jock, both as a fearless 160-pound tight end on the St. Ben's football team and as an amateur boxer. Sports bored him, though, and after his junior year he quit the football team and limited his fighting to an occasional scrap after school.

Boatnay Threkeld, on the other hand, was the greatest athlete in the history of the school, and one of the best the city had seen in a decade. In his senior year he averaged over two hundred yards rushing as a halfback, scored twenty-eight points a game playing center on a mediocre basketball team and, in the spring, set the New York City scholastic record for the hundred-yard dash. By the time he graduated, he was six foot four and weighed 220, and he was approached by almost every major college in the country.

Morgan Threkeld and John Flanagan took over the job of dealing with the recruiters. Assistant coaches from all over the country came to the Shrimp Hut. They found Morgan to be a slow, deferential colored guy who averted his eyes when he talked to white men and called them ''sir.'' ''I wants my boy to stay right here,'' he said to recruiters from out of town; and ''I wants my boy to get far 'way from this place,'' he told the representatives of local colleges.

Flanagan would appear on cue. Morgan introduced him as "Mr. John," Boatnay's best friend, and Flanagan would enthusiastically take the side of whatever recruiter happened to be there. Morgan's resistance would seem to weaken in the face of Flanagan's arguments, but never quite to the point of giving in. Afterward, Flanagan was invariably contacted by the coaches. "The old man listens to you," they said, white guy to white guy, and winked.

"I can convince Morgan," Flanagan told them, "but I got a problem with Boatnay. He knows his old man's a dimwit, and he doesn't want to leave him all alone."

"Something can be arranged," the recruiters said.

"Your campus sounds beautiful," Flanagan said. "I might like to go there myself."

"Something can be arranged," the recruiters repeated.

In April, Morgan, Boatnay and Flanagan sat down with a list of more than ninety offers. After due deliberation they settled on an Ivy League college that was offering two full scholarships, a new Oldsmobile for Boatnay, a used Ford for Flanagan, jobs for both of them keeping seaweed out of the football stadium, and carte blanche at a local clothing store. There was also a clause guaranteeing Boatnay five hundred dollars per touchdown and a flat five thousand dollars if the team made a bowl game. Finally, there would be a twenty-five-thousand-dollar nonrepayable loan to Morgan Threkeld from a school-spirited Wall Street alumnus.

Morgan poured each boy a small glass of champagne. "Mr. John," he said in his Stepin Fetchit voice, "you certainly is one smart white boy." He smiled broadly and sipped the champagne. "Yass indeed, you can be my jockey if you never win a race, you can be my gambler if you never pull an ace, and you can be my lawyer if you never win a case."

"Mr. Threkeld," said Flanagan, returning the toast, "it's a pleasure to be of service to such a deserving Negro scholar-athlete."

John and Boatnay lived together throughout college. Threkeld was a two-time all-American, and Flanagan editor of the college newspaper, which he used to promote Boatnay for the Heisman Trophy, sending clips each week to the wire services and putting together a brochure on Threkeld's career that he forwarded to sportswriters around the country. When Threkeld won the award, beating out an Italian quarterback from Notre Dame, both boys took it as a lesson on the power of the press.

After college, Boatnay Threkeld was drafted by the Detroit Lions. It was in the days before big contracts, and he actually took a cut in pay to play pro ball. He stayed with the Lions for six seasons, attended the University of Michigan Law School part time, and quit football the day he passed the bar. Flanagan, using his old man's contacts with the printers' union, got a job as a city reporter on the *Tribune*. When he returned to New York from Vietnam, Boatnay was already back in the city, one of the youngest—and by far the most famous—homicide detectives on the police force.

The two men picked up their relationship where it had left off. Flanagan made sure that Boatnay Threkeld's cases and career got maximum press coverage; in return, Threkeld provided Flanagan with scoops that left his competitors on other papers cursing. But this pragmatic cooperation did not obscure the genuine friendship they felt for one another. Flanagan was the best man at Boatnay's wedding, to a Jewish attorney named Arlene Lichtenstein, and he was godfather to their first son, Terrence. Boatnay, although he didn't know it, was the sole beneficiary of Flanagan's modest estate.

Morgan Threkeld interrupted Flanagan's train of thought by taking the empty glass out of his hand and setting a fresh Jameson's in front of him. "Hate to see a man daydream on an empty liver," he said, and Flanagan laughed. He touched Boatnay's massive forearm, and the cop, who had been talking to an old man about automobiles, turned toward him.

"Boatnay," he said, "I need a little help."

"Parking ticket, short-term loan or kidney donation?" he asked with a smile. Flanagan rarely asked for help, and Threkeld wanted to make it easy for him.

"Nothing that specific," Flanagan said. "It's more in the nature of keeping your eye on a situation." He hesitated for just a moment, not because he didn't want to go on, but to lend a dramatic touch to the conversation. "How much do you know about Spadafore, these days?"

"Luigi Spadafore?" said Threkeld. "Not much. Some. Why, you working on an organized-crime series?"

"Why do you think it would be a series?" asked Flanagan.

Threkeld laughed. "I know you're too smart to risk your ass for one measly little story," he said.

"Is he really that dangerous?"

"Does a big wheel roll?" said Threkeld. "Heck hell, yeah, he's dangerous. His line of work, you don't get to be an old man if you're not dangerous."

"Max Grossman died the other day," said Flanagan.

"Yeah, I read it in the paper."

"He was Gordon's uncle."

"Read that too. So what?" Threkeld sounded casual, but Flanagan could see that he was listening hard.

"Spadafore came to us with a proposition," said Flanagan. "A business-type thing."

Flanagan saw the lids on Threkeld's eyes drop halfway, not certain how much he wanted to hear. Boatnay was Flanagan's best friend, but he was also a police captain, and a lawyer. That was the difference between Threkeld and Gordon, Flanagan thought; Boatnay was a cautious man.

"What do you mean 'us,' John?" he finally said.

"Well, he came to Gordon first, and I'm acting as his adviser," said Flanagan. "Gordon's a good guy, but he's been abroad all his life. He doesn't have much experience with guys like Spadafore.''

"And you do? Listen, you ain't messin' with football coaches, man. You let your mouth start writin' checks, these guys gonna make your ass cash 'em." Flanagan just grinned and Threkeld sighed. "You better tell me what this is all about.''

Flanagan shook his head. "I don't want you involved. The deal is legal, at least in New York. But I don't think you really want to know any details and, anyway, it's still too early.''

Threkeld looked relieved. "What do you want, then?" he asked.

"I want you to keep that Chippewa ear of yours to the ground," Flanagan said. "If you hear anything unusual about Spadafore or Carlo Sesti, let me know. It's just a precaution at this point, but what the hell.''

Threkeld's gaze fell to the Borsalino perched on the stool next to Flanagan. "That your hat?" he asked. Flanagan grinned and nodded.

The police captain shook his large head in dismay. "Man, we're almost fifty years old," he said. "Almost fifty, and you're still out here playin'. When you gonna grow up, John?''

Flanagan reached over, picked up the hat and put it on his head. "It's too late for that, Boatnay," he said. "I'm too old to grow up.''

12

ON SATURDAY AFTERNOON AT FIVE O'CLOCK, THE caterer arrived with two assistants. He was a slender, self-important man, who asked Gordon to show him the kitchen, regarded the small room disdainfully and said, "I'm certainly glad we arrived early."

"It's only dinner for four," said Gordon.

The two helpers set boxes and cartons on the kitchen counter while the caterer, whose name was Armand, went into the living room. He stood, hand on hip, looking at the round dining table in the corner and shaking his head.

"Something the matter with the table?" Gordon asked.

"Not if you happen to be one of King Arthur's knights," said Armand. "Round table, round plates, round glasses. Circles, circles, circles."

"Work it out, Armand," said Gordon. "I'm going in the bedroom to watch the UCLA–Notre Dame game."

Through the door, Gordon heard the officious little caterer calling out orders to his helpers. There were sounds of furniture being rearranged, and china being set in place. Gordon remained in the bedroom, showering between halves, and changing out of his jeans and sweater into a quiet dark-blue business suit, he ventured into the kitchen for a beer.

Four large steaks were set out on the counter, four giant potatoes were wrapped in tinfoil, and china and silver were piled neatly on the Formica-topped kitchen table.

On the way back to the bedroom he saw Armand, hands on his cheeks, staring once again at the dining room table, which he had moved next to the sliding glass windows of the patio. A vase of yellow and red flowers stood on the table.

"It's beginning to come together," the caterer said. "Placing the tulips just off center softens the circular effect, don't you agree?"

"Yeah, good job, Armand," said Gordon.

Flanagan arrived at seven. He had obviously had a few drinks, and he immediately poured himself another from one of the bottles of Jameson's that Armand had set out. "I love a party," he said to Gordon. "I'm going in the kitchen to check out the food."

Gordon went back in the bedroom to put on his shoes, and the caterer, who had already sent his helpers away, fussed with the table, moving the flowers an inch or two in either direction. He and Gordon were both startled by the sound of Flanagan's voice. "Shit!" he bellowed.

Gordon raced into the kitchen and found a red-faced Flanagan already screaming at the caterer. "Smell these goddamn steaks," he said, thrusting one at Armand. "They're spoiled, you little fruit fly. They smell like shit!"

"There is absolutely nothing wrong with these steaks," said Armand. He bent over the meat, and suddenly wrinkled his nose in distaste.

"You see, you little homo, they smell like shit," yelled Flanagan.

Armand flushed. "I don't understand it," he stammered. "These are the finest cuts available. I picked them out this morning myself. I just don't understand—"

Enraged, Flanagan swept his arm over the table, knocking knives, forks, spoons and china cups to the floor. "Goddamn it, get this shit out of here, you moron," he screamed. Armand started to say something, thought better of it and bent down to gather the silverware.

"Wait a minute, John," Gordon said, looking at his watch. "They're going to be here in half an hour, what are we going to do without food?"

"You want to serve Luigi shit steak?" said Flanagan. Gordon couldn't remember ever seeing him so angry. "Damn, Gordon, I told you I'd take care of things and I fucked up." He kicked a piece of broken china all the way across the kitchen floor.

"Relax, relax," said Gordon. "There's still time to run out and pick up some steaks someplace." He turned to Armand. "You know a good butcher in this neighborhood?"

"I hope you don't think I'm going to prepare your meal now," said the little man with as much dignity as he could muster. "I don't enjoy being called a queer."

"I said 'homo,' you little homo," Flanagan bellowed. "I don't want you touching my food. Just take your little dishes and your little spoons and get the fuck out of here. Look, Gordon, help him clean up this stuff and I'll run out to the gourmet store, pick up something nice. Don't worry, it'll be all right."

Flanagan scowled at the caterer one last time, and banged out of the apartment. At the corner of Seventy-ninth and Columbus Avenue he stopped and reached into his pocket, taking out a small jar which he had filled with dog manure in Gramercy Park.

Who knows what evil lurks in the heart of man? Flanagan grinned to himself. The dog shit had been a last-minute improvisation, but he had been planning to torpedo the evening ever since his invitation to Spadafore. He wanted to pick a fight with Sesti, that smug, phony Englishman. "*Mano a mano*, consigliere," he said softly. "Just you and me."

Flanagan was aware that he had no good reason for want-

ing to take on the Spadafore Family, and he was too honest
with himself to pretend. He was going to war for the same
reasons that men have always gone—to test himself, to assert
the force of his will, and for the plain unadulterated hell of
it. He tossed the jar of dog shit into the trash basket and
began to hum to himself—"Don't cook tonight, call Pizza
Delight"—as he wiped his guilty fingers with a Rinse 'n'
Dry pad.

In the big brownstone in Brooklyn, Luigi Spadafore sat in
his padded armchair and waved his heavy arms to Vivaldi. It
had been months since his last trip into Manhattan, and
that had been a court appearance. He hadn't been out for an
evening in— He tried to remember the last time, but couldn't.
Seclusion was one of the burdens that a don had to bear. Not
only was there a safety factor, but there was also his dignity
to consider. At this stage of his career, he would no more
have eaten in a public place than defecated in the park.

Tonight, he reflected, would be a treat. When Sesti had
told him of Gordon's invitation he had been doubly pleased.
It indicated that Gordon respected him. And, although no
one, not even his sons or the omniscient Sesti knew it, tonight was his birthday. He was seventy-seven years old. The
Don considered birthday celebrations gauche, especially at
his age, but he nevertheless was pleased that he would not
be alone.

It was his wish to commemorate the event by giving gifts.
He had puzzled over just the right thing to bring to Gordon
and finally decided on three priceless bottles of Mouton-
Rothschild '29. At the end of the evening, he planned to
present Gordon with a gold signet ring that had once belonged to King Emmanuel of Italy. He wondered if Gordon
was planning to give him something in return.

There was a soft knock on the door, and Carlo Sesti entered, dressed in his impeccable evening clothes. "The car

is ready, Don Spadafore,'' he said. He helped the old man into his coat, and held the door for him as he climbed into the rear seat of his armored Bentley. The driver, an ex-prizefighter named Rudy Parchi, already had the address.

The Don and his consigliere sat in silence, side by side, as the big car flowed through traffic. Sesti knew that the old man disliked idle conversation. He was more than a little nervous about the evening. Perhaps, he reflected, it had been a mistake to accept. It had been he, after all, who had brought the invitation to Spadafore, and in their world, that was tantamount to a recommendation. Gordon didn't worry him, but Flanagan was obviously mentally ill. Nothing else could explain his erratic behavior. Still, he had Gordon's ear, and at this point he had to be placated.

The Bentley rolled up to Gordon's building at seven-forty, just as Sesti had planned. Rudy held the door for Spadafore, who looked around him with curiosity, as if he had just been deposited in a foreign country. Jimmy the doorman buzzed them in, and then called up to let Gordon know they were on their way. ''You got some company, boss,'' he said in his confidential tone. ''Real heavy hitters.''

Flanagan wasn't back yet, and Gordon cursed him as he opened the door for Spadafore and Sesti. ''Mr. Spadafore, Carlo, come in,'' he said, hoping that they couldn't read the anxiety on his face. ''Please, sit down, let me fix you a drink.''

Gordon was in the kitchen filling the ice bucket when the doorbell rang. He walked quickly through the small apartment, opened the door and saw Flanagan, his arms laden with thin pizza boxes and paper bags. ''What the hell. . . ?'' Gordon said, but Flanagan winked and brushed past him into the living room. He set down his packages and turned to face the guests.

''Hello, Carlo,'' he said warmly. ''And you must be Mr. Spadafore. I've been looking forward to this for a long time, sir. I'm John Flanagan." He extended his hand to the Don who, still sitting, took it limply.

"I guess you already heard about the shit steaks," said Flanagan. "Christ, these fucking poofters. Luckily, we happen to be right around the corner from one of the truly great pizza places on the East Coast, Rocco's Pizza Delight. You know Rocco, Carlo? I mean personally?" The consigliere, icily composed, shook his head.

"Well, you're gonna love his 'zahs. I didn't know exactly what you guys like on 'em, so I got an assortment, pepperoni, anchovies and mushrooms, sausage and green pepper and a plain. I know, I know," he said, holding up one hand, "there's more here than we can eat, but, what the hell, it's better to have some left over than not enough. Oh, and I got some side orders of ravioli, and salad. He was out of the cannelloni."

Flanagan walked to the side table and poured himself a tumbler of Irish whiskey. "Freshen anyone's drink?" he offered.

"John, let's take the food in the kitchen," said Gordon.

When they reached the kitchen, Gordon grabbed Flanagan roughly and pushed him up against the refrigerator. "What the fuck are you trying to prove, John?" he said.

Flanagan loosened Gordon's grip on his jacket, looking at him steadily. Then he smiled, embarrassed. "Shit, kid, I'm sorry. I went down to the gourmet place but all they had was quiche and soufflés. Can you picture us giving Luigi quiche? I didn't know what to do, honest to God. I don't blame you for being pissed, it's my fault, but let's not fight about it now." He gestured with his head in the direction of the living room.

Gordon pushed Flanagan hard against the refrigerator, and walked back into the living room. "Mr. Spadafore, I'm really sorry about this. Let's go out for dinner. Where would you like to go?"

"I don't care for restaurants," said Spadafore, speaking for the first time since Flanagan had come in.

"Obviously this is an inconvenient time," said Sesti smoothly. "Perhaps we could do this another night—"

Gordon could hear Flanagan opening the stove in the kitchen, whistling the radio jingle for Pizza Delight. He started to laugh. "This is the most ridiculous thing I've ever heard of," he said. "Let me send out for something. We could order Chinese food from the Peking Pavilion, or maybe Barney's would send us over some steaks—"

"Pizza will be fine," said Spadafore. When Flanagan had come in with the boxes, he had wondered if this was an intentional slight. But the stricken look on Gordon's face told him that it really was a mishap. More than ever he was certain that the newsman would never succeed in his world, and the thought pleased him. "I'd prefer mine with anchovies and mushrooms," he said.

To Gordon's amazement, dinner went well. Flanagan opened a bottle of the Rothschild '29 and offered a toast to new friendships. Spadafore praised the pizza, and told several stories about the old days, when the dish had first been introduced to New York. Even Sesti lost some of his frosty demeanor, eating three pepperoni slices. When Flanagan chided him about his appetite, the consigliere patted his flat stomach and shook his head ruefully.

Luigi Spadafore realized that he was having a good time. The pizzas reminded him of his last active campaign, more than thirty years ago, against the Marinis and their allies from Detroit and Arizona. He had eaten with the troops then, often out of cardboard containers. Max Grossman had done the same. Now, a lifetime later, he was here, in Max's nephew's apartment, and it took him back.

He also found that he enjoyed the company of Gordon and, especially, Flanagan. Italian men, he reflected, were either sweet, like Pietro, or sour, like Mario. But Flanagan was tart, irreverent and yet somehow deferential at the same time. The Don wondered if there might be a use for him; he seemed to be an altogether interesting fellow.

Gordon and Sesti were discussing possible countries of opportunity. "I think that Uruguay is promising," Gordon said. "I know the president, and I've had dinner with his chief of staff a few times. I think he'll do business."

"The chief of staff? Or the president?" asked Sesti.

"Both, but I was thinking of the chief of staff. They say he bribed his way into office."

"A man who will give in the morning is a man who will take in the evening," intoned Spadafore oracularly. Gordon and Sesti nodded respectfully but Flanagan looked quizzical.

"What do you mean by that?" he demanded.

Spadafore seemed taken aback. "It is merely a saying," he said stiffly.

Flanagan laughed. "You guys and your sayings, you kill me," he said. "Where do you come up with this stuff?" Gordon shot him a warning look, and saw that Flanagan was feeling the whiskey. "What horseshit," Flanagan mumbled.

Suddenly the doorbell rang. Gordon had no idea who it could be, but he didn't care. Saved by the bell, he thought. It never occurred to him to wonder why Jimmy hadn't buzzed.

The reason was that Flanagan had given the doorman ten dollars to let four men in tuxedos and a six-foot cake on a dolly come upstairs. Gordon opened the door and saw the men and the giant cake. "Mr. Flanagan sent us," said one.

Gordon was too astonished to protest. He merely stepped aside as they wheeled the cake into the living room. Spadafore and Sesti looked with uncomprehending eyes as the four began to snap their fingers, harmonizing doo-wop style: "Birthday, birthday ba-ba-ba-birthday, birthday, birthday, ba-ba-ba-birthday." One of them stepped forward and began to sing in a flat, nasal tone: "Happy birthday to you, happy birthday to you. Happy birthday, Luigi, happy birthday to you.''

Suddenly a young woman, totally nude, burst out of the cake. In a Marilyn Monroe whisper she crooned, ''How o-old are you, how o-old are you, how old are you cappo di tutti cappo, how old are you?'' She broke off a piece of the white cake, lowered herself onto the broad lap of the astonished Spadafore and popped it into his open mouth.

''Many happy returns of the day, Luigi,'' said Flanagan expansively. ''You thought we forgot, right? I got the date from a pal of mine at the FBI.''

For a long moment Spadafore said nothing. Then, his face mottled with rage and vanilla frosting, he turned to Sesti and muttered something in Sicilian. The consigliere stood, and helped the old man to his feet. Without even bothering to pick up their topcoats, they walked out of the apartment.

Flanagan shrugged and staggered a little. Gordon had never seen him so drunk. ''If they can't take a joke, fuck 'em,'' he said. ''You know who these guys are?'' He pointed to the singers.

Gordon looked at him blankly, still trying to grasp what his friend had done. He shook his head. ''Sunny and the Original fucking True Tones, that's all,'' Flanagan said proudly.

''Sunny and the True Tones!'' screamed Gordon, reality sinking in all at once. ''Goddamn you, Flanagan, you set me up! You're a fucking lunatic!'' He grabbed the tall Irishman by the shoulder and spun him around. Flanagan, still grinning, pulled back as Gordon threw a looping right hand at his head. Flanagan shifted his weight, slipping the punch with surprising agility, and clipped Gordon on the jaw with a straight right. He was out cold before he hit the beige carpet.

Flanagan bent down and put his head against his friend's chest to make sure he was still breathing. Then, with a slow, deliberate movement, he pushed himself upright, turned toward the stunned doo-wop singers and raised his clasped hands over his head in a champion's salute. "The winner, in a knockout over the Pulitzer Kid, and still champeen, Mad Dog John Flanagan," he proclaimed in a ring announcer's voice. "Put him to bed, Sunny. And, fellas—thanks for the memories."

13

IT WAS PAST ELEVEN WHEN GORDON WOKE UP. HE had a splitting hangover and the feeling of dread associated with irrevocable setbacks.

Gordon couldn't remember much about what happened after Spadafore left but he did recall taking a punch at Flanagan, and felt the tender spot on his chin where Flanagan had socked him. He vaguely recollected awakening in the middle of the night, vomiting and throwing an empty bottle of Wild Turkey off his balcony. He had no idea what had happened to the True Tones or the naked girl.

Gordon felt a stabbing headache and a wave of nausea. No more drinking, he said to himself. Ever. He gingerly climbed out of bed, massaging his eyelids tenderly, and went to the bathroom for three extra-strength Tylenol. The water made him gag, and he staggered to the kitchen for a glass of cola. Then, hoping that relief was on its way, he crawled back into bed and tried to decide what to do next.

As Gordon saw it, he had three options. First, he could try to patch things up with Spadafore and Flanagan and go on with the plan. Or, he could get rid of Flanagan and carry on alone. Finally, he could ditch the whole idea.

The first option was out of the question. Even if Luigi

Spadafore was prepared to forget what happened—a big if— Gordon no longer wanted to do any kind of business with Flanagan. Last night he had seen just how out of control his friend was. No matter what, Flanagan was out.

Which led to option number two. Getting rid of Flanagan might well appease Spadafore. The old man liked him, after all, and Sesti obviously was hot to do business. The problem was, Gordon did not want to be on his own, adrift in their world without allies. In his penitent hung-over state it was easy for him to admit the truth—he was scared to death of the possible consequences of becoming Spadafore's partner.

All that was left was the third option—call the whole thing off. Since his uncle's funeral he had inherited and lost a fortune, proposed marriage to Jupiter, bought a pistol, quit his job and had a Mafia chief to dinner. In ten days, he had gone from the secure life of a journalistic celebrity to the dangerous world of Luigi Spadafore. But, he realized, the trip had been largely in his head. He was still here, in his old apartment. The paper would take him back in a second; in fact, he wasn't due to leave until the first of next month. He could drop the pistol into a river someplace, laugh off his proposal to Jupiter and go back to being the old William Gordon. It was as simple as that.

Of course there wouldn't be any money, but Flanagan had been right about that—money didn't mean that much to him. He was making close to two hundred thousand dollars a year, counting lecture fees and magazine articles. Random House was after him for a book on the USSR, and that would bring in at least a hundred thousand. And when his father died, there would be a considerable estate. It was nothing like the millions that Sesti had dangled in front of him, but he wouldn't wind up with ulcers—or in prison—either. There was only one sensible course. Later in the day he would call Sesti, apologize, and call the whole thing off.

The decision enabled him to forgive Flanagan. Flanagan

had seen all along what he was only realizing now: that the very notion of two journalists becoming gangsters was ridiculous. He had treated the whole thing as a joke from the beginning. Gordon, on the other hand, had allowed himself to dream. Now that he was awake, he could see the humor of it all. He thought about the look on Luigi Spadafore's face when the girl jumped out of the cake and grinned through his hangover. After he talked to Sesti he would call Flanagan and meet him for a drink somewhere. This will become a legendary story, he thought to himself.

Carlo Sesti smashed a hard overhand serve just inside the baseline, inches past Shelby Strothers's outstretched racket. "Game," called Strothers, breathing hard. "That's enough for me. You're too tough for me this morning, Carlo."

Sesti smiled thinly. Fifteen years ago, Strothers had played on the U.S. Davis Cup team, but he was out of shape now, and not hard to beat. Sesti felt contempt for the former tennis pro's lack of discipline.

It was almost noon, and Sesti had a one o'clock meeting at his office. He showered and shaved for the second time that morning, put on his weekend clothes—a white shirt, gray wool slacks, gleaming cordovan loafers and a dark blue blazer—and walked up Madison Avenue. He disliked Manhattan on Sundays; with the stores and offices closed, there didn't seem to be any real point to the city.

Carlo Sesti's firm occupied the top floor of a skyscraper on Fifty-seventh between Fifth and Sixth. That afternoon the floor was deserted, and Sesti's footsteps echoed as he walked down the corridor to his office. Although he was the firm's senior partner, his large room was spare, almost spartan. The walls were lined with bookshelves, the floor was covered with a thick carpet and the room was dominated by a gleaming oak desk. It was Sesti's trademark that, no matter how much work he had to do, the desk was always clean. Not even a single paper was allowed to remain overnight unattended.

The lawyer's mind worked the same way. He confronted each problem as it arose, solved it with dispatch and then dismissed the matter. That was what he intended to do with the Flanagan question.

He had already laid the groundwork. On the way back to Brooklyn the night before, when the Don had bitterly cursed Gordon in Sicilian, Sesti had delicately pointed out that it was Flanagan, and not Gordon, who had been responsible for the outrage. At first Spadafore had been unreceptive; he had, after all, a boss's perspective that naturally fixed guilt on the senior partner for the behavior of his subordinate. But gradually, Sesti could see, he had gotten through. He knew that in his heart the old man wanted to blame the Irishman, and not the nephew of his friend. Sesti, himself, had to protect Gordon. Without him, there was no plan.

Once Spadafore weakened, Sesti knew what had to be done. A less expeditious man might have waited until Monday, but the consigliere did not want to postpone the execution of a decision, once taken, even for a single day.

In this case, Sesti also realized that delay could be dangerous. He had witnessed the humiliation of Don Spadafore. In some sense, because he had brought Gordon's invitation to the Don, he could even be considered accountable. But the main thing was, he had seen the injury to the old man's dignity, and this, he knew, Spadafore would find hard to forgive. Only swift, brutal retaliation would mollify him.

Sesti knew all this without being told, just as he knew that Spadafore would never give him an order to avenge his honor. The Don, who prided himself on his sense of proportion, could not ask his consigliere to have a man killed because that man had arranged for a naked girl to sing "Happy Birthday." It was Sesti's role to understand this, and to act on his own.

In Sesti's personal view, what had happened the night before was of no importance whatsoever. He considered Don Spadafore to be a primitive man with the same romantic, childish attitudes as his own father. To Sesti every sort of pride—national, ethnic or personal—was merely a foolish irrelevance. A man above pride would always best a proud adversary, just as a sober man had the advantage over a drunk.

Sesti felt contempt for Spadafore's weakness, but he in no way underestimated the Don's power or ruthlessness. He never forgot, for example, that the old man would have no compunction about killing him in order to protect his own sons. This, too, he saw as a foolish kind of sentimentality, but it was, nevertheless, a fact.

The consigliere looked at his watch. In less than half an hour he would meet with Grady Rand, and order the execution of John Flanagan. Rand was a professional assassin from South Carolina, a man who specialized in making murder look like an accident. Sesti had used him before and been impressed by his meticulous attention to detail as well as by his discretion. Most of the Family's so-called button men were simply unreliable thugs, and Sesti avoided employing them whenever possible. The contract that he intended to offer was a simple one—follow Flanagan and kill him as quickly as possible—but it had to be done elegantly. Flanagan was, after all, still a deputy editor of an important newspaper, and he could not be gunned down in the street like a common criminal without raising a tremendous fuss.

There were several advantages to Flanagan's prompt execution. It would win Sesti a temporary reprieve from the old man's wrath. It would concentrate Gordon's mind wonderfully. Finally, it would simplify his future dealings with the journalist by establishing a precedent. Sesti smiled with satisfaction at this last consideration. As a lawyer, he regarded precedent as the very cornerstone of an orderly society.

* * *

Rudy Parchi sat in the front seat of the Bentley with the windows rolled up, listening to a Connie Francis cassette on the tape deck and cutting long, wet-sounding farts. Rudy liked the way they smelled when they mingled with the fresh, saddle-soap aroma of the leather seats. A lot of people thought the habit was disgusting, but a lot of those same people, he had noticed, had no problem with belching in public, which was only farting through your mouth as far as he was concerned.

Rudy had enjoyed farting for as long as he could remember. In the service, during his first days of boot camp, a smartass sergeant had called him up in front of the whole platoon during barracks inspection and made fun of him for it. "Soldier, quit stenching up the area," he had screamed. "You got a problem with your plumbing or what?"

"It's a habit I got," Rudy said, and spat on the floor.

"Wipe up that spit, soldier!" the incredulous sergeant screamed.

"OK," Rudy said. He hit the sergeant with a looping right, knocking him unconscious. Then he gathered up the limp body by the legs and, with the entire platoon watching in awed silence, methodically wiped the floor with the sergeant, like a mop.

Parchi spent six months in a military stockade before receiving a medical discharge for mental instability. Then he came back to Brooklyn and resumed his career as a prizefighter. In the ring, inhibited by rules and referees, he was only fair; he beat slow heavyweights, lost to quicker ones. In the street he grabbed shifty boxers by the throat and hit them with a pipe.

Basically, Rudy didn't care much about boxing. It was just a way to mark time until there was an opening in the Spadafore Family. He was inducted at twenty-five, young for a neighborhood kid without blood connections, and he had been with the Family for twenty-one years. Sometimes he ran errands; occasionally, like last night, he drove Spadafore someplace, but usually he just hung around the house waiting. Half a dozen times in the past twenty-one years he had been asked to kill a guy, usually with a gun, and he had done it. Each time he had been given a cash bonus of a thousand dollars.

Rudy had no opinion of Luigi Spadafore other than that he was the boss, and a Man of Respect. He despised Carlo Sesti, with his fancy manners and sissy accent. He had grown up on stories about men going to the mattresses, but throughout his years with the Family he had been pretty much a peacetime soldier, and he blamed Sesti for that, feeling the grunt's contempt for the cookie-pushing diplomat.

Parchi saw Mario park his Cadillac across the street from the Don's house, and he tooted the horn softly. Mario saw him, waved and headed in his direction. Of all the brass, he was the only one who paid any attention to Rudy. Sometimes Mario would sit with him in the Bentley and they'd talk about the fights. They agreed that Rocky Marciano would have torn the head off Cassius Clay, that LaMotta was robbed in his losing fights with Sugar Ray Robinson, and that, in general, niggers were OK in the ring but on the street, where what counted was balls and heart, they didn't have a thing. Thinking about it, Rudy was sometimes amazed by how much he and Mario had in common.

Mario opened the passenger door and slid into the front seat.

"Hey, Rudy," he said.

"Hey, Mario."

"Hey, how's it goin'?"

"Real good, how's it with you?" said Rudy. It was always easy for him to talk to Mario.

"How come you in a car? The old man goin' someplace?"

"Naw," said Rudy. "He's probably still steamin' from last night."

"Yeah? What was last night?"

Rudy shrugged. He knew that sometimes Mario gave him little tests, pretending not to know what his own father was up to. Parchi figured it was a way to check out his loyalty. He didn't mind; when Mario took over, he might have a chance to get his own living. Rudy knew that the Don wouldn't be around forever.

"On the way back," said Rudy. "From dinner. The Don was cursing up a storm about that guy Gordon."

"Gordon?" said Mario. "You sure it was Gordon?"

"Yeah, the Don and Sesti had a whole big argument about it. Sesti says it was some guy named Flanagan's fault, the Don says no, it was Gordon's fault."

"What happened?" asked Mario, his eyes glinting with curiosity.

Rudy shrugged again. "I dunno, but it must of been something, like, really serious for the Don to be steaming like that. I ain't never seen him so mad."

Mario lifted his thick leg and cut a loud fart. That was another thing Rudy liked about him. "Listen," he said. "I'm going in there to see the old man. You wait here, don't go nowheres. I might have something I want you to do for me later."

14

GORDON SAT WATCHING THE REDSKINS-COLTS game, sipping a Bloody Mary. His "no drinking" resolution had lasted until the second quarter, when he fixed himself one medicinal Mary, heavily laced with Worcestershire sauce. It had made him feel so healthy that he drank two more during halftime, and he was now on his fourth. The vodka and the decision to call off his crazy adventure with Spadafore put him in a glowing mood.

He had been trying to reach Sesti all afternoon, but the lawyer was out, and his housekeeper had no idea when he would be back. He looked at the clock on the table next to his bed. Three-fifteen—Flanagan would be up by now. He picked up the phone and dialed. Flanagan answered on the second ring.

"John?"

"Gordon! I was just thinking about you," said Flanagan. He heard the note of forced joviality. Jupiter was wrong, he thought; Flanagan was a terrible actor.

"That was some night we had," said Gordon. "You really know how to throw a party, chief."

Flanagan laughed, and Gordon sensed his relief. "I thought you'd be pissed," the Irishman said. "Shit, kid, I'm sorry. I didn't want to hit you, but you wouldn't stop pushing me, and there wasn't anything else to do. You all right?''

"Hell, yes," said Gordon, rubbing his tender jaw. "You punch like a girl."

"I owe you one. Free shot," said Flanagan. "You, ah, didn't hear from Spadafore, did you?"

"You mean did he call up to thank me for the swell evening? Naw, I've been trying to reach Sesti, but he's not home."

"You better let me do that, boychik," said Flanagan, his spirits restored. "I'll explain that it was my idea, you had nothing to do with it. Let me handle it, OK?"

"Forget it, John," said Gordon. "It's all over. I'm gonna tell Sesti that the deal's off. I don't feel like playing anymore."

"You mean because of last night? Hey, come on, you're taking this too hard. It's not that big a deal, believe me, I can straighten everything out—''

"No," said Gordon, "if it wasn't last night it would have been another night. Those guys come from a whole different planet. It was fun while it lasted, but it's over, John. That's final.''

There was a long pause. "You got any plans for later?" Flanagan finally asked.

"Not really," said Gordon. "I want to see the end of the game, maybe watch a little of the Rams-Raiders. Nothing after that."

"Let's get dinner, then," said Flanagan. "We might as well celebrate the end of the Mishpocha."

"Yeah, OK," said Gordon. "You wanna come up here, or you want me to come down there?"

"Why don't you meet me at O'Dwyer's, around eight. Dinner's on me tonight," said Flanagan. "It's the least I can do."

* * *

Rudy Parchi stood in front of the Cancellation Shoes show window on Twenty-third near the corner of Lexington and looked at the latest models. Nigger shoes, he thought to himself; only a jig would buy shoes at a store with a name like Cancellation.

For an hour and a half he had been walking up and down the almost deserted block, pretending to be a window-shopper and hoping no one would notice that he kept doubling back, always keeping the front door of O'Dwyer's within view. He had followed Gordon down here from his apartment. His original plan had been to shoot him when he came out of his building, but there had been a crowd—a doorman, the waiting cabbie and a couple walking a dog. Mario had said to wack him out, not do another St. Valentine's Day massacre, so Rudy and his driver, Tubby Calabrese, had chased the cab all the way to O'Dwyer's in Tubby's untraceable Toyota with the phony plates.

Except for O'Dwyer's the whole block was dark, all the way up to Park. Across Lex, on the corner, a Korean fruit store was open, but Rudy didn't want to walk all the way over there and maybe miss Gordon coming out. Besides, he didn't want to be seen by anyone, although he doubted very much if a Korean could tell the difference between white guys any more than white guys could tell the difference between Koreans.

It wasn't particularly cold, but Rudy stamped his feet, trying to keep busy. He figured Gordon must be finishing dinner by now. Idly, Parchi tried to imagine what he was eating. He wondered if you cut a guy's stomach open right after dinner if pieces of food would fall out, like gumballs spilling out of the glass vending bowls he used to break open as a kid. He could picture Gordon standing there, watching, as a whole order of spaghetti and meatballs came pouring out of him onto the sidewalk. Thinking about it made him hungry, and he began considering where to stop to eat on the way home. . . .

Suddenly the door to O'Dwyer's opened, and he saw, framed in the light, Gordon and a tall guy he didn't know. Rudy walked down Twenty-third in their direction. He could picture the hit in his mind. He would wait until Gordon stepped off the curb to look for a cab, race toward him, blow his brains out from the shortest range possible and then run into the sparse traffic, across Twenty-third and around the corner, where Tubby was waiting.

Across the street, Parchi saw a blue Mustang parked at the curb with a man sitting at the wheel. The driver looked familiar, but Rudy couldn't remember where he had seen him. Rudy was almost directly across from Gordon and the other guy now. They looked up the deserted street for a cab, and then stepped off the curb, just as Rudy had pictured.

Parchi drew his pistol and began to run across Twenty-third. Suddenly the blue Mustang leaped from its parking space and headed straight for him. From twenty feet away he could see the driver clearly. "Hey!" he screamed, but it was too late. Gordon and Flanagan jumped back on the curb just as the Mustang smashed into Rudy Parchi, knocking him down. It took him about ten seconds to die, and in that time he saw the faces of his mother and father, his brothers and sisters, Don Spadafore, Mario and Sesti. And the driver. He looked like one of the Everly Brothers, Parchi realized. Either Don or Phil, he could never remember which was which. . . .

Flanagan recovered first. "Hit-and-run," he yelled. Gordon looked around dazed, and saw a man lying in the street and a blue Mustang tearing up Twenty-third. There was no doubt that the man was dead. "We better call the cops," he said.

"You call the cops, I'll call the paper," said Flanagan, leading Gordon back into O'Dywer's. Neither man saw the pistol that was lodged under the broken, bleeding body of Rudy Parchi.

Albert Grossman opened his eyes and cursed the daylight, pale and fragile, that filtered into his darkened bedroom. It was 6:27 A.M. He knew this without even looking at the clock on the nightstand because he got up every morning at exactly 6:27. It annoyed Grossman to awaken so early and so exactly, as if he were on some special old people's time that had nothing to do with how his body actually felt, whether he was still tired or rested. And it positively drove him crazy to look at the digital clock every morning and see the same ridiculous hour: 6:27.

Grossman felt a stirring next to him. Beverly Friedman. Forty-two years old, the same age as his son. Widow of Dr. N. Shelby Friedman, MD, who dropped dead one day in his office. Two kids in college, but she had the body of a college girl herself, Grossman thought. Twice, three times a week he dropped by her place. She grilled fish or a chicken, they watched a little TV and then they spent the night together. Grossman scratched between his legs and sighed. What a world, he thought, where a good-looking young broad like Bev was willing to shtup an old guy like him for free.

Grossman lowered himself out of bed and padded into the kitchen, where he put on the instant coffee maker and dropped two pieces of rye bread into the toaster. Then he went to the front porch and picked up the *Times*. He glanced at the headline, something about Argentina, and opened the paper to the sports section. He found the Knicks in the standings, three and a half games behind the Celtics, and checked last night's results. Since his retirement, Grossman rarely bet on sports, but he liked to keep an eye on the point spreads, just to see when something funny happened.

Al Grossman hated the *Times* and its lousy sports section. Until a few years ago, he read the *Post* and the *News* every

morning in the backseat of his limo, on the way to work in
the city. Now, if he wanted to buy those papers, he had to
go to the mall, which was where he had first met Bev Friedman.

She had been standing in front of a display of paperbacks
at Walden's, on tiptoe, squinting at the books on the top
shelf. Grossman noticed her automatically, the way he noticed all good-looking women; one of the few pleasant surprises about getting old was that he was just as horny at
seventy as he had been at forty. The difference was that now
he could do more about it. Never in his life had he been
surrounded by so many willing women. They seemed to be
everywhere, survivors of the internists and tax attorneys, oral
surgeons and CPAs who keeled over every day from over-
work and too much exercise. The women inherited their hus-
bands' money, and he inherited them, at least the ones who
were still in decent shape. Over the years he had modified
his taste—he didn't mind gray pubic hair, and he barely noticed varicose veins, but he still hated droopy tits, or big
flabby asses.

The lady on tiptoe had a mop of curly brown hair, dark
almond eyes, full lips, high round breasts and a tight-looking
bottom. Looking at her, Grossman got hard. Unexpectedly,
she turned and caught him staring at her. He averted his gaze,
snuck another look, and saw that she was smiling.

Grossman wandered around the store, waiting for the
woman to pick out a book, and then followed her over to the
counter. He had never been shy with women, but old age
made him bold; what's the worst that can happen? was his
motto.

"I noticed you over there looking at the books," he said.
"What did you get?"

"Just some trashy novels," she said, as though she had
been expecting him to talk to her. She showed him the pa-

perbacks, a Judith Krantz and a Sidney Sheldon. "Escape literature, they call it."

"You on the lam?" he said, smiling, but putting a little gravel in his voice. She laughed and looked at him more closely, really seeing him for the first time.

"No, I just don't like daytime television," she said. "Even these are better than those stupid talk shows."

They walked together to the parking lot, where she opened the door to a white Mercedes XL. "Your husband must do pretty good, car like this," said Grossman.

"My husband passed away last March," she said.

"Sorry to hear it," he said. "Kids?"

"A boy, nineteen, and a girl, eighteen, both away at school," she said. "They're great kids. I miss them." Grossman sensed she was stalling. Probably she had no place to go but home, and there was nobody there. "How about you?" she asked.

"My wife's dead," he said. "I've got a son around your age."

"Really?" she said, smiling, showing nice natural teeth. "You must have been a child groom."

"I'm seventy," Grossman said, making it a flat statement, no apology. He saw something in her eyes, but he couldn't tell what it was. There was an awkward silence.

"I've been thinking about buying one of these," he said, patting the car's roof. "Are you happy with it?"

"It's a wonderful car. If you can afford the insurance and the upkeep, that is."

"I think I'm going to get one," he said. "By the way, my name is Al Grossman."

"I'm Bev Friedman," she said. "Listen, would you like to take a sort of test drive sometime? See if you like the car?"

"Thanks," said Grossman. "Yeah, it would be a good idea probably. When would be a good time?"

"Anytime," she said. "Now, even, if you're not busy, I mean. Or you could call me. Do you live nearby?"

"Stratton Road," he said. "Across the street from the golf course. How about you?"

"I live on Harvest," she said. "Practically neighbors."

Grossman looked at his watch, making a show of it. "I've got some time," he said. "I'll take you up on the test drive, if you're serious."

She smiled, and raised herself lithely over the gear box to the passenger seat. "Hop in," she said, "you're going to love it."

They stopped for lunch at an old-fashioned roadside tavern on the way to Connecticut. During the drive Grossman let her do most of the talking, telling him about her husband, her kids and various friends he couldn't keep straight. It sounded like a pretty boring life, and he noticed she hadn't mentioned any romantic attachments. Grossman volunteered little about himself, not that he wanted to hide anything, but he figured his best shot would be the strong, silent approach.

At lunch she surprised him. "Are you Max Grossman's brother?" she asked.

"Yeah, as a matter of fact," he said. "How did you know that?"

"Well, you mentioned that you have a brother named Max, and your last name's Grossman, so I put two and two together," she said, laughing. "Are you a gangster too?"

"A retired businessman," he said, allowing his face to show he was lying. Broads, he knew, were attracted to gangsters, especially Jewish suburban broads who didn't know any better.

"Do you carry a gun?" she asked, her eyes sparkling with interest.

"Naw," he said. "What would I need a gun for out here, shoot at the squirrels?"

"I understand," she said, putting her finger to her lips. "Code of silence."

Grossman winked, took a bite of his lamb chop and washed it down with some beer. "I want to ask you something, a personal question," he said.

"Go ahead," she said.

"You think I'm too old for you? Be honest, there's no point in kidding each other."

She reached across the table and touched his arm. "I've been wondering that myself all morning," she said, giving him a level, appraising look. "My husband was fifty-four. You could almost have been his father."

"Yeah," said Grossman. "Well, I told you I have a son about your age."

"I wanted you to talk to me in the bookstore," she said. "You looked interesting. Different from the kind of people you meet out here. At least from the kind of people I meet out here."

"You gonna answer my question or what?" asked Grossman, smiling to soften it, but not letting her off the hook. He could tell that she was attracted to him, but some women had rules they made for themselves—no this, no that, whatever. If she had a rule about age, he wanted to know about it up front.

"Yes," she said. "I mean no. No, I don't think you're too old for me. I think you're very sexy."

That was almost a year ago. Since then they had settled into a pattern that was convenient for both of them. She had her own money, didn't bug him about his diet, didn't mind watching sports on television and was always ready to make love. She was good in bed, too, passionate and open without being a stunt girl. They never discussed it, but Grossman didn't see other women, and he didn't think she saw other men.

He heard the water running in the shower. She was a clean

girl, too, another thing he liked about her. He picked up the sports page again, and his eye fell on a small item in the lower left-hand corner.

FORMER HEAVYWEIGHT CONTENDER
VICTIM OF HIT-AND-RUN

(AP) Rudy Parchi (46), a former heavyweight boxer, was killed Sunday night in a hit-and-run incident on Manhattan's 23rd Street. There are no leads regarding the identity of the driver, according to a police spokesman.

Parchi, who was once the 10th ranked heavyweight in the country, was employed in recent years as a salesman for the Taste-Rite Potato Chip company in Brooklyn.

Grossman grunted. He remembered Parchi, a big dumb wop with a right hand and no defense. He had been so crooked he would have fixed his sparring sessions if somebody had offered him two bucks. He vaguely recalled that Parchi worked for Luigi Spadafore, although he didn't know any details, and he didn't really care. Grossman wasn't surprised that Parchi had been run down by a car. It figures, he thought; the guy never had any footwork.

Bev walked into the kitchen barefoot, hair still wet, wrapped in a terry-cloth robe. Grossman put his arm around her slender waist and pulled her close. "You smell good enough to eat," he said.

"Forget it, Big Al," she laughed. "I've got to be in the city by nine. You're going to have to settle for cream cheese and lox this morning." Grossman sighed. He'd spend the morning at the health club, then maybe go to the track in the afternoon. He had already forgotten Rudy Parchi. He had no idea that Parchi had saved his son's life.

* * *

Late that afternoon, Flanagan got a call on his private line at the paper from Boatnay Threkeld.

" 'Member what you asked me the other night?'' he said.

"You mean about Spadafore? Yeah. I think you can forget it, though. The deal's off.''

"I'm glad to hear that, John,'' said Boatnay. "Now you're using your brains for once.''

"Why, though, just out of curiosity?''

"Well, it probably doesn't mean much, but last night his driver, guy named Rudy Parchi, was killed. Hit-and-run.''

Flanagan felt a jolt of electricity run through his body. "Hit-and-run? Whereabouts?''

"Thirteenth Precinct, near the corner of Lex and Twenty-third. The guy used to be a fighter, there was something in the paper about it today.''

"You think it was an accident?'' Flanagan asked.

"Maybe. Something strange about it, though,'' said Threkeld.

"What's that?''

"Well, we found a loaded Smith and Wesson in his hand,'' said Threkeld easily. "Course he could have been on his way to the gun show, you never know.''

"I didn't see any gun,'' said Flanagan.

"You were there?''

"Yeah, right there. Gordon and I were coming out of O'Dwyer's and a Mustang almost numbered us. Would have if Rudy hadn't gotten in the way. We talked to the cops, didn't you see my name in the report?''

"I didn't see the report,'' said Threkeld. "Man, you mean you were standing right there? That's quite a coincidence.''

"Could be,'' said Flanagan.

"Could be that Parchi was intending to shoot your ass, too.''

"It's a possibility,'' said Flanagan.

"John, I think the time has come for you to tell me what the hell's going on," said Threkeld. "Not that I want to know, but I guess I better."

"Let's hold off on that, Boatnay," said Flanagan. "I'm gonna check this out my own way. It's probably just a false alarm. No point in getting New York's finest into it."

"What if it ain't no false alarm?" said Threkeld, using street dialect for effect. "I done warned you, white boy, 'bout fucking 'round with the man."

"Boatnay, I love you when you're being ethnic," said Flanagan in a prissy voice. "Thanks for the tip, and I'd be obliged if you let me hear anything else that comes up."

"John, seriously now—"

"I gotta go, Captain," said Flanagan. "Say hi to Morgan. And, Boatnay—thanks again."

Flanagan had only one sister, but many cousins. Most of them were lace-curtain Irish—insurance agents, junior high school principals, chiropractors and municipal employees. One, Terry Flanagan, was a drug addict and petty crook. He was Flanagan's favorite relative.

Flanagan gave his cousin Terry fifty dollars to sneak into the parking garage in midtown where Carlo Sesti kept his pearl-gray Rolls and slash all four tires with a knife. Then he waited across the street from the garage until he saw Sesti enter. Flanagan went to the phone on the corner. By the time the consigliere reached the wounded Rolls, his car phone was already ringing.

"Hi, Carlo, I was just calling to see if I could give you a lift someplace," said Flanagan in a jovial tone.

There was a moment's hesitation. "Who is this?" said Sesti finally.

"This is the voice of your conscience, you pizza-eating hump," said Flanagan. "Next time you fuck with me, I'm gonna cut your head off and put it in Luigi's bed."

"I haven't the faintest idea what you're talking about," said Sesti in a cold voice. "I think you must be insane."

"I'm talking about Rudy Parchi," said Flanagan.

"Rudy was killed in an accident last night," said Sesti.

"Yeah, I was there. You ought to run a remedial street-crossing course for the troops, Carlo."

"What were you doing there?" asked Sesti.

"Cut the bullshit, consigliere," said Flanagan. "I know you sent him down there to hit Gordon and me. You and Luigi can't take a joke, you know that? OK, fuck it. I'm warning you—if anything weird happens from now on, the Mishpocha is going to the mattresses."

"You are insane," said Carlo, hanging up the phone. He clicked the button on the small recorder attached to the receiver and heard Flanagan's voice, tinny but unmistakable: ". . . warning you—if anything weird happens from now on . . ." Sesti cut off the machine, took out the tiny cassette and put it in his pocket. Then he walked out of the garage and hailed a cab. "Brooklyn," he told the driver.

Luigi Spadafore looked at the thick, round face of his elder son and wondered what he had done to deserve such a child. When he had listened to the tape Sesti brought him, one word kept flashing through his brain: "Mario." Spadafore knew, even before Mario confessed, that he must have been the one who sent Parchi to kill Gordon and Flanagan. No one else could have been so stupid.

"It was a matter of honor, Pa," Mario said. That word, on the rubbery lips of his son, snapped the Don's icy self-control.

"Who are you to talk about honor?" he demanded. "You try to commit murder against the nephew of my oldest friend, and you call this honor?"

"He dishonored you, Pa," said Mario petulantly. "Rudy

told me. I can't have people goin' around dishonoring my own father."

"I am perfectly capable of defending myself, you moron," his father said. "Who gave you the authority to give such an order?"

"I'm the son," Mario said stubbornly. "I'm the number two, and I made a decision. I did what I thought was right."

Spadafore sighed. Nothing got through to his idiot son. "Mario, hear me well," he said. "You are my son, and someday you will be my heir. Then you will run your affairs as you see fit. But, for the moment, you are not in charge and you will do as I say. If a single hair on the head of Gordon is touched, I will personally chop off your hands. Is that clear?"

"You wouldn't talk like that to Sesti," said Mario.

"That is the first correct thing you have said today," said Spadafore. "I would not talk this way to Carlo Sesti because he is a man I respect. I respect his intelligence, his loyalty and his judgment. I would not talk to him this way because he would give me no cause to do so."

Mario reddened and tried to speak, but no words came out. Spadafore could see that he was in a murderous rage. "One more thing, Mario," he said. "If something happens to Carlo Sesti, I will cut off both your hands. But first I will cut off both your balls. Now, get out of my sight, and don't come back until you're sent for."

"But, Pa . . ."

"Do not answer me!" Spadafore screamed in Sicilian. "Do not answer me! Go." Mario rose and slammed out of the room. Spadafore looked at the heavy oak door for a long moment, and then let his heavy head droop into his hands.

15

WHEN HE WAS FOURTEEN, CARLO SESTI HAD ONCE been rebuked by a master at Downside for his cynicism. "Boy Sesti, you are too clever by half," the white-haired old man had said. "And a gentleman, although he may be educated, perhaps even intelligent, is never clever. That is the attribute of Jews and Gypsies."

Carlo realized that the old man was trying to wound him, but he took the implication that he was a foreigner as a compliment. Although he had been born in London, and trained to act and talk like the other boys of the monied class, he had no illusion that he was an English gentleman, and no desire to be one. Cleverness to Sesti was a virtue; he considered the English sense of fair play to be a crippling affectation.

All his life, Sesti used his cleverness the way a celebrated beauty relies upon her appearance. Even as a small boy he had been aware of his ability to think faster and more clearly than others, and he had seen the practical benefits of such an ability. It had propelled him through Downside, Cambridge and Harvard Law School with a minimum of effort; it gained him a fortune by the age of thirty; and, most important, it

enabled him to navigate the shark-infested waters of the Spadafore Family.

Thus, where others might have regretted the failed attempt
on Flanagan's life, Sesti saw opportunity, and even destiny.
The idea of taping Flanagan's idiotic threats had been in-
spired improvisation, but the rest of the plan was a masterpiece of cunning.

Spadafore, he understood, would naturally see that the
attempt on Flanagan and Gordon had been ordered by his
son. So when Mario was gunned down three days later, coming out of a midtown restaurant, the old man assumed, as
Sesti knew he would, that Flanagan had found out about
Rudy Parchi and made good on his threat. As an extra bonus,
Sesti had not even paid for Mario's assassination; Grady Rand
had felt so bad about botching the previous job that he did it
for free.

Sesti had, of course, comforted the old man in his grief,
and swore to help him take his revenge on the two journalists.
Like God, Sesti saw the future. First, Flanagan would be
killed in a street mugging. Then, Gordon would respond by
having Pietro shot—Sesti had already told Rand to remain in
readiness. Finally, Gordon himself would die in an accident.
Rand could retire on the money he would earn, although it
would be a short retirement, since he would know too much.
And Spadafore, if the death of his sons didn't kill him, would
have no remaining heir. Except his loyal consigliere, Carlo
Sesti.

Pietro Spadafore stood silently in the small chapel of the
Fortuna Bros. funeral home, looking into his brother's open
casket. Mario made a good-looking corpse, Pietro thought.
Death had taken the cruel stupidity out of his face and replaced it with a bland, angelic look. It was, he reflected, the
advantage of the ugly man to leave life looking better than
before.

Pietro wondered what he would look like in his own casket, and the thought made him shudder. He was too young to even contemplate dying, and yet, standing in front of his dead brother, it was hard to avoid the notion. He wondered whether his father would give him a send-off as grand as Mario's—five thousand dollars' worth of flowers, a silk-lined ivory casket, the cardinal himself to deliver the eulogy. Probably, he decided; he was as much his father's property as Mario, and for Luigi Spadafore to do any less would be an act of disrespect to someone he loved—himself.

Pietro sneaked a peek at his watch. Eleven-fifteen. He had promised Debbie Hearns that he would meet her for lunch at the Plaza at one. He looked at the body of his older brother with theatrical grief, hoping his act would appease his father when he told him, in a few minutes, that he had an appointment. He knew he would have a problem with the Don, especially now that Mario was gone. The old man would want him to take over, and Pietro intended to use all his wiles to avoid that.

Luigi Spadafore would have been astonished to know that his younger son had a capacity for duplicity that matched his own. From childhood, Pietro had been a misfit in the Spadafore Family, like one of those human babies raised in the woods by wolves. He was oppressed by his father's harsh demands, and by the solemn, old-world atmosphere of the huge brownstone. He had realized that his only possibility of escape was to play dumb. It had been an easy enough role; his father, already used to one idiot son, had taken Pietro's stupidity almost for granted.

He looked at his watch again, and at his father's grim, stricken face. Five more minutes and he would make his departure. The Don's grief was, he knew, a pose; the old man cared nothing for Mario. Pietro mumbled what he hoped sounded like a prayer and thought about Debbie Hearns, who liked to make love standing in front of mirrors in public rest rooms.

For Pietro, women were an acquired taste. He had initially been drawn to them not for glandular reasons but to fortify his image as a foolish playboy. But as he gained experience, he made a surprising discovery; he, Pietro Spadafore, needed and loved women, and he had the capacity to evoke their need and love in return.

It was not just his looks—he knew hundreds of better-looking guys who couldn't get laid at a Playboy bunny convention. No, it was something deeper, more subtle. He understood women, knew instinctively how to approach them, what to say, when to act and when to hesitate. Women were not merely a diversion, as his father imagined. They were as crucial to him as a sunrise to a painter, or the song of birds to a composer. They were his inspiration, his medium of expression, each relationship a self-created world of its own, and his ability to bring such worlds to life gave him a power far greater than anything his father could possibly offer.

He knew the Don considered his passion for women to be an effeminate weakness, but his father was an old man, and limited. Women, Pietro knew, were not trivial, but essential. Throughout history they had humbled kings, made philosophers dumb with desire, caused honorable men to break oaths and spill blood. And he, Pietro Spadafore, conquered these wild creatures. He could never explain this to his father, not because the old man would not understand, but for fear that he might—might realize that his son Pietro had a dominating spirit and intelligence not too different from his own.

Pietro's meditations were interrupted by a rustle in the rear of the chapel. He turned and saw William Gordon, dressed in a somber black suit, walking toward his father. The old man looked up and saw Gordon approaching, and a look of amazement and rage mottled his face.

Gordon stopped briefly in front of the casket, mumbled

something, and then approached the Don. This man has balls of brass, thought Pietro—either that or a serious death wish.

"Mr. Spadafore, I want to offer my condolences," said Gordon, extending his hand. Spadafore ignored it, looking intently into his face but saying nothing. Gordon, misunderstanding, withdrew his hand. "I want to apologize, too, sir, for the other night. I don't know what got into Flanagan to pull a stupid prank like that. I know that this isn't the best time, but I just wanted to say that—"

"You . . . come . . . here?" Spadafore interrupted him in a voice choked by emotion into a soupy whisper. "You . . . come . . . here, to the body of my son, the son you have taken from me, to offer your sympathy?"

"Who, me?" Gordon exclaimed. He sounded so boyishly astonished that Pietro nearly laughed out loud. "You think I had something to do with Mario's death?"

Spadafore turned to Sesti. "Get him away from me," he commanded. Sesti took Gordon by the elbow, and began walking him quickly toward the door. On the steps of the funeral home Gordon pulled away.

"Carlo, what the hell is happening here?" he demanded. "You can't really think that I—"

"Ah, but we do," said Sesti. "In fact, we think precisely that."

"*You* think that? Or just Spadafore?"

"You are very lucky," said Sesti. "The period of mourning is sacred to Sicilians, otherwise you would have been killed just now."

"Carlo, you didn't answer my question. Do you honestly believe that *I* could possibly have had anything to do with Mario's death?"

The consigliere shrugged. "What I believe is irrelevant. The point is that Mr. Spadafore believes it."

"But *why*? What possible reason could I have?"

"Why don't you ask your consigliere," said Sesti.

For a moment, Gordon looked blank. "My consigliere? Who? You mean Flanagan? What the hell did he do now?"

"He threatened Mr. Spadafore, three days before the death of his son. I have a recording of that conversation."

"I don't believe it," said Gordon. "Can I hear the tape?"

"You can go right now, with your life," said Sesti.

"Carlo, you've got to talk to Spadafore, tell him that this is a ridiculous mistake. We're reporters, Flanagan and I, not gangsters. We've been play-acting, that's all. You've got to make Mr. Spadafore understand that."

"I'm afraid I'll have a rather difficult time convincing Mr. Spadafore that two of New York's most distinguished journalists have been merely play-acting. And, Mr. Gordon, frankly I don't believe it myself."

"You mean, you actually think—"

"Yes, I think your Mr. Flanagan is capable of any sort of lunacy. In any event, as I've said, it isn't important what I think. Good-bye, Mr. Gordon."

"But, Carlo, what's going to happen? I mean, how do we make a truce, or whatever?"

Sesti gave him a wintry smile. "You still haven't understood, have you, Gordon? For a man like Luigi Spadafore, there is no possibility of declaring a truce with his son's murderers."

"Meaning what?" asked Gordon with a distinct tremor in his voice.

"I can do nothing for you," said Sesti. "It is out of my hands now. Good-bye, Mr. Gordon."

16

GORDON DROVE BACK TO MANHATTAN FEELING numb. He had often wondered what it would be like to hear from the doctor that he had a terminal disease. Now he knew. Sesti's message had been unmistakable—a death sentence had been passed on him. Gordon's instincts told him there must be some process of appeal, but he didn't know what it might be. Clearly Sesti was no longer an ally. He would have to find out what to do from someone who knew Spadafore's world and its rules.

Gordon knew he couldn't go home; there might be people waiting for him there right now. Flanagan would still be at the paper, but he wasn't ready for Flanagan at the moment. He was too scared to be mad, but he realized that Flanagan was more of a problem than a solution.

Gordon pulled into a gas station near Chinatown and dialed his father's number. The old man answered on the second ring: "Grossman." The sound of his father's gruff voice made Gordon feel safer than he had since leaving Brooklyn.

"Dad, it's me," he said.

"Yeah, right. You ain't been around much, Velvel."

"Listen, Dad, I'm in trouble. I need your help."

There was a frightened tone in his son's voice that Grossman had forgotten. The kid was such a hotshot, always calling from some foreign country, 'Don't worry about a thing, I'm fine,' no matter where he was, and then, when he got home, the stories about the battlefields and the dictators. Grossman was supposed to be impressed, but he never was; his son was a spectator, a tourist to other people's tsuris with a passport and credit cards.

"What kind of trouble? You knock up that les, or what?"

"Dad, can you meet me someplace? I mean right now?"

"I'm busy right now, boychik. You don't call for what, two three weeks, and then you expect me to slide down a poll like a fireman and meet you? Forget it."

"Dad, honest to God, I really need you."

"Yeah, OK, it's touching a boy needs his dad. I'm a sucker for sentiment. I'll meet you at six, same place as last time. But don't plan on wasting my evening, I got tickets to the Rangers-Bruins."

"Thanks, Poppa," said Gordon, and Grossman realized that his son had stopped calling him Poppa when he was seven years old.

Around noon, Flanagan got up from his computer and slipped into his jacket, walked down the long corridor leading out of the city room, and stuck his head into Corry Rosen's office. "I'm going out to get some lunch," he told the city editor. "I'll be back in time to go over the Queens zoning thing." Rosen nodded and waved. "Have a good time," he said.

Flanagan took the elevator to the lobby and walked into the street, turning left on Forty-ninth and heading briskly toward Broadway. Mario's murder puzzled him; maybe, he thought, the Spadafores are on the brink of a war with some other Family. If so, it could screw up his own plans. Flanagan decided to get in touch with Boatnay Threkeld after lunch, and to see what the cops knew about the hit on Mario.

Halfway up the block, Flanagan saw a tall man in a tan

jacket. The man had a broken nose and a longish dirty-blond ducktail. It was the haircut that caught Flanagan's attention; he hadn't seen one like it since the fifties, in Brooklyn.

The man approached Flanagan. "Scuze me, mister, you got the time?" he asked in a Southern accent.

"Yeah," said Flanagan, looking at his watch. "Twelve-fifteen."

"Thanks." Suddenly the man's arm flashed and Flanagan felt a sharp pain in his stomach, just below his rib cage. "Shit!" he screamed, grabbing the wound and sinking to the sidewalk. He called for help, but he could barely hear his voice over the pounding in his ears. He lay in his own blood, looking up at the patch of blue sky between the tall buildings. It was a beautiful day. There were people in the offices above who didn't know a thing about what was happening to him. Flanagan felt an overpowering rage. Goddamn it, I'm going to die, he thought. Right here on Forty-ninth Street.

The man with the beaky nose and the dirty-blond hair stood above him, and suddenly he was gone. Flanagan heard voices, and then he stopped hearing them.

Gordon called Jupiter. He had four hours to kill and he wanted to spend them with her. But she was out and her service said that she had left no message. Probably just as well, he thought; seeing Jupiter might make him even shakier.

He left his car in a parking garage near Chinatown and hailed a cab. He was afraid to hang around downtown, near Little Italy. The streets looked dirty and corrupt, like Saigon or Bangkok or Munich after dark. Gordon wanted to be around rich white Americans, people in tweed clothing with dogs on leashes. He told the driver to take him to the Providence Club, on Seventy-fourth off Madison.

Gordon had been a member of the Providence Club for close to twenty years; Cy Malkin put him up after his first

Pulitzer. During his time abroad, he often stayed there during home leave, but since coming back to the city he had rarely used the place. Most of the members were journalists or television executives, and he found their smug certainties about the world to be silly and sometimes offensive. Once, soon after returning from Tehran, where he covered the overthrow of the Shah, he had met a senior editor from the *Daily News* in the reading room. "I saw your stuff from Iran," the editor told him. "I think you went a little overboard on the Islamic fundamentalist angle. What the people over there really want is Coca-Cola and color television." On another occasion, a syndicated columnist, full of vodka and Perrier, had assured him that African nations would never be able to develop modern economies. "No sense of technology," he said. "The only things that blacks ever invented are the peanut and the zip gun." Normally this kind of wisdom kept Gordon away from the Providence Club, but today he was anxious to be among members of his fraternity, safe on familiar ground.

At three, the dining room was empty, but there was a crowd at the bar in the wood-paneled saloon. Gordon joined a group of reporters, who greeted him with good-natured banter about the soft life he was living as a columnist. No one seemed surprised to see him. None of them had any idea of the life he had been living for the past few weeks, or that right now swarthy men with weapons under their topcoats were cruising the city looking for him. He wondered what they would do if a couple of hoods burst into the cozy room. Who would stand up for him, defend him? He looked at his colleagues and felt an inward chill. None of them would lift a finger. He was on his own. The only person he could count on was his father.

Gordon sat listening to the reporters brag and bullshit. Once, long ago, he had been flattered to be included in these sessions, and anxious to hold up his end with combat stories and rueful tales of memorable benders. He had seen something colorful and heroic in these men, insiders who knew the secrets of the world, intrepid witnesses to history. Now, listening to them drop the names of overrated Third World hotels—the Commodore and the Colony, Raffles and Mena House—they sounded to him like so many Midwestern tourists with stickers on their suitcases.

"I was in Cairo one time and this U.S. senator was supposed to check into the Sheraton," said Wharton, a bibulous Texan with a red nose and walrus mustache. "So I gave the desk clerk a ten and told him to call when the guy arrived. One hour, two hours, I don't hear anything, so I call him up. Anything happening, Mohammed? The senator get there yet? All of a sudden, Mohammed says, 'Wait a minute,' and leaves me on the phone. A few minutes later he comes back on and says the senator isn't there yet. The next day I found out where Mohammed went." He paused, allowing them to wonder. "Seems somebody just assassinated the prime minister of Jordan, Wasfi Tal, on the steps outside. He went out there to see what happened, but he didn't bother to mention that. It wasn't part of the deal."

There were chuckles from the other reporters. They all had a headful of tales about the Mohammeds and Pedros and Shin Lis of the world. "Fuckin' wogs," said the Texan, savoring the story.

"Hey, Jack, you ever been to the Hobbit in Manila?" a man in a bow tie and suspenders asked the Texan. "What a place. Everybody's a midget. Bartenders, band, waiters, even the bouncer—all midgets. One time I was over there, and we went over to the Hobbit, me and Harvey McKenzie and Gary Lauffer, from the AP. Anyway, we walk in and see all these midgets, and McKenzie goes over to the bar and says, 'Double bourbon on the rocks, and go easy on the thalidomide.' "
The reporters laughed. "Easy on the thalidomide," the bow tie repeated, eyes dancing with mirth.

"Fuckin' midgets," said the Texan.

"Gordon, remember the time we were in, where was it, Tel Aviv, or Jerusalem, must have been in Jerusalem because we were with Cy Vance, staying at the King David, I think, which has got to have the worst fucking room service in the world, nothing but cold little kosher sandwiches after midnight. Anyway, we're in the bar and these two hookers come in, and Dave Gershenson from the *Post* takes one upstairs. So, about half an hour later, he comes down with this shit-eating grin on his face. Turns out the hooker's got a stack of telex receipts she picked up from her sister, who works at the post office. Gershenson's got one, made out for international telex charges, one hundred dollars. Remember that, Gordon? 'I'll take the whole thing off expenses,' Gershenshon says. And, you know what? Three days later, he comes down with the clap. And you know what Artie Simms told him? He says, 'That only proves that when it comes to pussy, you get what you pay for.' " The group roared once again.

"Fuckin' Israelis," said the Texan. "No offense, Gordon."

"Yeah, right," said Gordon. He looked around and saw Todd Dorfman rush into the room. "Hey, you guys, you hear what just happened?" he said. "John Flanagan got stabbed on Forty-ninth Street on the way to lunch."

Gordon felt a freezing terror in the pit of his stomach. "Stabbed? What are you talking about?" he asked.

"I don't have all the details, but apparently he was walking down Forty-ninth and someone tried to mug him. He's in critical condition."

"Is he going to make it?"

Dorfman shrugged. "They don't know yet. He lost a lot of blood, they said. It's on the radio."

"Where is he?" asked Gordon, hoping no one could hear the panic in his voice. Dorfman shrugged again. "Didn't say. Hey, Gordon, I'm really sorry."

"What for, you didn't stab him," said Gordon. "I gotta get back to the paper."

"This city's a goddamn jungle," said Wharton. "It's worse than Beirut. Fuckin' New York."

"Hey, speaking of Beirut, did I ever tell you about the time the Shi'ites tried to kidnap Cassie Rutherford, when she was with Reuters in Lebanon. . . ?"

17

PIETRO SPADAFORE WALKED INTO THE PALM COURT of the Plaza a few minutes after one, and he was immediately warmed by the appraising gazes of several of the women waiting for tables. After his grim getaway scene with the old man, he needed female company and admiration; Debbie Hearns, a red-haired actress with long legs, an upturned nose and a way of listening with her lips slightly parted, would do nicely.

Pietro was pleased and a little excited to find her with Jupiter Evans. The two women had made a movie together the previous year, and Debbie sometimes spoke of her. Pietro couldn't help contrasting Debbie's pert, somewhat shallow beauty with Evans's strong, sensual face and piercing eyes. He had heard that she was gay, but Pietro didn't really believe that there was such a thing, any more than he believed in nymphomaniacs or ball busters. To him, each female was a unique fascination; unlike other men, Pietro never classified them.

"Peter, I have bad news and good news," said Debbie with a smile. "The bad news is that I have to stand you up—my accountant has something urgent to go over with me, and it's now or when he gets back from Jamaica two weeks from

now. The good news is that Jupiter is my stand-in this afternoon.''

"That is, if you don't mind," Evans said in a low, melodious voice.

"Delighted," said Pietro, meaning it. He had wanted to
meet Jupiter Evans for a long time.

"Don't be too delighted, Peter," said Debbie Hearns. "I'll
call you later. Maybe we can get together tonight.''

"I've got something to do tonight," said Pietro, keeping
his eyes on Jupiter. "I'll call you tomorrow. And good luck
with the accountant.''

Pietro and Jupiter used Debbie Hearns as a conversational
shoehorn, agreeing at more than normal length that she was
a delightful girl. Another man might have wondered if the
two actresses were lovers, but Pietro knew they weren't. His
instincts about women were almost never wrong. He had
once read about certain baseball players whose eyesight was
so good that they could actually see the stitches on the ball
on its way to the plate. That's the way it was for Pietro with
women; he saw and understood them in slow motion, as
though they were larger than life.

For twenty minutes or so they kept the conversation light,
chatting about new films and the sensational divorce of a
local tycoon. As they spoke, Pietro watched Jupiter's brown
eyes soften, and her body lean involuntarily toward him
across the table. It was time, he sensed, to lead things in a
more personal direction.

"I've got a confession to make," he said, speaking in an
easy tone. "I feel nervous just sitting here with you. I've
admired you for a long time.''

"Really? What have you seen?" she asked.

"It's not the plays and movies, it's you," he said. "Sometimes I watch you act and I feel that you're special, a person
with a secret.''

Evans searched Pietro's face for signs of stupidity. Only a

very stupid man, or a very smart one, would say such a thing. She had been eager to meet Pietro Spadafore because Gordon had talked so much about his father; she thought it would be fun to surprise him with some inside information of her own. She had been expecting a Brooklyn hood, but Pietro, with his blue eyes and long lashes, soft skin and well-made sensitive hands, was anything but a greaser.

Jupiter followed Pietro's lead, allowing the conversation to take on a more intimate tone, and she found him almost eerily attuned to her moods. When she came to a difficult subject, he opened the door for her with a graceful word, and then stood aside to allow her to enter. Unlike most men, who tried to impress her with their anecdotes and opinions, or attempted to play on her vanity, Pietro drew her out, made her want to reveal herself. She found herself wondering what it would feel like to lick the smooth skin of his neck, run her hands over his body. It was a sexy thought, and scary; for the first time in many years, Jupiter Evans truly wanted a man.

Pietro leaned forward and looked intently into her eyes. "I know who you are," he said. "I know you." Those were the words that Claudette Lawton had said to her at camp, near the lake. Jupiter felt light-headed, a bit dizzy. For a moment it seemed to her that Pietro was Claudette reincarnated in a man's body.

"Would you like to go to my place?" Jupiter asked suddenly, not even trying to hide the sudden urgency she felt. She had to find out right now about Pietro: whether she was simply responding to his charm and technique, or if her attraction was more profound. "We could have a drink, or, well, we could make love."

Pietro smiled—it was the most disarming, gentle smile she had seen in her life. "We've been making love all afternoon," he said, and Jupiter had to admit that, yes, that was just what she and Pietro Spadafore had been doing.

18

WHEN GORDON SAW HIS FATHER SITTING IN HIS usual rear booth in the Emerald Isle, he was so relieved that tears sprang to his eyes. Thank God he's here, he thought; he'll know what to do.

"Dad," he blurted out, "they stabbed Flanagan."

"I heard," said the old man. "On the radio, coming in."

"He's going to pull through, though," said Gordon. "I talked to Rosen at the paper, and he said that he's going to be OK. Apparently the knife missed his heart by an inch or so."

His father said nothing, and his face remained expressionless. "Dad, it was Spadafore who set this up," Gordon continued. "I went out there today to pay a condolence call, and Sesti told me that he thinks we had Mario killed. He practically said that they were going to take revenge."

"Yeah, I figured it was Spadafore," said Grossman. "And?"

"And I was right. I wouldn't want to be the goombah who messed up the hit, I'll tell you that."

"That's all you've got to say? I'm telling you that they tried to kill Flanagan and they want to get me too, and you're feeling sorry for some Mafia guy you don't even know?"

"It was just a figure of speech, Velvel. What the hell do you want me to say? I warned you, goddammit. We sat right here, in this booth, and I told you to keep away from Spadafore. I told you he was poison, but you're a hotshot, you know everything."

"OK, you were right," said Gordon. "You want me to kiss your ass, fine. But right now I'm in trouble. I need your help, Dad. Don't make me beg for it."

"Last time we talked you called me a bastard for helping you, if you remember."

"That was different," said Gordon, trying hard to keep the exasperation out of his voice. "I was talking about interfering with my career. This is a matter of life and death. Jesus, listen to me, I sound like a soap opera, only it's not, it's real. There could be guys out there right now, waiting for me."

"Yeah, and I could get caught in the cross fire, ever think of that?"

Gordon stared at him. The thought that he was endangering his father had never entered his mind. Grossman saw it in his son's eyes. "How old are you, anyway? Forty-one, forty-two?" he demanded gruffly. "You got important friends, you go to dinner at the White House. Why don't you get Ronald Reagan to give you a hand? Get him shot."

Gordon squeezed his fingers together until the knuckles were white. He longed to reach across the table and grab his father by the throat and choke the arrogant meanness out of him. "You're not going to help, fuck you," said Gordon. "I'll fight these guys myself." He rose to go, but Grossman signaled with a nod of his head for him to remain seated.

"If you want my help, Velvel, from now on we do things my way. You send me out to Katmandu, wherever, I'd probably screw up, spell the names all wrong. But this ain't South America, boychik, it's New York, and Luigi Spadafore ain't some Hottentot. So, you want me in, I'm in, but I run the show. Deal?''

Gordon could feel the heat rising in his cheeks. All his life he had resisted this domineering man, and now, in the prime of his adult life, he was turning himself into his father's little boy again. But there was no choice, really; no one else to go to. ''OK,'' he said thickly.

''OK, what?''

''OK, goddammit, it's a deal.''

''Fine,'' said Grossman. ''Now, first thing, I want you to tell me what's happened. I want to know everything, every little detail. Don't leave anything out. You can take your time; I already sold the Rangers tickets.''

Instinctively, Gordon organized his story into a news report, giving a full, concise account of the events of the past two weeks. At every turn he could see how his greed and his inability to control Flanagan had led to disaster. ''I just don't understand John,'' Gordon said. ''I mean, he's always been a wild man, but never like this. That stunt with the cake, threatening Spadafore—it's like he was looking to start a war or something.''

''Now you're talking, boychik; that's exactly what he was trying to do.''

''But why? Flanagan knows we wouldn't have a chance. Two reporters against the Spadafore Family? It just doesn't make sense.''

''Why?'' said Grossman. ''I'll tell you why. Because your buddy Flanagan is a burnt-out alcoholic Irishman who probably can't get a hard-on anymore.''

''Dad, I don't think that ethnic generalizations—''

''Who's generalizing? You think I don't know about generalizations. Jews are supposed to be smart, and look at you. I got nothing against Irishers who drink. The bars are full of sweet old guys with watery eyes playing darts and singing Toorah Loorah Loorah. But your pal Flanagan ain't one of them. He's got a death wish. Look, Velvel, I seen this plenty of times before. You ever hear of Ben Siegel?''

"You mean Bugsy Siegel?''

His father nodded. "Ben Siegel was just about the best operator in this city. He and Lansky began to run together around the same time Max got started. We were friends, all the Yidden—Lepke, Gurrah Shapira, even Dutch Schultz, although personally I thought he was an asshole. We helped each other out.''

Gordon realized that this was the first time he had ever heard his father explicitly discuss his underworld connections. For a moment, his professional curiosity overcame his fear.

"What kinds of things were you into?'' he asked.

"Never mind that, we're talking about Ben Siegel,'' said his father. "He was always crazy—you don't get a nickname like Bugsy for nothing—but it was a smart craziness, cautious. If Ben said he was going to rob a convoy in broad daylight, you could be sure that he already knew how many guns were aboard, what was the police protection, everything. In other words, he did things that sounded crazy but weren't really so crazy when you looked closer.

"The thing is, Ben was a cowboy. He needed the excitement. Broads, booze, opium, betting, you name it, Ben was there. But there's a catch—the older you get, the less that stuff does for you, except to give you the clap or screw up your liver. After a while, the only thing that still got him going was danger.''

"I thought Bugsy Siegel founded Las Vegas,'' said Gordon.

"Yeah. He didn't found it, there was already a town out there full of hayseeds, but Ben set up the first casino. He was a smart cookie. Until he started skimming. He was stealing from his partners—Lansky, Max, Genovese, Luigi Spadafore. Why, 'cause he needed the dough? Get outa here, Ben

Siegel was a rich man. He did it for kicks, for thrills, so he could still get a hard-on. You think he didn't know what would happen? He hadda know, he was around these guys all his life. But he didn't care anymore. He was like a junkie.''

"So they shot him," said Gordon.

"How old's your buddy Flanagan?" asked Grossman.

"Forty-seven. Six years older than me," said Gordon.

"There you are," said Grossman. "See, Velvel, this ain't a matter of ethnic generalizations. This business is like pro sports, you judge a guy by how he performs. Max had been the commissioner of baseball, Jackie Robinson would have been in the majors in 1920. Flanagan is a type. He's going down in flames, like a Jap kamikaze pilot during the war. You happened to be on board when he decided to plow into the battleship."

"I gave him the keys to the plane," said Gordon. "This never would have happened if I hadn't got involved with Spadafore. I take the blame for that."

"Spilled milk now," said Grossman. "They know how soon Flanagan's going to be back on his feet?"

"Rosen said about two weeks. Why?"

"Because we're going to need him, that's why."

"Need him? You just got done saying how dangerous he is."

"Yeah, under normal conditions. But things could get rough now, and Flanagan is a warrior. I want him with us."

"You're planning to fight Spadafore? Come on, Dad, you know we wouldn't have a chance. We've got to find a way to convince him to call this off."

"Velvel, you ever hear of NATO?"

Gordon gave him a surprised look. "NATO? What about it?"

"What's the point of NATO? Deterrence, right? I know we can't beat the Spadafores in a fight, but you deal with a guy like Luigi, you need some deterrence. Otherwise, he's a wolf and you're a lamb chop.''

''And Flanagan is our deterrence?'' asked Gordon with a twinge of envy. In a fight his father wanted Flanagan, not him. ''What am I going to be doing while all this is going on?''

''For now, you're getting out of sight. I got a lady friend out in Scarsdale, Bev Friedman. She's got a big house and she's all alone. I want you to go there right now. Don't stop to pick up anything at your place, whatever you need she'll go out and get for you. You get there, stay in the house. No shopping in the mall, no drives around town, not even a walk. Stay put.''

''Does your friend know what this is all about?'' Gordon asked.

''No details, and don't discuss any with her. Another thing, you got any pals on the police force?''

Gordon shook his head. ''Flanagan's got a friend, a captain named Threkeld. Why?''

''Good, get in touch with Threkeld, use a pay phone. See if he can get some off-duty cops to guard Flanagan. I'll take care of the bill, whatever it is.''

''How long do I have to stay in hiding?'' asked Gordon.

His father shrugged. ''A week, two weeks. Maybe longer. I'll let you know.''

''Let me know? Where will you be?''

Grossman smiled. ''Me? I'm going to Florida.''

19

IT WAS DARK WHEN GORDON DROVE UP TO BEVERLY
Friedman's big Colonial house on Harvest Drive. He parked
in the circular driveway and rang the bell. "Who is it?" a
voice called from the other side of the door.

"William Gordon," he said, feeling foolish. "My father
is Albert Grossman."

The door swung open and Gordon saw a woman about his
age in a pair of tight-fitting jeans and a white T-shirt that
outlined her nipples. A blue band held her curly hair off her
forehead, and she was barefoot.

"Hi," he said. "I think your mother is expecting me."

"I doubt it," said the woman. "My mother's been dead
for nine years." She laughed at the confusion on Gordon's
face. "I'm Bev Friedman," she said, extending her hand.
"I've been waiting for you. Please, come in."

Gordon followed her into the spacious living room. "Can
I get you something to eat?" she asked. "I didn't know if
you'd be hungry or not, but I've got a steak I could toss onto
the broiler."

"No, thanks," said Gordon. "I'm not really hungry."

"How about some coffee, then? Or a drink?"

"Bourbon, if you have any," said Gordon. "Or Scotch."

"One bourbon coming right up," she said brightly. "On the rocks?" Gordon nodded. "You sit down and make yourself at home, I'll be right back."

Gordon inspected the records near the stereo. *Jackie Wilson's Greatest Hits, Aretha Franklin Live at the Fillmore West, The Best of Van Morrison.* He tried to imagine his father with Bev Friedman. Did they go out to nightclubs? Was he keeping her? What did they look like in bed together? Christ, he thought, this girl is my father's mistress.

Bev returned with two glasses. "Music?" she asked.

"Sure."

"You like Bruce Springsteen?" Gordon nodded, and she hit a button on the tape deck. *"The River,"* she said. "It's my favorite album." She sat cross-legged on the semicircular couch. Gordon sat at the other end.

"I'm really sorry about all this inconvenience," he said.

"Are you kidding?" she laughed. "I love having a celebrity for a house guest. I've heard so much about you from your father that I feel like I know you, but otherwise I'd probably be too intimidated to talk."

"Intimidated?" said Gordon. "If anyone's intimidating, it's my father, not me."

"Al? He's a pushover," she said.

"A real pussycat," said Gordon. "Have you, ah, known each other long?"

"For a while," she said. "We met at the mall. I've wanted to have you out to the house for dinner, but according to your father you're always away somewhere, or busy. You must have a fascinating life, adventures, famous people, it seems so exciting."

"It's like anything else, you get used to it," said Gordon. "Most famous people are dull when you get to know them."

"Only if you're famous, too," she said. "Then you get to be blasé. Your father told me you're friendly with Jupiter

Evans. I think she's wonderful. What's she like? I mean personally. That is, if you don't mind talking about her.''

"She's just the girl next door," said Gordon, and laughed. "I don't want to keep you from whatever you're doing. Don't feel you have to entertain me or anything."

"I'll show you your room," she said. "It's my son Arthur's room really, but he's away at school. You can freshen up, and if you feel like it, come back upstairs and we can talk, or watch a movie. I rented some videos, just in case."

"Did my father tell you why I'm staying with you?" Gordon asked.

"Not really. He said you were working on something and needed to get out of town. That didn't sound like the real reason to me—I mean, after all, you must have better places to get away to than this. But it doesn't really matter. I love having company, and if Al thinks it's important, well . . ." She shrugged and Gordon saw her breasts swell together for a moment.

"I think I'd like to take a shower, if you don't mind," he said. "It's been a long day."

"Sure," she said, leading Gordon down carpeted stairs to a boy's room decorated with football posters and college banners. Bev gave him some towels and a pair of her son's pajamas. The towels were soft and fluffy, and the pajamas smelled slightly of laundry powder.

"I'm afraid I won't be around tomorrow," she said. "The Temple sisterhood is having a bazaar, and I'm in charge, if you can believe that. But I'll be back around five. I didn't do any special shopping because I didn't know what you'd want, but I'll stop tomorrow on the way home. What kind of things do you like to eat?"

"Please, don't fuss on account of me. I can heat something up or—"

"Don't be silly, I love to cook. It'll be fun. How about

roast beef? There's a great butcher in town. And I can make us a nice salad, maybe baked potatoes.''

"Sounds wonderful," he said.

"And you need some clothes, right? There's a Brooks Brothers at the mall."

"I'll go over tomorrow and get whatever I need," said Gordon, but Bev shook her head. "Your father said not to let you out of the house." She smiled. "Just tell me what you want and I'll pick it up."

"All I need are some shirts and underwear, socks and sneakers," said Gordon. "And a couple pairs of jeans. The shirts are sixteen-thirty-three, and the pants are a thirty-four waist."

"Any particular kind of jeans?"

"I'll trust your judgment," Gordon said, feeling foolish.

"OK, I'll get Levi's," she said. "You don't look like a designer-jean type. By the way, Al calls you Velvel. Is that what you like to be called? I mean, as long as we're living together." She laughed, not quite hiding her embarrassment.

"Call me Will," said Gordon. The name just slipped out. It was Jupiter's name for him.

"OK, Will. You take a shower and get some rest. If you want anything, the refrigerator's stocked, pretty much. I wind up throwing out half the stuff I buy, but when you've had kids, an empty refrigerator seems depressing. So help yourself, and feel at home."

"I don't know how to thank you," said Gordon.

"Don't," she said. "I love having a man around the house again."

Gordon took a shower and put on the pajamas. Usually he slept in his underpants, but for some reason the pajamas fit his mood that night. He climbed into the soft queen-sized bed and closed his eyes; he couldn't remember when he had been more tired. He wondered where Jupiter had been the past few days, and decided to call her the next day.

Just before dropping off, he thought about Bev Friedman—her almond eyes, her slight overbite, the arch of her bare feet, the tight jeans stretched across her small rear. She looked warm and juicy, like ripe fruit. Gordon hugged the pillow and felt his eyelids grow heavy, falling off to sleep thinking about his father's woman.

2⃝0

AL GROSSMAN SAT ON THE BENCH ALONGSIDE A tennis court in the Century City complex and watched Harry Millman lob yellow balls over the net to a grandmother with a Billie Jean King headband and legs that looked like a relief map of the Mississippi River and its tributaries. Millman stroked the balls effortlessly, and ran the baseline with short, energetic strides, barely sweating. Grossman saw him in his little white tennis shorts and T-shirt with the alligator on the pocket and recalled a younger, less elegant Harry Millman, bashing a rubber spaldeen with a broomstick on Hester Street.

"Game, set and match!" Millman finally called out, sounding like a country-club pro. He walked off the court with a white cotton sweater wrapped around his shoulders, and his racket under his arm.

"Where'd you learn to play tennis?" Grossman asked.

Millman laughed. "Tennis? In the joint. My last stretch, I was a ranked player. Number three racket on the Jackson squad. Would have been number one if they hadn't caught two guys from Grosse Pointe on a bank fraud."

The green expanse of the village square was crowded with old Jews in T-shirts and shorts tossing Frisbees and chipping golf balls. In the distance Grossman heard happy shouts and splashing from the Olympic pool. "Do these alter kockers know you were in the joint?" he asked.

"What alter kockers, they're the same age as us," Millman said, sounding hurt. "And I'll tell you something, Al, there's a lot of flanken down here. I could fix you up. You'd be surprised."

"Yeah," said Grossman sourly. "You didn't answer my question, though. Did you tell them you were in the joint?"

"No point in broadcasting it," said Millman. "Not that it would matter. The people around here are pretty broad-minded about the past. That's why they come down here, most of 'em, to get away from the past. And their kids."

"You ever get bored?" Grossman asked.

"Bored? Hell, no. This place is summer camp—parties, a health club, guys to play cards with, whatever. Plus you can go into town and see the ponies run, or catch a Dolphins game. This is the life, believe you me."

"Yeah," said Grossman, making his voice bland. "I thought maybe you were a little bored down here, but I guess I was wrong."

"Look, Al, if you're thinking about moving down yourself, trust me, you won't regret it. There's empty units, I could take you over to the management office right now, get you fixed up. Jeez, it'd be like the old days having you around."

Millman's enthusiasm told Grossman what he wanted to know. "Not me," he said. "I'm not the old-folks-home type."

"Ah, get outa here," said Millman, flexing his stomach muscles. "This look like an old man's stomach?"

Grossman punched his gut lightly. He had to admit that Handsome Harry was still in good shape. "Forget it," he said. "I'm down here on business. I just dropped by to say hello."

"What kind of business you doing in Florida?" asked Millman. "I thought you was retired."

"Something came up," said Grossman.

"Like what?" Millman asked.

Grossman lowered his hoarse voice to a confidential whisper. "Nothing that would interest you anymore," he said. He knew that Millman would identify the tone, a sound he had heard for more than half a century on the streets and in prison—the sound of conspiracy.

"Al, are you back in the life?" he asked. "You are, aren't you?"

Grossman sighed. "OK, you figured out that much, I may as well tell you the rest. You remember my boy, Velvel?"

Millman nodded. "Sure, I saw him at Max's funeral. He looks good, Al."

"Yeah, well, he's had a little misunderstanding with Luigi Spadafore. Nothing that won't go away eventually, but right now he needs some protection. I came down here to find a couple of tough Cubans, somebody don't know who Spadafore is."

"Cubans," said Millman incredulously. "Al, what about me?"

"You?" Grossman laughed so hard he began to cough. "Harry, you? You live in a summer camp, for Christ's sake. I need a tennis lesson, I'll give you a call; for this job, I need somebody a little younger."

"Rat momzer bastard," said Millman. "You're as old as me. You think I can't handle myself anymore, you're full of it."

"Harry, it's been, what, eight, nine years since you got out of the joint? And what have you done since then, besides lie in the sun and shtup Hadassah ladies. No, this isn't for you, believe me."

"Al," said Millman, tightening his grasp on Grossman's wrist. "I want in. I mean this, Al. I'm going bananas down here, it's worse than the joint. At least in there you figure someday you're coming out. Here it's a life sentence. I'll work for free, I'll even pay my own way. Honest to God, Al, for Max's sake, I'm in, OK? Forget about the Cubans.''

Grossman deliberated for a long moment. Finally he looked at Millman. He no longer saw an old dandy with a tennis racket, or a dirty young kid with the broomstick on Hester Street. This was Handsome Harry, grayer and wrinkled, but the same guy who walked into the apartment house on Dexter Avenue and took out three hoods from the Little Jewish Navy with a submachine gun.

"Harry, it's against my better judgment, but OK, if you're sure you can handle it, you're in.''

Millman pulled Grossman to him and kissed him roughly on the cheek.

"Hey, cut that out,'' said Grossman in a gruff voice. "You want your girlfriends to think you're a fag?''

"Al, honest to God, I'll never forget you for this,'' he said. "How many more guys we need?''

"Half a dozen would do it,'' said Grossman. "You know how to get to the Cubans?''

Millman shook his head impatiently. "Al, forget the Cubans, that's what I'm telling you. Your boy's in trouble, Max's nephew, this is a family thing. You know who's down here? Not right here, I mean, but in the area? Mortie Zucker, Bad Abe, Sleepout Louie Levine, Steinie—Christ, there's a whole army down here.''

"You don't say,'' said Grossman through half-closed eyes. "You know, that never even occurred to me.''

Congregation Beth Israel was the last remaining synagogue on South Beach. Built around the turn of the century for merchants who needed a place to say afternoon prayers, it had once been a thriving little shul. Today it was kept going by a handful of small shopowners, most of them immigrants from Eastern Europe, who wanted somewhere to say Kaddish. On Pine Tree Drive, lined with Holiness churches, barbecue joints and party stores it stood out like gefilte fish at a clambake.

Grossman walked in out of the glaring Miami sun and blinked to accustom his eyes to the gloom. The place smelled of old prayer books, Lysol and phlegm. He remembered the odor from his boyhood on the Lower East Side. Christ, he said to himself, these guys must carry the smell around with them in bottles and spray it wherever they go.

There was a door off the tiny lobby marked RABBI'S STUDY. Grossman knocked and entered without waiting for an invitation. It was a small room crowded with cleaning untensils and dusty bottles of kosher wine. The walls were decorated with calendars featuring Israeli landscapes. An unmade cot stood in one corner. In the center of the room, behind a steel desk, a burly, gray-bearded man in a yarmulke sat, head bent, mumbling over a book.

"I'd like to talk to somebody about a Bar Mitzvah."

"We don't do Bar Mitzvahs," he said, barely looking at Grossman. "Try Temple Rodef Shalom out on Forty-first Street."

"How about banks? You do banks?" asked Grossman. The rabbi stared and suddenly a look of recognition spread across his broad, blunt face. "Al? Al, God bless you, goddammit, it's you!"

"Well, it ain't my sister Sadie," said Grossman, shaking the old man's hand. He noticed that the grip was still powerful. "I heard from Harry Millman that you were down here, I decided to look you up."

"Al, I was sorry to hear about Max alav ha-sholom," he said. "I read about it in the papers."

"Thanks, Zuckie. What the hell kind of scam you got going here?" Grossman asked, looking around the room. "Since when are you a rabbi?"

Mortie Zucker laughed, exposing two rows of misfitted false teeth. Grossman remembered the night he lost the real ones in a main-event brawl at the Garden, against Two-Ton Tony Belino. In those days, Mortie Zucker had been considered the toughest street fighter in Brooklyn. "I ain't exactly a rabbi," he said. "This neighborhood, the guys belong here couldn't get nobody to take care of the place, run the services. And you remember I could always doven, my old man learned me when I was a kid, and he kicked my ass if I didn't get up with him in the morning to go to shul. One of the guys, he's got a pawnshop around here, he asked me one day would I be interested. It ain't much, but what the hell . . ."

"So you sit here every day reading, what, the Talmud?"

Zucker grinned, showing the yellow false teeth again. "Naw," he said, holding up the book on his desk.

Grossman squinted. "*How to Win Money at the Races*, by Nate Perlmutter?"

"Don't laugh," said Zucker. "This guy used to be the head of the B'nai B'rith, a very big Jew."

"Yeah, a regular Ben-Gurion," said Grossman. "Tell me something, you like the rabbi business?"

"Well, it beats shining shoes at the Fontainebleau," said Zucker. "My time's my own, I got a place to stay and Mogen David on the cuff. They got my name registered as an official clergyman and everything. You need to get married sometime, I could do it. One time I even gave the prayer on TV, you know, the one they got on in the morning."

"Imagine that," said Grossman dryly. "Listen, Zuckie, how'd you like to take a leave of absence from being the chief rabbi of Coontown and come back with me to New York? I got a job for you."

Zucker's eyes widened with amazement. "A job? Are you talking about what I think you're talking about?"

"How the hell do I know what you think I'm talking about?" said Grossman. Zucker could be stupid sometimes, but the man was a professor when it came to street instincts. He could spot cops from a mile away, had a sure sense of who and when to push, and never made foolish mistakes. This was the kind of judgment and experience that would be invaluable to Grossman. Slowly, carefully, he outlined his plan to protect his son from Luigi Spadafore. When he was finished, Zucker chuckled and tugged on his white beard.

"Take a look up on the wall," he said, pointing to the calendar with a picture of the Bay of Haifa. "Read the year. You come twenty years ago, you got a deal. Today?" He shrugged.

"Yeah, Harry Millman said you'd be too old, but I wanted to see for myself," he said.

"Harry Millman's in on this?"

"Ground floor," said Grossman. "Well, Rabbi Zucker, it was nice seeing you—"

"Wait a minute," said Zucker. "Al, tell the truth, you don't think I'm too old?"

Grossman considered. "Yes and no," he finally said. "Yes, too old to go back to work full time. No, not too old for what I've got in mind. The whole thing should take a couple weeks tops, until I get things straightened out with the lokshen. Until then, simple bodyguarding, no rough stuff. Yeah, you could handle that. And, just as important, you could keep Millman under control."

"Pardon me for asking, but you didn't mention money," said Zucker.

"Ten thousand bucks for the first two weeks, and three thousand a week after that," said Grossman. The rabbi whistled. "*A sach gelt,* Al," he said. Grossman snorted. "What am I, a shnorrer? You want the best, you pay for the best."

"You really think that about me?" asked Zucker in a soft voice.

"I wouldn't be down here if I didn't," said Grossman.

"In that case," said Zucker, taking off the yarmulke, "you

got yourself a boy. I just hope to God you know what you're doing.''

Grossman called the office of J. Kenneth Weintraub, investment counselor. ''Tell him it's Mr. Foster from Internal Revenue,'' he told the secretary.

''Hello,'' said the man's voice.

Grossman noted the smooth tone superimposed on top of the Brooklyn honk, like a peanut butter and gravel sandwich. ''You J. Kenneth Weintraub?'' he asked.

''Yes, speaking.''

''I was wondering, Mr. Weintraub, does the *J* stand for jailbird by any chance?''

''Who the hell is this?'' Weintraub screamed into the receiver. The smooth inflection was gone, and only Brownsville remained.

''Relax, J. Kenneth, it's Al Grossman,'' he said.

''Al! *Vas macht a yid?*''

''Not bad, Kasha, not bad. I hear you're a big man these days, a regular k'nocker.''

''In your league I'm not, but I got no complaints. What can I do you for?''

''You don't seem too surprised to hear from me,'' said Grossman.

''Naw, Harry called, told me you were in town.''

''Did he say what I wanted?'' asked Grossman. ''It's OK if he did, I told him he could mention it.'' He had told Millman no such thing, but now would be as good a time as any to check on Handsome Harry's discretion.

''Yeah, he did mention something,'' said Weintraub. ''Listen, are you calling about me and this—''

''Wait a minute, Kasha, how's the phone? You sure it's OK?''

Weintraub laughed. ''Are you kiddin'? You're talking to a citizen, Al. The Torch Drive wants a buck, I give a buck.

UJA, Heart Fund, even the policemen's ball, whatever the hell they call it these days. The mayor sees me at the Chamber of Commerce, 'Hi, Kenny,' he says, like we went to cheder together. What I'm saying is, the phone is fine.''

"Well?"

"Al, it's been a few years, y'know? I got arthritis in my left hand. I go to the bathroom, it takes ten minutes, and I wind up dribbling on my shoes. I'm not embarrassed to admit it, you know what it's like."

"The hell I do," snapped Grossman.

"You still got a temper, you know that?" chuckled Weintraub. "You remember the time you and me and Bummy Katz took on those Kraut bastards up in Yorktown?"

"Yeah, and the one guy, the one with the red nose—"

"Un-huh, he busted out crying, 'I vant my mama, I vant my mama,' you remember that?"

"Like it was yesterday," said Grossman, his voice softer now, and a little dreamy.

"And after, we went by Polly's and spent the night with Lean Ilene and Jew Mary? Remember the look on Ilene's face when you handed her the guy's wallet with all that dough and told her that it was on Hitler? Christ, what a night—"

"Well, what the hell, Kasha, the mayor calls you by your first name now. You got it made down here. You're a citizen—"

"Al, I want in," said Weintraub. "I been thinking about it and fuck it, you only live once, right?"

"So I've heard," said Grossman.

"I'm not in the greatest shape in the world, I already told you, but I'm not a fucking invalid yet, either. I want one last roll."

"Yeah, one last roll," said Grossman. "Well, you got it, Kasha. We'll have some fun, I promise you that."

"What happens now?" asked Weintraub. "I mean, when do we start?"

"There's a few more guys I want to talk to down here," said Grossman. "I figure it'll be two, three days and then we'll head back up to the city."

"OK, I'll be ready anytime. And Al—thanks for including me in."

When Grossman got back to the Fontainebleau he found three little white message slips from Mr. Sleepout, Bad Abe and Indian Joe. "Sounds like a vaudeville act, don't it?" Grossman said to the bewildered message clerk.

The phone was ringing when he opened the door to his room.

"Al, it's Sleepout. I left word, you don't answer your messages?"

"I just walked in," said Grossman.

"I hear you're getting the boys back together, you don't call me?"

"Where did you hear that?" asked Grossman.

"Whattya mean, where? It's all over the place, everybody's talking. They call me up—'So what's the deal with Al?' I'm too embarrassed to say my pal Al is in town and didn't even call me."

"Hey!" said Grossman. "Cut that shit out, I ain't into guilt trips."

"Guilt trips, he ain't into guilt trips. You becoming a hippie or something?"

Grossman laughed in spite of himself; it was a phrase he had picked up from Bev. "Nu, you in or out?"

"Since you're asking, in," he said.

"Harry Millman will be in touch with the details," said Grossman.

"What's the matter, you couldn't take a few minutes yourself, tell me what's happening? I have to hear from Horseface Harry?"

"I told you, goddammit—" Grossman began, and then

heard the chuckling on the other end. "OK, OK, I don't have time to dick around. I'll see you in the city."

"Not if I see you first," said Sleepout, and hung up laughing.

Grossman saw eight more men in the next three days. Four were too old or too sick to make the trip to New York. One, Baboon Bernstein, had become a Seventh-Day Adventist and only wanted to talk about salvation. Three—Bad Abe Abramson, Indian Joe Lapidus, and Pupik Feinsilver—were in. Along with Millman, Zucker, Weintraub and Sleepout Louie he had seven guys. There was only one more person he wanted to see—Shulman.

Shulman's house was located on a street of neat three-bedroom bungalows in a neighborhood of retired school principals and Midwestern insurance salesmen, a few blocks off Collins Avenue. There were well-tended beds of flowers in front of the houses, and late-model Japanese cars in the driveways. Shulman could have afforded better.

Grossman rang the doorbell and waited. He had called ahead; Shulman was not the kind of person you just dropped in on unannounced. They hadn't seen each other in more than ten years, and Grossman wondered how he would look to Shulman. He had dressed with care for this meeting, in a sport shirt with some slack to hide his potbelly, a dark brown blazer, tan pants and polished loafers. As he had ever since he first met Jerry Shulman, more than fifty years before, he wanted to impress him.

Their first meeting was on the corner of Canal Street and East Broadway, when they were both twelve. Shulman sold the *New York World* on that corner; one day Grossman showed up with a stack of *Post*s. "This is my corner from now on, kid," he told Shulman.

"There's enough room to go around," said Shulman. "Besides, nobody can own a corner."

Grossman knocked Shulman's papers on the street. "You wanna make something of it?" he challenged.

"Nah," said Shulman. "I don't feel like fighting over a corner. If it's that important to you, there are other corners."

Grossman was infuriated by Shulman's blasé attitude, as if the little kike in raggedy clothes sold newspapers as a hobby. "I'm gonna kick your ass for you," he said.

"I won't let you do that," said Jerry Shulman. "I'll move to another corner, but you can't kick my ass."

Grossman set down his papers and charged. Shulman side-stepped and tripped him into the gutter. Several grown-ups passing by laughed, but nobody tried to break it up. Grossman got back on his feet and leaped at the newsboy, who backed away, forcing him off balance again. "What are you, some kind of a jujitsu guy?" Grossman asked through clenched teeth. "I'll show you jujitsu." He picked up the lid from a garbage can and heaved it at Shulman, who blocked it with a forearm. By now a large crowd had gathered and they were cheering the boys on.

"Let's quit," said Shulman. "There's no point in putting on a free show for these people."

"I'm gonna kick your ass," Al Grossman said, although for some reason he felt like crying.

Suddenly Shulman turned to the crowd. "You want to see us fight," he yelled, "you gotta pay." He took off his cap and circulated among the men on the corner, who grudgingly tossed in a few pennies or a nickel. Al Grossman stood there waiting, unsure of what to do.

"Winner take all?" Shulman asked.

"Yeah," said Grossman, trying to regain some of his attitude. "Come 'ere, kid, I'll break your neck."

Shulman walked toward him. Suddenly Grossman was on the ground, and the crowd spun above him. He struggled to regain his feet, and when he did, Shulman knocked him unconscious.

Al woke up a few minutes later. Shulman had propped him up, half sitting, against a brick wall, and was back on the corner hawking papers. Grossman rose groggily. "My brother's Max Grossman," he said. "He's gonna come down here and kill you." Max already had a reputation in the neighborhood as a hood, but Shulman seemed totally unimpressed. "If you tell on me, he'll laugh at you," he said, and Grossman realized that he was right. He stood on the corner, fists clenched, not knowing what to do next. Shulman reached into his pocket and took out a handful of coins. "Here," he said. "This is from the fight. You earned it."

"You hit me with a sucker punch," said Al Grossman. "I'll kick your ass next time."

Shulman looked at him evenly with warm brown eyes. "You can't," he said flatly.

Grossman saw Shulman around the neighborhood from time to time, but they never fought again. One day, when he was seventeen, he walked into the Cream of New York Deli and found Shulman sitting with his brother, Max, and Al Axelrod. They treated Shulman with respect, he noticed jealously—more like a contemporary of theirs than of his.

They were talking business, and Max ignored his younger brother. "You're going to need somebody to go with you," he told Shulman. "You can't do this alone."

"How about him?" Shulman said, gesturing toward Al.

"Him? He's a kid."

Shulman turned to Grossman. "How about it?" he said. "You want to take a truck ride with me to Michigan?"

They spent three days on the road, transporting a load of stolen radios and appliances to a dealer in Detroit. By the time they got back to New York, Jerry Shulman was Al Grossman's best friend.

It was an unequal friendship. Shulman was more like an older brother, someone Al came to with problems or asked for advice. He admired Shulman's quiet competence, his intelligence and his courage. He had class, never raised his voice or started trouble. For Max and Al and the other neighborhood wise guys, crime was a way of life; for Shulman, it was a boost out of the Lower East Side. On Hester Street there were two kinds of kids—good boys, who studied hard, helped their fathers and dreamed of being doctors; and wise guys, who carried guns and talked about becoming millionaires. Alone among the kids in the neighborhood, Jerry Shulman was accepted by both crowds, sometimes serving as an ambassador between them.

Shulman was the first person Grossman knew personally who attended college. He went to NYU and studied, of all things, American history. He also supervised Max's numbers operation. When he graduated, Max gave him a new Packard as a gift.

After the Japanese attacked Pearl Harbor, Al, who was by then working full time for his brother, received a medical discharge. Shulman refused a similar offer and joined the marines. He came home in 1945 with a Silver Star, a Purple Heart and the same softly self-confident manner he had before the war. He went back to school and earned a master's degree in history. To pay for it, he worked for Max as an organizer in the garment union.

During those years, Al and Shulman frequently hung out together. Although he was working and going to school, Shulman found the time to go up to Yankee Stadium for a ball game or to join Al at Jones Beach with a case of cold beer and a couple of girls. He never bragged about his wartime experiences or flaunted his education. He spoke quietly and sensibly, although Al knew that in dealing with the garment workers he did what needed to be done.

One day in the spring of 1948, Shulman came by the Cream of New York and announced that he was going to Israel to fight. At first Al tried to dissuade him, but Shulman wouldn't be talked out of it. "It's the right thing for me to do," he said.

"I suppose you think I ought to go, too," Al said, but Shulman shook his head.

"If you don't feel like it's your fight, you shouldn't get into it," he said.

"How come everything is your fight?" Grossman flared. "Who appointed you the avenging angel?"

"It's not like that, Allie," he said, laying his hand on his friend's cheek, a tender gesture that only Jerry Shulman could have gotten away with. "It's just the kind of time we're living in, that's all. Don't worry, I came back last time, I'll come back this time."

Shulman did come back, although it took him six years. After the war he completed a doctorate in history at the Hebrew University in Jerusalem and married an Israeli girl named Dina. When he brought her to New York, in 1954, Max greeted them at the airport with a new Cadillac and the keys to a duplex on Park Avenue.

For the next three years, Jerry Shulman was the only gangster in the United States with a Ph.D. During those years he undertook special assignments for Max Grossman, who kept him far away from anything dangerous. Once, when Al Grossman tried to involve Shulman in a diamond-smuggling operation, Max had vetoed the idea. "Smugglers are a dime a dozen," he told his younger brother. "Jerry's too valuable to waste. He knows how to talk to people."

In 1957, after the heads of the Mafia were rounded up at Appalachia and the McClellan Committee began looking into Max Grossman's affairs, Jerry Shulman quit for good. He moved his wife, Dina, and their four children to Florida, where he got a job teaching history at the University of Miami. As far as Al knew, he had been legitimate since then, but he never turned his back on his old friends. Whenever Max Grossman came to Miami, he was always invited to dinner, and often he and Shulman spent evenings together. His association with Jerry Shulman, whom he naturally and affectionately called "Professor," was a source of pride.

After Shulman moved to Miami, Al Grossman found it hard to spend time with him. He made Grossman feel crude and ignorant. Whenever he was around Shulman, Al dropped his wise-guy routine but he had nothing to replace it with. Gradually he let the friendship fade, but never lost his sense of admiration, almost awe, for his boyhood rival.

Now he stood on Shulman's front porch, wondering whether Shulman would be willing to come back with him to New York. The others, trapped in boring lives and staring death in the face, had been pushovers; as Weintraub had said, they were players looking for one last roll. But Shulman was a different story; and the appeal to him would have to be different.

The door opened and Grossman found himself staring into the face of a frail, emaciated old man; Jerry Shulman, he could see, was very sick. His even features seemed pinched, and the straight hair, once brown, was entirely white. Only the soft, intelligent brown eyes looked the same.

The old man took Al's hand in a weak grip. "Hello, Allie," he said. "It's good to see you. Come in and sit down."

"Hello, Jerry, how've you been?"

Shulman chuckled. "I've been better, I suppose. I'm dying. You look great."

Grossman cleared his throat in embarrassment. "Ah, you'll live forever," he said.

"Now, there's a sobering thought," said Shulman. Grossman looked around the book-lined living room, searching for something to say. "You read all these books, Professor?"

Shulman shrugged. "In my line of work, you pick up a lot of books. For some reason people think it's an appropriate

gift. That set of the Britannica over there came from Max,
as a matter of fact. Someday he'll probably be in there.''

"Max? In the encyclopedia?'' The thought amused Grossman and he smiled.

"Sure, Max was a historical figure,'' said Shulman.

"My boy, Velvel, has an Irish friend who said the same
thing,'' said Grossman. "Somehow I can't picture it.''

"Well, no man is a hero to his valet,'' said Shulman and
frowned. "Or,'' he quickly added, "to his brother. How is
Velvel? I see his stuff in *Foreign Affairs* from time to time,
and of course on television.''

"Velvel's in trouble, Jerry. That's why I'm down here.''

"What kind of trouble? I thought he was back in New
York.''

"You don't think you can get in trouble in New York? You
been down here too long.''

Shulman laughed. "You're probably right,'' he said. His
face turned serious. "Tell me what kind of trouble Velvel's
in,'' he said.

Shulman listened to Grossman's account with an intense,
concerned expression. When Grossman came to the part
about the death threat and Flanagan's stabbing, he winced
and shook his head. "It's hard to believe that Luigi Spadafore
would do something like that,'' he said. "Of course it's been
years since I've seen him, but even so, it doesn't sound like
him.''

"People change as they get older,'' said Grossman.
"Anyway, that's the story. Now you know.''

"I don't understand Velvel. How could he have gotten
involved in something like this?''

Al sensed Jerry Shulman's implication; it was his fault
for letting his son get into this mess. "I warned him,
Jerry, but you know how, ah, attractive the life can be.
They waved big bucks at him and he bit. After all, you're

a smart guy too, and you weren't exactly a saint when you were Velvel's age.''

Shulman smiled faintly. ''Touché, Al. Anyway, what brings you down here? Shouldn't you be back in New York with Velvel?''

''I've got him holed up with a friend,'' said Grossman. ''Until I can get some protection for him. There's nobody left in the city, the guys are all down here.''

''The guys?'' asked Shulman, puzzled. ''What guys?''

''Harry Millman, Zuckie, Weintraub, Indian Joe—''

''My God, I didn't even know Indian Joe was still alive,'' said Shulman. ''Come to think of it, I didn't know any of them were still around. But what good can they do you? I mean, Indian Joe must be seventy-five, and the others are pushing seventy.''

''Seventy's not so old anymore,'' said Grossman. ''Harry Millman looks like Bill Tilden. Weintraub—he's a rabbi now if you can believe that—is in good shape. Most of them are.''

''Maybe for seventy-year-olds, but I assume that Spadafore's people are a little younger. Doesn't sound like much of a fight.''

''That's just the point. Who could I get in New York to buck Spadafore? Anybody with any brains would know what the odds are, and even if I could find some guys, Spadafore could get to them. I'd be left with the psychos, and that's all I need. No, the most important thing is guys who know how to handle themselves, and I can count on their loyalty. We're not talking about a real war here; I'm pretty sure Spadafore doesn't want that. I just need a few guns and some time.''

''You think you can talk him around?'' asked Shulman. His voice was weak, and Grossman could see him growing tired.

''That's the problem,'' Grossman admitted. ''Spadafore has no respect for me, he never had. You know that as well as I do. To him I was always Max's kid brother; he never took me serious—ah, seriously. Neither did Max, for that matter. You were more like his brother than me.''

''Aw, Allie—'' Shulman began, but Grossman cut him off.

''Let's not bullshit each other, Jerry,'' he said. ''Maybe Millman and Zuckie and the others thought I was the crown prince, but you knew the score. I'm out of my league when it comes to dealing with Luigi Spadafore and I know it.''

''You've always underestimated yourself, Allie,'' said Shulman. ''You'll handle Spadafore all right.''

Grossman shook his head. ''That's why I came to see you,'' he said. ''I thought that you, well, you could come up, just for a day or two, and talk to him. He always respected you, just like he did Max. You could convince him that the whole thing is a mistake, that Velvel had nothing to do with Mario—''

Shulman began to cough, his eyes watering and his slender body jerking back and forth. ''I'm sorry, Allie, you see how it is with me,'' he said.

''Just for a day, Jerry,'' he said. ''I never asked you for a thing—''

''Except my corner,'' Shulman said.

''Yeah, except your corner, and I didn't get that. I'm not gonna say you owe me one—you don't owe me a thing. But I'm gonna tell you something I couldn't say to another person; I'm scared for my boy, Jerry. He's counting on me to fight for him, and I don't know how. Except to ask you for help.''

Shulman sighed and Grossman heard the phlegm rattle in his chest. He stared into space for a long time. Finally he focused his brown eyes on Grossman. ''It's too late, Allie,'' he said. ''I just don't have the strength for what you want. I'd never make it back from New York.'' Shulman saw the disappointment and fear on his old friend's face. ''Listen, even if I don't talk to Luigi myself, we could work out some strategy together. I've got an idea or two. Let me rest on this, come back tomorrow and we'll talk some more. We'll come up with something, don't worry.''

Grossman stood. ''I'll be back tomorrow,'' he said. ''In the meantime, think hard, Jerry. Velvel's life depends on it.''

21

THAT NIGHT GROSSMAN CALLED BEV. "HOW'S MY favorite baby-sitter?" he asked.

"Just fine," she replied in a bright voice. "I miss you, though."

"Glad to hear it. Can I talk to Velvel?"

She passed the receiver to Gordon. "Dad? How's it going down there?"

"Good. You been staying in the house?"

"Yeah."

Grossman had expected Gordon to complain about being cooped up. "No cabin fever?"

"It's all right," said Gordon neutrally. "When are you coming back?"

"Day after tomorrow. How's Flanagan?"

"Much better. I talked to him today."

"Didn't I tell you not to use the phone?" said his father gruffly. "Well, what the hell. When's he coming out?"

"Tomorrow. He's going to stay with that friend I mentioned to you."

"That's fine. You got the number at his place?"

"I got it. You find what you were looking for down there?"

"Yeah, everything's under control. Lemme talk to Bev again."

"Dad, what about—"

"No more questions, boychik. I'll give you the full report when I get back. Gimme Bev for a minute."

She came back on the line. "You and Velvel getting along all right?" he asked.

"We're having a ball," she said.

"That a fact? Well, I'll be back day after tomorrow, so don't get too attached to him. Anything you want from down here?"

"Not really," she said. "I'm all set."

Bev spent the day after Gordon arrived at her house at Temple Beth Shalom, where she supervised the most successful bazaar in the history of the sisterhood—eleven thousand dollars raised for charity and, everyone agreed, a lot of fun, too. She sent Madge Thalstein to the bank to deposit the money, called Rabbi Simon to report on the results and then bought three ounces of Northern California grass from Clarence the janitor.

On the way home she stopped at the butcher shop and picked up a four-pound sirloin wrapped in pork fat and bound by an intricate web of string. Down the street, at Moran's, she bought a head of lettuce, vegetables, popcorn, a bag of potato chips, a round of Gouda cheese, a wedge of Roquefort, two dozen assorted chocolate bars, a fudge cake, an apple pie, a case of Miller High Life, six bottles of Cabernet and three fifths of Wild Turkey 101. "Having a party?" the checkout girl asked.

From Moran's she drove to Brooks Brothers in the mall, where she picked out half a dozen striped button-down shirts, two cashmere sweaters, three pairs of prewashed straight-leg Levi's, white deck shoes, sweat socks and a dozen pairs of colored bikini underpants. The sweaters and the underpants were her gifts to Gordon.

Heading home, she popped Eric Clapton into the tape deck and sang along. The shopping spree reminded her of the days when she used to buy clothes for her kids and refreshments for the parties that she and her husband Norm threw on the weekends. In those days, though, it had been Norm who bought the dope.

People who knew Norm from his clinic, the temple or Weeping Rock Country Club considered him a solid, somewhat unimaginative guy; several times, at social functions, she had heard men wonder aloud what a great-looking girl like her saw in old Norm. Those were not the people who attended their private parties, however; if they had, they would have known a different Norm Friedman.

During their first years of marriage, Norm sometimes asked her in a kidding way if she ever thought about other guys. At first she denied it, but when she realized that he was disappointed, she confessed that she did, indeed, sometimes fantasize about making love to other men. "Like who?" he asked in a thick voice.

"Oh, Robert Redford, Paul Newman, I don't know," she said.

"How about someone we both know?" he asked.

She had ducked the question, but the next time he brought it up she said, "Marty Roth is cute."

"Cute or sexy?"

"Well, sexy, I guess."

"You think Pam is sexy, too?" he asked. They were naked in bed and she could feel that her husband's feet were cold as ice.

"She's got a great body," Bev said.

"Maybe we should invite them over sometime," he said. She paused. It wasn't hard for her to imagine what he had in mind, and she was surprised to find that she wasn't shocked.

Bev had been raised to feel a connection between sex and sin, but she was also alive to the link between sin and excitement. "Maybe," she said.

That weekend they sent the kids to her parents'. Marty and Pam brought a bottle of good French wine. Bev cooked rice pilaf. Norm supplied a bag of grass, an ounce of cocaine and a dozen little vials of laughing gas. By the end of dinner, everyone was stoned.

Norm went to the stereo and put on Sam Cooke's *Music for Sentimental Lovers*. "Let's dance," he said, leading Bev into the living room. He pressed her close and she could feel his penis throbbing against her. After a moment, Pam and Marty joined them.

The song ended and another began. Norm took Pam in his arms, leaving Bev with Marty. She knew what would happen next and she felt so nervous and excited that she could barely swallow. She saw Pam grind her thin, athletic body against her husband. Marty saw it too. She felt his hand run down her back and rub her ass. This is it, she thought, and put her tongue in his ear.

That night with the Roths was the beginning of a long, secret portion of the Friedmans' marriage. Outwardly they were a conventional suburban couple, and they derived a delicious satisfaction from their little deception. A few times they seduced other couples from the club. Occasionally they cruised the swingers bars in the city, often coming home with a girl to share or sometimes a young guy who made love to Bev in front of her husband—Norm wouldn't touch other men, but he enjoyed watching. These sessions, once every few months, were enough to keep their sex life full of fantasy and heat.

And then Norm had dropped dead, not, as she sometimes feared, from sexual exertion, but in his office, peering at an X ray. At first she got calls from some of the couples they had played with, but she turned them down; without Norm, she would have felt like a sex toy, and she didn't want that. She was only forty-one, still a beautiful young woman, but she spent her nights at home, and, after the kids went away to school, alone.

What she wanted was a new life, but it wasn't easy in the couples world of Scarsdale. Since Norm's death, she had had exactly three blind dates—a professor of biology at a junior college who spoke with a lisp, a friend's cousin who came over with Shelley Berman records and laughed raucously at the punch lines, and a man with a huge head and tiny body who had opened his fly at the movies and tried to force her hand inside. When Al Grossman had picked her up at the mall that morning, she had been very ready indeed.

Compared with the others, Al was the prince of her dreams. He was surprisingly good in bed, had a gruff sense of humor she found diverting and was generous, although she didn't need the gifts he brought. On the other hand, he didn't talk much, especially about himself, and he rarely wanted to go anyplace except to some sports event. His idea of a great movie was *Somebody Up There Likes Me*. And, of course, Al was seventy; he wouldn't be around forever.

She had been curious about Gordon ever since she had learned that he was Al's son. Bev was no intellectual, but she read the papers and watched television, and she knew that William Gordon was one of the best-known journalists in America. Several times she had suggested inviting him over for dinner, but Grossman had always waved the idea away. At first she had been offended, supposing that he didn't think she was interesting enough for his famous son, but she soon realized that the problem was with Grossman—he didn't feel comfortable with Gordon.

When Al had asked her to let his son stay with her, she had tried hard not to show that she was elated. She saw possibilities—not necessarily romantic—in the arrangement: if she and Gordon became friends, he might welcome her into his world, a place, she imagined, of embassy parties and country homes full of famous, sophisticated people and clever talk. There she would find fun and laughter and men, unattached or detachable. She hoped it wouldn't be necessary to seduce Gordon in order to win his friendship—she genuinely liked Al, and an affair with his son would be messy—but she was prepared to do it if necessary. She would do anything to get out of Scarsdale, the big silent house and the bleakly cheerful shopping malls.

Gordon had been a surprise. From what she had read and seen, she had been expecting a younger, more refined version of Al—a tough, confident man of the world. But he had showed up on her doorstep looking shaky and uncertain, like a little boy. Putting him in her son's room, instead of the guest suite, had been a stroke of inspiration. So had the pajamas. She wanted to make Gordon feel warm and safe.

When her kids were little, Bev Friedman occasionally allowed them to stay home from school. Those days she turned into events, stocking up on goodies, cooking their favorite foods, allowing them to watch television until all hours and stroking their backs with gentle fingers. Her kids called this "making nice," and she had loved doing it for them. During Gordon's first three days with her, she had done the same for him. She enveloped him in a cloud of warm luxury, poured him drinks and fixed him delicious meals, encouraged him to tell her stories about his foreign adventures and listened with flattering attention. It wasn't a disagreeable task; Gordon could be charming when he wasn't feeling sorry for himself, and he was an excellent raconteur.

On their fourth morning together, Bev sensed a change. Gordon came to breakfast with an appetite, joked with her as if he were an old friend instead of a diffident house guest, and asked what they would do that day. She heard the "they" loud and clear; he was thinking about them together, as a couple.

"We've still got those W. C. Fields movies I rented," she said. "We could watch those, have a film festival."

"Just like in college," Gordon said.

"You did that too?"

"Are you kidding? One semester that's all I did. Yeah, let's watch some flicks. Think it's too early for popcorn?"

"Never too early for popcorn," she laughed. "Since we're skipping class, you want to get high?"

"High? On what?"

"I've got some grass," she said, trying to keep her voice even and natural. "But I hate to smoke alone. I haven't gotten high in a long time."

"Me either," said Gordon. "Yeah, what the hell."

They sat on the sofa in the den, passing their second joint between them. Gordon stared at the movie, but Bev could tell he wasn't really paying attention. When he thought she wasn't looking he glanced at her out of the corner of his eye.

"How do you feel?" she asked. "Are you stoned?"

"Yeah," he said after a long pause. "How about you?"

"God, yes," she laughed. "I'm completely wasted."

"How does it make you feel?" he asked, looking at her directly for the first time. She giggled and put down the joint. "The truth is, dope always makes me horny."

There was a long silence. Gordon felt the sexual electricity in the air. He wanted Bev, and he was sure—almost sure—that she wanted him. But if he was wrong, it would be a disaster. He was stuck here with her and a misunderstanding would make things awkward. And, she might tell his father that he had tried to seduce her, making him appear ridiculous. It never occurred to Gordon to wonder how his father might feel about it.

Bev sensed his dilemma. This was the moment, she thought. She looked at Gordon and found that she really *was* horny. Her nipples were hard, and she felt wet and warm. "Will," she said softly.

"What?" Gordon answered, his voice heavy with excitement. Bev got up and stood between his legs. Slowly, she knelt in front of him and, unbuckling his Levi's, took him in her mouth. She felt him run his hands through her curly hair, and heard him breathe, "Oh God."

They spent the next two days making love, eating cheese and crackers in bed, smoking cigarettes and making up stories for each other about what they thought and didn't think, felt and didn't feel. They pretended they were stranded on a desert island, a place where Luigi Spadafore and Al Grossman, Jupiter Evans and the crushing loneliness of suburban widowhood didn't exist. But it was precisely those things that fueled their lovemaking, making it an act of heated healing and forgetfulness.

Al Grossman's phone call from Florida broke the spell. "What do we tell him?" she asked Gordon.

"What do you think we should tell him?"

"Nothing, right now," she said. She wanted to be sure she had the son before losing the father.

"I think you're right," said Gordon, afraid of antagonizing the old man just when he needed him most.

"We don't want to hurt him," they said to each other.

22

ON TUESDAY, AL GROSSMAN RETURNED FROM MIAMI. Bev and Gordon woke up early, made love in the shower and then ate breakfast. "I'm going into the city," she said. "I don't want to be here when your father comes."

Grossman arrived at noon, accompanied by three elderly men whom Gordon vaguely recognized but couldn't place. "Velvel, you remember Zuckie, don't you?" said his father, gesturing toward a heavyset old guy with dentures and a beard. "And you saw Harry at the funeral." Gordon recalled him, all right—Handsome Harry, the one with the tan who had killed those guys in Detroit. "I don't believe you know Louie Levine."

"Call me Sleepout," said Levine, a small man with a pockmarked face, prominent nose and huge hands that hung from long, thin arms.

"Sleepout?"

"Louie never liked to go home very much," said his father in a dry tone. The others, including Levine, laughed.

"Velvel, get your things. I got us a place in town. These old bastards are your new roommates."

"You play pinochle?" Zucker asked. Gordon shook his head. "OK, we'll learn you, won't we, Harry?" he said with a sly grin. "By the time we get done learning you the game, you'll be a regular Cincinnati Kid."

"I saw that," said Harry. "Edward G. Robinson played the old man. Remember him in *Scarface*? They don't make 'em like that anymore."

"Wasn't it poker?" asked Gordon. "I mean, in *The Cincinnati Kid*?"

"We don't play poker when we're on the job," said Levine. "It leads to hard feelings."

"It's one of the first things you learn," said Millman.

"And no craps," said Levine, pinching Zucker's cheek. The others laughed again; apparently it was an old joke.

They reminded Gordon of foreign correspondents on a big story, full of good humor and adrenaline. By contrast, he felt constrained and sour. When he had agreed to put himself in his father's hands, it had never occurred to him that he would wind up being guarded by a bunch of characters out of *Guys and Dolls*.

"Enough shmoozing, let's get the show on the road," growled Grossman. "We got things to do and people to see."

They drove into the city, Gordon wedged between Zucker and Sleepout Levine in the backseat, Millman in front with Grossman. At Sixty-third and Second they pulled to the curb. Zucker and Millman climbed out of the car, but Levine put a restraining hand on Gordon's shoulder. "Let them check the street first," he said. Up the block, under a green awning, Gordon saw an old man in an overcoat and fedora look their way and nod. Levine tapped him on the arm. "All clear," he said.

The apartment was on the third floor in the rear. "It should be a walk-up, according to Hoyle," Sleepout said as they crowded into the elevator. "This way you gotta watch the stairs *and* the elevator."

"Yeah, OK, but I didn't want you guys dropping dead on me," said Grossman.

"Very thoughtful," said Zucker, but Levine was not appeased. "You do it, you do it right," he muttered.

The apartment was a dark, stuffy two-bedroom flat with plastic slipcovers on heavy old-fashioned furniture and cheap reproductions on the yellowing walls of snowy landscapes and apple-cheeked children. The aroma of boiled meat and stewed vegetables permeated the place.

"Very haimish," said Zuckie, looking around approvingly.

Gordon wandered into a small bedroom, where he found a man in a white sleeveless undershirt squinting through bifocals as he oiled an old-fashioned-looking revolver. He ran a small cloth through the long barrel and whistled under his breath. Gordon recognized the song: "How Much Is That Doggy in the Window?"

"Hi," he said, feeling like an intruder. "I'm William Gordon."

"Velvel!" said the man, rising slowly as if his back hurt. "I remember you from when you were a pisher. Kasha Weintraub."

"Hello, Mr. Weintraub," said Gordon. "It's been a long time."

"Call me Kasha," he said. "You wanna bunk with us? Joe Lapidus is staying in here and Abe Abramson. This is the best room, believe me. Zuckie snores like a bastard."

"Where do we all sleep?" asked Gordon. There were two cots and a narrow bed in the room.

"It's a two on, two off," said Weintraub. "But you're not part of the rotation, so you get the bed. We take turns on the cots."

"I'd like to take a shift along with everybody else," said Gordon, but Weintraub shook his head. "That's not the way it's done," he said. "You're the body, we're the bodyguards."

"I'd still like to take a turn," said Gordon. "It would give me something to do."

"It's up to your father," said Weintraub, "but I don't think he'll go for it. There's a right way to do things and a wrong way. Maybe some of these young punks—no offense, Velvel, I mean some of your younger wise guys—they don't know how it's supposed to be. But your true pros from the old school, it's our second nature. Just stick with Uncle Kasha, you'll learn the ropes in no time."

"How many of you are there?" Gordon asked.

"Seven," said Weintraub. "That was Joe Lapidus you passed downstairs, we call him Indian Joe. Pupik Feinsilver and Abe Abramson are in the kitchen, I think."

"Why do you call him Indian Joe?" asked Gordon. "He didn't look like an Indian to me."

"Naw, he's a Galitzianer," said Weintraub. "He got Indian Joe because he had this habit of scalping guys."

"You mean like tickets, at the ballpark?"

Weintraub chuckled. "Naw, the real thing." He made a cutting gesture. "Like you see in the movies. Only I guess you don't see too much of that anymore. They don't make so many Westerns nowadays, and if they do, the Indians are the good guys."

"He actually scalped people?" asked Gordon, incredulous.

"They were dead first, though," said Weintraub. "Why don't you go in the kitchen, say hello to Pupik and Abe. They've been waiting to see you."

Gordon found the two old men sitting at the kitchen table with a copy of *Jennie Grossinger's Cookbook*. Kitchen utensils, many of them still in their plastic wrappers, were strewn around, and several large pots stood on the counter. When he came in, they looked up and smiled shyly.

"You like Jewish food?" asked Feinsilver. He was a small, round-shouldered man with a fringe of gray hair and bifocals perched on a button nose. "We're thinking about making kugel."

"I don't think we got the right-sized baking pan for ku-gel," said Abramson. His hooked nose and drooping white mustache reminded Gordon of the fierce, sad-looking old Turks he had seen in Istanbul.

"We could use two smaller pans," said Feinsilver. "Or we could make the kugel as a side dish, and cook the roast."

"Wouldn't it be easier just to order in something?" asked Gordon.

"Naw, cooking's half the fun," said Feinsilver. "Besides, what can you order in? A pizza? Chinese? For this kind of work, you need something that sticks to the ribs."

"How about sending somebody over to the Carnegie?" Gordon asked. "They've got Jewish food over there. It'll be my treat."

"Why spend the money when you can cook yourself?" asked Feinsilver reasonably. "Believe me, I've cooked for more than eight before, plenty of times. Once, in the old days, I fixed a whole Pesach seder, the works. You remember that, Abe?"

Abramson smacked his lips, and Gordon heard his den-tures clack. "Yeah, just like Mama used to make. Pupik is a great cook, believe you me."

"You guys had a seder during a war?" asked Gordon. He was pretty sure they were putting him on, but Feinsilver looked serious. "Of course a seder. A holiday's a holiday."

"Here you are, Velvel," said Al Grossman, walking into the kitchen. "You meet everybody? Good. I'm going out for a while, I'll be back by five, six o'clock. In the meantime, just sit tight. There's color TV in the living room, anybody wants to watch, but make sure you keep it down in here. I don't want the neighbors complaining."

"Hey, Al," said Abramson. "You think you gotta tell us that?"

"Don't be so touchy," said Grossman. "I just thought I'd mention it."

On the way out to Brooklyn, Grossman congratulated himself on the way things had gone so far. Velvel was temporarily safe; now it was time to make things right with Luigi Spadafore. Thanks to Jerry Shulman, he had a plan. Jerry was dying, but he was still brilliant. Albert Grossman was not, by nature, an envious man, but he envied his old friend's learning and originality.

As he pulled up to Spadafore's mansion, Grossman noted the hoods on the corners and in front of the house. It had been years since he had been to the brownstone, and never had he been invited on his own. He hadn't seen or talked to Luigi Spadafore since his retirement, and he hadn't missed him. Grossman knew that it was mutual; in the old days, the Sicilian had barely tolerated him, and made little effort to hide it.

He parked at the curb and took a small piece of paper out of his breast pocket. There, in Jerry's spidery, precise handwriting, he read: "Canossa, Gregory, Henry." "Canossa" he repeated to himself. He was afraid that he might get it mixed up with Canarsie.

Grossman was admitted to the tomblike house by Carlo Sesti. He had seen the consigliere at Max's funeral, but hadn't bothered to say hello; Sesti gave him the creeps. Now they shook hands solemnly. "Mr. Spadafore is expecting you," he said. "He's in the library."

Spadafore, dressed in a silk smoking jacket, sat in his easy chair puffing a DiNobli. Classical music that Grossman couldn't identify played softly. The Don took Grossman's proffered hand, but remained seated, a calculated act of rudeness.

"Luigi," Grossman said, "I was sorry to hear about Mario."

Spadafore nodded silently, but his face told Grossman nothing. He gestured to his guest to take a seat. Sesti remained standing behind Spadafore's right shoulder. So far he was playing it just as Shulman had predicted, like a fat wop potentate.

"There's been a misunderstanding, Luigi, and I've come here to clear it up," said Grossman. "I know you think that my boy had something to do with Mario's death, but you're wrong. I want you to know that."

"Why do you imagine that I think such a thing?" asked Spadafore softly. "Have I done something to threaten your son?"

"My son has been in hiding, which you know very well," said Grossman, trying unsuccessfully to match the Don's formal, old-world cadence. "He's still hiding, and I intend to keep him hid until I know you don't believe this bullshit about him being involved."

"I ask again, why do you imagine that I would believe such a thing?"

"Logic," said Grossman. "Mario gets hit. Then, Sesti here threatens my boy. And that afternoon, Flanagan gets stabbed on the street. I don't need a billboard to tell me what's happening."

"I had nothing to do with Flanagan," said the Don. "As for your son . . ." He let the phrase dangle in the air.

"Luigi, I come here today like King Henry came to Pope Gregory," said Grossman, the unfamiliar names clumsy in his mouth. "I have come to Canossa, on my knees."

"I am familiar with the story," said Spadafore. Carlo Sesti was alarmed to see that the old man's face registered quiet pleasure at the analogy.

"King Henry came to ask forgiveness for a crime; you say your son is innocent," the consigliere interjected.

"I'm not talking about Mario. My boy is a famous journalist, not a murderer. I swear to you, on Max's memory, that he had nothing to do with the death of your son.

"No, I'm here to appeal to you to forgive my boy's foolishness," Grossman continued. "Velvel had no business getting involved in our world. I apologize for his nutty Irish pal, too, for the way they both behaved toward you. I understand from Velvel that he's got some papers you want—OK, you say what they are, they're yours. For free. But you've got to believe that the rest of this is just a misunderstanding."

Sesti saw that Grossman was getting through to the Don's most vulnerable spot—his damnable vanity. Pope Gregory, indeed. He suspected that Gordon was behind the comparison; certainly the father hadn't thought of it alone. It was extremely important to Sesti that Don Spadafore believe that Flanagan and Gordon were the cause of his son's murder; otherwise, he would inevitably cast about for another explanation.

Sesti cleared his throat. "Since you raise the example of King Henry's trip to Canossa, you must know that it was merely a subterfuge. Eventually King Henry raised an army and deposed the pope."

"Yeah, well, I ain't no king, boychik," Grossman flared, fixing the consigliere with a fierce scowl. "I'm an old man with a son in trouble and I want to make peace." He turned back to Spadafore. "I'm willing to do whatever you say, Luigi. There's no excuse for Velvel's disrespect to you, but I'm asking you to forgive him. I've come to you for, ah, clemency."

Spadafore puffed his cigar, considering. Despite Carlo's tape, he still had his doubts that Gordon and Flanagan were behind Mario's murder. He would look into it, perhaps use someone from one of the other Families to double-check his consigliere. If it turned out that Gordon and Flanagan were guilty, there would be plenty of time for retribution. Indeed, bringing them out of hiding would make the task all the easier. As for the notion of King Henry's subterfuge, Spadafore considered this merely a case of Carlo parading his erudition; he had known Albert Grossman for fifty years, and considered him to be a vulgar, harmless fellow, certainly not capable of deceiving him.

"Your trip to Canossa has been unnecessary," he said to Grossman. "I have no reason to suspect that your son is involved in the death of mine. Should I believe that, no plea of yours could prevent me from doing what would be necessary. But, as I say, there is no reason to suppose it is so."

"Do I have your word that nothing will happen to him?"

"You have my word that I will not punish an innocent man," said Spadafore stiffly. "Carlo will arrange to collect the papers you mentioned. And now, if you will excuse me . . ."

Grossman stood and pulled the creases of his trousers straight. "Thank you, Luigi," he said. "I hope you catch the bastards that hit Mario and string them up by the balls."

"One more thing," said Spadafore, ignoring the remark. "You have come to me with assurances that your son is innocent. I accept those assurances because I have no reason to doubt them. But you have made yourself a party to this affair, and unlike your son, you understand the rules of our world."

"Sure, I understand," said Grossman. He felt a great surge of relief; he had succeeded, dealt with Spadafore on his own terms and won a reprieve for his son. He wished that Max could be here to see his little brother in action. "Don't worry, Luigi," he said. "You won't be hearing any more from the Grossmans."

23

GROSSMAN STOPPED AT A COFFEE SHOP JUST ACROSS the bridge and called Bev. "Things are under control," he said. "I'll try to get out there tonight."

"Great," she said. "How's Velvel?"

"Last time I seen him he was making matzoh-ball soup with a cat burglar," said Grossman. "Wear something sexy tonight, I'm in the mood."

Grossman drove to the hideout. He was annoyed to find that there was no guard downstairs. On the way in, a stooped Hasidic rabbi pulled the sleeve of his sport coat. "Can you give me a dollar for charity?" he mumbled in Yiddish.

"Get outa here, you old shnorrer," Grossman snarled in English, brushing past the rabbi. "Go back to Williamsburg, where you belong."

"I hope your dick falls off," the rabbi said in Yiddish.

Grossman spun around and burst into laughter. "Louie, where the hell did you get that outfit?" he demanded.

Sleepout Levine grinned through his false beard. "Zuckie brought up three suits," he said. "Camouflage. The beards we got at the costume place on Times Square. You know what? I been out here two hours, I already collected thirty-one bucks."

245

Grossman went upstairs, where he found his son sitting in the living room with Handsome Harry, Kasha Weintraub and Indian Joe. "Al, come on in, we just were talking sports here with Velvel," said Kasha.

"They were telling me about Jackie Malka," Gordon said.

Grossman's face lit up. "The greatest crooked basketball player in the history of the sport," he said. "Played for NYU, all-American, and a couple years in the pros. What a gonif. You heard of the jump shot? He invented the dump shot."

"Hey, Al, you remember that game against Seton Hall?" said Indian Joe. "NYU's down one point, five seconds left and a rebound hits Jackie right in the hands. He can't drop it 'cause it's already there, see. And he's got a guy under the other team's basket, all alone. 'Hey, the ball, the ball!' he's screaming. Jackie rears back and heaves it into the stands, damn near in the upper deck. 'I guess I got nervous,' he tells the sportswriters. Nervous. Christ, the kid had a thousand beans down on the Hall. What an operator!"

"You think they still fix ball games?" asked Gordon.

Kasha shrugged. "The kids they got today, they're so stoned on shmeck you can't rely on 'em to be crooked."

"Nothin's like it was," said Indian Joe. "These young punks don't have no pride of accomplishment. Take Harry here," he said, gesturing toward Millman. "Remember him in court, bitching 'cause he was only sixth-ranked in the most-wanteds? That's pride."

"And sixth-ranked in them days wasn't peanuts," said Kasha. "Waxy Gordon, Longy Zwillman, Bugs, Lepke, the Purples in Detroit, Al Axelrod, Jake Shapira . . ."

Millman shrugged modestly. "Don't forget the Blumenthal brothers in Minnesota," he said. "They were some tough fellas."

"For my money, the toughest was Charlie Workman and Abe Reles, out of Murder Incorporated. What a crew," said

Indian Joe. "You know what it was, sixth-ranked with them guys around?"

"Weren't there any Italians in the Mafia?" asked Gordon, amused and a little touched by their nostalgia.

"Lokshen? Sure there was lokshen," said Kasha. "Luciano was a smart cookie, and Anastasia, Genovese. But between you and me, Velvel, they were never in our league."

"The movies made them heroes," said Indian Joe, with a touch of resentment. "All them big Jews, your Rabbi Wises and whatnot, got to the Warners and the other Yiddlach in Hollywood, they shouldn't put Jewish gangsters in the movies. Better they should be Italians."

"I still say *Scarface* was a great movie," said Millman. "You wanna tell me that Capone wasn't a rough character?"

"Capone? Yeah, he was right up there," conceded Indian Joe. "But how come nobody ever made no movie about Handsome Harry Millman, for instance? Answer me that. I'll tell you why—discrimination."

Gordon laughed. "Why don't you complain to the Anti-Defamation League?"

"Nah, that's your style, Velvel," Kasha said affectionately. "You could write about it sometime."

"Yeah, make a book up about our exploits for a change," said Millman.

Grossman saw that the boys were having a ball entertaining his famous son. The kid loved it, too. He felt a touch of resentment. All those years when he had kept his mouth shut around the boy, not wanting him to be ashamed of his old man, and it turns out he's a regular camp follower. The hell with it, he thought; it's better this way.

"Listen to you alter kockers," he said. "One carload of these young punks today would mow down the whole Purple Gang, for Christ's sakes."

There was a chorus of protest. "How can you say something like that?" Millman demanded angrily.

"Stands to reason," said Grossman. "Look at sports. Kids today are bigger, faster and stronger than our generation. You think Joe Louis could take Muhammad Ali? No way."

"Yeah, but who was smarter, Al, Ty Cobb or Joe Montana?" demanded Weintraub.

"Apples and oranges," said Grossman. "What are you, senile?"

The kitchen door opened and a red-faced, sweating Pupik Feinsilver emerged. "Dinner is served," he announced in a mock formal tone.

They took their places around the large table in the living room. "I thought tonight we could eat, ah, buffet," Feinsilver said, pronouncing the *t*, "but Abe wanted it should be family style."

"Family style is nice," said Indian Joe.

"What's on the menu, Chef Boyardee?" asked Kasha. Feinsilver smiled broadly. "We got kugel," he said. "Tsimmes, a nice roast and a leafy salad," he said.

"Oy, the cholesterol," said Kasha. "You couldn't make something a little more healthy?"

"Whaddya think this is, Grossinger's?" demanded Abramson, emerging from the kitchen with a large pot in his hand.

"I hear Grossinger's is closing down," said Millman. "What a spot that was. Christ, the broads they had up there . . ."

Despite himself, Grossman felt a flush of affection for these men. He had planned to tell them that Velvel was out of danger and they could all go back to Florida. But seeing them together, the kibbitzing, even the taste of Pupik's awful cooking, brought back memories. Why spoil their fun? he thought. They're not in any hurry. He decided to wait awhile to send them home. A few more days, he told himself. What difference can a few days make?

* * *

Jupiter Evans rolled over in the satin sheets and ran her hand along Pietro's thin, surprisingly smooth thigh. He stirred and opened his eyes. When he first woke up, Pietro looked like a deer, she thought—warm, frightened and very sweet.

Pietro wriggled lower in the bed and took her nipple in his mouth. She felt a flush of pleasure. He didn't gnaw it like most men, or lick it, as if it were some kind of lollipop. She had no idea how he knew exactly where and how to touch her, but he knew.

Never, not even that first time with Claudette Lawton, had Jupiter experienced such an erotic excitement as with Pietro. It was as if he had opened a locked place inside her, and all the anger and frustration and fear had come spilling out, mysteriously transformed into lust. I can't get enough of this man, she said to herself. I can't get enough of this . . . man.

As usual, Pietro responded to her mood, tracing a soft hand across her belly and touching her with feathery fingers between her legs. Sometimes she felt that he was reading her thoughts, but she didn't care. She wanted him to know, to see her hidden places. Perhaps it would give him pleasure to feel her excitement but she didn't care about that, any more than a ravenous woman cares about giving pleasure to a lamb chop. She was a performer, and she needed an audience— someone to witness the salvation of Jupiter Evans's sexuality.

For a fleeting moment she saw Gordon's face. What he would give to be here instead of Pietro, she thought; how unfair. But, after Pietro, she would never sleep with Gordon again. He was too large, too hairy and coarse, rough even in his most desperate attempts to be gentle. Besides, the woman he had known was dead; and the new Jupiter didn't want Will Gordon around to remind her of who she had been.

Pietro kissed her neck, just a wisp of a kiss, and she felt herself rising slowly, almost involuntarily. He slid inside her, but by some trick of gravity, she could barely feel his weight. She knew that Pietro would take his time, find just the right rhythm, allow her to get hot and wild until she wanted to tear the pillow apart. "Fuck me, Pietro," she said in a low moan, "fuck me like a man."

Pietro felt Jupiter's thin, muscular thighs tighten around his ass. Soon she would begin to moan and cry, and call out filthy words. When she did that, it was a sign that she wanted to be taken faster. He stole a glance at the clock on the night-stand—six-nineteen. With a little luck she'd climax by six-thirty, which would give them time to shower and dress and drive into the city. Coming to his father's farm had been a good idea, but he wanted to be back in town by ten, when Julie Morganfield got through rehearsing. He licked her neck the way she liked it, and felt her respond. "God, you're a sexy woman," he groaned. He wondered if there would be a parking spot near the theater, or if he'd have to leave the Jaguar in the lot.

At seven-fifteen, Pietro and Jupiter emerged from the farmhouse. The sun was setting and she could hear the moo-ing of cows in a distant field. Everything was so still, so beautiful, so perfect. Even this, she thought, Pietro had known, had sensed her need to make love in a rustic place, a spot, she recalled suddenly, not too different from the lake where she had first been awakened to sex.

Jupiter felt the lust rising in her once again. She knew what she would do. When Pietro climbed into the car she would lean over, open his pants and take him in her mouth. She was thrilled at her own boldness—she had never before tasted a man.

Pietro helped her into the red Jaguar, walked around the car and slid into the driver's seat. As he put the key in the ignition she leaned over and touched him between the legs. She felt his hips move, and his penis grow hard. Jupiter gently opened his fly, eased him out of his trousers and low-ered her mouth onto the head of his cock. Pietro Spadafore sighed happily, turned the key in the ignition, and six pounds of TNT attached to the Jaguar's starter blew them both into a million pieces.

It took the Massachusetts state police laboratory twenty-four hours to positively identify the bodies of Jupiter Evans and Pietro Spadafore, and the media twenty minutes to flash the news around the globe. "Movie Queen Killed in Mafia Love Nest," read the *Tribune*'s headline. "Police Suspect Gangland Slaying."

In gangland, war was declared. Within an hour of Pietro's identification, the area around Luigi Spadafore's mansion looked like Fort Dix. Dozens of heavyset men in overcoats patrolled the streets, or stood stonefaced at the intersections leading to the house. Half a dozen sharpshooters were deployed on the roof, with orders to fire at suspicious automobiles first and ask questions later. These orders came directly from Spadafore himself. The murder of his younger son reawakened in him a ferocious thirst for blood that he had long forgotten, and could now barely control.

"They must be killed," he commanded Carlo Sesti. "Hunt them down like wild dogs and destroy them. Gordon, Flanagan, the father—I want them all dead."

"Justice demands it," agreed Sesti. "You have always been a man of peace, Don Spadafore, but there is no other way."

The phrase "man of peace" grated on Spadafore's ears. This was the thanks he got for the long and prosperous Pax Luigi that he had imposed on the East Coast underworld. Like his hero Augustus Caesar, his sons had been murdered, not, in his case, by the devious Livia, but by the even more treacherous Grossman. He had been too trusting, too soft. But that was all over now. Luigi Spadafore, at the end of his illustrious reign, had no intention of going down in history as the don who allowed himself to be humiliated by an old Jew, a reporter and an Irish madman.

Spadafore shot Sesti a sharp look. "There is no need, consigliere, for you to tell me what kind of man I have been. I am perfectly capable of evaluating my own character," he said. "I remind you that it was you who brought these people into our world. I hold you responsible."

"Yes, Don Spadafore," Sesti said quickly. "I have already called a council of war; this afternoon I will meet with the captains, and we will formulate a plan. There is only one small difficulty. . . ."

"Yes?"

"Flanagan and especially Gordon are eminent men. A highly public execution would focus unbearable attention on our affairs, particularly following the death of the movie star. How shall we handle that?"

Don Spadafore was impressed in spite of himself. Carlo had a cool head. Maybe too cool; he was, after all, the chief beneficiary of the death of his sons. The old man knew that his consigliere was perfectly capable of engineering the murders, but this knowledge did not in any way alter his resolve to take revenge on Gordon and the others.

Over the course of his long career, Spadafore had learned that honor was largely a matter of public perception. In his world, it would be assumed that the journalist and his friends were guilty, and thus his honor could be preserved only if they were executed. In the meantime, he would quietly look into Carlo's connection with the affair. In the event that the consigliere was indeed a traitor, there would be time to deal with him later. But until Gordon and the others were dead, Sesti was as inviolate as a nun. The Don knew that should anything happen to his consigliere now, it would be interpreted as yet another defeat for the Spadafore Family.

"You are correct, Carlo," he said. "I want these men killed discreetly. When you have the bodies, take them to the waste-treatment plant in New Jersey and have them ground into fine powder. Then it will be my pleasure to personally flush them down the toilet. Does this answer your question?''

Sesti nodded, regarding Spadafore with real admiration. The Don had already been an old man when Sesti was appointed consigliere, and this was a side of him he had never seen. ''I will meet with the captains,'' he said, ''and your enemies will be destroyed.''

At five o'clock the war council gathered in the massive brownstone: Bertoia, head of the Bronx regime, Fazzio from Queens, Rizzoli from Staten Island and Negrone from Long Island. Sesti was the youngest man in the room. During the long years of peace, Spadafore had promoted his captains according to seniority and executive ability rather than ferocity or military prowess. Now, seated around the table, Sesti saw four bland elderly men who could be counted on to carry out orders, nothing more.

Fortunately, thought Sesti, wartime preparedness was not necessary. He knew, as Don Spadafore did not, that Gordon and Flanagan were perfectly harmless. Still, the pretense that they were dangerous assassins was necessary; otherwise, suspicion could focus on him. Thus did Carlo Sesti deploy his troops as if they faced a major campaign.

Sesti spoke to the captains in Sicilian dialect, the language of war. ''As I see it, we are up against a serious enemy,'' he told them. ''Not because they have many guns, but precisely because they are few, and unpredictable. They do not follow the established rules of war, and they have no scruples. Gordon murdered Mario, and then brazenly offered condolences to Don Spadafore. His father came to this house and swore a blood oath of innocence while, at that very moment, he was planning the assassination of Pietro. Only lunatics would strike out this way at a superior force, and lunatics can be dangerous foes.

''You have, among you, almost one thousand men,'' he continued. ''Let each regime provide fifty soldiers to protect the house; Nestore Bertoia will command the guard.'' Bertoia nodded, proud of the confidence that such an assignment reflected.

"Next, I want another fifty men from each regime to conduct a citywide search for the filth who killed Mario and Pietro. This force will be commanded by Bruno Rizzoli. Following this meeting I will provide you with pictures of Grossman, Gordon and Flanagan, as well as the information we have about them.''

"Where should we concentrate our efforts?'' asked Rizzoli. "Two hundred men are not enough to cover the entire city.''

"Keep a watch on their houses and on the newspaper,'' said Sesti. "Also, have some people at the airports and the railway stations. Within a few hours I hope to have more specific information.'' Sesti had already spoken to a friend in the police department, who had promised to use his resources to find the fugitives. He also had Grady Rand on the streets. Unlike these jowly men, Rand was a true professional, and Sesti was counting on him to track down Gordon and the others. Dispatch was the key. Prompt action would make Spadafore eternally grateful to him; and, in the case of the seventy-seven-year-old Don, eternity would not last forever.

Gordon and his bodyguards heard about Jupiter's death on the six o'clock news. "Film star . . . reputed Mafia figure . . . Spadafore Family . . . romantic connection . . . explosion''—the words rattled in Gordon's uncomprehending brain like beans in a bag, refusing to stick together. Jupiter and Pietro Spadafore? She didn't know Spadafore. What could they have been doing together, how could she have been caught up in a bombing. . . ?

Then, in a flash of clarity, he saw the entire picture. Jupiter had gone to Pietro Spadafore to plead for his life. There could be no other explanation, no other reason. He could picture her piercing brown eyes fixed on Pietro, begging him in her husky, melodious voice to spare her man. Gordon didn't know who or what had caused the explosion, but he was certain of one thing—because she had loved him and wanted to protect him, Jupiter Evans was now dead.

He was possessed with a furious urge to avenge her. He saw now how badly he had underestimated Luigi Spadafore. The old man was a demon, a nemesis who had killed Jupiter, attempted to murder Flanagan and forced Gordon himself to hide like a criminal.

Gordon had a sudden impulse to pick up the phone and call the head of the FBI or the chairman of the Joint Chiefs of Staff. Hell, he could probably get through to the President. But, what would he say—that he was hiding from the Mafia, and could they possibly send a platoon of marines to Brooklyn? No, it was up to him; he would have to act alone.

"There's gonna be blood on the streets now," said Sleepout Louie. Gordon spun his head in Levine's direction, shocked that the old man had read his thoughts.

"Relax, kid, we can handle the lokshen," said Handsome Harry Millman grimly, but Gordon didn't hear; his brain was already fogged with steamy thoughts of remorse and revenge. Thus it was that William Gordon, two-time Pulitzer Prize–winning journalist, was the only man in the room who missed the lead of the story; it was not the death of Jupiter but the murder of Pietro Spadafore that mattered.

24

AL GROSSMAN SAT IN THE WOOD-PANELED SALOON of the Grand Central Oyster Bar and methodically ate his way through a bucket of steamers. A few blocks away, Velvel and the boys were having dinner, but Grossman hated Pupik Feinsilver's cooking, and he wanted to spend some time alone, savoring the events of the past twenty-four hours. He knew it was a cliché, but he felt like a new man.

The more he recalled his meeting with Luigi Spadafore, the prouder he was of himself. He had faced the Don as an equal, carried out his plan and saved his son. No one, he thought, not Jerry Shulman, not even Max himself, could have done better.

Grossman had celebrated his triumph the night before with Bev. In bed he had performed like a teenager—twice during the evening, once again this morning. "Florida agrees with you," she said.

He stayed with her until about noon, just lazing around the house in his pajamas. Then he got dressed, came into the city and spent the rest of the day pampering himself—a svitz and rubdown at the New York Athletic Club, followed by a long nap; haircut, shampoo and manicure at the Waldorf barbershop; and now ice-cold martinis and steamers. After dinner he planned to stop by the apartment to say hello, and then go on to the Lakers game. Not bad for a seventy-year-old, he thought; who says you can't live forever?

Grossman was too absorbed in his own thoughts to pay attention to his fellow diners. He did not notice the man with the broken nose and dirty-blond hair who sat at a table near the entrance staring at him. Even if he had, it wouldn't have meant anything to him; Albert Grossman had never seen Grady Rand before.

Rand kept his eyes on Grossman out of curiosity, not necessity. He wasn't afraid that the old guy would try to give him the slip. Obviously Grossman had no idea that he was being followed.

Finding him had been a snap; Rand simply gave a doorman at the athletic club twenty dollars to call him when Grossman showed up. He had done the same at half a dozen of Grossman's other haunts. Rand knew from experience that men, especially men as old as Al Grossman, were creatures of habit; they went back to the same places, mostly because they couldn't think of anyplace new. This sort of insight into human nature was what made Rand an efficient practitioner of his art; to be an assassin, he always said, you have to be a people person.

Grady Rand loved his work. The money was good, the hours undemanding, and he was his own boss. But there was more to it than that. Contract killing enabled him to come into contact with fascinating people, and gave him a special, almost divine role in their lives. Death, like birth, was a great existential moment, and he, Grady Rand of Columbia, South Carolina, was its agent.

For that reason, Rand was choosy about his victims. In eleven years of more or less steady work, he had killed politicians and corporation heads, union officials and high-priced call girls, a professional basketball coach, the head of a major philanthropic institution and two left-wing priests. He had taken time with each one, tried to understand their characters and aspirations. Such personal involvement was, in Rand's view, the difference between the true agent of death and a mere butcher.

That is what had made his present contract with Carlo Sesti so frustrating. Shooting Mario Spadafore through a telescopic sight at two hundred yards and blowing up his brother, Pietro, had been little more than technical exercises; he had never even seen their faces.

And then there was Flanagan. Rand didn't really blame himself for missing the lanky Irishman twice; your average layman didn't understand how difficult it was to kill someone. Like any other assassin, Rand had his share of failures, and he accepted them philosophically. In a few minutes, with Grossman, he would get back on the scoreboard.

Grossman looked to Rand like a tough, lonely man. From the way his lips moved slightly when he was lost in thought, Rand could see that Grossman talked to himself, a trait they shared. He wondered what was going on in the old guy's head right that second. Certainly he had no idea that he was going to die within minutes. Only he, Grady Rand, knew that, and the knowledge made him feel like God Almighty.

Rand felt no remorse and he knew he would feel none later. Grossman had to die eventually; death was simply a part of the natural scheme of things. It was better, he reflected, for the old guy to go out with a painless bang. It pleased him that he could do Grossman that favor; he looked like the kind of man that Rand would have liked as a friend.

The thought took him back to boyhood. After graduating from high school, Grady Rand had worked briefly as an ambulance driver. One day he had been called to the scene of a suicide. The victim was a girl he had gone to school with, an ex-cheerleader named Connie Berlow. Rand thought she was one of the cutest girls around, but he never found the nerve to ask for a date. She was the kind of girl who went out with football stars and rich kids, not with Grady Rand.

As Rand placed her body in the back of the ambulance, he noticed once more that she was very cute—and still warm. He knew what some guys would have done in that situation; they would have stopped on the way to the morgue, crawled in back of the ambulance and fucked her. Maybe, he reflected, that was the natural thing to do. But Rand had a different impulse. He found a deserted spot, lugged the inert Connie Berlow off the stretcher and propped her up in the front seat, next to him. Then he put his arm around her shoulder and drove, slowly and deliberately, through the Dairy Queen, where his pals hung out. He was proud that she was with him in death, which, to his way of thinking, was a far more important time for her than, say, prom night. It made him feel very close to her, gave him a thrill of intimacy that he never achieved with living people.

That's the way he felt about Albert Grossman. Of course Grossman was technically still alive, sucking the juice out of his clams, but Rand knew that for all intents and purposes he was already dead, like a zombie. And who was here with him, sharing his last moments on earth? Not his famous brother or his illustrious son but him, Grady Rand. He wished he could make his face look like a skull and grin at Grossman. He decided to kill him from the front, just to share a private moment with the tough old bird.

Al Grossman raised his hand for the check and glanced at his watch. There was plenty of time to go by the apartment and still make the game. He hated the Lakers, especially since they got Magic Johnson. He tried to picture the Knicks with Johnson in the backcourt, and he felt a flash of annoyance. How the hell could they have screwed up the franchise this bad?

Grossman walked out of the restaurant, past the arcade of shops, toward the escalator. The corridor was deserted except for a few derelicts looking for a warm place to sleep. Suddenly he heard someone call his name, and turned. He saw a tall, thin man in a tan windbreaker. Grossman had no idea who he was, but that wasn't unusual. He knew a lot of people, and he had a poor memory for faces.

"Yeah?" he called. The man was perhaps twenty feet behind him.

"You're dead, Al," said Grady Rand, and pumped two bullets into his chest. The shots thundered in the underground passage. Rand saw the winos scramble in terror as Grossman hit the ground. Normally he would have gone over to check the corpse, but there was no time; the noise of the gunshots would soon draw a crowd. Besides, he had seen both bullets hit the old man directly in the heart. Rand holstered his revolver and walked briskly toward the Lexington exit.

A minute later, when Albert Grossman opened his eyes, he saw a circle of unwashed wino faces peering down at him. He could smell their foul breath. Jesus, he thought, heaven stinks.

"He ain't dead," he heard someone say, and Grossman realized that it was true. He tried to sit up, but his legs were leaden and the bulletproof vest that had saved his life seemed to weigh him down.

Suddenly Grossman felt a sickening pressure in his chest, and the room began to spin. "Call an ambulance, shmendrick," he murmured to the closest wino. "I'm having a goddamn heart attack."

25

FLANAGAN LAY IN BED AND STARED VACANTLY AT
the pictures of Martin Luther King and David Ben-Gurion
on the wall of the Threkelds' guest room. He had been staying with Boatnay and Arlene for a week, recuperating, and
he was itching to leave. He had enjoyed spending time with
his godson, Terrence, and the twins, but he felt better now,
and he wanted to get back into circulation. Flanagan was
certain that Boatnay would try to force him to stay another
week or so, but he was planning to escape. With Pietro Spadafore and Jupiter Evans dead, this was no time to be an
invalid.

Arlene knocked lightly and opened the door. She was a
big, handsome woman with a strong nose, prominent jaw
and no sense of humor. Her marital policy was total ethnic
parity—Ben-Gurion next to King, a Barbra Streisand record
for every Otis Redding, this year's trip to Kenya offset by
next year's vacation in Israel. Arlene also insisted that Boatnay do exactly one half of the housework and what she called
parenting, and the big police captain accepted the arrangement with a docility that astonished Flanagan. Several times
he had remarked on Boatnay's dishpan hands or compli-

mented him on his fluffy towels. Each time he had noticed that Arlene was not amused.

"Boatnay's on the phone," she now said. "He wants to talk to you."

Flanagan picked up the receiver. "Hey, Boatnay," he said.

"John, how long will it take you to get packed?" Threkeld asked in a peremptory tone.

"About ten minutes," said Flanagan. "What's the matter, is it Arlene's turn to have a houseguest?"

Threkeld ignored him. "Get your things together, and I'll be there in half an hour," he said. "I'm going to take you up to Dad's place."

"Boatnay, will you tell me what the hell's going on?"

Flanagan heard muffled voices in the background, and someone call Threkeld's name. "What's going on? You tell me. All I know is that they just found Albert Grossman in the basement of Grand Central Station. Shot, a professional job. You could be next, and I don't feel like having my kids in the middle of some Mafia shooting gallery."

"Is he dead?"

"Would have been if he wasn't wearing a vest. They took him to Bellevue. Looks like he had a coronary. They got him in intensive care."

"Does Gordon know yet?" Flanagan asked.

"I don't see how he could," said Threkeld. "It just came in about five minutes ago. But it'll probably be on the radio anytime now. Where is Gordon?"

"I can't tell you that," said Flanagan. "But I'll get in touch with him right away. Look, don't bother to come all the way out here, I'll take a cab. I'm not going to Morgan's."

"Well, you sure as hell can't go home," said Threkeld. "Besides, I want you where I can find you. This isn't just your business anymore, it's a mob hit, and I want to know what you know about it."

"Right now I don't know anything," said Flanagan. "Give

me a few hours and maybe I will. I'll call you when I get where I'm going, let you know what I find out.''

There was a pause, and Flanagan knew that Boatnay was considering his options. ''OK,'' he said finally. ''It's a free country, you can go where you want. But, John, I'm warning you as a friend, there's a limit to how far I can go with you on this. If you try to take things into your own hands, you're gonna wind up with me on your ass, you understand?''

''Don't worry about a thing,'' said Flanagan. ''Oh, and, Boatnay—I didn't want to say anything about this before, but I think you're putting a little too much starch in the sheets.''

Flanagan hung up and began getting his clothes together. The stitches in his stomach still hurt, causing him to move slowly, but his mind was racing. Somebody had killed Mario and Pietro Spadafore. The same person had tried to kill him. And now a hit on Grossman. But who? The old man, Don Spadafore? Why would he murder his own sons? A rival Mafia Family? What interest would they have in Grossman and him? There was only one possible answer—Sesti. With the sons out of the way, he would take over when Luigi died. He must have put the blame for Mario and Pietro on Gordon and his old man. And on him. Carlo, you clever bastard, he thought; wait'll I get my hands around your fucking Limey dago neck.

Flanagan dialed the apartment, and an old man's voice answered. ''This is John Flanagan,'' he said. ''I want to talk to Gordon.''

''He's asleep,'' said the voice. ''Are you the guy came with Velvel to Max's funeral? This is Abe Abramson talking.''

''Bad Abe! Yeah, I'm the one. Give me the address over there, I got to see Gordon right away.''

''Not so fast, wise guy,'' said Abramson. ''What's the password?''

''Your mudda done it,'' said Flanagan.

"Yeah, you're the guy, all right," said Abramson. "You want me to wake up Velvel?"

"First give me the address, I want to get going. Then wake him up. Tell him that somebody just shot his old man at Grand Central Station."

"Shot what? Somebody shot Al?"

"That's right, he's in the hospital. Tell Gordon before he hears it on the radio, and then keep him there. Don't let him go running out. I should get there in half an hour. Tell him I said not to make a move without me."

"Wait a minute, what the hell are you talking about? Is Al all right? What hospital? Who shot him?"

"Not on the phone, OK? I'll be there in half an hour and tell you everything I know. Just keep the lid on things." Abramson heard the phone click.

"Was that Al who just called?" asked Harry Millman. He was sitting at a card table playing pinochle with Pupik Feinsilver, Sleepout Levine and Kasha. "You should of told him to bring over some broads."

"No, it wasn't Al," said Abramson in a flat tone. "Al's shot. Spadafore's guys got him in Grand Central Station. He's in the hospital."

In the shocked silence, Abramson could hear Sleepout Levine's dentures click, and Millman nervously shuffle the cards. Pupik Feinsilver was the first to speak. "Somebody's got to tell Velvel," he said. "Poor kid. First his girl, and now this."

"Yeah, poor Velvel," said Sleepout. He was already wondering what time the next plane to Florida was.

John Flanagan climbed out of the cab in front of the nondescript apartment building on Sixty-third. He looked up and down the street and saw no one. Satisfied, he squared the Borsalino on his head, and took the elevator up to the third floor.

Abe Abramson opened the door, and Flanagan saw the look of relief on the old man's face. "I'm glad you're here," he said. "Velvel ain't taking the news too good. He's in the bedroom."

Beyond Abramson, Flanagan saw six dejected-looking old men sitting in the living room. The only one he recognized was Harry Millman. "I'm John Flanagan," he said in a strong, confident tone. "I'm in charge now. First thing I'm going to do is talk to Velvel. Then I want to meet with all of you." The old men looked at him vacantly and nodded; no one said a word.

He found Gordon lying facedown on the bed. "Kid, it's me," he said, putting an arm around Gordon's shoulder. "I'm sorry as hell about your father."

Gordon raised himself on one elbow. Flanagan could see from his swollen eyes that he had been crying, and smell from his breath that he was drunk.

"Jesus, John," Gordon mumbled. "They're killing everybody. I can't believe it's happening, right here in New York. It's like a nightmare. How could things have gotten so out of control?"

Flanagan was tempted to slap Gordon across the face. He loved those scenes in the movies where the combat veteran snaps the young kid out of his battle shock with one quick blow. But Gordon looked too beaten to respond. Flanagan realized that he would have to keep him away from the troops while he rallied them; there would be time to bring him around later.

"Listen, kid, your father's going to be OK," he said. "Tomorrow, we'll go see him in the hospital. Honest, everything's going to be all right now. I can handle it."

"My father said you were a warrior," Gordon mumbled.

"Did he?" asked Flanagan, delighted. "Well, your old man was right. We're going to kick the shit out of these humps, I promise you."

Gordon grinned weakly and closed his eyes. "Wake me up when it's over, chief," he said, and fell back into a drunken sleep.

Before going back into the living room, Flanagan looked at himself closely in the mirror. He *was* a warrior, by God. You're fucked, Sesti, he said to himself. Your ass is grass and I'm the lawn mower.

Flanagan knew he needed a plan. Taking on the whole mob was out of the question, but somehow he had to think of a way to get to Spadafore and Sesti. He had no doubt that he'd come up with something, but whatever it was, he'd need help. Right now, his only allies were the frightened old men sitting in the living room. Somehow, he'd have to shore up their morale.

Flanagan strode into the living room. "The only guy here I know is Bad Abe," he said in a strong voice. "Let's go around the room and introduce ourselves." One by one, formally and a bit shyly, they mumbled their names. No one, he noticed, used his nickname. Even Sleepout referred to himself as Louis Levine. Flanagan knew who they were, although he gave no sign of recognition; Grossman had gathered quite a group.

"I'm John Flanagan," he said when they had finished. "You can call me Mad Dog." The old men raised their eyebrows and shrugged at one another, unsure of how to react to the tall goy in the hat.

"Right now I'm the proudest guy in New York," Flanagan continued. "Why am I proud? Because I've just been introduced to the goddamnedest collection of tough guys in the history of this city. Kasha Weinstein. Zuckie Zucker. Indian Joe Lapidus. Pupik Feinsilver. Sleepout Louie Levine. Bad Abe Abramson. And Handsome Harry Millman. This is the goddamn Hall of Fame here," he said, letting his voice rise to a near shout. "A lineup of legends. Fucking superstars. It will be an honor to lead you men into battle."

Feinsilver coughed. "Look, Mr. Flanagan, it's nice of you to say so and all, but there ain't gonna be no battle. We're going home."

"Yeah," said Levine. "No offense, but we ain't never heard of you. We was hired by Al to do a job, and Al's not here now. That's that."

"You were hired by Al to protect his son," said Flanagan.

"It's no good, Mr. Flanagan—"

"Mad Dog."

"Yeah, Mad Dog," said Weinberg in an ironic tone. "We were only kidding ourselves. A bunch of old men, up against the Spadafores? Forget it. We don't have a chance and neither does Velvel. The best thing he can do is make a run for it. That's my opinion." Most of the others nodded in agreement, but Flanagan noticed that Indian Joe and Millman looked grim.

"How about it, Handsome Harry," said Flanagan. "You too old to fight?"

"Goddammit, I never punked out in my life," said Millman.

"Me neither," said Indian Joe. He turned to Weinberg. "You should speak for yourself, Kasha. Not everybody here is yellow."

"I'm not yellow, I'm sensible," said Weinberg in a hurt tone. "We got nothing, no plan, no leader except this character, nothing. How the hell we gonna fight Spadafore?"

The phone rang, and Abramson picked it up. The others fell silent, afraid of more bad news. They saw a look of astonishment come over Bad Abe's face.

"Who is it?" asked Flanagan, annoyed that the momentum of his pep talk had been interrupted.

Abramson put his hand over the receiver. "It's Jerry Shulman," he said in a thick whisper. "He heard about Al on the radio. He says he'll be here tomorrow."

Flanagan had no idea who Jerry Shulman was, but he could tell from Abe's urgent tone, and the amazed looks on the faces of the others, that he was someone special. Flanagan scowled; this was his show and he wasn't in the mood for intruders. "Tell him we're not receiving visitors," he said loudly.

Abramson ignored him. "Sure, Jerry," he said into the mouthpiece. "They're all here. . . . Tomorrow at eleven? . . . I'll tell them. . . . God bless you, Jerry. Good-bye."

He hung up and everyone began speaking at once. Abramson held his hand up for silence.

"Jerry said to ask you all to stay until he gets here," he said. "He says we owe it to Al."

"Christ, I thought he was dead," said Harry Millman in a dreamy voice. "Jerry Shulman . . ."

"Jerry'll know what to do," said Zuckie. "Jerry always knew what to do."

"I still say we don't have a chance," said Weinberg. "Shulman's as old as the rest of us. With or without him, taking on Spadafore is suicide."

"Suicide my ass," snorted Millman. "What are we doing down in Florida? I'd a hell of a lot rather go out fighting like a man than wind up in the Hebrew Home for the Aged with oatmeal dribbling out of my nose. Besides, we got Jerry now."

The others nodded; resentfully, Flanagan saw that Shulman's name was magic. Well, he thought, if you can't fight them, join them.

"Goddammit, with Jerry Shulman here, how can we lose?" he demanded in a strong voice. He would find out later who Shulman was and what he wanted; right now, he had no other card to play. "I'm not gonna let Jerry come all the way up here to find a bunch of quitters. Every man here has to decide right now. Either you stay, same deal as before, or you leave, no hard feelings. Harry?''

"I'm in," said Millman.

"Me, too," said Indian Joe. "Harry's right, I got nothing waiting for me in Miami."

"Count me in," said Abramson. "Allie would have done the same for me."

"You're sure Shulman's coming?" asked Zucker.

"That's what he said," Abramson said.

Zucker nodded. "OK, then. You got me."

"You're all nuts," said Weintraub. "You don't have a chance."

"Goddammit, Kasha, you yellow momser, shut up," snapped Millman.

"How about it, Kasha?" asked Flanagan, staring directly into Weintraub's eyes. "Yes or no?"

Weintraub looked at the faces of the others and sighed. "Yeah," he said. "You only live once, what the hell."

"What about you, Sleepout?" said Flanagan.

"Did Jerry say he had a plan?" asked Levine. Abramson shook his head. "He just said to wait."

"Jerry Shulman says to wait, I wait," said Levine.

"That's it, then," said Flanagan. "Everybody's in."

"In that case, we might as well eat,"' said Pupik Feinsilver. "How about some latkes? I could whip some up in a jiffy."

"Great idea," said Flanagan. He went to a side table, poured himself a double shot of Seagram's and raised his glass. "To the men of the Mishpocha," he said grandly. "All for one, and one for all. Today we eat latkes; tomorrow, we conquer the world."

26

THE FIRST THING FLANAGAN DID AFTER DINNER WAS
to call Mike Collins, a retired crime reporter from the *Trib*.
He and Collins were old drinking buddies. "Who's Jerry
Shulman?" he asked.

"Jerry Shulman," Collins said in a fond tone. "Where'd
you come up with that name?"

"I'm working on an organized crime piece, and somebody
mentioned him. What can you tell me about him, Mike?"

"Last I heard, he was down in Florida, dying of cancer,"
said Collins. Although he was retired, Collins liked to keep
up; occasionally he and Flanagan met in a midtown bar and
swapped stories.

"I'm more interested in his past," said Flanagan. "I hear
he was connected with Max Grossman."

"You hear right," said Collins. "He's been retired for
years, though. Teaches history in a college, if you can believe
that."

"A professor? Is he smart?"

Collins cleared his throat. "Jerry Shulman is the smartest
guy I ever met," he said.

"Smarter than Max, or Lansky or, I dunno, Luigi Spadafore?" asked Flanagan, trying to sound offhand.

"Smarter than Henry Kissinger," said Collins with a finality that dismayed Flanagan. "Hell of a lot more trustworthy, too."

"If he's so smart, how come I never heard of him, then?"

"You just answered your own question, John," said Collins.

Flanagan hung up, feeling angry and a little intimidated. Goddammit, he thought, this is my operation. He felt Pupik Feinsilver's latkes rumble in his stomach and thought of Morgan Threkeld. Morgan could help keep an eye on Shulman; he could also prevent them all from dying of food poisoning. He picked up the phone and dialed the club in Harlem.

"M.T., here with thee," Morgan Threkeld whispered in his Isaac Hayes voice. Obviously he had been expecting a woman.

"Morgan, it's John," Flanagan said. "I need your help. Do you think you could get away for a few days, come downtown and cook for me and some friends?"

The old man chuckled. "What's the matter, John Flanagan, you turnin' green from the bean cuisine of Big Arlene?"

"I'm not at Boatnay's anymore," Flanagan replied. "I'm holed up with seven old Jewish hoods, and I need a combination cook and chief of staff. You game?"

"Does a cat have a tail? Yass, Morgan will be there, just hold the chair. By the way, does Captain Threkeld know about this venture in community living?"

"No, and don't say anything to him about it. I don't want to get him involved."

"You very thoughtful for a tall white man, John Flanagan. Who's running your intelligence-gathering operation?"

"No one right now. Why do you ask?"

"Well, I thought you might be interested to know that Captain Bernard Threkeld has put himself in charge of the investigation into the shooting of one Albert Grossman."

"Oh, shit," said Flanagan. "Look, maybe you better not come down here, after all."

"Naw, it's cool. Boatnay don't mess in my business and I don't mess in his. Onliest thing is, I can't be getting involved in any er, ah, illicit activities."

"I just need you to cook and help me plan. And to keep up the morale of the troops. Nothing on the street."

"In that case, as the little hand said to the big hand, see you in one hour's time."

The next morning, Flanagan arose early and found the tiny apartment bustling with activity. Pupik was in the kitchen preparing a spread of bagels and lox, pickled herring and Bloody Marys. Morgan Threkeld sat on the side of Gordon's bed, helping the reporter work on his hangover with a home-made recipe of black coffee laced with rum, honey and garlic. Handsome Harry ran an old-fashioned stand-up vacuum cleaner over the living room rug, and hollered at Kasha Weintraub to take out the trash. The others, faces covered with lather, jostled one another in front of the mirror in the cramped bathroom, or whistled as they spit-shined their shoes. By a quarter to eleven, the flat looked like a marine barracks on inspection day, and the septuagenarian men of the Mishpocha sat fidgeting in the living room, like school-boys awaiting the visit of a beloved headmaster.

Precisely at eleven the doorbell rang. Abe Abramson rushed to answer it, and a moment later reappeared in the living room accompanied by a frail-looking, breathless old man. "It's Jerry," Abramson announced grandly, and then pointed to the others. "Jerry, look who's here."

Slowly, Shulman moved from one man to the next. They rose and shook his hand with great formality, displaying none of their normal banter. Shulman said a quiet word or two to each man, eliciting pleased, bashful reactions.

When Shulman reached Flanagan, the Irishman remained

in his chair. Even seated, he was almost as tall as the old man, whom he regarded warily.

"Jerry, this is John Flanagan, Velvel's friend," said Abramson.

"Pleased to meet you, John," he said, offering a surprisingly strong hand. "I've heard a lot about you."

Flanagan blinked in surprise, and then regained his composure. "Yeah? From who?" he asked skeptically.

"From Al, down in Florida," said Shulman mildly, ignoring Flanagan's tone.

"He says to call him Mad Dog," said Kasha Weintraub with a mocking grin, pointing a thumb at Flanagan. The others chuckled, but Shulman's expression remained serious. "From what Al told me about him, the name fits," he remarked in a respectful tone. The men looked at one another with raised eyebrows, and Flanagan felt himself relaxing. Shulman was all right; maybe they could do business after all.

"Where's Velvel?" asked the old man. "I expected him to be here."

"He's a little under the weather this morning," said Flanagan. "Nothing serious. He's in the bedroom."

"I'd like to go in to see him, if that's all right," said Shulman. "John, will you help me?" Leaning on Flanagan's arm, he left the living room.

They found Gordon sprawled on his bed, with Morgan sitting nearby reading a copy of *Jet* magazine. "This is Jerry Shulman from Florida," Flanagan said. "Morgan Threkeld, my friend and adviser, and you know Velvel."

Threkeld's hangover remedy had worked, but it had left Gordon a bit groggy. "Jerry who?" he asked Shulman thickly.

"Jerry Shulman," said the old man. "I'm a friend of your father's."

"My father's not here," said Gordon. "He's in the hospital."

"I know," said Shulman. "I called there from the airport, and they said we could stop by this morning for a short visit. I'd like to go with you if you don't mind."

"They told us no visitors," said Gordon.

"One of the doctors there is the son of an old friend," said Shulman blandly. "He'll arrange it. Why don't you take a shower and get dressed, and we'll go over for a little while. And, John, if I could make a suggestion, maybe you should ask one or two of the boys to come along, just in case."

Without a word, Flanagan picked up the phone and dialed Boatnay Threkeld. "Hey, Boatnay," he said, "I need a favor."

"John, where the hell are you?" demanded Threkeld. "I got half the damn police force looking for you."

"Don't worry about me, Officer," he said airily. "I'm staying with friends. Listen, Boatnay, Gordon wants to go down to the hospital to see his old man, and he needs some protection. Could you send somebody to drive us over there?"

"Call a cab," said Threkeld. "I'm not running a damn chauffeur service."

"Look, Boatnay, drop the Kojak routine. This is my ass on the line, and I'm asking for help." He heard the police captain sigh.

"All right, give me the address and I'll take you down there myself. But I want some answers from you, John. I'm not playing."

Suddenly Flanagan remembered Morgan Threkeld. "We'll meet you on the corner of Sixty-fifth and Lex in forty minutes," he said.

"Yeah, all right," said Threkeld.

Flanagan put down the phone and turned to Shulman. "You wanted protection, I got us protection," he said. When the old man said nothing, he added, "New York City police captain."

Shulman made a low whistling sound, and Flanagan was gratified to see that he was impressed. "You're not the only one with friends in this city," he said.

There were police guards at the door of Al Grossman's private room, but a nod from Threkeld was enough to get them to open the door. "I'll wait out here with Boatnay," Flanagan said to Gordon and Shulman.

They found Grossman lying under an oxygen tent. The shower and the drive downtown had sobered Gordon up, but he was still woozy, and the sight of the long tube sticking out of his father's arm made him feel faint. "Hello, Pop," he murmured.

"What the hell took you so long?" Grossman said in a surprisingly loud voice. "You been busy, or what?" Then the old man saw Shulman and his eyes went wide. "Jerry," he said in a softer tone. "You're a little late."

"I'm sorry, Allie," he said. "You were right, I should have come when you asked me. This is my fault."

"Aw, the hell with it," Grossman said. "I ain't dead yet. Thanks to you. You were right about that bulletproof vest."

"The doctors say you'll be fine, Pop," said Gordon.

"I stopped believing in doctors when *Ben Casey* went off the air," said Grossman. "Look, Jerry, it was Spadafore got to me. You gotta stop him before he hits shmendrick, here. You talk to him. He didn't listen to me, but he'll listen to you."

Shulman shook his head. "It's too late for that," he said. "We got a war on our hands now."

Gordon saw his father's face flush. "Maybe we shouldn't talk about this now," he said. "Don't worry, Pop, whatever it is, Flanagan and I can handle it. You just concentrate on getting better."

"Handle it, my ass," Grossman snapped. "You stay out of this—it ain't your kind of situation." He looked at Shulman. "Jerry, keep him out of it, OK? He's a good kid. I'm putting him in your hands, Jerry."

Shulman looked at his old friend for a long moment. "I don't think I can do that, Allie," he said. "There may be a way out of this, but we're going to need Velvel and Flanagan."

Grossman smiled under the oxygen tent. "You got a plan, then? I knew you'd come up with a plan."

"Let's say I have an idea," said Shulman. "Look, Allie, I'm going out now. You take a minute with Velvel. I'll be waiting in the hall. Maybe I'll see you tomorrow."

Grossman struggled to a sitting position. "I knew you'd come, Jerry," he said. "I knew you wouldn't let me down."

Shulman walked slowly to the door and opened it with difficulty. "I'll do what I can," he said softly.

The door closed and Gordon found himself alone with his father. "Come 'ere, hotshot," Grossman said. "I don't feel like shouting all the way across the room."

Gordon moved to the side of his father's bed. The old man slid his free arm out from under the oxygen tent and took his son's hand in a weak grip.

"Pop, honest to God, I'm sorry about all this," Gordon said.

"Spilt milk, boychik," said Grossman. "Just do me a favor and listen to Shulman. He's the only chance you got. Promise me that you'll listen to him and do what he says."

Gordon nodded. "I'll listen to him, I promise," he said.

"Good. By the way, how'd the Knicks do last night?" he asked.

Gordon shrugged. "I'll ask the nurse to bring you a paper," he said.

A soft, faraway look came into Grossman's eyes, and he pressed his son's hand. "You know, I've always loved the

Knicks," he said. "They were always my team. A lot of times I'd sit in the Garden and give them a hard time when they screwed up, but I was proud of them, and I never stopped loving them. Know what I mean?"

Gordon felt a lump in his throat and swallowed hard. "I know what you mean, Pop," he said. "I've always loved you, too."

Boatnay Threkeld was gone when Gordon emerged from his father's room. He found Shulman and Flanagan sitting in the visitors' area. "Let's get a cup of coffee in the cafeteria," Shulman suggested.

They found a table near the back of the room, and Gordon brought over three cups of steaming coffee in Styrofoam cups. For the first time that morning, he noticed that Flanagan was in an uncharacteristically subdued mood. "Don't worry, John," he said. "It looks like my father's going to be all right."

"Yeah," said Flanagan. "That's great. Now we've got to start thinking about our next move. The way I see it, Luigi and that prick Sesti think they've got us on the run, which means that we need to counterattack, catch them off guard—"

"Wait a minute, chief," said Gordon. "Jerry's got an idea. I'd like to hear what it is."

"Actually, it's more like a premise," Shulman said softly. "I think we need to examine the inner motivation of a man like Luigi Spadafore. He comes from a particular tradition— you might even say that he exemplifies that tradition—and there could be some leverage in that . . . ."

"Inner motivation, tradition, my ass," exploded Flanagan. "The man's a Brooklyn greaser, I've been dealing with them all my life." He glared at Shulman and then turned to Gordon. "Look, kid, no offense to pops, here, but we don't need a lecture in Goombah Anthropology 101. We need to make some serious plans."

"I'd like to continue," Shulman said evenly. "It won't take long, and, of course, the final decision is up to you."

"Goddamn right," said Flanagan. "Look, Shulman, I know your reputation. Everybody thinks you're smarter than God. But this is New York, 1982, not 1932. Your kind of brains went out with spats and the tommy gun—"

"Shut the fuck up, John," said Gordon. "Mr. Shulman, I want to apologize for Flanagan. He's been under a lot of pressure—we all have. Please, I'd like to hear what you've got to say."

Unperturbed, Shulman placed a hand on Flanagan's sleeve. Gordon could see the blue veins and the liver spots. "I think that John is right," he said without rancor. "He's put his finger precisely on the solution. This is New York, 1982. It's your time, your city. My kind of thinking is out of date—and so is Luigi Spadafore's."

"Go on," said Gordon. Flanagan, placated, remained silent.

"You see, until now, you've been playing according to Luigi Spadafore's rules. Midnight dinners in Brooklyn—yes, your father told me about that—hit men, blood oaths, the whole Mafia mystique. As long as you go along, Spadafore will win. Because he's a master of his game, and you're not."

"So, what we do is change the rules," said Flanagan, interested in spite of himself.

"Exactly," Shulman agreed. "You're not criminals, you're prominent citizens of an open society," he said. "Nothing compels you to take Spadafore on frontally. Play the game on your turf, your way, and you can exploit your strengths against Spadafore's weakness."

"You mean turn him in to the police?" asked Gordon.

Shulman shook his head. "That won't help," he said.

"You have no evidence of anything. And even if you did, his people would still be able to get to you. No, what we need is a decisive victory, something to convince him to call off the war. And to do that we need to hit him where he's most vulnerable. We need to strike at his pride."

"Now I've heard everything," Flanagan exploded. "You think that if we hurt Luigi's feelings, he'll give up and go home? Listen, Gordon, let's get out of here—"

"John, you can go if you want to, but I'm staying," said Gordon. "I told you a long time ago that this was my deal, and you'd do it my way or not at all. That's the way it is. If you can't accept that, I'm sorry."

"Fuck you, kid," said Flanagan, rising to go. "You want to handle things your way, go right ahead. I'll see you around."

"Sit down, John," said Shulman in an icy tone of command that froze Flanagan halfway out of his seat. "It's time you calmed down and stopped being so touchy. Now, listen to me. When I say hit Spadafore's pride, I don't mean hurt his feelings. We're talking about a man who's spent a lifetime inventing himself as a Sicilian aristocrat. Threaten that and you've struck at his most vulnerable spot. It can be done, but not without you."

"What do you need me for?" asked Flanagan, still half standing. "You're the genius, you do it."

"I'm a dying old man," said Shulman mildly. "Tomorrow I'll be on a plane back to Florida. I can give you advice, but you and Velvel will have to refine it into a plan, and execute it. Besides, you have the power, not I."

"The power?" asked Gordon. "What power?"

"That's obvious," said Shulman, looking from Gordon to Flanagan. "The power of the press."

Shulman spent the next two hours huddled with Gordon and Flanagan in the basement cafeteria, fleshing out a battle plan.

Finally, exhausted, the old man asked to be taken back to the apartment. When they arrived, he found the men of the Mishpocha waiting nervously in the living room. He asked Gordon and Flanagan to wait in the bedroom while he said good-bye.

"I wish I could stay longer, but I've got to get back to Miami," he told them.

"And leave us here?" demanded Sleepout Louie. "Jerry, we only stayed because we knew you were coming."

"Velvel and Flanagan know what to do," said Shulman. "We've worked out a plan."

"No way," protested Kasha Weintraub. "You go, we go. I'm not taking orders from these kids."

"I want you all to stay here," said Shulman in the same icy tone of command that he had used at the hospital. "And I want you to do exactly what Velvel and Flanagan say. They have my confidence. If you trust me, then you can trust them."

"Velvel's a nice boy, Jerry, but he's a reporter. And this Flanagan guy's a nut," protested Zuckie.

"That's exactly right," said Shulman. "And that's what's going to win this war. Look, give them two days. Do exactly what they tell you, no matter how strange it seems. If you're not convinced by then, you can come home. Will you do that for me?"

"Two days," said Sleepout, looking at his watch. "Forty-eight hours, and then, good-bye Manhattan."

After Shulman left, Flanagan called Kasha Weintraub into the bedroom. "Kasha, what do you know about credit cards?" he asked.

"What does Willie Shoemaker know about horses?"

"Do you think you could get me the American Express and Visa numbers for a guy named Carlo Sesti?"

"Visa I can get you right now," he said. "I got a friend

at the company. American Express will take me until tomorrow.''

In the meantime, Gordon dialed a Brooklyn phone number. It answered on the third ring and he heard a familiar voice.

''Jacob Gurashvili?''

''Is speaking in person.''

''This is William Gordon. I, ah, purchased something from you the other day?''

''Ah, Tiflis!'' the cabbie exclaimed happily. ''You need another merchandise?''

''I might,'' said Gordon. ''I was wondering, do you ever do any private driving?''

''You mean free?'' asked Gurashvili cautiously.

''No, private. I want to hire you and your cab privately for a week. I'll pay you one thousand dollars.''

''Where you want to go? California?''

''No, right here in the city. Is it a deal?''

''A deal,'' said Gurashvili happily. ''Good deal. Business is business.''

Gordon hung up and winked at Flanagan. ''I got us a driver, chief,'' he said.

''Yeah, and Kasha's going to get Carlo's card numbers. Looks like we're ready to roll. Let's go in and tell the troops.''

Flanagan and Gordon strode into the living room. ''Let it be noted that the great war between the Spadafore Family and the Mishpocha began today, December eleventh, at six-forty-five P.M.,'' Flanagan intoned, looking dramatically at his watch. ''Now, with your permission, Don Velvel here will put you in the picture.''

Briefly, Gordon outlined the plan, based on Shulman's original premise, with embellishments by Flanagan. When he was finished, seven pairs of watery old eyes gleamed with admiration. ''I been in this racket all my life, and I ain't never heard nothing like this," said Pupik Feinsilver, speaking for everyone else.

The next morning, armed with Carlo Sesti's credit card numbers, the members of the Mishpocha fanned out to public phones all over the neighborhood. Each had a copy of the yellow pages and thirty dollars in quarters. Between eleven in the morning and two-thirty in the afternoon, they ordered 419 large pepperoni pizzas from 281 pizza parlors throughout the city. The address and time of delivery were all the same— Luigi Spadafore's mansion at 4:00 P.M.

Flanagan himself scanned the yellow pages for businesses that advertised same-day service. He ordered sixteen collections of doo-wop records, twenty-one bouquets of flowers, three male strippers and a complete set of the *Encyclopaedia Britannica*. All were sent to Luigi Spadafore and charged to Carlo Sesti.

Next, Flanagan called a friend at the *Daily News*. "Mike, this is John Flanagan. Yeah, you heard right. I left the *Trib*. The cheap bastards wouldn't take care of my hospitalization. Listen, I got a great story for you. You know Luigi Spadafore? Yeah, that's right, the Mafia guy. Well, he's holding a New York championship pizza-eating contest out at his house today in Brooklyn. . . . I don't know why, maybe it's like Columbo, when he did that Italian Anti-Defamation thing, you know, for the PR . . . Yeah, I know, it is an incredible story. The address? Yeah, I got it right here. . . ."

At four o'clock, when the first of the delivery vans began pulling up alongside Luigi Spadafore's mansion, they were greeted by five TV news crews, a dozen press photographers and reporters from every newspaper and wire service in the city. Jacob Gurashvili was there too, equipped with a speaker system that blared the Dean Martin rendition of "That's Amore" over and over.

Spadafore's guards tried to move the cameras away from the mansion, and scuffles broke out between the reporters and the hoods. Enraged delivery men, their vans caught in a colossal traffic jam, joined the fray, and within a few minutes, half a dozen squad cars, sirens screaming, arrived to restore order. The camera crews turned their attention to the melee, forcing the hoods to flee, hats over their faces, into the large brownstone.

Luigi Spadafore sat in his heavy armchair and looked out the window with uncomprehending eyes at the chaos in front of his house. The phone rang, and his private secretary buzzed.

"Someone named Mad Dog Flanagan," he said.

Spadafore picked up the phone. "Hi, Luigi," said a voice he recognized instantly. "What's new?"

"I should have known you were behind this," he muttered.

"Yeah, Flanagan's back. Tell that to your consigliere. Flanagan's back and you're going down. I'm coming out there and burn your mansion to the ground. I'm gonna rape your women and slaughter your cattle. I'm gonna crucify you on a telephone pole, you disgusting greaseball. I'm gonna—" Flanagan heard the click and smiled to himself. "Temper, temper, Luigi," he said.

At six, Flanagan gathered the Mishpocha in front of the TV set in the living room. Gordon remained closeted in one of the bedrooms, where he had spent the entire day. The aroma of Morgan Threkeld's fried chicken and biscuits wafted out from the kitchen.

"This afternoon, a quiet Brooklyn neighborhood became the scene of what police are calling the Bensonhurst Pizza Riot," intoned anchorman Jack LeDuff. "The riot broke out when an angry mob of pizza delivery persons gathered in front of the mansion of reputed crime lord Luigi Spadafore, who, they say, ordered more than four hundred pies and then refused delivery." A picture of Spadafore flashed on the screen. "Police believe that the mass order may have been a hoax, but investigators are not ruling out the possibility that Spadafore himself ordered the pizzas to create a diversion in front of his home. No motive is yet known, and Spadafore refused to comment. Maybe tomorrow, Luigi will order a few hundred cases of beer, to wash down the pizza. Over to you, Linda . . .''

A cheer went up, and Flanagan smiled happily. ''We're on the scoreboard,'' he said. ''Wait till you see what we got planned for tomorrow.''

Around seven, Gordon emerged with half a dozen sheets of paper in his hand. ''Tell Jacob to run these down to the *Trib*,'' he told Flanagan.

''How did it go?'' Flanagan asked.

''A masterpiece of disinformation and innuendo, if I do say so myself. Walter Lippmann is spinning in his grave.''

Flanagan glanced at the first sheet. ''My War with the Mob,'' by William Gordon. ''For the past several weeks, some of New York's most vicious mobsters have been waging war against this reporter and his family,'' it began. ''Apparently under the mistaken impression that my uncle, Max Grossman, left me valuable papers, the Brooklyn-based Spadafore Family has sworn to kill me, my relatives and friends—''

''Hell of a lead,'' said Flanagan. He scanned the article with an editor's practiced eye, pausing here and there for an appreciative chuckle. ''I love the part where you accuse Sesti of being behind Mario's murder,'' he said. ''Luigi will love it too. I just hope the paper has the balls to run it.''

''Piece of cake,'' said Gordon. ''You'll see.''

An hour later the phone rang. It was Morrie Birnkrant, the editor in chief of the *Tribune*. ''You don't expect us to run this thing, do you?'' he shouted into the receiver.

''Why not?'' asked Gordon. ''It's an eyewitness account

of the Spadafore Family. I'd say there's another Pulitzer in it."

"Pulitzer, my ass," said Birnkrant. "There's a lawsuit in it."

"Morrie, give me a break. You know what kind of disclosure you have to make in a libel suit. We're talking about the Mafia here, not Mobil Oil."

"Sorry, William," said the editor. "We can't use it."

"Fine," said Gordon. "In that case, I quit. By the way, do you happen to have the phone number of *The New York Times*?"

There was a long pause. "You think you have me over a barrel," squawked Birnkrant. "Well, goddammit, you do have me over a barrel. But I'm warning you, Gordon, you better be right. If they sue, Pulitzers or no, you'll be lucky to get a job on the *Ankara Gazette*."

"Morrie, don't worry, it'll be sensational," said Gordon. "And that's not all. I have another one for tomorrow—Carlo Sesti, mob lawyer."

"Lawyer? Christ almighty, I must be crazy."

Gordon put his hand over the receiver and smiled at Flanagan. "We got him, chief," he said. "I can't wait for the early-bird edition."

Flanagan called Boatnay Threkeld. "Got any leads on the Grossman case?"

"Not much," said Threkeld. "Couple of winos saw the hit, and they think it was a tall white man with long hair. That could be a whole lot of people. It could even be you."

"Bet you a dollar I can pick him out of your book," said Flanagan. "How'd you like that?"

"You think he's the same guy that knifed you?"

"Sounds like it."

"How come you couldn't pick him out last time I showed you the book?" asked Boatnay suspiciously.

"Boatnay, you're my best friend and I'm not going to jive you," said Flanagan. Threkeld waited, but there was only silence on the other end of the line.

"What is that supposed to mean?" he finally asked.

"It means I'm not going to tell you a lie, and I'm not going to tell you the truth, either. You want me to pick this guy out for you, OK. No explanations."

Threkeld sighed. "Man, you are the most difficult mother fucker I ever met in my entire life," he said. "All right, come down here and finger this guy. No, on second thought, I'll come over there. Could be dangerous for you to be cruising around town right about now. And give me the real address this time."

Flanagan went into the kitchen, where Morgan was teaching Pupik Feinsilver and Bad Abe to play tonk. He noted that there was a large pile of dollars in front of Boatnay's father. When it came to stereotypes, he thought, these Jews are definitely antis. "Boatnay's gonna be here in a little while," he said. "Maybe you fellas ought to make yourselves scarce. And make sure the guard downstairs wears a Hasidic outfit. I don't want this to look too much like a scene from *The Untouchables*."

"Where do you want us to go, boss?" asked Feinsilver. Ever since the Pizza Riot made the evening news, Flanagan had noted a new respect from his troops.

"Why don't you get some fresh air. I may have something for you to do in a while."

Suddenly, Flanagan noticed a strange aroma in the kitchen. "What's that?" He sniffed.

"That is a new recipe that Pupik and I invented," said Morgan. "Southern-fried kreplach."

"You gotta be kidding," laughed Flanagan.

"You makin' fun of us now," said Morgan, "but we're gonna have the last laugh when this stuff hits the market, packaged under the R and J label."

"R and J?"

"Rhythm and Juice," said Morgan expansively.

"Juice, Jews, get it?" said Pupik. "The slogan was Morgan's idea."

"No kidding," said Flanagan.

"You won't be singing the blues when you cook with rhythm and juice," Morgan sang, scooping his tonk winnings into the large pocket of his white apron. "I think I'll go out with the boys for a bit of air. There's a pool hall over on First, might could use a visitation from the geriatric nation."

"It would be a sensation," said Bad Abe with a grin.

"My man," laughed Morgan. "Gimme five."

Flanagan was alone in the living room when Threkeld arrived with three large leatherette-bound folios under his arm. "The bad ass file," he said.

Flanagan had looked through the file the day after his stabbing. He had been pretty sure then that he had seen the picture of his attacker, but he hadn't said a word. Better to wait till I'm not so doped up, he had told himself; no point in making any moves when I'm not thinking straight.

Now, leafing through the pages, he looked for the man with the long, dirty hair and the beaky nose, and in the second folio he found him. There could be no doubt—this was the guy. He looked at the caption under the picture: Grady Rand. He had forgotten the name in his sedated condition, but he wouldn't forget again.

"Sorry," he said to Threkeld when he had finished looking through the last book. "I don't see the guy."

"Why do I have the feeling that you're bullshitting me, John?"

"Because life on the streets of this city has made you suspicious and cynical," grinned Flanagan. "I don't know what's happening to you, Boatnay; you never used to be this way."

"John, I'm asking you straight. Did you see the guy or not?"

Flanagan looked directly into Threkeld's eyes. "Boatnay, I swear to you, he's not in there," he said. "If that's not enough for you, then you better put an ad in *New York* magazine for a new best friend."

"All right, don't get offended. I just wanted to make sure," he said. "If you say you didn't see him, I believe you."

"Well, that's more like it," said Flanagan. "You want a dish of Southern fried kreplach before you go?"

"No, and I don't want any chili con tofu, either," said Boatnay. "Unlike you, I've got a job to get back to. I'll see you later, John. And be careful, whatever you do. The guy that shot Grossman's still out there."

Boatnay Threkeld took the elevator down, handed a quarter to an old Jewish beggar standing outside the apartment building and walked over to a white Ford Escort parked down the street. "Here's a picture of John Flanagan," he said to the detective sitting in the driver's seat. "He goes anyplace, you follow and let me know. Don't lose him. I think he knows who shot Al Grossman."

27

GORDON'S ARTICLE CAUSED AN IMMEDIATE SENSA-
tion. Within minutes, the wire services spread the story across
the United States and around the world. Television news
teams cruised the city like hit squads, searching for Gordon
and Flanagan. The mayor issued a statement, assuring the
journalists around-the-clock protection, and the district attorney promised a full investigation.

Gordon placed a call to ABC News. "Peter, it's William
Gordon," he said.

"You're the talk of the town," Peter said.

"Think your viewers might be interested in a firsthand
account?" he asked.

"Are you kidding? Can you be at the studio at six?"

"On two conditions. First, nobody knows, not even your
producer. It could be dangerous."

"No problem," said Peter.

"And I want ten minutes," said Gordon. "At the top of
the show."

"Ten minutes is impossible," said the anchorman. "Ten
minutes on network news is a lifetime."

"You got Dan Rather's number handy by any chance?"
asked Gordon.

"OK, ten minutes, but that's counting commercials," said Peter.

Gordon placed one more call, to Bev Friedman. "I'm so scared," she said. "Do you think I should stay here? I could go stay with my sister in California."

"That's a good idea," said Gordon. "Don't leave from here, though; they might be watching the airports. Drive down to Philadelphia and fly out from there. Give me your sister's number and I'll call when things calm down."

"Will, I think you're incredibly brave. Maybe I should come to wherever you are. Do you need me?"

"We'll have plenty of time later," he said. "Right now, get out of sight and stay there."

"OK," she said. "You know something, Will? Just now, you sounded just like your father."

It took Kasha Weintraub less than an hour to find Grady Rand's address. "Would you mind telling me how you did it?" asked an impressed Flanagan. "Just out of curiosity."

"Well, since you're asking, I found him in the phone book."

"The phone book? Under what, Rent-a-Thugs?"

"Naw, a guy I know did a job with him a while back. He told me that Rand's got a security company in Paramus, you know, something for the income tax guys. The number's in the book."

"Is it a real company?"

"Seems to be. He handles building sites, warehouses, that sort of thing. It's easy work. You just round up some ex-GIs, give them little blue uniforms, and presto, you got security guards."

"Thanks, Kasha," said Flanagan, snapping the notepaper with the phone number between his fingers. "Ask Zuckie to come in, will you."

* * *

Zucker dialed the number. "Mr. Rand? This is Rabbi Morton Zucker of Temple Beth Momser in Newark calling," he said.

"What can I do for you, Rabbi," Rand drawled.

"We got a problem here with the shvartzers," he said in a thick Yiddish accent. "They write dirty words on the walls outside. They pee in our bushes and break windows at night. People are afraid to come anymore. Maybe you could help?"

"Why me?" asked Rand. "Where did you get my number?"

"I found you in the yellow pages," said Zucker. "I don't want a Newark company, they're all cousins around here. May I ask what you charge?"

"I don't usually work with houses of worship," said Rand.

"We'll pay whatever it takes," said Zucker. "We got a special account, the tochis fund." He waved his hand for Gordon and Flanagan to stop giggling.

"Well, why don't you come out to my office, and we'll discuss the whole package," said Rand. "Around four would be all right."

"I don't finish with the afternoon prayers until six," said Zucker. "I could meet you maybe around seven o'clock?"

"Yeah, all right," said Rand. "My office is in Bergen Mall on Route Four. Nobody's there at that hour, so ring the bell and I'll let you in."

"You're a good man, Mr. Rand," said Zucker. "May God bless you and shtup you."

Detective Pete Moore unwrapped the Big Mac and stared at the sandwich. "Doesn't it seem like these things are getting smaller?" he said to his partner, Dan Murphy.

"There's more meat in the Whopper," agreed Murphy, "but there isn't a Burger King around here."

"That's life," said Moore. "You can never find a Whopper when you need one." The two men laughed comfortably.

They had only an hour or so before the next stakeout team took over at seven.

"See anything while I was gone?" asked Murphy.

"Nope, the usual. Oh, there's a pack of old Hasidic Jews went by. Don't see too many of them in this neighborhood."

"Must be collecting for something," said Murphy.

"I guess," said Moore. "Hey, you got any ketchup for these fries?"

At two minutes to seven, Flanagan took a big sip of Jameson's and picked up the telephone. "Carlo, it's John Flanagan," he said. "How the hell are you?"

"I have nothing to say to you," said Sesti. Flanagan detected a jagged note in the consigliere's normally smooth voice.

"Having a rough day, are we? I won't keep you, then. I just called to tell you to turn on ABC News. I think you'll see someone you know-o," he said in a teasing voice.

Sesti hung up the phone and pressed the television button. William Gordon's bearded face stared back at him. ". . . would be funny if it wasn't so dangerous. This Luigi Spadafore is a ridiculous old man who sits around in a smoking jacket covered with spaghetti sauce and talks in parables that would embarrass a third-grader."

"Was it Spadafore who threatened you?" asked the anchorman.

"No, that was his so-called consigliere, Carlo Sesti. He's a lawyer, if you can believe that. Sesti told me that if I didn't turn over these imaginary papers, he would have me killed."

"What did you say in reply?"

"Well, naturally I told him I didn't know what he was talking about."

"And did he attempt to make good on his threat?"

"Well, all I know is that there's been a series of amazing coincidences. First, I was almost killed by a hit-and-run driver coming out of a restaurant. Then, my fiancée, Jupiter Evans, was murdered, and my close friend, John Flanagan, was . . .''

Sesti stared at the screen in disbelief. That contemptible liar, he thought, deliberately twisting the facts to protect himself. And ABC—how could a responsible network broadcast such libelous charges? He had seen abuses of power in his life, but this was the most brazen, outrageous . . .

He was interrupted by the telephone. "Carlo," growled Don Spadafore, "are you watching the news?"

"Yes," said Sesti. "I was just planning to place a call to the head of the network, demanding an apology."

"They're crucifying me on television, consigliere, and you speak of apologies. I have already received calls from our friends in Detroit and Philadelphia. They say that this attention could be ruinous, and they are right. To them I said that it will soon stop. To you, consigliere, I say that you were the one who brought Gordon into our world, and he is your responsibility."

Sesti felt a chill at the menace in Spadafore's voice. "I assure you, as a lawyer, that Gordon has nothing whatever that could incriminate us," he said. "The only papers he saw were fictitious. I anticipated that he might—"

"You anticipated nothing," said Spadafore. "We are being publicly humiliated and you do nothing to stop it. If I wanted a moron for consigliere, I would have appointed Mario. Perhaps if I had, he would still be alive." He hung up, leaving Sesti with a dead receiver next to his ear.

Sesti forced himself to stay calm. He hadn't heard from Grady Rand since noon, and he wanted an immediate status report. Perhaps he could pick up Gordon's trail from someone at ABC. Rand had told him that he would be at his office between seven and eight. He dialed the number and let it ring fourteen times, but there was no answer. Maybe he's already on his way to the studio, Sesti thought hopefully.

* * *

Shortly after eight, Indian Joe, Zuckie and Handsome Harry returned to the apartment. They wore black Hasidic outfits, and Zuckie carried a hatbox. Jacob Gurashvili was with them, dressed in a Barry Manilow–type suit.

"Everything go OK?" asked Flanagan.

"A piece of cheesecake," said Millman, showing his white teeth. "It's like riding a bicycle. You never forget how."

"What do we do with this, boss?" asked Zuckie, gesturing to the hatbox.

Flanagan turned to Abramson. "Abe, you think that you could break into Carlo Sesti's office? It's in a building on West Fifty-seventh."

"I imagine I could handle it," said Abramson. "I've broken into better places."

"Good," said Flanagan. "I've got a little errand for you."

The following morning, Carlo Sesti arrived at his office shortly before eight. A night's rest had restored his spirits and his self-confidence. The storm of publicity was bad, of course, but it would blow over. The main thing, he told himself, was that Flanagan and Gordon had no proof of anything. When this fact came to light, he was quite certain that he could extract public apologies from ABC and the *Tribune*. This, he hoped, would go a long way toward mollifying the Don's outraged dignity.

Sesti realized that Spadafore was his major problem at the moment. The old man was positively crazed with a desire for revenge, but the consigliere saw that it was now impossible to strike at the two journalists. If something were to happen to them it would constitute prima facie evidence that he and Spadafore were responsible. Somehow he would have to find Grady Rand and tell him to call off the contracts temporarily.

Sesti entered his private office and sensed, before he actually saw, that something was awry. His gaze wandered around the large room, and rested on his gleaming desk. He saw something that hadn't been there the night before—a white plastic dummy's head, of the kind used to display wigs. Perched on the head was an unruly mop of yellowish hair.

Carlo moved closer, and saw that there was caked blood around the scalp. He also found a note, attached to his desk. Printed in neat block letters, it read: "Carlo had a little lamb, his fleece was dirty blond; and if he wants to look for him, he better drain the pond." It was signed, "The Mishpocha."

Sesti looked at the bloody scalp in horrified disbelief, and felt his stomach rise in a rush. "My God," he said to the empty room, and vomited all over his two-thousand-dollar suit.

28

THE MEDIA WAR AGAINST THE SPADAFORE FAMILY
reached a climax over the weekend. First, *Saturday Night
Live* ran a skit called "Fat Luigi and the Spaghettifore Family" about a gang that stole food to feed their insatiable
leader. Then, the following morning, on *Meet the Press*, Senator Danworthy announced the creation of a Senate subcom-
mittee on organized crime to look into the Gordon Affair, as
it was already being called on the national news.

Half an hour after *Meet the Press*, Carlo Sesti's phone
rang. "Be at my house at five this afternoon," said Luigi
Spadafore curtly.

Sesti took a Valium and put on a black business suit. He
anticipated a rough session with the Don, and the worst of it
was, he had no real solution to their problem. The media
were like a swarm of vicious bees, and the consigliere had
no idea of how to fight back. Given time, he was certain that
he could find the answer; but Don Spadafore was manifestly
running out of patience.

When Sesti arrived in Brooklyn, he noticed that the extra
men were no longer on duty in front of the brownstone, and
the sharpshooters had been removed from the roof. "Who

gave the order to reduce the guard?'' he demanded of Nestore Bertoia, who was waiting for him outside the house.

"I did, Carlo," he said. There was an annoying familiarity in the capporegime's voice.

"On what authority, may I ask?"

"You mean, who told me to? The Don. You got a beef, take it up with him."

Sesti let himself into the mansion and went directly to the Don's study. As usual, the old man was seated in his easy chair near the fireplace. Sitting next to him was John Flanagan.

The consigliere felt a stab of annoyance. Somehow Spadafore had captured Flanagan, succeeded where he himself had failed. Probably he had found the Irishman by dumb luck, but even so, it was a humiliating turn of events. Sesti gave the Don a warm, boyish smile. "I see, Don Spadafore, that you have caught one of our elusive butterflies," he said in Sicilian. "There is still much a young man can learn from the master. Now we must decide how to dispose of him. I have some—"

"Speak English, Carlo," the old man interrupted harshly. "Mr. Flanagan does not speak Sicilian."

"Yes, of course," said Sesti in a chastened voice. Obviously the Don planned to rub it in. "I was just going to offer a suggestion about what to do with him."

"That decision has already been made," said Spadafore. Flanagan, brazen as ever, nodded in affirmation.

"May I inquire what you have decided?" asked Sesti.

"You may. I have just appointed Mr. Flanagan to the position of counselor."

Sesti looked at Spadafore with dumb amazement. "Counselor?" he stammered. "I don't understand."

"That's the English word for consigliere," said Flanagan, speaking for the first time. "You should get yourself a dictionary, Carlo."

"Surely this is a joke," Sesti said, trying to recover his poise. "You do not actually intend to appoint this, this lunatic, to the post of consigliere?"

The Don shook his large head slowly and allowed himself a smile. With his heavy eyelids and large, yellow teeth he looked to Sesti like a dull, malign mastiff. "Not consigliere," he said. "Media counselor. I believe that is the appropriate term, is it not?"

"But I do not understand," said Sesti. "Media counselor?"

"The last few days have taught me that we are living in the electronic age, Carlo, and a wise man adapts himself to the times. Mr. Flanagan and his friend, William Gordon, have given me a lesson in the power of the media; and I intend to harness that power for my own purposes. Now do you understand?"

Sesti threw his arms open in a Sicilian gesture of admiration. "It is a brilliant strategy, Don Spadafore. I am ashamed that I did not think of it myself, but, as I said before, there is much to learn from the master." He turned to Flanagan and extended his hand. "Welcome to our Family," he said. "It will be a pleasure to work together."

Flanagan took the outstretched hand in his own, and tickled Sesti's palm with his middle finger. The consigliere jumped in surprise, and Flanagan winked.

"Perhaps the reason that you did not think of this yourself is that you have been too busy with other matters recently," said the Don. "Murder is a very time-consuming business."

"Murder?" said Sesti, keeping his face expressionless by an act of will. "Ah, you mean Grossman. But of course, Don Spadafore, he is not dead. And, in any event, that was carried out on your orders."

"I do not mean Grossman," said Spadafore in a tight voice. "I mean the murder of my sons."

Sesti felt a cold chill in the pit of his stomach. "Surely

Don Spadafore, you don't believe that *I* could have been involved with the murders of Mario and Pietro. Here is the murderer,'' he exclaimed, pointing dramatically at Flanagan. ''This man whom you wish to appoint counselor and his friend took the lives of your sons. You must believe that.''

''We have played that comedy long enough,'' said Spadafore. ''You are an analytical man, Carlo, and so I will explain my reasoning to you. That is,'' he added with fine irony, ''with your permission, consigliere.'' Sesti, speechless, merely nodded.

''First, may I say that I never entirely believed that Gordon and Flanagan killed Mario. At my age you learn that people rarely act out of character, and murder is not in the character of two journalists. And so, from the beginning, my suspicions were aroused. That is the reason I accepted Albert Grossman's assurance of his son's innocence.''

''But Pietro,'' said Sesti. ''You yourself told me after Pietro's death that Gordon and Flanagan were to be held accountable.''

''That is true,'' said Spadafore. ''At the time, it appeared the most probable explanation. But that was before Gordon's article appeared. I had no idea that the girl, Jupiter Evans, was his fiancée. I asked myself, why would a man murder his own future bride, simply to kill my son. It seemed illogical.''

''That bothered me, too,'' said Sesti quickly. ''But of course, these men are amateurs. Perhaps it was simply an accident that the girl was there.''

''Possible, I grant you,'' said the Don reasonably. ''Unlikely, but still possible. On the other hand, I began to think—who is the true beneficiary of this string of murders? And to that there was only one answer—it was you, Carlo.''

''And on the basis of such reasoning, you accuse me of killing your sons?''

''I am a cautious man, consigliere, and, I hope, a just one.

Certainty required more, and luckily, Mr. Flanagan has provided it.''

"Flanagan? What has he told you?''

"Carlo, do you know a man named Grady Rand?''

For a split second, Sesti considered lying, but he realized that the old man would not have asked if he did not already know the answer. "Rand was an assassin. I used him for the Grossman job,'' he said.

"Yes, it is in here,'' said Spadafore, producing a small leather notebook. "This belonged to Rand. On the day that Albert Grossman was shot there is a notation—'A.G.' It may interest you to know that 'M.S.' appears on the day that Mario was shot, and 'P.S.' on the day that Pietro was blown up. What is your explanation for this, consigliere?''

"Where did you get that notebook?'' Sesti demanded.

"Mr. Flanagan brought it to me early this morning,'' said the Don.

"He could have written those initials himself,'' Sesti sputtered. "This is a forgery. I'm certain of it.''

The Don shook his head. "I asked Arturo Pasterno to check the writing against the other notations in the book,'' he said. "It is identical.''

"Dum de dum dum,'' Flanagan sang the ominous first notes of the theme song to *Dragnet*. "He's got you there, Carlo old chap.''

"You, bastard!'' Sesti spit between clenched teeth. "You did this.''

Flanagan stared at him with ingenuous blue eyes and shook his head. He had to admire the consigliere's fighting spirit and his quick, devious mind. Sesti had figured out right away that the initials were forged; whereas it had taken Flanagan himself half an hour to come up with the idea, and another hour for Sleepout Levine to actually copy Rand's handwriting.

"Don Spadafore, this man is lying. I give you my most solemn assurances—"

The door opened and Sesti saw Bertoia and Rizzoli. "You may save your assurances for God," said the old man. "Good-bye, Carlo. In many ways you were a good consigliere. Perhaps we will meet someday in heaven." The pleasantry was insincere. Although Don Spadafore feared that it might be blasphemy, deep in his heart he believed that God had a special part of heaven reserved for Men of Respect.

29

GORDON SAT AT THE LONG TABLE IN THE FRONT OF the wood-paneled private dining room in the Waldorf, and fiddled with his silver butter knife. It had been two days since Flanagan's meeting with Spadafore, two days since Flanagan had reported on that meeting over drinks at O'Dwyer's. Now, watching the lanky Irishman, resplendent in his shining black dinner jacket, greet his guests, Gordon still couldn't believe that conversation.

"He offered you what?" Gordon had asked in an incredulous tone.

"You heard me, pal," said Flanagan. "As of this morning, you're looking at the new media consultant of the Spadafore Family. Of course, it's really the consigliere job, but Luigi is too traditional to appoint an Irishman. But it amounts to the same thing." Flanagan raised his glass of Jameson's. "L'chayim, kid," he toasted himself.

"Flanagan, of all the insane shit that's happened the past few weeks, this has got to be the craziest. What the hell does Luigi Spadafore need with a media consultant?"

"Are you kidding? After the job we did on him, image is his biggest problem. He's got a Senate committee on his ass, and Eddie Murphy doing bits on him on television. He figured that if I could get him into this, I can get him out. He's right, too, that smart old bastard. By the time I'm finished, half the country's going to be calling him Uncle Luigi.''

"What about Sesti? What's Luigi going to do with him?''

Flanagan grinned broadly. "I think he's already done it,'' he said. "See, I explained to him that Carlo was the one who had his kids numbed. Which, by the way, happens to be true, not that it matters all that much. And you know how sentimental Luigi is about his boys. So, good-bye Carlo, hello Mad Dog.''

"We're off the hook,'' said Gordon, more to himself than to Flanagan. "I can hardly believe that this nightmare's over.''

"One man's nightmare is another man's daydream,'' said Flanagan, rubbing his stomach lightly; the scar was still tender. "I'm really sorry about your father, and Jupiter, but I've got to admit that from my point of view, this could have ended a lot worse.''

"You really think you can get good PR for Spadafore?'' Gordon asked, intrigued in spite of himself.

"Well, not right away, not directly. See, the real problem is that people have the wrong idea about organized crime. They picture it as a bunch of, I guess you could say, criminals. The thing is to let them see the warm, human side of the underworld, the kind of things we've seen the last few weeks.''

"What I've seen are half a dozen murders and a bunch of crazed thugs combing the city with automatic weapons,'' said Gordon. "I don't think even you could make that play in Peoria.''

"Yeah, but you've seen some other things, too,'' said Flanagan. "Those old guys your dad rounded up are some of the most lovable characters around. When I told them the war was over, you should have seen how disappointed they were about going back to Florida. They still don't know that old Mad Dog Flanagan has other plans for them—''

Suddenly a heavy hand on Gordon's shoulder snapped him out of his reverie. He looked up and saw Mortie Zucker's yellow-toothed smile. ''This is a hell of a going-away party, Velvel,'' he said, gesturing broadly toward Flanagan. ''I'll give that guy one thing, he's got class.''

''You're not just beating your gums,'' said Handsome Harry, joining them. Millman gave his dinner jacket a fastidious tug and took a noisy sip of champagne. ''Hell of an evening—black tie, bubbly, the whole shmeer. Reminds me of way back when.''

''Yeah,'' said Zucker. ''How's Al doing, Velvel?''

''A lot better,'' said Gordon. The mention of his father's name made him uncomfortable. Ever since their reconciliation at the hospital, he had been feeling distinctly guilty about Bev, and uncertain what to do next. Not about Bev—he had no intention of seeing her again—but about his father. A part of him wanted to confess, apologize and gain absolution. But, Gordon realized, a part of that part wanted to do this just to see the look on the old man's face when he found out.

Gordon heard the tinkle of silver on crystal; Flanagan was calling on the guests to take their seats. ''Just look for your card,'' he said.

Next to each plate was a formal place card inscribed with a nom de guerre: Sleepout Louie, Indian Joe, Pupik, Bad Abe, Handsome Harry, Zuckie the Rabbi, Kasha and Morgan the Magnificent. Gordon rose, found his own card and grinned in spite of himself. It read, ''The Pulitzer Kid.''

''Gentlemen, before we begin the evening, I want to ask our spiritual leader, Rabbi Zucker, to lead us in prayer,'' said Flanagan.

Zucker stood, fished a black yarmulke out of his pocket and placed it over his bald spot. He clenched and unclenched his powerful fists, and then placed his right hand over his heart, like a Boy Scout. "Um, *Baruch ata Adonai, Elohaynu melech ha-olam,* thanks for everything, God, amen," he said, and sat down to appreciative cheers and laughter.

"Hey, that's not supposed to be funny." Zucker scowled, and the men laughed harder. Only Flanagan kept a straight face. He let the laughter go on for only a few seconds before tinkling the room back to silence.

"Thank you for those inspiring words, Zuckie," he said. "And thank all of you for coming here tonight. Men of the Mishpocha," he intoned solemnly, raising his glass and gesturing for them to raise theirs, "I salute you. You came, you saw and you conquered!" Flanagan gulped his champagne, and then threw his glass against the wall with a powerful gesture. The others did the same.

Flanagan faced them, legs spread, hands on his hips. "Men, it has been a pleasure to lead you in battle. Together, we have made history. Thanks to you, we have made the peace with the Spadafores."

A cheer went up as the old men slapped each other on the back and pounded the table. Flanagan held up his hand for quiet. "You have fulfilled your part of our bargain, and I have some envelopes here," he said, tapping his breast pocket. "Believe me, nobody ever earned their money more than you guys."

"Yeah, you and Velvel weren't so bad either," said Sleepout Louie, and the others applauded. Gordon shook his head modestly, but Flanagan beamed.

"For some of you, tonight is a good-bye party," said Flanagan. "But no party is complete without a few surprises. Bad Abe, will you get the door?"

A murmur went up as Abrams walked across the thick red carpet and opened the polished oak door. The murmur turned into a cheer as Al Grossman entered the room in a wheelchair, pushed by a blond nurse of about thirty, dressed in a tight-fitting white uniform.

"Al, you look great," hollered Handsome Harry.

"Look at him, just like FDR," bellowed Indian Joe.

"Who's the chippie, Al?" called out Kasha Weintraub, and the others, including the nurse, laughed appreciatively. Gordon noticed that his father's color had returned; he looked as healthy as ever. He also noticed that the young blonde was gently stroking the back of Grossman's neck.

"Behave yourselves, you galoots," Grossman growled affectionately. "Say hello to Nancy the nurse. Velvel, come over here a minute."

Gordon felt Flanagan gently pushing him to his feet. He walked over to the wheelchair, bent over and gave his father a kiss on his rough cheek. "I didn't know you'd be here, Pop," he said.

"I wanted to surprise you," he said. "Wheel me over to the corner there, I want to talk to you. Nancy, sit next to Handsome Harry and have some bubbly. But no hanky-panky."

Gordon pushed his father to the far end of the room, and pulled up a chair next to him. "Not bad, eh?" Grossman said, gesturing toward Nancy. "You know something? It's true what they say about nurses."

"Pop, don't you think that it's a little early—"

"Yeah, I got all the time in the world. Listen to me, boychik, I decided that I need a change. I'm moving to Florida. And I'm taking Nancy the nurse over there with me."

"Florida? With her? What for?"

Grossman gave him an amused look. "A bedside romance, boychik, what's the matter, you never saw *General Hospital*? Don't worry, I'm not planning to marry her, I just want some hands-on health care while I'm recuperating."

"What about Bev?" Gordon blurted, hoping that his voice didn't betray any guilt.

"Yeah, Bev," said Grossman, looking at his son steadily. "I was hoping you could help me out there."

"Me? How?"

"I got the idea that you and Bev got to be on good terms while I was away," Grossman said. "She's a good-looking broad, you're a nice young guy . . ."

Suddenly Gordon saw the whole picture. It was the Pulitzer Prize all over again, his old man trying to arrange his life. He waited for the angry lump to rise in his throat, but to his surprise, there was only a warm feeling of affection. Jewish fathers, he thought with an inward sigh; they never quit, but they only want what's best for their kids.

"Listen, Pop," he said. "Bev Friedman's a nice woman, but she's your friend, not mine. Besides, I'm leaving in two weeks. I asked the paper to send me back overseas." Sure-footed in Beirut and Baghdad, Gordon felt out of his depth in Brooklyn. He knew that Flanagan would try to drag him into his new life, and he had had enough of the world of the Spadafores.

"Overseas, eh?" grunted Grossman. "Well, it's your life. Listen, boychik, I don't feel so hot. Ask Nancy the nurse to come over, I want to head back to the hospital."

"Sure, Pop," said Gordon. He signaled to the nurse, who put down her glass and hurried to Grossman.

"Let's go, honey," he said, running his thick hand down the outside of her thigh. "I'm getting tired, and I want a sponge bath."

"Your dad's a devil," Nancy giggled, wheeling the chair in the direction of the door.

"Take good care of him," Gordon called after her. "I'll be by tomorrow to see you, Pop."

"You do that, boychik," called Grossman over his shoulder, "I'll be looking for you."

The heavy door closed behind them, and Grossman slumped in his chair, a smile on his face. In the lobby, near a bank of pay phones, he told Nancy to stop and dial a number for him. It began with an L.A. area code—213. After the third ring, he heard a familiar voice.

"Bev, it's Al," he said.

"Al, where are you? I just called the hospital and they said you went out."

"Yeah, I'm over at the Waldorf, at Velvel's going-away party," he said.

"Going-away party?" Grossman could hear the surprise in her voice. "What do you mean, going away?"

"He decided to go back overseas. The Middle East or some damn place. I think he's trying to get over that broad of his, the les. Didn't he tell you?"

"I haven't spoken to him," she said in a tight voice. "Are you sure?"

"Sure, I'm sure, he just told me," Grossman said. "Listen, that trouble we had? It's all taken care of. I'm heading down to Florida for a month or so, gonna stay at Harry Millman's place, near Miami. Wanna join me?"

Grossman heard the pause, so brief as to be all but indiscernible. He could guess at the disappointment in that pause, but it didn't bother him. All's fair in love and war, he thought to himself; that, and age before beauty. It wasn't Shulman's kind of wisdom, but what the hell.

"Of course I'll come," Bev said brightly. "And Al . . . I can't wait to see you."

On the way back to the hospital in the front seat of Nancy's Saab, Grossman took five one-hundred-dollar bills out of his wallet and handed them to her.

"I guess it went all right, huh, Mr. Grossman," she said.

"Yeah," said Grossman, flipping on the radio to look for the Knicks game. "You're a hell of an actress, honey. You ever play Century City, don't forget to look us up."

". . . So there's the deal," said Flanagan, looking at the rapt faces of the old men and at Gordon. "It's up to you—you want in, you're in, same as the last time. Anybody wants to leave, well''—he patted his pocket—''your money's right here, and God bless you.''

''Now wait a minute,'' said Pupik Feinsilver. ''Let me get this straight. You want us to appear in a movie?''

''Not appear in a movie—star in a TV docudrama,'' said Flanagan. '' 'The Glory That Was Hester Street' is the working title, although that could change. Like I said, it'll be a documentary, about your life and times.''

''For this you need young actors,'' said Harry Millman. ''For example, I could see what's-his-name, Robert Redford, playing me.''

''Redford's a goy,'' protested Feinsilver.

''He's half Jewish,'' said Millman, ''same as Cary Grant. Besides, so what, this is show biz.''

''How about Jack Nicholson as me,'' yelled Kasha Weintraub.

''Yeah, and I could be Steve McQueen,'' hollered Zuckie.

''McQueen's dead, shmuck,'' said Sleepout Louie.

''Dead? When did that happen?''

Suddenly the air was thick with the names of movie stars past and present. Flanagan listened for a moment, and then held up his hand for silence.

''You guys are missing the point,'' he said. ''This isn't about then, it's about now. I'm talking HBO, a two-hour film showing you lovable gents to the American public. You know, people have the wrong idea about gangsters. This way, we can set the record straight.''

''And after the movie, what?'' asked Feinsilver.

''The sky's the limit,'' said Flanagan. ''A regular network show, guest shots on Johnny, Mishpocha T-shirts. By the time I'm finished with you guys, they'll be putting up statues in Central Park.''

''Speaking of statues, how about the statue of limitations?'' asked Indian Joe.

"Good question," said Flanagan. "I'll refer it to our attorney."

"Since when do we have an attorney?" asked Feinsilver.

"Since this morning," said Flanagan. "I'm pleased to announce that Mishpocha Films has retained the services of one of New York's finest lawyers, ex-police captain Bernard Threkeld."

"Boatnay?" said Morgan. "Boatnay gonna be your lawyer?"

"It's a day of surprises," Flanagan said merrily. "Don't worry, Morgan, this deal is strictly legit. Besides, I need someone I can trust."

"John Flanagan, you one amazing white man," said Morgan. "OK, in that case, count me in. Onliest thing, who am I supposed to play—Bugsy Siegel?"

"Nope, you play yourself, just like everybody else. Interracial is in this year—look at *The Cosby Show*."

Slowly, Bad Abe Abramson rose from his seat. He cleared his throat, and the others fell silent. "Give the boys and me five minutes to talk this over," he said.

"Sure," said Flanagan. "I want a word with Gordon anyway. We'll take a walk, be back in a few."

"How about it, Velvel, are you in?" asked Levine.

Gordon shook his head. "I'm a foreign correspondent, not a movie star," he said. "I'm going back overseas."

As soon as they were outside, Gordon turned to Flanagan. "Jesus, John. Do these guys know that they're gonna be working for Spadafore?"

"Not for Spadafore, for me," said Flanagan. "Mishpocha Films, Inc., is an independent company. My arrangement with Luigi is between me and him; it doesn't concern them."

"Until the next gang war, or the next grand jury. I thought

you loved these old guys, John. You can really be a prick sometimes.''

''I do love 'em,'' said Flanagan with a grin. ''Not that this is about me loving them, but since you bring it up, OK. They need five minutes to decide? Bullshit, they don't need five seconds. They're in there right now jumping up and down. I'm keeping the gang together, giving them something to live for.''

''And yourself.''

Flanagan nodded. ''That's right. And myself. But this is about more than having fun now. Spadafore's all alone—no sons, no Sesti, just me. When the old bastard croaks, we'll have a real shot at taking over the business.''

''You will, maybe; I've had enough. Look, we were lucky to get out of it this time, but I'm not pushing it. I'm sorry, you're on your own, John, but that's the way it is. I told you the other night I was going back to the paper, and I meant it.''

''Yeah,'' said Flanagan with a grin. ''You told me, and I told Luigi. Funny, he got it right away, and he doesn't even have a Pulitzer.''

''Got what?'' asked Gordon.

''That you're my protection. You know how, in the movies, when the good guy's got something on the bad guy, and if anything happens to him, a letter with all the information automatically goes to the cops? Well, you're my letter. Something happens to me, you get Luigi.''

''What?''

''In the paper. Shit, that's the only thing he's afraid of these days anyway. I, ah, told him that was the reason you were going back.''

Gordon stared at the grinning Flanagan. ''I don't believe this,'' he said finally. ''You're using me to threaten Luigi Spadafore. And you did it without even telling me.''

''I just told you,'' said Flanagan. ''Look, you were ready

to risk your ass for twenty percent of some foreign operation from Carlo Sesti. Well, I'm offering you a better deal—twenty percent of everything. And you don't have to lift a finger, just be yourself. Besides, you'll be in Beirut. What's the problem?''

Gordon paused, considering. No matter what he told Spadafore, the old man would never believe him. And, over the past few weeks, he had revised his opinion of Flanagan. With Boatnay and the old buzzards in the other room, he just might pull it off. The way he saw it, he had no choice. ''Twenty-five percent and it's a deal,'' he said, extending his hand.

''Twenty-five percent it is,'' said Flanagan, taking Gordon's hand in his and pulling him into a bear hug. ''You're a made man of the Mishpocha now, Velvel—your uncle Max would have been proud.''

For a moment Gordon struggled against the hug. Then, without really intending to, he threw his arms around Flanagan's narrow back, pulled him close and kissed him on the cheek.

''Hey,'' said Flanagan, ''What the hell was that for?''

''For you, chief,'' said Gordon. ''You mind?''

''Mind, hell,'' said Flanagan with a grin. ''I'm a sucker for a happy ending.''

ACKNOWLEDGMENTS

I would like to thank my agent, Esther Newberg of ICM, for her help and support, my friends Danny Sanderson and Arthur and Harriet Samuelson for their encouragement and editorial advice, and, finally, my editor, David Rosenthal, for his invaluable contribution on this book.